THE LAST TO LET GO

Also by Amber Smith

The Way I Used to Be

THE

AMBER SMITH

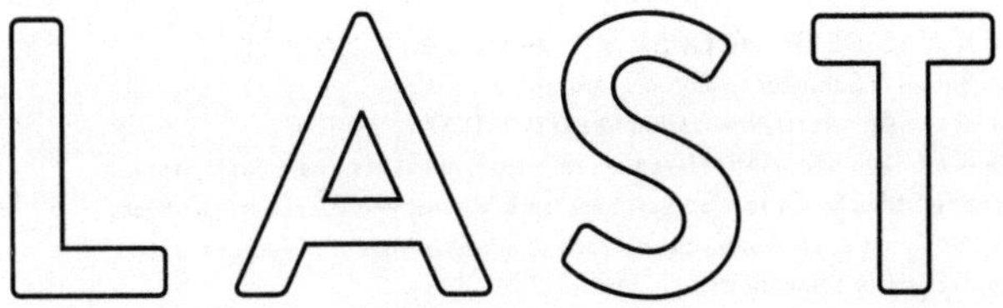

Margaret K. McElderry Books

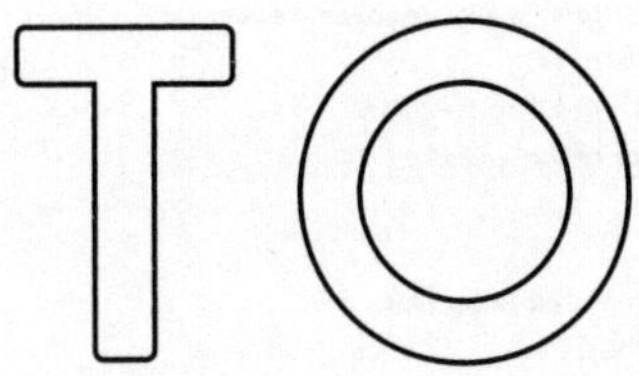

New York London Toronto Sydney New Delhi

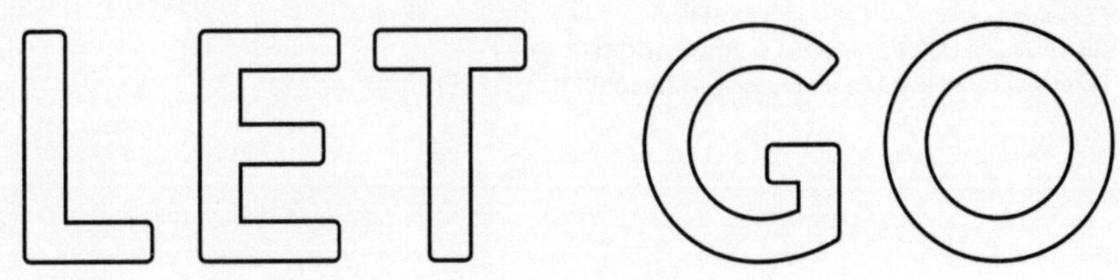

MARGARET K. McELDERRY BOOKS
An imprint of Simon & Schuster Children's Publishing Division
1230 Avenue of the Americas, New York, New York 10020

Book design by Debra Sfetsios-Conover
The text for this book was set in Minion Pro Regular.
Manufactured in the United States of America
First Edition
10 9 8 7 6 5 4 3 2 1
Library of Congress Cataloging-in-Publication Data
Names: Smith, Amber, 1982- author.
Title: The last to let go / Amber Smith.
Description: First edition. | New York : Margaret K. McElderry Books, [2018] | Summary: "When her mother is arrested for killing Brooke's abusive father, Brooke must confront the shadow of her family's violence and dysfunction"—Provided by publisher.
Identifiers: LCCN 2016058211 | ISBN 9781481480734 (hardcover) |
ISBN 9781481480758 (eBook)
Subjects: | CYAC: Coming of age—Fiction. | Brothers and sisters—Fiction. | Family violence—Fiction. | Murder—Fiction. | Abused women—Fiction. | Sexual orientation—Fiction.
Classification: LCC PZ7.1.S595 Las 2018 | DDC [Fic]—dc23
LC record available at https://lccn.loc.gov/2016058211

For anyone who has ever been caught between
wanting to hold on and needing to let go

THE LAST TO LET GO

SUMMER

SHADOWS

IT'S THE END OF JUNE. A Friday. Like any other day, except hotter. I take my usual shortcut home from school through the alley, where the air is dense and unbreathable, saturated with the raw smell of overheated dumpster garbage. I can taste it in the back of my throat like an illness coming on.

But this is the last time I'll ever need to take this route, I remind myself. Almost instantly that invisible yet ever-present straitjacket begins to loosen its grip just enough for me to breathe a little easier. I've been counting down the days for years. Not that school itself was ever the problem. It's all the people *in* the school who are the problem. Or maybe, as I sometimes think, the problem might have been me all along. Occam's razor, and everything. Isn't it simpler that the problem should be one person versus hundreds, rather than the other way around? Logically, maybe. But then, if I'm really going to think about it—which, I've decided, I'm *not*—me being the problem is the opposite of simple.

As I step out of the shaded alley and onto the sidewalk, the sun blasts down in a cascade of heat and light. I stop and roll my jeans up to my knees, while my shadow pools at my feet like a small gray puddle. When my brother, Aaron, and I were little, we always kept a vigilant watch over our shadows, convinced that one day they'd splinter off like in *Peter Pan* and run amok, committing all sorts of treacherous deeds without our consent.

But that was a lifetime ago. I doubt he even remembers.

As I stand up, my forehead is instantly beaded with sweat, the back of my shirt dampened under the weight of my backpack. Usually I can't stand the heat, but today it doesn't bother me. Nothing can right now. Because I just aced my AP Bio final. I'm officially done with Riverside High. And I'll be starting my junior year, the most important year, at Jefferson—the special charter school that's had me wait-listed since eighth grade—with all new people. Where no one knows me. Where I can focus, get ahead, and start my life already. I've wanted to go there ever since I found out about all the AP classes they offer.

I've thought about it for roughly a million hours. I worked out a plan and now it's finally happening: I'll graduate from Jefferson, get in to an amazing college somewhere far away, and then get out of this hellhole for good. I feel a hitch in my step. I involuntarily skip ahead on my toes. This feels like a moment I should be celebrating with my friends, if I had any. Because I'm free, almost.

A siren chirps once.

Twice.

I look up just as the red and blue lights begin spinning, in time to watch the patrol car go from parked to sixty in a matter of seconds, the noise shifting the heavy air around me. The heat radiates from the pavement through the rubber soles of my flip-flops as I skip over the crumbling blacktop, sidestepping the potholes I've practically memorized over the years. The sirens fade into the distance, but within seconds that patrol car is followed by five more, then a fire truck, then an ambulance, leaving the air too still in their wake.

I follow the procession of emergency vehicles, systematically reviewing my answers on DNA and RNA and the endocrine system, and cell division: prophase, metaphase, anaphase. For six blocks of brick and cement and glass-window storefronts, the sun beats down on my hair and face, my shadow following along behind me the whole way. I only wish I could've known that these were the last relatively carefree moments of my life, because as my heel turns ninety degrees on that last corner to our apartment, nothing will ever be the same again.

The six police cars and the fire truck and the ambulance are all jammed into the narrow alley next to our building. Although there are seven other apartments in our building, I can feel it in my bones and skin and blood, this is not about any of the other people behind any of those seven other doors.

This is about us.

I try to run but it feels like I'm moving through water, my feet sinking into wet sand, my legs getting tangled up in strands of seaweed wanting to pull me under. I don't care that I've lost my flip-flops, or that the sunbaked asphalt is boiling the soles of my feet, or that somehow my backpack has shuffled off me and is now lying in the middle of the road like a dead animal, with all those precious study materials inside. I race through the door and up the stairs, calling her name over and over again.

Mom.

I make it up only to the first landing before I'm caught by the waist, a voice shouting in my ear to "calm down, calm down." I try to fight him, but it's no use. "*Brooke*," he says firmly, calling me by my name. "Hold still, all right—wait!" I know exactly who it is without even having to look. Tony. He told me I could call him that when I was in fourth grade and one of our neighbors had called the cops on us. It was the time Dad broke Mom's collarbone and Mom convinced the police she had fallen down the stairs. That was one of the few times I'd ever seen him cry about what he'd done; he melted into a puddle, and swore—swore to all of us, swore to a god I'm not sure he even believed in—never again. I didn't know which version of him scared me more, the crazy one or the sorry one.

We've been through this enough times to know that the cops don't pull out all the stops like this for a simple noise complaint from a neighbor, especially when that neighbor is a cop himself. Which can mean only one thing: *It's finally happened.* Aaron always said it was only a matter of time.

Tony opens his mouth, the words to explain escaping him. Mrs. Allister, in 2B, inches her door open, the chain-link lock pulled taut in front of her face. She stares out at me with her wide, red-rimmed eyes, her chin quivering, her mouth turning downward as she whimpers my name. "I didn't know what to do," she pleads in her own defense. "I didn't know what else to do." Mrs. Allister was always the one to call the cops, until the one time when I was in seventh grade and I barged into her apartment, yelling about how even though she thought she was helping, she was only making things worse. Calling the police never did any good, I tried to make her understand, because *he* was one of them. Mrs. Allister cried then, too. As far I know, she never called again. Until now.

"Ma'am, back inside right now!" Tony demands. And Mrs. Allister retreats like a turtle back into its shell. The door clicks shut, the dead bolt sliding into place.

Then suddenly a whole swarm of cops in bulletproof vests barrel down the stairs toward us, shouting, "*Outta the way, move, outta the way, get her outta here.*" I think they mean me at first, but before I even know what's happening next, Tony has my back pinned against Mrs. Allister's door, shielding me as they pass by us like a hurricane of bodies.

That's when I see her, my little sister, like a ghost encircled by these gray uniforms, each one with a hand on her. Her hair swings forward over her shoulders as the cops jerk her body down the stairs. She's still wearing her baby-blue T-shirt and her favorite cutoff jean shorts, which she isn't allowed to wear to school, just like she was when I left this morning. I remember because she kicked her feet up and sprawled out on the couch, grinning in that stupid, goofy way of hers, taunting me because she was already finished with her exams. "Summer starts now, sucker!" she said as she flipped on the TV. But now her eyes stare ahead, wide and empty, unfocused.

"Callie?" I call after her. "*Callie!*" I shout her name as loud as my voice will let me. She doesn't even look back. I struggle to get out from under Tony's arms, but he holds me in place.

"What did he do?" I want to scream it, but the words drown in my throat. I search Tony's eyes for an explanation, but I can't force myself to ask the real question: *Is she dead?* But I need the answer. I need it now. Because even though I know she has to be dead, there's this hope still chiseling away at my heart. His arms envelop me, and for maybe the billionth time in my life I wish that *he* were my father, that he were taking me out of here. For good. Away from all of this. I feel myself slinking down against the wall and melting into the floor, my legs twisting under me, suddenly unable to support the weight of my body.

Tony crouches down next to me, instructing, calmly somehow, "Breathe, Brooke. Breathe." Over his head a figure has emerged. I blink hard. There, on the landing at the top of the stairs—alive. She's alive, and life can continue, and we'll be *fine*, we'll be fine because she's there and alive, and that's all that matters. "Mom," I whisper, scrambling to my feet. "Mom!" I yell.

She lifts her head as I call out to her. Her face is tear-and-mascara streaked. I break away from Tony, my flimsy arms and legs struggling to crawl up each step. I reach out to her, but she doesn't reach back. I watch as she unfolds in bits and pieces, like my brain is suddenly working in slow motion to understand, unable to take it in all at once.

There's a legion of cops surrounding her, holding her arms behind her back as they walk down the stairs in rigid, jerky movements. Her eyes hold mine as she comes closer, mouthing the words, "I'm sorry, I'm sorry," as if she no longer has a voice. And I'm shoved out of the way like I'm not even there. As she passes, I see her arms twisted behind her back, the shiny silver handcuffs locked around her wrists. Her hands look like she dipped them in red food coloring and didn't wash it off before it stained, the way our fingertips used to look after coloring Easter eggs when we were little.

I think my heart actually stops beating. I swear, I die. A temporary little death. Because that's when the whole picture shifts into focus, the puzzle pieces fitting together, yet the picture they form making no sense at all.

"No," I breathe, trying to shout the word. But no one's listening. No one understands.

UNDERWATER

UNDERWATER THE WORLD IS SOFT. Life is gentle, easy. The smell of chlorine, the burn of sunscreen in my eyes, muffled splashing, and rippled lines of refracted light—that's what summer is supposed to be.

We were planning on going to the community pool after I got home—I had promised her. Even though it's not particularly nice or updated in any way, it's still our favorite place, mine and Callie's. Last year we went nearly every single day. The three-block trek was torture, especially in the afternoon with the sun at its peak, but as Callie always insisted, it only made her first cannonball into the cool blue water all the more worth it.

There was a day last summer when something changed between us and it felt like we were friends, rather than a big sister babysitting her little sister. On the walk there she was talking nonstop, as usual. And I was humoring her weird, random questions, which would often begin with "If there was a zombie apocalypse . . ." And, like every day, even though I warned her not to, the second we walked through the gates, handing our passes over to the attendant, she'd run ahead of me alongside the pool, causing the lifeguard to blow on his whistle and shout, "No running!" But it only made her run faster, screaming at the top of her lungs as she leaped into the air. Her goal was to make waves, always.

Before I could set our things down and lay our towels out, Callie was splashing me. "Stop it, Callie!" I scolded, though I didn't care about the splashing so much as the attention she was drawing.

"Dive in," she said. "Please?"

I ignored her as I set our bag down and tried to maneuver out of my shorts and baggy T-shirt.

"Do it!"

"You do it," I countered.

"You know I don't know how. Show me again," she demanded in that annoyingly adamant eleven-year-old way of hers. "Last time, I promise." That's what she said every time.

I looked around; there were hardly any other people there, and no one was watching. I hated when people stared at me any time, but while wearing a bathing suit, I might as well have been naked. "Fine," I relented. "This is the last time."

I tiptoed my way over to the deep end, set my toes along the edge of the pool, testing my feet and knees and ankles with a couple of practice bounces. Then, springing off the balls of my feet, I threw my arms over my head and transferred my weight forward, airborne for a split second. My body cut through the cold water, gliding in a smooth, straight line, making me feel so light and sleek and nimble I could almost forget about the rest of my life waiting for me on dry land.

When I came back up to the surface, Callie was holding both of her hands up high out of the water, all five fingers on each hand spread wide. "Ten!" she shouted, then, "Race you to the shallow end."

Before I could even respond, she was gone. She always pretended to be a mermaid, swimming right along the bottom, waving her body while keeping her legs and feet suctioned together like a tail. She made it all the way across the whole pool like that and was waiting for me on the other side. When I reached her, she said, "Go under, I gotta tell you something."

I rolled my eyes but did it anyway. Underwater her voice was high pitched and garbled, bubbles flowing out of her mouth, up to the surface. We came back up, and I said, "Birthday card inside out?"

She wailed, "*No!*" and we went under again.

"Same thing," I told her. "Birthday card. Inside out."

"You're terrible at this!" She splashed me again. "Lifeguard. Checking. You. Out."

"No he isn't!" I said, without even bothering to see whether it was true or not. I didn't want to know either way. How many times had I told her that I didn't care, wasn't interested in looks, didn't want guys being interested in me, and how many times would she try to convince me otherwise, tease me, try to make me feel uncomfortable?

"He so is!" she giggled, her eyes already turning red from the pool chemicals.

"No," I said. "He's not."

I dunked my head underwater then and kicked my feet against the side of the pool, darting away from her, away from her games and her words, away from the way they made me feel. Or *not* feel.

I wasn't interested in some random lifeguard, or any other guy for that matter, and that was not something I was ready to think about in too much depth. I swam until I lost count of the laps. Until my arms and legs refused to go any farther. Until I could almost forget who I was. Then I turned over onto my back and opened my eyes; I gazed up at the clouds floating in the blue sky just as I was floating on the blue water. My thoughts had finally slowed to a crawl. This was around the time I'd expect Callie to stealth-mermaid her way beneath me, grab my leg, and pull me under—I'd flail and spring back up to the surface with a gallon of water up my nose—but that's not what happened that day.

She was already out of the pool, lying down on her towel, my too-big sunglasses shielding her eyes. I climbed up the ladder, my body heavy out of the water. My wet footsteps slapped against the concrete as I made my way over to our spot. I spread my towel out and lowered myself down onto my stomach next to Callie, resting my head on top of my folded arms. She lifted my wet hair and flopped it over my shoulder. A cool breeze flowed over my bare back as her finger pressed against my skin, drawing a hook shape, like the beginning of a question mark, on one side, then its mirror image on the other: a heart.

We used to do this all the time when we shared a room. She'd often wind up in my bed, scared, with our mom crying and our dad yelling on the other side of the door. I'd write out silly invisible messages on her back until she fell asleep.

I smiled and whispered, "Sorry I got mad."

Then she drew a circle followed by three sharp lines: *OK*. Then two dots and a curved line: smiley face.

She lay back down next to me, and although we didn't say anything to each other, it felt right. Like we didn't *need* to say anything, like maybe she finally got something about me that I wasn't even quite sure of myself yet. I closed my eyes and let my body soften against the hot, hard cement, that good ache in my lungs, the gentle strain of muscles after swimming as strong and hard and long as I could, the slow fog settling over my thoughts again.

THE REAL WORLD

TIME SKIPS FORWARD SOMEHOW, and when I snap out of it, I can't tell if it's been seconds or hours or years. I push through the front door, and the sun blinds me in one giant flash. I can feel tears burning behind my eyes. Then time drops back again, drawing everything sharply into focus: all these flashing lights, the pop and buzz and static of two-way radios wafting out from open police car doors, emitting a sequence of cryptic numbers and letters, and people running all over the place, the heat a physical presence that stands like a million invisible walls between me and the real world.

My head pounds like there's a small hammer tapping against the inside of my skull. The water from my eyes shakes loose, drawing a kaleidoscope of prisms across all that I see. Then the minutes jump ahead again and I'm suddenly standing next to Callie, who's sitting on the back of the ambulance, her legs dangling off the edge lifelessly. Two paramedics are patting her down, touching her everywhere; they shield her eyes from the sun with their hands and then shine a small flashlight into each eye. It takes a second longer than usual for my brain to realize that there's something not quite right about her. She's not moving, not making a sound, not actually looking *at* anything.

Suddenly I know—just know, somehow—that this all has to be some kind of a nightmare. So I turn around and look. Turning, faster and faster, in circles, looking fiercely, scanning, watching for any signs, some bizarre, out-of-place detail, a clue that I'm about to wake up. Any second I'll be back in reality, and maybe I'll have to do this whole day over, retake the stupid AP Bio exam. But that's okay. I don't mind. I'll ace it a second time. I'll shower. I'll eat another bowl of cereal. I'll walk to school again. I'll sweat. I don't care. I'll do it all over if that's what it takes.

That's when my roving gaze catches Aaron. His body jerks to a halt as he rounds the corner, and he stands still for a moment. That's my sign. There's no reason in the real world Aaron should be here right now. Then he's running toward me. Fast.

I raise my arms over my head, signaling to him. I want to call out, *Don't worry, this isn't even real*, but he arrives so quickly, ramming into me as he grabs hold of my arms. I feel the squeeze of his hands, feel the weight of his body crashing into mine, feel my feet anchored to the ground like they're made of cement. I see the panic in his eyes, I hear his voice, loud and real—this is definitely my brother. He's here, right now, in the flesh.

"What's going on?" He takes my face in his hands. "Brooke, look at me. What happened? Mrs. Allister called me."

I can only shake my head. I don't know what's going on. I don't know what happened. When I don't answer, he pushes past me, rushing to the paramedics. They yell at him to get back, but he doesn't listen. "Oh my God, Callie—what the—what's wrong with her?" he shouts at them.

"Calm down, you need to let us—" one of the paramedics tries to say, coming between him and Callie.

"This is my sister!" he shouts at them. "Don't you dare tell me to calm down. What's wrong with her? What happened?"

I slowly walk up behind him, reality gaining on me with every step.

"She's in shock," I hear the other one answer.

"Is she hurt?" Aaron asks, his voice breaking like glass.

"No," the first one tells us. "I don't see any physical injuries."

Aaron starts looking around exactly as I did, like maybe he's searching for dream cues too. But then something in his face changes. It hardens and cools as he blinks away the tears that were on the verge of spilling over, and—just like that—he grabs on to the guy's collar. "What the fuck is going on here?" he demands with this intensity that makes him look and sound so much like our dad it scares me.

Another pair of hands pulls him back by his shoulders. And then he's on the ground. Tony's on top of him. Aaron's struggling, throwing punches, nothing connecting.

"Enough!" Tony yells, holding Aaron's arms down against the blacktop. Then quieter, "That's enough. Pull it together, all right? Your sisters need you."

Aaron goes still, like some kind of tranquilizer has been injected into him and is in the process of being dispersed into his bloodstream, calming his limbs into submission. He looks at me over Tony's shoulder, his face changing back to normal. Tony slowly loosens his grip and climbs off him, reaching out to help pull Aaron up. They sit on the burning pavement. Tony looks over at me and Callie. Then back to Aaron. The four of us jumbled together in the middle of the street, the calm in the eye of a swirling storm. "You kids," he says, breathless, "you keep me up at night, you know that?"

"Tell me," Aaron demands, able to ask the question I couldn't. "Did he kill her?"

Tony shakes his head and points to the patrol car. I follow the direction of his arm to my mom's face in the window. He puts his hand on Aaron's shoulder. "She stabbed him. Your mother stabbed him. I don't know anything else. There must have been some kind of struggle. That's all I know right now."

The words are dull and thick and slow to sink in.

"That's impossible." Aaron's voice trembles, and he looks at me as if he's asking whether or not I believe it.

Callie makes no movement. They have her wrapped in a blanket even though it has to be about 195 degrees out here. They start putting her inside the ambulance. They're strapping her to a gurney. "It's okay," I call out to her. "It's okay," I lie.

The driver turns on the lights and shouts to us through the open window. "Taking her to General!" Then the double doors are slammed shut and the ambulance speeds down the street, sirens wailing.

"I will do everything I can," Tony says as he starts jogging toward the police car. "That's a promise, all right?" Then he climbs into the passenger seat of the police car and it starts to pull away too. My mom keeps mouthing, “I’m sorry, I’m sorry.” I run alongside, as far as I can, until the car drives too fast for me to keep up.

“Wait,” I hear myself say, but there’s no volume behind the words. “Wait!” I try again, but it’s barely more than breath escaping my lips. Aaron and I are left in the street all alone, watching the car grow smaller and smaller in the distance, watching our lives slowly slip away. The fire truck rolls past us quietly, as if the truck itself is disappointed there were no fires to extinguish. I look at our building. It seems so normal. I pick my backpack up off the street, along with my sandals, several feet apart from each other.

Aaron stands still, breathing heavy, then he sprints for the door. “Stay here!” he calls over his shoulder.

But I don’t. I race inside, though I’m not sure why. I only know that I don’t want to be left alone out here. I start up the stairs behind him; the third step creaks, as it always has. I approach the door to our apartment. It’s open. I hear voices. I take one step inside and Aaron is standing there like his feet are stuck to the floor.

“Brooke, get out!” he yells. “Don’t look,” he says, throwing his arm out to block me.

But it’s too late. I already see.

He’s lying on his back in the middle of the kitchen floor like he’s asleep. Except there’s a small, dark puddle beneath him, almost black, like his shadow is seeping out of his body, the source a giant burgundy stain in the center of his stomach. My eyes focus on his hand, lying there against the linoleum floor, palm facing up, fingers slightly curled. Gentle, somehow. I’ve never seen my father’s hand look so powerless.

“Hey! You can’t be in here!” someone shouts, just as another cop steps in front of me and Aaron, strong arms pushing us back toward the door. My body moves so easily it doesn't even resist.

"That's our dad," I say to no one in particular.

"We have to go," Aaron tells me. "Let's go to Carmen's. Come on, hurry."

"Okay," I hear myself reply as I follow behind him.

FRESH MEAT

THE FIRST TIME I MET Carmen was at school in ninth grade. She was older than me, a senior like my brother should've been. He had been held back in his freshman year, so he was a year behind. Dad was furious, told him he was stupid, useless, never going to amount to anything. I knew that wasn't true, though. Aaron was really smart. He just didn't care about school, not the way that I did. I was actually happy that he'd been held back because that meant we'd be together for an extra year, and then I didn't care so much about transferring out.

When I walked into the cafeteria the first day of high school, I was hoping I'd see him. We'd compared our schedules that morning and he'd assured me we were in the same lunch. But, as I would soon learn, he spent so much time in in-school suspension for one thing or another that it hardly felt like we even went to the same school at all. After one lap around the cafeteria I gave up and sat down at a table in the corner by myself. That was when Carmen came over and introduced herself, inviting me to sit with her. "This is Brooke," she told her table, which was filled with seniors. "It's her first day, so be nice."

"You're a freshman, right?" one girl asked as she slid over to make room for me.

Then the guy next to her cupped his hands around his mouth and megaphoned, "*Fresh meat.*"

Before I could answer, Carmen intercepted the conversation and told the guy, "She might be fresh meat, Mark, but she's already a million times more mature than *you*."

Carmen tried to include me in the table's conversation, asking about my classes, whether or not I was planning to join any teams or clubs. I was not. I could feel myself blushing, all awkward and plain and boring, the complete opposite of everything she seemed to be: confident, smart, beautiful. I barely spoke. I was too stunned that she had even noticed me in the sea of fresh meat, let alone singled me out to take under her wing. There must have been something about me, something she saw that I couldn't, I thought. Something special, even.

For all of five minutes I thought she actually liked me.

"Dude!" Mark shouted, looking somewhere behind me. "What is up, man? We thought you got busted already."

I turned to see my brother leaning over Carmen, wrapping his arms around her like he was going to scoop her up and take her away. She turned her head and smiled through the words "Hey, you," and then they kissed. A deep, serious one.

Something inside of me ground to a halt. Of course this wasn't about me. I was stupid to think otherwise. After they disentangled themselves, Aaron straightened up and grinned, patting me on the back before tumbling into the last open chair. "Thanks for rescuing my kid sister," he told them. Then he looked at me. "So, how's the first day so far?"

I shrugged while I tried to find my voice. "Okay, I guess."

"Dude, she's really chatty," Mark interjected. "Couldn't get her to shut up this whole time."

"Yeah, maybe you should take a lesson from her," Carmen said, blowing on the end of her straw so that the wrapper launched across the table, hitting Mark square in the forehead.

"She's just a loner, is all," Aaron said. I gave him my deadliest eyes. "What? Nothing wrong with that." Then he added, hitching his chin to point in Mark's direction, "Some people *should* be loners." He knocked his shoulder into mine, and then everyone started laughing.

Mark looked around, taking a second too long to get it. "Fuck you," he finally said, hesitating before he joined in the laughter at his expense, which, I realized, was for my benefit.

I was grateful to Aaron, of course. He was only trying to look out for me. But damn, it had felt good to think that I'd made some friends all on my own for once, to think, for even one minute, that someone had actually, voluntarily, wanted me.

It was weird to see Aaron like this. Part of me wondered if he was only pretending. We never laughed like this at home anymore, never joked around or even spoke too loudly. But when I saw the way that Carmen and Aaron looked at each other, I knew, somehow, this wasn't pretend. He had friends, and a girlfriend who clearly cared about him enough to gather up a lowly freshman on his behalf. He had a life. He had all the things I never thought I'd have.

I was envious; I knew that even then. I thought he'd found a way to get out from under the weight of our family, found a way to be happy. It gave me hope that maybe one day I could too.

But now I know he was never out from under anything, that weight was just building pressure, slowly crushing him, like it was crushing all of us. I just didn't see it then, didn't *want* to see it.

possible, as many times as possible, before he'd spin ar
yell, yet we'd both be laughing so hard we couldn't breathe.

I found him up there, but he wasn't smoking. He was there, passed out and cold as ice because it was December an was wearing only a T-shirt and jeans with holes in the knees, a socks without shoes. His lips were purple. He was barely breathing by the time the ambulance got there. Even though it was pretty obvious what he had done, I convinced myself it was some kind of freak accident. But that wasn't the truth, and as much as I wanted to pretend, deep down I knew it was never that simple.

They pumped his stomach, and he had to stay here in the psych unit for a week. Then he came home and everyone acted like he was okay. But he wasn't really okay, I knew. He was simply alive. Things changed after that. I had to be careful with him, like he was made of porcelain. I had to watch what I said and how I looked at him. He moved out a few weeks later. And he's lived with Carmen's family ever since. We've never talked about it. I don't know why. It felt off-limits. Still does.

As I watch Aaron and Carmen sitting here together, I become very aware of this dull, steady pain in my chest, throbbing, aching for something—some*one*. I've never been in a relationship. Never been kissed, either. Not unless you count that time in seventh grade when some random kid ran up and gave me a dry, papery peck on the lips at my locker on a dare, which I don't. I've had infatuations, fantasies, a few crushes, but that's as far as it ever goes. Maybe I even had a crush on Carmen at one time. I try not to think about it, though. There's no point anyway. Because how would I have time for that with everything else that's always going on? How could I

SHUTTING DOWN

THE SMELL OF HOSPITAL: a sickening combination of dise disinfectant, and stale vending machine coffee. Carmen drove here in her mother's car.

After we filled out Callie's paperwork in the ER, we w directed to the seventh-floor waiting area, the psych unit. Aa sits across from me, gnawing on his thumbnail like a cannibal, j gling his leg up and down at warp speed. Neither of us mentions last time we were here.

Carmen sits next to Aaron and takes his hand. I wonde she's thinking about the last time too. That time when Aaron alm died.

That time two winters ago when no one had heard from hi the entire day and no one else except for me seemed to be worrie When he didn't show up for dinner that night, a strange sick feeli told me to go to the roof. I knew sometimes he would smoke ci arettes up there, and sometimes, if I managed to be quiet enoug I could sneak up behind him and punch him in the arm as hard ever find the space for another person in my life when I barely even have enough room for myself?

I check the time on my phone. Another hour has passed. I don't understand how time keeps doing that. Moving forward when all I need is for it to stop, to give me a chance to work back through all that's happened today, which is impossible to do when the seconds keep marching ahead, piling new minutes on top of all the old minutes, building a landfill of lost time.

There's only one other woman in the waiting area, sitting with her back to us, facing the row of windows that overlook the downtown city buildings, their lights beginning to blink on as the sun finally lies down for the day, the sky darkening slowly, like a long sigh. She's flipping through a five-month-old copy of *Good Housekeeping*, her fingers turning the pages too rapidly to be actually reading. She's probably our parents' age. Heavy makeup, hair dyed dark red, a little plump, but strong. Tough. Weathered. Still pretty somehow. A no-nonsense person, I'd imagine. I wonder vaguely, for a second, whom she's here to see.

She looks up from her magazine and catches me staring. I quickly look down at my lap. When I raise my eyes again, she's looking at me this time, her mouth held slightly open. I give her my best fake smile and try to act like there are lots of interesting things to be paying attention to in the waiting room.

Just then, interrupting the quiet vigil of the seventh-floor psych ward waiting room, something slams into one of the windows like a bullet, making each one of us jump in our seat.

"Oh my God!" the woman gasps, clutching at her chest and nearly dropping the magazine.

"What the hell was that?" I breathe.

"Bird," Aaron answers immediately, as if he's witnessed a million of these.

Carmen's voice is muffled as she buries her face in Aaron's shoulder. "Oh no, poor thing."

The sound—that hollow thud—echoes through my head. It sends a tingle down my spine. I can feel those delicate hollow bird bones crushing somewhere inside of me. I draw my arms around my midsection.

In the wake of silence that follows I hear the woman say, "Hello?" like that one word was the result of long, hard contemplation. I turn to look at her once more. Her eyes are so wide I can see white all around her dark irises. She has these massive black eyelashes that make her expression even more dramatic.

"Brooke?" she asks. "And *Aaron*? Is that you?" Hesitantly, she sets the magazine down and stands, adjusting her shirt and the waist of her pants as she does so. Her smile reveals two rows of perfectly straight extra-white teeth—the kind that make me feel self-conscious about mine being not so straight, not so white.

Aaron looks at Carmen, then at me. Sitting up straighter, he lets go of her hand. "Who are you?" he says, not particularly nicely, putting on his tough-guy face once again.

"I can't believe how grown up you are," she says, more to herself, as she begins walking toward us. Her gaze alternates between me and Aaron, and her eyes glisten like she might start crying. "I'm here to help," she says, hand over her chest like she's making some kind of pledge of allegiance to us.

Aaron's squirming, preparing to get all fiery and worked up.

"Who. Are. You?" he repeats, not quite raising his voice yet.

She stops midstep, her face collapsing into a frown as she points a finger at her chest and says, "It's Aunt Jackie. You—you don't remember me?"

Aunt Jackie.

In my mind I do that age progression thing, like you see in those flyers for missing people, comparing what they looked like when they were last seen with what they would look like today.

We used to call her Aunt Jackie when we were kids, though she's not really our aunt at all. We never had any aunts or uncles, no cousins, and all our grandparents are dead—except for our mother's mother, but they hate each other and we've never even met her, so she doesn't really count either. Jackie was the only "relative" we'd ever known. Our mom's best friend. Or she used to be, anyway. When we were kids, Mom would walk us up to Jackie's Coffee and Bakeshop after playtime in the park. Aaron would hold my hand, and then with his other hand he would hold on to the side of the stroller Mom was pushing, with Callie inside. I can remember Jackie reaching across the counter, smiling that toothpaste-commercial smile as she handed me and Aaron little chocolate doughnut holes wrapped in sheets of wax paper.

"Oh," Aaron finally says, his face softening. He stands up and walks toward her. "No, we do. We remember you," he says, speaking for us both.

"Your mom wanted me to meet you here." She starts rubbing her hands together nervously. "To check on Callie. Make sure you were okay," she says, tears filling her eyes as she reaches out for Aaron's hand, maybe to stop herself from fidgeting.

Okay, my brain echoes. How can we be okay? How could we possibly be okay?

"Thanks for coming," Aaron tells her solemnly, taking the hand she offers.

It's beyond annoying how one moment Aaron can be on the verge of raging out of his mind and in the next he's like some kind of patron saint of compassion and gentleness. I've always felt like he had the potential to be either a ruthless dictator or a sequestered monk, have a life of chaotic tyranny or peaceful contemplation. Nothing in between. The main problem with that is I never know which Aaron is going to show up. Just when I need him to be skeptical and cynical and tough, he goes soft on me.

I roll my eyes. Look around. Am I the only one who's suspicious of Jackie? Even Carmen—levelheaded, calm, wise-beyond-her-years Carmen—greets this woman, this supposed friend who dropped out of our mom's life years ago for no apparent reason.

"You'll stay at my house," Jackie continues. "Until everything gets sorted out."

I have to say something. "Wait. Hold on, how did you even know we were here?"

"Allison, your mom, I mean. She had her police officer friend call me. I'm—I'm so sorry, kids. I'm so sorry this happened," she says, her voice caving into her throat. "I can't express to you how sorry I am. Really." She blinks back the tears that are getting caught in her spider-leg eyelashes.

No one knows what to say. Thankfully, we don't have to, because the doctor comes out right then. "Callie's family?" she asks softly.

"Yes," I answer, standing up and pushing my way past the others to meet her in the doorway.

"Let's sit." She directs me back to the seating area. "We're all together here?" she asks as we huddle around her.

I look at Carmen, then Jackie, and reluctantly answer, "Yes."

"All right. So, I've had a chance to examine Callie and run some preliminary tests. She's doing okay, she's stable. But I would like to keep her here for a few days, just basic evaluation—a chance to figure out how to best help her."

"What's wrong with her?" Aaron asks.

"Well, she's been traumatized. It's expected that she would have some symptoms of posttraumatic stress. Witnessing a death, particularly the death of a parent, particularly when it's a violent death, is a tremendous experience for *anyone* to process, let alone a twelve-year-old girl. She is alert and responsive, but she's not speaking—at least, I haven't been able to get her to speak *yet*. This kind of mutism is not entirely unusual in situations like this."

"But why? What does this mean?" I ask her.

"It's like shutting down—it's all too much for her to process right now. She doesn't feel safe, which is understandable after what's happened. This is her mind's way of saying, *I need a break*. It means that she's going to need time and space to recover. It could be a long process. Or not. It's hard to tell at this point."

"Can we see her?" Aaron asks.

"Not yet. We're admitting her. And what we like to do is keep the patient for seventy-two hours. It's only so we can get a clear picture of what's actually going on."

I laugh, and everyone looks at me like I'm the crazy one. "Sorry, but we can't just *not* see her. I mean, that's out of the question. She's going to be scared. I don't want her to think she's alone. What if she doesn't understand what's going on?" I say, the words tumbling out of my mouth, too fast.

"It will be okay. She knows why she's here—she understands what's going on. She knows you're here. What she really needs right now is rest."

This is all wrong. I feel my pulse racing, my thoughts spiraling. "Well, so she'll come home in a few days?" I try. "Right?"

"Maybe. We may need to keep her longer. Could be a week. We need to see how she does. That's all. Really, the main idea is to ensure that she's not a threat to herself or anyone else."

That makes us all go mute.

The doctor allows the moment of silence to wash over us, and then continues, gently. "There's honestly nothing left for you to do here. Not right now. And I'm sure you're all exhausted after . . . the ordeal. I will certainly give you an update tomorrow."

She stands and leaves. And eventually we do the same.

SALT

JACKIE'S HOUSE WAS NOT even fifteen minutes away, across the river that divides our town in half. Carmen went back to her apartment, but Aaron, thankfully, agreed to come to Jackie's with me, although I suspected he would rather have gone home with Carmen. As Jackie drove us in, her neighborhood came up suddenly after we crossed the bridge, a shiny little village that dropped from the sky, out of place, out of time.

I take inventory of Jackie's living room: her pretty photo frames on the mantel, our glasses of lemonade collecting condensation on the ceramic coasters that have a special wooden holder and a special place on her special, perfect little coffee table. There are nice curtains in the windows, the furniture crisp and unworn. There's a gentle rumble through the walls as the central air kicks on.

I keep thinking someone is about to bust through the door, or something, and tell us it's all been a big mistake and everything's fine and we can all go back home. But the only person who comes is Jackie's husband, Ray, who wanders aimlessly into the room for about the hundredth time, asking us if we need anything, giving us pitiful charity smiles each time.

Aaron watches Jackie with wide eyes as she paces between the rooms, while we hear only one side of multiple phone calls. He chews on his fingernails and jiggles his leg and keeps clearing his throat. I can feel the anxiety vibrating off him, and it makes me feel like *I'm* going to burst out of my skin.

"She needs a *criminal attorney*?" Jackie shouts, enunciating the words like they're in a foreign language. She's talking to her cousin who's a lawyer, but not the right kind, I gather. "You know someone? Great. Okay, spell that again?" she asks, hunched over a pad of paper, pen furiously scribbling out names and numbers.

One of the ice cubes in my glass cracks, except it feels like something in my skull cracking instead, splintering. The tiny hammer I know so well, smacking into that tender spot, the one right near the temple. Another headache coming on. I close my eyes, yank the couch pillow out from behind my back, and pull it over my face, blocking out the light, muffling the sound of Jackie's voice.

I'm not sure what I'm supposed to be feeling. How can I feel anything about something that I don't even understand? I don't need feelings right now. I need facts. I need information. But the facts are these: My mom is locked up and no one has a clue what happened. Callie is zombified in some padded room across town. And my dad—a man I've never had much use for, a man I've hated the majority of my life, a man, I realize only now, right at this moment, I must also love somehow—is dead.

"My birthday," Aaron suddenly says quietly, as if he's answering a silent question he posed to himself.

I pull the pillow away from my face and open my eyes. "What?"

"My wish," he whispers, looking at me like I'm supposed to understand.

"What are you talking about?"

He stretches his arms out and leans forward, gripping on to his knees to steady himself, bracing for whatever he's about to tell me. "The last time I saw Dad was for my birthday last month." He stops and leans in closer like he doesn't want anyone else to hear. "And as usual, he started on me the second I walked through the door. You remember? How I'm wasting my life away. How nineteen is too old to not have my shit together. How when he was my age . . . blah, blah, you know?"

"Yeah, I remember."

"And I sat there through dinner and candles and cake while he railed on me, like always." He hesitates, the beginning of a small, sad smile taking shape at the corner of his mouth. "Know what I wished for?" He looks at me, waiting for me to guess, before he continues. "That I'd never have to see him again," he admits, his voice barely audible.

I hold my breath. There's this giant pause between us, an intermission. I'm not sure what I'm supposed to say. I'm not exactly sure what *he's* even saying.

"I was only wishing that I could finally stand up to him once and for all. By not coming back. Like, if I could not give him the satisfaction, the opportunity. I was just thinking . . ." He trails off, shaking his head. "I don't know, how much more am I expected to give? How much more am I expected to take?" he asks, like there are answers to these questions.

"Yeah," I whisper. "I know."

He nods, and then we're left in our silence again. I let my head fall back against the couch and stare at Jackie's popcorn-textured ceiling.

I don't tell him about any of my wishes, any of my secrets.

Like how often I imagined what it would be like if Dad weren't around. Not necessarily if he died, but if he'd never even existed. Mom would be safe. Callie could have sleepovers like a normal twelve-year-old, without worrying if that would be a night Dad would start some explosive fight and go batshit on us. Maybe Aaron would be graduating high school in just a few days like he was supposed to have been. Maybe he'd still live at home with us. And me, maybe I'd finally have some time to worry about myself instead of everyone else, and maybe I'd actually have a life—friends instead of a GPA.

Dad was the problem, his absence the solution to everything that was wrong with our whole world. If he were gone, things would finally be the way they were always supposed to be. But I was wrong. This is not the way things are supposed to be at all. This was never my wish, either. I don't tell Aaron any of these things, though.

At last Jackie hangs up the phone. She shuffles into the room, looking as if there's a hundred-pound weight on her shoulders, and then she falls down onto the couch next to Aaron with an enormous sigh. Placing her hand on his knee, she gives us both a weak smile. "How you guys holding up?"

Aaron shrugs.

I don't offer a response.

"All right. So . . ." She rubs her forehead for a moment before continuing. "My cousin gave me the name of a colleague of his who's going to work with us. Apparently, he's very good and this is exactly the sort of thing he specializes in. Criminal law."

"She's not a criminal," I mutter, but no one hears me.

"Okay," Aaron says, leaning forward. "That's good news, right?"

"Right," she answers. "But the bad news is it looks like your mom has to wait until Monday, until the arraignment."

"What?" I hear myself shout. I turn to Aaron, wanting him to share in my outrage.

But he just sits there quietly next to Jackie, shaking his head. As he drags his hands across his face, letting the heels of his palms dig into his eye sockets, he murmurs, "Shit."

Jackie stares at me for a moment, opens her mouth, but then closes it, averting her eyes like she's trying *not* to say something. "Look, it's been a long day for everyone. It's going to be okay," she attempts to reassure us. "Let's all try to get some rest."

"Right," Aaron agrees, letting his hands fall to his lap. "I'm gonna take off. Brooke—you're okay here? For tonight."

I look at him as he stands, and I open my mouth to answer, this sickening panic sinking its familiar roots deep inside of me, stealing all the words I need to be able to tell him how much I'm not okay here by myself. Jackie meets my eyes, seeming to understand, which I both appreciate and despise somehow.

"Aaron, you know you're welcome to stay. I mean, if you don't feel like schlepping back into town at this hour."

"Uh, I don't know," he says uncertainly, blinking his eyes tightly, like he's only just now letting himself feel how tired he is. "You sure?"

“Of course. Let’s regroup in the morning.” She turns to me. “Sound good?”

I hate the way she’s looking at me. Like she has X-ray vision and can detect all the terrible stuff that was never supposed to see the light of day, like she can see all the secret places it lives inside of me. It’s like having a thousand bandages ripped off simultaneously, exposing a thousand open wounds. Her pity and her charity and her gentleness are the salt that only makes it all hurt a million times worse than I ever thought it could.

“Sounds good,” I lie.

I raid Jackie’s bathroom for some ibuprofen, aspirin, Tylenol . . . anything. But her medicine cabinet is filled with things like Saint-John’s-wort and vitamin C and valerian root. As I lie down in one of the spare rooms, which Jackie made up for me, in this bed that should be really comfortable because it feels nice and new and clean and safe, I am awake.

It’s too quiet here. I’m used to the gentle hum of traffic or voices drifting in through open windows, or muffled television sounds traveling through the walls and floors and ceilings of our building, or, on an extra-quiet night, the lapping sounds of the river that runs alongside the park across the street. This kind of quiet doesn’t feel peaceful at all. It makes me focus on my thoughts instead, which is the last thing I want right now. I hear them mobilizing, feel them lining up one after the other into formation, building a loop, a reel that begins playing in my head before I can stop it. Frames of Mom in handcuffs, Dad on the floor, Callie in the ambulance, Aaron running, Jackie, Tony, the doctor, police car, ambulance, fire truck. Going over everything, repeating, repeating, repeating, again, again, again.

I pull the pillow over my face and hold it there, hearing my own pulse thumping in my ears. I try to think about something else. Anything else. I think about my exam, all those right answers I knew by heart. I think about Darwin and evolution. Survival of the fittest and natural selection. I think about cellular processes. And genetics. Chromosomes. Kingdom, phylum, class, order, family, genus, species. I think about this time next week, this time next month, this time next year, five years, ten years from now, measuring out the distance to a time when things will be normal, when things will make sense, when things will be right again.

LOCAL WOMAN

STUPID. PATHETIC. WEAK. LOSER. I think I've heard my mom called every name imaginable. From cops to ER nurses to grocery store cashiers to waitresses and bus drivers—all strangers who could see through her lies and her constant cover-ups and outlandish excuses. They shook their heads and silently cursed her, dismissing her as someone who deserved what she got. Whispers from people who thought they knew, thought they understood something even though they didn't have the slightest clue what it was really like, their words always some variation of "Why doesn't she just leave him?" or "Ever hear of a restraining order?" or "What kind of a mother would let her kids witness X, Y, Z?"

This is the first time she's been called a killer.

Last night's news: "Local woman awaits arraignment after being arrested for allegedly stabbing her police officer husband to death." Jackie immediately grabbed the remote, pressing a few wrong buttons before the TV went black. "We don't need to hear this," she said.

But that was yesterday and now it's Monday. Aaron and I sit

next to each other on the couch in Jackie's living room, waiting for dinner to be ready. I'm thankful that Aaron is here, even if there is this awkward silence hanging between us. If I had to be alone with Jackie and Ray for another second, having Jackie ask if I needed anything, if I was okay, if I wanted to talk, and did I like salmon, was I allergic to anything, I would implode. All weekend long she and Ray were trying so hard to make me feel welcome, but it was only making me feel like more of an outsider, more of a burden.

I pull my phone out, checking for the latest updates on final exam grades. No news yet. I close out my e-mail and return my phone to my back pocket. But I pull it out again to check one last time. Aaron sighs loudly and gives my phone the dirty look he really wants to be giving me.

"Will you stop that?" he finally mumbles, nudging me in the arm. "Making me nervous."

I want to ask if he saw the news last night, if he knows what they're saying about Mom, but I don't. Just then Ray appears in the entryway of the living room, clapping his hands together once. "All right," he announces, "I think we're about ready in here."

Aaron and I sit across from each other, with Jackie and Ray at either end of the table. When I set my phone facedown next to me, Jackie clears her throat and says, "Brooke, one of our house rules is we always unplug at the dinner table. This is pretty much the one and only time we get to really be together and catch up, so that's what we do."

"Oh. Right. No, I wasn't—" I begin, but stop because we're talking over each other.

"No, I know you weren't using it *right now*," she says, her voice higher than usual. "I'm just taking the opportunity to let you know, that's all."

"There aren't many rules," Ray chimes in, shaking his head slowly. "But boy, is she serious about that one. I was in the doghouse for a week over one text message."

"Stop it, you were not!" Jackie swats at him, showing all her teeth. Ray laughs on mute: no sound, with his face scrunched up and his shoulders bobbing up and down. "He's teasing," Jackie says, looking at him like they're the teenagers, in goofy sappy-sick love.

I glance over at Aaron. He offers a tight smile, but his eyes are glaring at me. We rarely ever made it through a meal with a conversation that didn't end in a major blowout. So we'd learned simply to be quiet. His eyes are telling me, *Put the damn phone away now.* I do. I slide it into my back pocket despite the fact that it's now digging into my flesh as I sit. I try not to move too much.

But that's hard when there's this elaborate foreign ritual of passing dishes and spooning sauces and picking the right utensils, and the stress of saying "please" and "thank you" and acting normal and polite, like we ever had dinners like this at our house. There are fresh biscuits Jackie made from scratch, steamed vegetables and roasted potatoes, salad with sliced strawberries and little wedges of mandarin orange, and grilled salmon that looks and smells expensive. They even have a white tablecloth that's embroidered with flowers and lace, and a tall white candle lit in the center of the table. I know I'm going to spill something on the tablecloth. I try to make my movements as small and careful as possible, which is only making me feel clumsier—I accidentally drop my biscuit and I can feel Aaron tense up next to me.

I pick at the salmon with my fork. It's pink. I'm sure this is how it's supposed to be, but I'm scared to eat it. The only fish we ever had at home was in the form of sticks. I look over at Aaron to see if he's as lost as I am. He's eating normally, but maybe he has meals like this at Carmen's all the time. I feel so uncivilized.

"Well, the whole point of our family dinnertime is to talk about our day," Jackie begins, like this is something she's rehearsed. "So I went over to the courthouse today for the arraignment. And I also had a chance to meet with Allison's lawyer, Mr. Clarence."

"When is she coming home?" I ask.

"Well," she says, carefully setting her fork on the edge of her plate. "She's not coming home, at least not for a little while, anyway. The judge denied bail."

I look back and forth between Aaron and Jackie, but no one says anything. "What does that mean?" I finally say.

"It means she's going to have to stay in the county jail until"—she pauses, looking up as if trying to locate her next words—"the next hearing, which will determine if they have enough evidence to move forward with a trial."

"What are the charges, exactly?" Aaron asks, twisting up the cloth napkin in his lap.

"There are a number of factors coming into play." Her words are precise, prepared. "The lawyer said that this could potentially be high profile. From his perspective, I guess it's not as open and shut as we'd like it to be. It involves a police officer, minors, assault with a deadly weapon"—she ticks off the reasons on her fingers—"and the doctors say Callie doesn't remember what happened, so as of right now there are no witnesses."

"But what are the charges?" Aaron asks again, this time flattening his napkin and smoothing it out over his legs.

"This sounds bad, I know," she cautions us. "It's voluntary manslaughter, second-degree murder, and first-degree murder."

"She didn't *murder* . . . ," I begin, but the word sticks in my throat, my voice catching on its jagged edges. "She was defending herself. It was an accident. I mean, it would be ridiculous to charge her with that."

"I know, I agree with you. Her lawyer is fully aware of everything. We *all* know that, honey." She exchanges a loaded glance with Ray before continuing. "The lawyer had to explain it to me, and so now I'm explaining it you. They always include more-serious charges, in hopes that we'll plea down to one of the lesser ones to avoid a trial. It's just how it's done, apparently."

Aaron remains silent. I wish he'd say something, anything. There's a tightness taking hold of my insides, everything in me wanting to constrict. I try to breathe in deeply, but my lungs feel like they're made of rusty metal.

When I turn to look at Aaron, he's covering his face—I hear him mumble something through his hands, but the only word I can make out is "fucking." Somehow, I manage to push away my own feelings and put my arm around him like I'm the big sister.

Jackie shakes her head slowly and brings her napkin to her face. "I'm sorry, I know this isn't what anyone wants to hear." Ray reaches out and places his hand on her shoulder and looks down at his half-eaten salmon.

FAMILY PORTRAIT

IT'S BEEN TEN DAYS. Callie stands in Jackie's living room, clutching the handles of her oversize plastic hospital bag like she's holding on to a roller coaster safety bar. They let her leave so she could attend the funeral, which we've had to reschedule three times while we waited for the police to "release the body." A phrase that makes my stomach twist.

She was talking at the hospital but still doesn't remember anything about what happened. The doctor said that's not unusual. She hasn't spoken a word to us, though. She's given us no indication that she intends to go to the funeral, and in fact, she hasn't moved from this spot for about ten minutes.

"Nice house, huh?" I ask stupidly, trying to find any words that will mask how weird this feels, how much of a stranger she suddenly seems to me.

She doesn't answer. Instead she walks over to Jackie's fireplace and picks up one of the picture frames that sit on the mantel. It's silver and has elaborate molded edges. It looks expensive. More expensive than any five-by-seven picture frame has a right to be. She holds it close to her, then at arm's length, as if it's multidimensional and will somehow change its appearance if she holds it at different angles. Silently she sets it back down on the mantel where she found it, except she places it facedown. Then she walks away, drifting down the hall and into the guest bedroom that we'll be sharing, even though we haven't shared a room in years.

I look over my shoulder to see if Jackie was watching us from the kitchen. She wasn't. She's sitting at the dining room table with Aaron, who's already wearing his black suit and black tie, and they're talking in hushed tones, being too obvious about trying to conceal the topic of conversation. Which is Mom. Or Dad. Or Mom and Dad. Or me and Callie—what they're going to *do* with us. I pick up the frame and unfold the arm that's attached to its back with a thin satin ribbon. As I set it back in its place, I look at the picture itself, standing there, perched among the other photos that line the narrow shelf. It's a family. A family that could be any family—a mother, a father, and three kids, their heights measured in perfect increments, smallest to tallest.

The smallest could be a boy or a girl. It's that toddler age where it's hard to tell. There's a messy mass of wild hair sticking out in all directions, a smile that looks like a film still of a belly laugh, the face slightly blurred from the motion. And the boy, the tallest—while still small—has a shyness about him, a quietness, a stillness with his hands clasped together, his arms somehow twisted in front of him at impossible angles as he glances backward at the mother and father, who stand behind all three kids and exchange a knowing look. A familiar, easy smile, a gaze of love and admiration.

The one in the middle, she holds her arms out at her sides, as if saying, *Ta-da!* and her smile is real and her eyes are closed. Not a single one of them looks at the camera.

It could be any happy family.

Except it's not. It's us. And the one in middle, that's me. Eyes closed. And maybe my eyes are still closed, because I've been in this house for ten days and I swear I've even looked at these pictures, but I never really saw this one until now.

My fingers leave tiny smudges on the glass. I can hold it in my hands, see it with my own eyes, yet I can't quite believe there was ever a time when this family existed. But the digitally printed date in the lower right-hand corner is evidence, that on New Year's Eve, ten years ago, they were here—the people in this picture, this family—they existed. I quickly do the math: I had just turned seven, Aaron was nine, Callie was two, and our parents hadn't destroyed everything good in each other yet. I don't know these people. They are all strangers.

Maybe we were all only playing parts; we just didn't know it at the time.

"Great picture, isn't it?" Jackie says, standing right next to me all of a sudden. "One of my favorites." She sighs, gently touching the surface of the glass with her index finger. "Well, we probably need to start getting ready, don't you think?" She has this way of framing statements as questions, and I can't tell if it's annoying or endearing. Or annoyingly endearing.

"Yeah," I agree, unable to decide. "Jackie, do you think we can see her this week?"

"Let's just get through today, all right?"

"All right."

Soundlessly, Callie reenters the room and stands in front of us. Sans plastic bag, she holds on to herself instead, arms folded tightly one over the other. Then she goes and sinks down into the couch cushions, pulling a pillow onto her lap, and stares out the window.

"Callie, you should probably start getting ready too," I say to her, but she only glares in response.

Aaron sits next to her and says something to her, softly. I can't tell what.

She lowers her chin, almost a nod—a half nod.

"I'm going to get in the shower," I announce, though no one seems to hear me.

When we're trying to leave, Callie refuses to move. When I try to convince her to stand up and come with us, Jackie pulls me aside and says, "Maybe it's for the best she doesn't come," as if she somehow knows my sister better than I do. "Ray can stay home with her. It'll be fine."

JUST IN CASE

JACKIE TOOK ME TO the mall to shop for a black dress yesterday. I didn't try it on. I wish I had now, though, because it sticks to me around the hips and it's too loose in the stomach. The fabric is thin, and it's sleeveless. It doesn't look like anything I'd ever allow to be anywhere remotely near my body, but I didn't care enough to look any farther than the first rack of clothes.

I was sweating on the car ride here, but inside it's freezing. A deeper shiver runs through my entire body when I realize why. A place that houses dead bodies would need to be cold. I linger behind Jackie and Aaron as we walk down the wide hall plastered in the most depressing wallpaper imaginable: sick, pale peach and pink flowers against a deep-navy-blue background. Everything about this place screams death. It shouts it from every inch, every corner. From the dark, heavy drapes that block out all the sunlight in the world. *Death*, it whispers as we pass empty rooms on either side. The hard floor, covered in a carpet that's so thin there can't possibly be any padding underneath. *Death-death*, it seems to squeak under my footsteps. The carpet feels more like what I would imagine the green felt on a pool table would be like if you walked on it. I guess there's no real reason for a funeral home to have any luxuries or comforts. Like my dress, it doesn't matter.

I hold my breath as we near the last room—our room. I know because each room has a frame affixed to the wall outside the door, and in it, behind the glass, a sheet of marbleized paper with an unfamiliar name printed in calligraphy.

Until we reach the last one: PAUL WINTERS.

Aaron stops short when we reach the doorway.

Jackie enters first. When Aaron follows, his steps take on a zigzag path, walking like he's drunk, like he doesn't know which way to go, like his feet are arguing with his brain.

I exhale slowly, then suck in another deep gulp of air as I cross the threshold for myself. My eyes are immediately pulled to the opposite end of the room. The casket is laid out like a centerpiece, surrounded by flowers, some kind of morbid banquet. Immediately to the left of the door stands a podium that holds the guest book; I turn around and grip on to it with both hands, my thumbs making imprints in the crisp paper. I can't do this, I realize, I don't want to. I wish I had stayed home with Callie.

I glance over my shoulder, nearly losing my balance completely. Jackie's standing in front of the casket. Aaron stands in the very center of the empty room, craning his neck like he's trying to see, at a safe distance, how bad this is. As I'm watching him, waiting for some sign to tell me how bad it is, he turns to look at me. Like he can read my thoughts, he holds his hand out. Carefully I release my grip on the podium one finger at a time. Force my feet to move toward him, left-right, *death-death*. I force my eyes not to look anywhere except at my brother. He reaches for my hand the way he used to when we were kids, crossing the street. That small gesture makes me feel a little safer, like maybe he'll be my big brother again. Starting now.

We walk together, slowly, cautiously. I can't tell if it's his hands that are shaking or mine. I look down at my feet until I have no choice, until there is nothing left to do but raise my eyes.

We weren't brought up with any kind of religion. So maybe that's why I've never thought too much about the soul. Never knew how to define it, how to recognize it. But looking down at my dad's face, I know exactly what a soul is, and I know for sure that it exists, because I can see that his is gone. He doesn't look real. Like whatever made him *him*, whatever made him a person, a human being, is no longer there.

As I stare, I keep thinking he's about to open his eyes. I keep thinking that he moves, just slightly, that I can see him breathing. I blink hard, trying to reset my vision. But it happens again. And again.

"Aaron?" I whisper. I want to ask what he looks like to him. *Do you see him breathing? Do you notice his soul is gone? Are you scared?*

"Yeah?" Aaron answers, not taking his eyes off our father either.

But I can't utter any of those questions. And he doesn't ask me again. So we just stand there. It seems too surreal even to cry.

One second it's only us and the next there are tons of people filling in the empty space behind us, the air crowded with chatter, with signs of life that only accentuate all the nonlife, making all those markers of death scream louder, more dead somehow.

I hear Carmen's voice close by, whispering, "Sweetie?" As Aaron turns to her, they pull each other into an embrace. Carmen faces me, her chin propped on Aaron's shoulder. We're the exact same height, so as we stand eye to eye, I can see it clearly now, living there inside of her the way it lives inside of me. Fear. That Aaron won't be able to handle this, that she won't know the right thing to do or the right thing to say. That he'll go off the deep end again. I want to tap him on the shoulder and spin him around and look him in the eye and tell him: *For once just be here for me, Aaron. Because I'm afraid I might be the one to go over the edge this time.*

But I don't say that. I don't do anything. Because Carmen's mother is suddenly there, pulling me into a hug so tight my lungs don't have room to expand. I start to feel dizzy as I extract myself from the vise of her arms.

Most of the people are Dad's police friends. I recognize the captain and Dad's partner, and Tony is there, of course. There's Carmen and her mom and Aaron's friend Mark. Three of Callie's friends come with their parents. Callie's JV soccer coach comes with a man I assume is her husband. I take a good look around. That's when I realize that no one is here for me. Not a single person.

I'm caught, all alone, in this whirlwind of comments and declarations that swirl around me like a cloud of fog moving through the room, accompanied by hugs and shoulder squeezes and pats on the back: "He was a great guy . . . generous . . . hardworking . . .

loved his family . . . so sorry . . . so sorry . . . so sorry," they say. I guess it's natural that when people die, when they're no longer here to defend themselves, the temptation to idealize them is stronger than the pull of reality. That acute desire to pretend they didn't have a single flaw—I feel it too. No one mentions the way he died, as if there are unspoken rules dictating what you can and cannot say at a funeral.

It's like in *Peter Pan*, how Peter's shadow separates from him, and Wendy has to sew it back on. Here we pretend my father was divorced from his shadow. And it's nice. I wish I could make the shadow of him stay separate, like it is right now, forever. I want to throw it away, or lock it up and make it disappear inside a dark dresser drawer where no light can reach it. I want to destroy it altogether. But that's not how real life is. In real life there's no way to tear that seam that kept it tethered.

I want to play along, because it would make me feel so much better to pretend that the person they're talking about is the real, the one and only, Paul Winters. But there are two different people. There's Paul, the hard worker, the generous great guy who loved his family, in his way. The one who was a cop and protected other people. But then there's his shadow. The part that no one here ever knew, the one that I never understood—*that* was the part of him I wanted gone, his shadow that could take over in an instant.

I'm thinking about how I *shouldn't* be thinking about this when I see someone new, this old woman standing in the doorway, surveying everything. Or rather, a woman who may not be all that old but looks like life has beaten her down, aged her prematurely. Tall and thin, her face sharp angles, she wears a navy-blue pantsuit that matches the wallpaper and looks like something that would've been on sale several decades ago. Her movements are rigid and jerky as she enters the room, as if each step is painful.

She has a long gray braid that swings back and forth with her footsteps as she makes her way through the room, drawing the attention of every last person here. She walks up beside me and places both hands on the edge of the casket. She looks down into my father's face. She nods, as if he addressed her somehow.

"Had to see it for myself," she mumbles. Then she takes a sniff of air through her nose. "You don't know me; she never wanted you to know me," she says, still looking down at my dad. "Your mother." She slides her gaze to me then. I motion for Aaron to get over here because she's making me nervous. "All because I didn't approve of him. Well, can you blame me?" she says, coughing as she loses her breath by the end of the sentence.

I look at Aaron. Though we've never so much as seen a picture of her, we know who she is—I see a flash of something familiar, something that I can't quite name but that reminds me of Mom, reminds me of myself, even. She's our grandmother.

"I have to say," she begins, the line of her mouth quirking up at the corner, "I predicted this. I *predicted* it would end this way. One of them would be here."

Jackie quickly steps in and puts her hand on the woman's shoulder. "It's time for you to leave, Caroline. That's really enough."

She shrugs Jackie's hand off. "She was like a dog all those years, you know," she says to Jackie, her expression twisting her already-harsh features, like she's catching the odor of something rotten. "So desperate for his love and attention and approval that she'd let herself be kicked and kicked. Always went crawling back, licking his hand." She looks up at me and Aaron. "Everyone wanted to make me out to be the bad guy."

"You need to leave," Jackie repeats more firmly. "You're causing a scene, and Allison would not want you here—*no one* wants you here. Please go."

"Well, she finally bit back, didn't she?" she says, shaking her head.

She pauses, letting her words sink onto my skin, finding their way inside of me, like a drug into my bloodstream. We're not supposed to be talking about any of this, not here, not now, not out in the open, not ever. But she won't stop.

"She was going to be trapped forever, and she knew it. *You* know what I'm talking about, don't you?" she asks, looking directly at me.

I open my mouth, but . . . no words. I shake my head, or at least I think I do.

"I think you should go," Aaron says, taking a step toward her.

She holds her hands up in front of her, surrendering, then she reaches for my hand. As her fingers graze my palm, they feel cold and soft and bony. She turns, and leaves exactly the way she came.

I look down at the small, folded piece of paper she's left in my hand. I open it slowly. In handwriting so impeccable it looks like a scrolling font, ten numbers are lined up in a perfect row, along with the words *Caroline. Just in case.* I close my fist around the paper, crunching it in my palm like it's a secret.

I want to follow her, tell her not to leave. I want to know what she knows. But I can't do any of those things. I can barely feel my hands and feet. The world seems to tilt on its axis just a little too much. I have to sit. Because my thoughts are racing in a million different directions and I'm sure my brain is short-circuiting one region at a time, neuron by neuron. I move to the hard couch along the wall, Aaron and Carmen and Jackie following me. And the paper in my hand: *Caroline. Just in case.*

DROWNING

MY BRAIN FIGHTS AGAINST my body, but I have to open my eyes. And as soon as I do, I'm forced to remember everything all over again, all at once. The way he looked lying in the casket, his face, his hands crossed over his chest like he'd been sculpted out of something other than flesh. When I think of him, this seems to be the only image on file in my head. Better not to think of him at all.

It's been three weeks since Dad died.

My mind ticks off one more day. Another Monday, Tuesday, Wednesday, Thursday, come and gone. Check. No news. Check. Friday again. Check. Callie stays silent. Check.

July is now in full effect. Nearly every day this month has reached record highs. I kick the sheet off the bed and roll over. Jackie replaced the big bed that was originally in here with two twins, like Callie and I used to have back home when we shared a room. Her bed is empty, made up perfectly neat. I look at the clock; it's already noon.

Just in case. I think of the scrap of paper tucked away in my change purse, sliding around the bottom of my backpack. And now the thought that, every morning, inevitably comes next: *In case of what? What more can possibly go wrong?*

I pull the pillow over my head and will myself to fall back asleep. I try to tell myself it's only the heat zapping all my energy, evaporating the life force right out of me. It's the kind of weather that makes me long for the slow, cold seasons, for wind and snow. Right as I'm at the edge of dreamland, something jolts me back: a knock on the door.

Three dull, soft taps, a sound you could almost ignore.

I pull the pillow away from my ears and listen.

"Is someone there?" I call, my voice scratchy as I utter my first words of the day. "Come in."

The door pushes open. Callie stands there. A doughnut wrapped in a napkin in one hand, Jackie's cordless phone in the other.

"Hey." I clear my throat. "What's up?" I ask, even though I don't expect an answer.

She steps inside the room and sets the doughnut down on the nightstand. She holds the phone out at arm's length. It's become like this massive game of charades trying to communicate with her. I try to keep my patience, but it gets harder every day.

I take the phone and bring it to my ear. Callie walks away.

"Hello?"

"Brooke, is that you?"

Something inside me releases like a pressure valve with the sound of her voice. "Mom!" I shout, suddenly completely awake.

"I don't have long. Please, tell me. Tell me everything. What's happening? How are you? What about your brother? And Callie?

We have a lot to talk about, I know. How are things at Jackie's? Tell me the truth. Please believe me, I think of nothing else but you kids. Brooke, hello?" she asks frantically, as if she thinks maybe she's lost me, though she hasn't given me a chance to respond to her series of rapid-fire questions.

"I'm here." My own voice echoes back at me, a delay on the line that I once heard somewhere means your call is being recorded.

"I love you, do you know that?" she says.

"I love you, too. How are you? Do you have any news?"

Silence.

"Mom? Are you there?" I ask, feeling my blood begin to pump faster through my veins.

"Just tell me you're okay," she says, not answering my questions.

"I'm okay," I lie. "We're all okay. But no one's telling us anything."

"I know, I know and I'm sorry." She stops, and I can feel this vibration in her voice, weaving its path through the air and space, through the telephone lines, coiling its way around the inside of my ear—she's about to start crying.

"When can we see you?" I ask, feeling her desperation quickly becoming mine.

"I don't want you to see me here," she says quietly. "It will only make me feel worse."

"But I miss you." I wait, but she doesn't say anything. "Mom, I . . ." I want to tell her just how hard all this has been on me. But I don't. Because this isn't how things work between us. Sometimes I wish it were, but I know now is not the time to try to make it about me.

"You have every right to hate me," she gasps, and I hear the tears fully emerging now, distorting her voice, making it high, then low, then whispery, then loud, the words being pulled under by an ocean churning up from the deepest part of her. "It's—it's so hard to explain. I can barely get my head around it myself, I just . . ." Unable to catch her breath, she pauses midsentence.

I know what I need to do, what I need to say. "Mom, stop, it's okay." I take a breath and set my own murky ocean of needs and fears aside. "Look, everything is going to get straightened out and you'll be home in no time." Though I have no way of knowing whether or not that's even possible, I try to reassure her, and myself. "Stop talking like that. Everyone knows it was an accident, okay?" I lie again.

"Brooke," she whispers. "I don't even know that."

I feel this sharp piercing in my chest, like someone has just stuck me in the heart with a tiny hypodermic needle, and now a small but steady stream of blood is leaking out with every beat, every pulse.

"*Mom*," I say firmly, trying to snap her out of it, "I think you just need to take a breath, okay? You'll be back home with us soon enough. Hold out a little longer, and it will all be over."

"No, no, no," she whines over me, like she's the child and I'm the parent. "No, you don't—you don't understand."

"None of this is your fault," I tell her, but as those words pass across my lips, I have trouble believing them. And I hate her for making me doubt—doesn't she know that my belief in her is all I have to hold on to?

I hear a click on the line, a pop. "Brooke, I have to go, okay?"

She sniffles. "They're telling me I have to go. I love you, okay? I love—"

I try to answer her—"I love you, too"—but the line is dead. I hold the phone in my lap and stare at it, waiting for my head to stop spinning, waiting for my thoughts to clear up. And when they do, I remember what's important, what I have to do: I have to protect her, protect her from herself, even. She's unraveling and she needs me to be strong enough for the both of us, for all of us.

I carry the phone in one hand and the stupid doughnut—which is the source of the five extra pounds I've put on since we arrived here—in the other as I make my way to the living room. Jackie sits on the couch with a basket of laundry next to her, folding clothes into neat piles that line the coffee table like towers in a skyline.

"Oh great, you got to talk to her," she says, gesturing to the phone in my hand. "She sounded good, didn't she?" Jackie says, smiling, nodding.

Of course she sounded good to Jackie—she saved up the real stuff for me. "Yeah," I lie. "Jackie, I know she says she doesn't want us to visit her, but I need to see her."

"I hear you," she tells me. "We'll figure something out, all right?"

I nod. Then I look at Callie, folded into the cushions of the couch, absently picking at a pastry from Jackie's shop. Jackie's eyes meet mine, her lips pressed together into a hard line, her head shaking slightly back and forth. We share a silent moment of communication that somehow conveys how I've been feeling too: hopeless, frustrated. Callie's been going to see this therapist once a week—Dr. Greenberg, a highly recommended child psychologist, according to the doctors at the hospital—except I don't see any improvement, and if anything, I think she may be getting worse.

That night Jackie invites Aaron and Carmen over for dinner. I think it's going to be another announcement, but dinner goes as usual. Unplugged, we all take turns talking about our day, except Callie. Aaron and Carmen brought dessert: a cake that Carmen's mom baked. Jackie makes a huge deal about how she wants her mother's recipe and maybe she will add it as a seasonal special at the shop.

We're all sitting in the living room afterward when Jackie suddenly stands up and says, "Oh! Hold on," and rushes out of the room. Ray shrugs. I hear her opening and closing the closet door in the hall, then she comes back, toting a stack of board games in her arms. "Game night!" She sets them down on the coffee table like an exclamation point. "Kids, this is what us old folks used to do for fun before video games and all that computer stuff came along."

"Back in the Stone Age," Ray adds as he leans forward in his chair to take the tattered lid off the Scrabble box.

"We've played Scrabble before," Carmen says, nudging Aaron. "Right, babe?"

"Yeah," he agrees.

"So have we," I add, gesturing to myself and Callie.

"*This* kind of Scrabble?" Jackie asks, holding a wooden *L* tile between her fingers. "Or the one they have on the computer?"

We all look at one another; she has us there. We have video games, of course, but I've never been any good at them. That's

Aaron and Callie's thing more than mine. I don't mind; I've never had much use for games anyway.

We choose our tiles and arrange our letters. Ray insists that Jackie is making words up. "'Appliqué,'" she argues. "It's a design, like in sewing. It's a word—look it up if you don't believe me."

"I will!" he counters in that good-natured teasing way of his.

I wish I could call my mom back right now and tell her that being here with Jackie and Ray, with their clean sheets and perfect marriage and balanced meals and game night, only makes *me* feel worse. I know I don't belong here and I never will. It's like being underwater and not knowing which way is up, like drowning slowly, even though you're trying so hard to find your way back to the surface.

I get stuck on my turn; there are no words to be made. "Pass," I say.

"If you have an *S*, you can just add it to the end of one of the other words," Jackie offers.

"Come on, just take your turn," Aaron says.

"You could add on to this word right here," Jackie says, leaning over to peek at my tiles like I'm some kindergartner who doesn't know how to play the game.

"Pass," I repeat.

"You can't pass," Aaron says, losing his patience with me.

"Do you have an *S*?" Jackie repeats. "If you do, then you can just—"

"I know," I interrupt. "I don't have one," I tell her, pulling my row of tiles closer to me.

"Here, let me see," she says, reaching for my little wooden tile tray.

"I don't have a damn *S*, okay?" I don't mean to yell, I don't mean to knock over my tiles and mess up the whole board. I don't mean to stand up and storm out of the room. But I do.

"Brooke, what the hell?" Aaron calls after me.

As I'm shutting the guest room door, I hear Jackie tell him, "No, leave it. It's fine, really."

KEEPING SCORE

ANOTHER WEEK, COME AND GONE. Jackie, Ray, and Aaron are all in the kitchen talking in hushed tones. No one ever said anything to me about the Scrabble incident, which only makes me feel worse. Because now I'm positive they're keeping score against me, they're just doing it silently. They enter the living room in single file, each taking turns flashing me and Callie fake, uncomfortable smiles, looking back and forth between one another.

"What's going on?" I finally ask as they form a semicircle around us.

Jackie reaches for the TV remote and mutes it. That gets Callie's attention, finally causing her to look at them. I brace myself as Jackie takes a seat on the couch between us—this can't be good. Aaron sits on the arm of the recliner and it tips forward with a squeal. "Your mother's hearing was today—" she begins.

"I wanted to be there," I interrupt.

"Mom didn't want you there," Aaron says, quick to jump in.

"That's true," Jackie agrees, bowing her head. "And, well. It didn't exactly go in our favor." She takes hold of Callie's hand. I move mine before she can touch me. I hold my breath. "This hearing was to decide if there was enough evidence to proceed with a trial, or if your mom could come home, and they decided that the case will go to trial."

"What?" I try to shout, except my voice barely works.

"I know, honey," Jackie says. "But this isn't the end. It simply means this is all going to take longer than we wanted, that's all."

"How much longer?" I ask.

"I don't know, Brooke. It depends. And actually," Jackie adds, "that's one of the things we wanted to talk with you about."

"Okay," I mutter, the inside of me feeling like a slow-sinking ship, my heart a steel anchor that's been thrown overboard.

"They offered a plea bargain, but—do you know what that is?" she asks, interrupting herself. I nod, even though I'm not exactly sure, because I need her to finish. Aaron sits up straighter and doesn't seem to want to make eye contact with me. "It means they would drop the more serious charges if your mother pleaded guilty to one of the lesser ones—that way there wouldn't be a trial."

"That's a good thing, right?" I ask, looking back and forth between Jackie and Aaron, who's starting to get all twitchy and irritated, raking his hands through his hair.

"No, it's not a good thing, Brooke," Aaron says, looking up at me like I'm completely dense. "Because then she has to say that she's guilty, which means she'll have to serve time, no matter what." He pauses and takes a breath. "At least if there's a trial, she has a chance."

"Oh. Right," I agree, my brain processing this information too slowly.

Jackie continues, probably sensing the mounting tension between me and Aaron. "Well, her lawyer is working on building a case. He thinks we should go to trial instead. He thinks we can win," she tells us, her mouth halfway between a smile and a frown.

"Okay, but how long will *that* take?" I try to ask again.

Jackie shakes her head. "A while. Months. He says it could be a year, even, depending on all the different factors. He's not sure how long."

I feel my mouth drop open, my jaw suddenly unable to bear its own weight. I try to speak, but my tongue feels like a dull, flat rock in my mouth. My voice has to claw its way out of my throat. "And *what*?" I say, turning to Aaron. "We're just supposed to live at Jackie's house for a year?"

Aaron looks up at me from under his eyebrows, scrunching his forehead like I'm saying everything wrong. "Brooke, come on."

"No, you come on!" I check my volume, try to make my voice softer, but I can't. "You always do that. You act like *I'm* the one embarrassing everyone, but I'm only saying what everyone else is thinking!" I stop to take a breath. I look at Callie, wishing she could agree with me.

"You're wrong," he says, lowering his voice. "That's not what I'm thinking at all." He taught me that when we were kids: When you're being yelled at, you should get quieter rather than louder because then the other person—usually Dad—has to get quieter too, just to be able to hear you. It worked only sometimes. "I'm thinking you have it pretty good here and you should be grateful."

“That’s easy for you to say! You can leave and go back to your normal life.” My voice only gets louder, despite its shaking. “We’re stuck here.”

Jackie releases a short breath of air, and when I meet her eyes, they are cold. I’ve never seen her look like that before. She raises her eyebrows and inhales a deep, long breath of air, like she’s preparing to deliver a huge monologue, but she only whispers, more to herself, “Okay.”

Then she stands and walks into the kitchen. Ray follows behind her without so much as a glance at me. Aaron glares for a moment longer, then slides his eyes away, shaking his head. I throw my arms up and pull them tight around my stomach, clenching my teeth hard, not about to let any more words escape my mouth.

Later that afternoon Jackie and I are sitting in the waiting room of Dr. Greenberg’s office—Callie’s weekly appointment. This is the first time I’ve ever gone with them; Jackie said it would “do me good” to get out of the house.

She sets her magazine down and side-eyes me. If she’s waiting for me to apologize, she’s going to be waiting a long time. I’m straining to hear the words underneath the sound machine stationed on a table right outside the door. I can’t make any of them out, but I know that one of the voices belongs to Callie.

“Is she *talking*?” I ask Jackie.

She nods. “Yes. She has been.”

“Yeah, but she’s talking *a lot*,” I whisper.

"I know."

"Well, why doesn't she talk to us like this?"

She shakes her head. She doesn't have an answer.

I jerk myself back in my chair. I should be happy that she's talking, I guess, but I'm starting to really resent the fact the she still hasn't said a word to me.

"It's better than nothing," Jackie points out.

"I know," I tell her, my voice tight and closed off.

"I was thinking maybe you should try talking to Dr. Greenberg too, Brooke," she says cautiously, adding in that rehearsed way of hers, "And you know, it just so happens that he has an opening after Callie, so if you wanted to meet him and—"

"Oh, it just so happened that way, huh?" I interrupt, my tone all saccharine, so mean I can taste it on my tongue.

Jackie scoffs, shifting in her seat.

"Is this how it's going to be?" My pulse is gaining speed with every word. "Every time you don't like what I have to say, you're going to threaten to send me to therapy like I'm crazy or something?"

"Come on," she says, turning her head. "No one said that. It's sometimes helpful to talk to someone who's objective."

"There's no way some *stranger*"—I emphasize that word—"is going to understand anything about anything."

"Are you talking about me or Dr. Greenberg?" she asks, hurling some of my own attitude back at me.

I roll my eyes and mumble, "Forget it."

"Brooke, I'm trying to help you, that's all. Don't you see that?"

“I don’t need to see some doctor. I need to see my mom, which is what I’ve been saying for weeks now.”

Jackie looks at me like she wants to say something else, but she doesn’t.

“I’ll be in the car,” I finally say after a long moment of silence. I walk out of the office without another word.

THE VISIT

THE COUNTY JAIL IS forty minutes away. I keep looking at the clock on the dashboard in Jackie's car, my mind performing endless calculations of how long it will take to get there, as I double-, triple-, quadruple-check the traffic report on my phone.

Our appointment time is eleven o'clock, and we get only a half hour, so we can't be late, because Mom can have visitors only once a week. Yet Jackie drives too slowly, first navigating out of the twists and turns of her bizarre green-grassed, hedge-lined, subdivided world, and soon enough the scenery begins to look more familiar as we cross over the bridge and back to our side of town. We stop at Jackie's shop on the way, which isn't far from our old apartment—I could get out of the car and walk only a few blocks and be there in seven minutes, or cut through the park and be there in five. We keep the car running so we don't lose time. As soon as we pull up, a guy in an apron jogs out of the store, carrying a pink cardboard box to the car.

"Thanks, Owen," Jackie tells him as he deposits the box into Callie's hands through the window of the passenger-side door. "So how's everything going in there, or do I not want to know?" she asks, like we have extra minutes for small talk.

I look up when I hear the voice that answers her. Owen Oliver. We had the same homeroom last year. He's the superstar of the Riverside Ravens. Anytime he entered a classroom, there was always a crowd of people to yell his nickname: O. O for Owen or O for Oliver, I'm not sure. "O—O—OHHHHH," they yelled, like they yelled on the field at the Friday-night games. I think both the guys and the girls worshipped him—when he started growing his dreads out in freshman year, so did about ten other guys on the team.

Their chanting always made my head throb. Even now it pounds in my ears so loud I can barely hear what they're saying. When I look up again, he smiles at me. I quickly look back down, duck my head, try to escape any kind of recognition, focusing instead on texting Aaron:

Running late. There in two mins. Be ready.

My phone vibrates in my hand as the car shifts into reverse.

Aaron: K. I'm outside already

"One thing I learned a long time ago," Jackie says, her tone calm and cheerful as I meet her eyes in the rearview mirror. "Good old-fashioned comfort food can make any situation feel just a little bit better."

I force a smile and bite back any words that might give away how irritated I am. Callie lifts the lid and chooses one of the cream-filled ones, then passes the box to me. I set it down on the middle seat and cross my arms over my growling stomach.

Next we turn down Carmen's street—I could make out the roof of our building if I looked over my shoulder. But I try not to do that. Instead I focus on the road ahead of us. As we pull up next to the curb, Aaron's standing there, his hair wet, like he just got out of the shower. He slides into the backseat with me, an invisible cloud of smoke trailing in after him as he sits behind Callie.

"Hey, good morning," Aaron says to the car collectively. "Smells good in here. Doughnuts?" he asks, looking at the box.

"*Did* smell good," I mumble, waving at the air in front of my face. He clearly just finished smoking a cigarette, even though he supposedly quit after he moved out.

Then he reaches forward around the front seat, placing his hand gently on Callie's shoulder. "Cal? How you feeling?" he asks. She turns around to look back at him, and gives him a quick nod, a small smile, and touches his hand for a moment—more than I've gotten out of her this whole time—something real exchanged between them as their eyes meet in the side rearview mirror outside Callie's window. Like they have some secret language, a secret club to which I've not been granted access.

Somehow we make it on time. We approach a counter where a corrections officer stares us down until Jackie introduces us. Then she reads a series of numbers off a scrap of paper she's been holding on to. The officer gathers up Aaron's and Jackie's driver's licenses, then looks at me and Callie like, *Well?*

"Documentation for the minors?" he asks Jackie.

"Oh, right. Yes," she says, sliding several sheets of paper across the counter.

"And you're their legal guardian?" he asks, examining the forms with suspicion.

"Yes," Jackie answers again, and the man nods and begins entering information from the forms into the computer.

Aaron, Callie, and I share a look, all of us confused. "No you're not," I tell Jackie, using all my willpower to keep my emotions in check.

Jackie turns to face us, taking a deep breath and exhaling. "Actually, I am. At least for now. It was your mom's idea. It's only a temporary guardianship," she says quietly. "I had to get this paperwork filed before you and Callie could visit her—you can't come here without a legal guardian."

"And no one was planning on telling us?" I look to Aaron for some sort of backup, of which he offers none. He stands there nodding along as if Jackie's making sense.

"It's a formality, Brooke," she says, also looking to Aaron for some kind of support.

"Are you getting money for this, or something?" I blurt out. A low blow, I know. But it's the first thought that entered my mind.

Jackie flinches.

"Brooke," Aaron says close to my ear. "Shut up."

The man behind the desk peers out over the rims of his glasses at me, continuing to type, though he's not looking at the screen. "Problem?" he asks me.

I clench my mouth shut tight, so hard my back teeth throb, and I force myself to shake my head no and go against everything I'm feeling inside.

Reluctantly he hands Jackie her papers and the IDs. "Maximum of three people. Only one minor can visit an inmate at one time," he begins, like he's an actor spitting out lines he's said a thousand times—no emotion, no feeling, no idea how it twists my insides to hear my mother called "inmate." "Minors must be supervised at all times, so you'll have to take turns. You'll have thirty minutes."

Jackie and I go in first, while Aaron stays in the waiting area with Callie. It seems like a ridiculous rule that I can't see my own mother by myself, but if this is the only way, I'll take it. We're led into a small box of a room that has concrete floors and concrete walls. Empty, bare, and gray, with an overhead vent blasting cold air on us, so that it feels like we're in a walk-in refrigerator. There's a table, with one chair on one side and two chairs on the other. The guard has us sit down while we wait for Mom to be brought in.

The door opens and another guard walks alongside her, holding on to her arm. I think I stop breathing. I can barely recognize her—because her usually soft, shiny hair seems to have lost its sheen, pulled back in a ponytail, and her face is bare, without any makeup, pale, making her look sick. But as she comes closer, I start to recognize her underneath the too-big jumpsuit—I find her somewhere behind the eyes. The guard leaves after Mom sits down. She's crying before anyone has spoken a word, and as she reaches out, the metal handcuffs clang against the tabletop. The skin on her hands looks transparent and papery, like she's aged ten years since the last time I saw her. I reach across the table, but the guard bangs on the door and yells, "No touching, please!"

I pull my hand back. "Mom . . . ," I begin, but I haven't a clue what to say next.

"I'm sorry." She wipes her eyes and pulls herself together. "I know I look like hell," she says, scooping the loose strands of hair behind her ear.

"*Ally*," Jackie coos.

Mom smiles at her and says, "I can't thank you enough for everything you're doing—I don't deserve you."

"Stop that right now," Jackie tells her, waving her hand through the air and shaking her head like it's no big deal. "What are best friends for? And you don't look like hell, by the way."

"Liar!" They both start laughing like we're in some high school cafeteria.

I make myself count to five before I begin. "Mom, it's really good to see you." *Start slow*, I tell myself. *Ease into the big questions.*

"You too, honey," she tells me. "Listen, I don't want you to worry. Everything's going to be okay," she says, spitting my own words to her back at me.

As I look at her, I see a whole other world in her eyes. She doesn't believe things are going to be okay. Not for a second. She's only saying that because Jackie's here. I feel tiny pinpricks behind my eyes, tears building up. I wipe them away before they can fall, though. It's time to get serious. "Mom, what are we going to do?" I whisper. "What's going to happen now?"

"Let's not talk about that today," she says, trying to smile, trying to act like everything's okay, as usual—you would think if there were one time she could drop the act, it would be now.

"But how much longer do you think—" I try again, but she interrupts me.

"I'm not sure."

There's this exchange between her and Jackie, like they're trying to protect me from the truth, like *I'm* the one who needs shielding. Jackie doesn't know my mom at all.

"Mom, what is this guardianship thing?"

"Brooke, please," she says, as if I'm being inappropriate, like I don't have a right to know what's going on in my own life.

"But—"

"It's temporary," she interrupts, losing her patience with me. "It's just a six-month arrangement so that I know you're being taken care of—that's all. Can we drop it now?"

"Does that mean you could be here for six months?" I ask.

"I don't know, Brooke. Really, I'd rather not talk about this." She widens her eyes at me, in a silent flash, then her face melts back into a soft fake smile. "Tell me about Jackie's house. I haven't seen it in ages."

"No," I argue. "I need to know what the plan is—what's going on? What does your lawyer say?"

She sighs and shakes her head. Then she interlaces her fingers and I can see that her hands are trembling, that she's bitten her usually polished nails down to the quick.

We all sit in silence for what feels like too long.

"Why don't you tell your mom about your exams?" Jackie suggests, trying to diffuse the tension.

I roll my eyes. "I got As on all of them."

"Very impressive," Jackie offers.

"Yes," my mom agrees, trying too hard to sound enthusiastic, but she and I both know her real thoughts are a million miles away from me and my grades. "Brooke always does well," she adds. I hate when she says stuff like that—it feels so dismissive. Like me doing well is something that happens automatically.

I despise the fact that Jackie is here, because I know my mom is holding back. She doesn't want Jackie to see her fall apart. So no one really says much else. Jackie comments on the unusually hot weather several times. And Mom says that they keep it cold in here day and night. And I sit there, stewing inside, until our fifteen minutes are up.

Jackie stands and tells Mom, "Hang in there," before walking over to the door.

"I miss you," I whisper to my mom. "And I want you to come home," I try to tell her quietly so Jackie doesn't hear, so that maybe she can actually answer me.

She grabs my hands tightly, breaking the rules; she leans in and whispers, "I'm sorry," like it's a secret meant only for my ears.

ILLUSIONS

WE DROPPED AARON BACK off at Carmen's, even though I was hoping he'd come over. So now it's just me and Callie and Jackie, sitting in her living room once again, each of us picking at a doughnut from earlier—even me, despite my plan to boycott them.

"Hey, Callie?" I call across the room, though she gives me no sign that she's heard. "Callie?" I repeat, louder. She looks up. "Why don't we go take a walk, get some fresh air?"

She shrugs but finally gives me a small nod in response.

Only a couple of weeks ago I would have missed a gesture that tiny, but I've had to train myself to pay closer attention. She stands and brings her half-eaten doughnut into the kitchen.

Jackie mouths, "Thank you."

Outside, our slow footsteps flip and flop against the sidewalks that line the clean streets as they twist and curve into one another like a maze to which there seems to be no exit.

People talk about being scared in cities, scared of crime,

scared of getting lost—but here it's like you have no choice *but* to get lost. Every street looks the same, like every house looks the same, like every SUV in every driveway looks the same. What's scarier than that? I always used to harbor a silent complaint about our neighborhood. It was old and drab and shitty; I'd rather have had something new and shiny, somewhere else, somewhere quieter, with softer edges, more green and less gray. Somewhere like this, I thought. But after spending these last weeks at Jackie's, I'm beginning to understand why my parents hated places like this. Our neighborhood really wasn't so bad, considering the worst things that ever happened there involved us.

We turn left or right at each corner without speaking. A middle-aged couple power walk toward us like they're on a mission, their movements synchronized as if they've been programmed that way. The man tips his head and says, "Good afternoon." And the woman, "Beautiful day."

I hold my hand up in a greeting. Callie bows her head politely. They would never know that she wasn't some ordinary twelve-year-old—they might notice that her hair looks more red than blond in the sun, or that her legs have grown so fast they suddenly seem too long for her body, and they'd attribute her awkward, shy manner and her crossed arms and her downcast eyes and her disinterested shuffle as typical of any girl her age. For some reason I want to tell them, *No, this isn't her. She's not shy, she's not quiet, and she doesn't try to make herself small; she owns every space she enters, she's full of life and is annoyingly honest and has a sharp tongue and would be ruthlessly mocking your matching hats and sunglasses and sneakers under normal circumstances.*

But they march on by, never knowing, and somehow that makes me the most sad I've been all summer, which is saying a lot.

Callie looks at this group of kids across the street who appear to be her age, maybe slightly younger, playing on a perfectly manicured lawn that lies out before a gingerbread-looking house. There's a sprinkler that streaks across the yard, ticking off aggressively, like a machine gun as it rotates, the kids screaming and cheering as they run through in their bathing suits and bare feet. A square-shaped bulldog sits on the porch, tied to a post, and though it looks like it's melting from the heat, its folds and flaps sagging a little more than seems natural, it lets out a low, obligatory woof as we approach.

"Haven't we passed them, like, five times already?" I ask with a laugh, breaking the silence. I crane my neck to see Callie's face—she tries to hide the beginning of a smile, but I can see the dimple in her cheek, tugging at the corner of her mouth. We stop for a moment on the sidewalk under the shade of a gigantic tree to catch our breath and wipe the sweat from our foreheads. "Can we sit for a sec?" I ask, though I'm already lowering myself down to the curb.

"I always thought I'd like to live out in the burbs. But this place is weird, isn't it?" I try to laugh again, but it sounds too fake, too much like Mom, and certainly not a comment worthy of a response.

She shrugs, focusing her attention on the kids. A warm breeze blows a mist off the sprinkler and carries it across the street to where we sit. It hangs in the air just beyond the arc of the sprinkler's reach, catching a rainbow in its invisible net. I watch her watching it, and I can almost see her eyes light up as they take in the spectrum of colors.

"Pretty, huh?" I offer.

She nods.

"It's the water."

Finally she turns her head to look at me, meeting my eyes for what feels like the first time in years.

"It's like a prism," I continue. "The ordinary light that we see all the time is white, but when the light passes through the water, it bends it, so all the colors that make up the white light get refracted and reflected out—that's the rainbow. It's the only way our eyes can see all the colors. But the really cool part is that it's not actually there at all. It's only an illusion created by our eyes and our brains. So even though we both see it, what I'm seeing doesn't look the same as what you're seeing because it's not really, physically there."

She looks back at the rainbow, thoughtfully, and smiles ever so slightly. Sometimes she appreciates my little anecdotes, sometimes not.

"Cool, huh?"

She nods again and lowers her eyes, studying her hands.

I try to wait, I hold out as long as I can, but—"Callie?" I begin, my voice trembling. She turns her head to look at me, a faint smile still lingering on her lips. "I want you to talk to me. Please. Tell me what I need to do to help you and I'll do it." I take her hand. She lets me. Maybe it's the blue sky, or the rainbow, or the sun—that bright white light washing out all the shadows and the hiding places—that fills me with this desperate need for truth, this need to be honest, to *speak*, myself.

"I just—I can't take this. This silence." I hear my voice fracturing into individual syllables, the words breaking down like the sunlight passing through mist. Her hand suddenly goes slack in mine, her attention back to the rainbow still hovering in space.

"I mean, we need to stick together," I continue. "We need to be there for each other right now. I know it's scary—I'm scared too. And I'm sorry. I'm so sorry," I tell her, no idea if she's even listening. "Look," I say more firmly, shaking her hand, trying to get her back. "I wish it had been me there that day and not you. I wish I could trade places with you, okay? But I can't. And I need you. I need you to get better and . . ." I have to stop to catch my breath.

Her gaze seems to find some breach in the physical world, a resting place somewhere beyond the street and the kids and the house, the dog and the rainbow. I can see her only in profile, but I can tell she's squinting like she's trying not to cry, like maybe something I'm saying really is reaching her. This is the time. *Now*, I tell myself. I take a deep breath and ask what feels like the most important question in the world. "I need to know what happened, Callie. What did he do—what did he do to make her do it?"

It's as if by knowing the actual chain of events that led up to it, maybe I can unravel this jumbled mess, untie all these knots, rewind it, start it over. Have it make sense. Even if I can't make it end differently, if I can at least understand, then maybe other people will understand and then Mom will be able to come home.

"What *really* happened?" I continue, spurred on by this need that's been harassing me for weeks. "I have to know, Callie. And you're the only one—"

But before I can finish, she snatches her hand back. She stands. She's walking away—seemingly all in one movement. The air goes still as I watch the shape of her receding down the street, that breeze falls dead and flat, the air sinks back into its own density. Across the street the rainbow vanishes as if it never even existed—and I suppose it didn't really.

The dog barks once more, having sensed this shift taking place in the atmosphere.

I sit there by myself for a long time, feeling like something has disintegrated inside of me as well. I'm jostled by a sudden crack of thunder in the distance. The kids across the street scream and scatter. The dog jumps up and yelps, begging to be let inside. An enormous black cloud rolls in fast, like a tidal wave in the sky, blocking out the sun. I stand, and for a moment I can't remember which way we came from. I pick a direction and start walking, the air around me taking form, like hands pushing me from behind, urging me to run. But before I can, the rain comes crashing down over me in heavy, sharp sheets.

No use running now. I'm caught.

STANDING STILL

I'M WEARING AN APRON and a baseball cap that says JACKIE'S on it, in case people stumble in and suddenly forget where they are. My ponytail sticks out through the hole in the back of my hat, making me look like some tragic softball team reject.

Jackie had the brilliant idea that I should work part-time at the shop, but I know it's only a way to keep tabs on me, to make sure I'm not sleeping until noon every day.

I've been assembling pink cardboard pastry boxes for the last forty-three minutes.

Fold, bend, tuck, close. Repeat. Fold, bend, tuck, close. Repeat.

We haven't had a customer in one hour and fifty-eight minutes.

Time is not warping, not jumping back and forth, not stalling, then speeding up. It's standing still, like every clock in the world has broken simultaneously. Maybe standing still is simply what happens to time in a coffee shop/bakery in the middle of a weeklong streak of summer thunderstorms.

I don't think we've spoken a word to each other in hours.

"Jackie," I hear myself say, "can I ask you something?"

"Yes, of course," she answers, holding her finger at a spot on the inventory sheet, pushing her glasses to the top of her head as she raises her eyes to look at me.

I try to frame the question in my mind first. "Where were you? I mean, why did you disappear? If you and Mom were really so close, why weren't you around? We've lived, like, five minutes away this whole time."

She lets her finger slide from its spot, tears suddenly flooding her eyes.

"I'm sorry," I admit, looking down at my hands in my lap. "I'm just trying to understand. I keep thinking, what if—"

"I know," she interrupts. "I keep thinking *What if* too. What if we hadn't lost touch? Could I have helped her get away from him sooner? I ask myself that every day." She leans forward, propping herself up with her elbows on the counter. "You know, we were all best friends in high school. We grew up together—your mother, your father, me, my high school boyfriend—we were inseparable. Ally practically *lived* at my house when we were your age."

"What happened, then?" I ask.

"They both had it rough, Brooke. I remember Paul would come to school with black eyes, cuts, scrapes, bruises, a broken nose once. Really bad stuff." She inhales deeply and shakes her head.

"I never knew that," I tell her.

"I guess I'm not surprised." She comes out from behind the counter and sits on one of the stools opposite me. "Well, your mother could relate. Her father used to beat up on her mother right in front of her. And her mother, *Caroline*"—she says her name like it's a bad word, and I wonder if she realizes that she's also just described my mother—"she was a nightmare. Really. Pills, alcohol, basically criminally negligent, in my opinion." Jackie looks up at me then and exhales before she continues. "I probably shouldn't have been so hard on her at the funeral. She is still your grandmother, after all. I'm guessing you never heard any of this, either?"

I shake my head, wanting her to tell me more, but also afraid of knowing the real story of where I come from, for once not sure I want the whole truth, if there even is such a thing.

"Well, it can't hurt to tell you now, I suppose. Now that it seems everything's out in the open." She chokes out a small, nervous laugh. "They both had a lot of pain in their lives. I think they thought they'd be different from their parents—they were madly in love at one time, believe it or not. It's almost like their pain took on a life of its own after so long. Until it was all they had left."

She pulls a paper towel from the dispenser on the wall and dabs her eyes with it. I try to think of something to say but come up with nothing.

"Don't think I didn't try, Brooke. I promise you, I did. I told her to move in with me when Aaron was a baby. She told me I couldn't understand. She forgave him somehow, made every excuse for him. It only started happening more and more, getting worse and worse. The more I tried to help, the more she pushed me away."

"So you just gave up?" I ask, feeling the words beginning to collapse in my throat.

"No, of course not. I never gave up. She did. It got to the point where I would call, she wouldn't answer. I would stop by, she'd pretend not to be there. Finally I told her I would back off, only because I thought maybe it was making it worse for her, but I let her know that I would always be here, that I would always be her best friend, and I would help her whenever she was ready. Except it was ten years before she ever called. And, well, here we are."

"Here we are," I repeat, looking around at the empty tables, so far away from everything I've ever known, far from all the things about my life I always hated, the things I only ever wanted to escape. I have the strongest urge to stand up and race for the door, to run through the rain, across the park, and down the block and up the stairs to home.

"Brooke," she says more firmly, regaining her composure. "We can ask ourselves *What if* all day long, every day, for the rest of our lives, but I couldn't help her because she couldn't deal with the fact that she *needed* help. I've managed to stop blaming myself over the years. I hope someday you can too."

I want to ask if she means that she hopes I can stop blaming *her* someday or stop blaming myself. But the tiny cowbell tied to the door with Christmas ribbon dings, interrupting us. A man walks in, shaking his umbrella off in the doorway.

"Hi there, I'll be right with you," Jackie calls out to him as she blots her eyes one last time.

I clear my throat and swallow hard, pushing those goddamn tears back down into the pit of my stomach—I imagine them being boiled away by acids and enzymes and chemicals. I refocus, with all my might, on the ever-important box assembly project.

I can't sleep at all that night. The silver moonlight shining in through the window is keeping me up. "Callie?" I whisper. "Are you awake?"

I climb out of bed and tiptoe across the room to where Callie is lying on her side with her back facing me. I crawl in next to her and tap three times on her shoulder. She turns her head to squint at me for a second, then rolls back over. With my index finger I draw a big heart on her back, like she did to me that day at the pool. I wait for her to say something. But she doesn't. She squirms and inches away from me, pulling the covers around her tighter.

As I lie here, staring at the ceiling, too tired to sleep, an old memory creeps in. It was sixth grade. I was at a sleepover. Cindy Irving's birthday party. I was only invited because her mother invited all the girls in our class; everyone knew that. But somehow I managed to have a little bit of fun anyway. We made our own personal pizzas and watched movies and ate lots of junk food, and I got to play with her dog, which I liked.

When it got late, we scattered throughout Cindy's living room. They had one of those foldout couch-beds, and so Cindy and three of her real friends slept there. There was a cluster of three more girls on an air mattress Cindy's father had inflated earlier. They were all involved in their own conversations, so I rolled out my sleeping bag on the other side of the room, where I could get some sleep, away from their voices and the light emanating from their phones as they compared the selfies they'd been taking all night long. To my surprise, Monica B.—there were two Monicas in our class that year—came and laid her sleeping bag on the floor next to mine. She was kind of quiet like me, did well in school like me, and, I thought, maybe like me, wasn't really invited. We hadn't ever talked much in school, but I'd always liked her, always noticed her.

As an icebreaker, I told her that I liked her hair—she had it in one of those fishtail braids that I could never seem to figure out. She had me turn around and she explained the steps as her fingers worked through my hair. Back then, whenever I found myself with those crushing feelings I sometimes got, I figured it was because I wanted to be *like* those other girls, not be *with* them. At least, that's what I always told myself. Until that moment—that small, innocent, sweet moment with Monica B.—that's when I first knew it had to be something more. Maybe it was the way her fingers felt in my hair, or the way her smile seemed a little too tender, the way it lasted a little too long.

When we lay down, I showed her how Callie and I would write out messages to each other on our backs. I spelled out *HI*, then a smiley face, then *THANKS*.

But then she giggled. I'm not sure why, I guess it must've tickled her. The light flipped on and suddenly Cindy was standing over us, hands on her hips, this evil grin on her face. "What are you *doing*? Oh my God," she snorted, "are you guys *lesbos* together?"

Monica B. looked at me, and for a moment I thought we were going to stick together, tell those little assholes off, and agree to form our own lunch table at school on Monday. But that's not what happened. Monica jumped up and, taking on the same exact tone as Cindy, said, "Oh my God! Ew, no—gross." And everyone started laughing before I could say anything, not that I would've known what to say had I been given the chance.

I called home. I told Mom that I didn't feel good, I begged her to ask Dad to pick me up, risking any argument that conversation might cause between them. I had never wanted to go home so badly in my entire life. I stood outside on the front steps by myself and

I ran my fingers through the braid, unraveling it strand by strand while I waited for Dad to pick me up.

When he arrived in the patrol car, having just gotten off duty, all he said was, "Hi."

I said "Hi" back.

He said, "Buckle up," and that was the end of it. I was grateful he didn't make a big deal about it or demand to know what had happened. Maybe he knew somehow that it was too humiliating to discuss, that there was nothing to be done about it anyway.

By Monday I'd gone from invisible geek to the rumor mill, and Monica B. was suddenly one of Cindy's minions. Needless to say, I was never invited to another slumber party.

I jerk awake, my body half falling out of Callie's bed. It's darker now, the moon having shifted its position in the sky. I make my way over to the other side of the room and lie down in my bed again, though I know it will never really be *my* bed. As I close my eyes, I vow never to think about braids, or Dad, or that night I missed home so bad I would've done anything to get back there, again.

CEASE-FIRE

IT'S BEEN NEARLY EIGHT weeks since I walked up these stairs. The third step creaks, as it always has. My hand slides easily along the well-worn molded wooden banister, like it has a million times before. I pass by the doors of the neighbors I've lived next to, side by side, for my entire life, trying to be as quiet as possible as I approach the door to our apartment. I put my key into the lock and turn, the familiar metal-on-metal rumble, the sound of the tumblers clicking into place—something inside of me clicking into place.

I push the door open a crack and a thin line of light spills out into the hall. I let the door swing all the way open, the old hinges squealing as it hits the wall with a dull thud and bounces back toward me. I quickly survey the room before stepping inside. After the cops had collected and documented everything, Jackie arranged for a special crime scene cleaning company to come and scrub the place down. As I take one step inside, I'm assaulted by the smells of strong, toxic chemicals unsuccessfully masked with potpourri-scented air fresheners, all being circulated and recirculated through the stuffy, overheated, oversaturated, used-up air. I walk across the living room and throw open the entire row of windows that line the front wall. The room seems to inhale deeply and exhale, the curtains sucked in, then blown back out.

I walk the perimeter of each room, examining its contents—was that ceramic vase always there on that end table? What about that stack of magazines sitting on the bottom level of the coffee table? Surely the pictures on the shelf above the couch have been rearranged. But no. Everything is as it always was. The same with my bedroom, formerly Aaron's room. And Callie's room—formerly my room too—everything looks the same. Our old bookcase in its old spot in the corner, our globe sitting on the top shelf like it used to. I walk over and give it a small spin, but it's barely enough force for even one revolution.

I move on to my parents' room. The door is closed as always, off-limits to us. Anytime I was in their bedroom for any reason I felt like I was in a museum—nothing was to be touched or moved or even looked at for too long.

The metal doorknob feels cool and slick in my hand. I hesitate but then turn it slowly. As I push their door open, the air that rushes out is of a different quality than the rest of the apartment, like it was somehow spared from chemical contamination, the air still fresh and many degrees cooler.

I step inside and am immediately engulfed by the scent of my mother—something like citrus and flowers, though not quite—rushing over me and around me and through me. It's just as comforting as it is agonizing. As I go one step farther, though, it hits me like a wall. Dad. Sandalwood and eucalyptus and spice, the combination of mysterious products he used daily, aftershave and soap and shampoo, obsessive as he always was with the appearance of order and cleanliness in all things. Unmistakably here, dense yet invisible—a ghost stopping me in my tracks.

A breeze floats through the room, raising the hair on my arms and the back of my neck. I hear people talking down below, from the courtyard of our building. The light in my parents' bathroom is on. The window was left open—the fan never did work properly, so they always kept that window cracked while they showered. I walk across the floor, the carpet changing to cold tiles against the soles of my feet as I enter the bathroom. All their things have been left out around the sink—Mom's hairbrush and makeup, Dad's electric razor still plugged in—like they knew for sure they'd be back, using everything again the next morning.

Just then a quick, sharp bolt of lightning cracks inside my head, splintering along the surface of my skull. It nearly knocks me off my feet. I stumble out of the bathroom and make it to their bed. Hunched over, I hold my head in my hands, pulling my stupid JACKIE'S hat off slowly, my hair snagging as it tugs my ponytail loose. I let myself lie down on my back, my legs dangling over the side. I close my eyes. Just a second, I tell myself. Only until the pounding stops.

Someone shouting "God—fuck—dammit, Brooke!" is what wakes me, sends me sitting straight up, my eyes wide open. Aaron stands in the doorway, brandishing an umbrella. "Don't ever do that again!" he shouts, tossing the umbrella to the floor and dragging his hands over his face. "I thought someone broke in. I thought you said we'd meet outside?"

"What?" I manage, still foggy as I look down at the hat clenched in my fist and remember how I came to be lying in my parents' bed.

"Do you know you left the door wide open?" he asks, still standing out in the hall, like he senses that same invisible barrier to this room, preventing him from entering.

"Shit, I did?" I ask, the ratio of profanity to regular words seeming to rise involuntarily whenever it's just us. I quickly get up off the bed and smooth my hands over the wrinkles I've made in the bedspread.

He moves aside so I can pass, eyeing me suspiciously. Then he follows me back out to the living room. "So, what are we doing here?" he finally asks.

I shrug. "I just wanted to check on things, since we're allowed back in now. I thought we could do it together. Plus, I wanted to see you."

"I've been meaning to stop by Jackie's place," he says. "I've been working a lot." Aaron always has an assortment of random part-time, sometimes under-the-table, seasonal, fill-in-for-the-regular-guy jobs. I can never keep track of where he's working or when.

"Thanks for coming," I tell him, turning around to face him. "Is this the first time you've been back?"

He crosses his arms and says, "Yeah." He takes a quick look around the room, his eyes twitching when they scan the doorway to the kitchen.

"I haven't gone in there yet," I tell him, because I know that's the question on his mind, the fear in his heart—I know because it's mine, too.

Keeping his arms tightly folded across his chest and his eyes on the floor, like he's concentrating on counting his steps, he walks slowly toward the dining room. He stands at the entrance to the kitchen for a second, the way he stood in the doorway at the funeral home, checking first to make sure it's safe. Or safe enough, anyway. He unfolds his arms like he's taking off some kind of protective armor, and steps inside the kitchen, so that I can't see him anymore.

My feet begin to follow but stop short at the dining room. "Well?" I ask, growing more nervous, more impatient by the second, but also thankful he's here, that he's the one checking it out first.

"It's okay," he calls back.

I take the final steps into the kitchen, still bracing myself as I assess the scene, examining the walls and floors, the countertops and the sink—everything shiny, cleaner than ever before, better than new. Wiped clean like my sister's memory.

"Do you believe her?" I finally dare myself to ask.

"Who?"

"Callie. Do you believe she really doesn't remember what happened?"

He sighs and leans against the counter, bringing his hand to his mouth like he's trying to prevent himself from answering. "*God*," he murmurs, drawing the word out into a sigh, a groan. Then, meeting my eyes, he says, "I don't know. I have no fucking idea what to believe anymore." He cracks a laugh but stifles it immediately, shaking his head. "Do you?"

I shrug, because that's the best, most honest response I can manage. Then I go stand next to him, and we both stare at the flour, sugar, coffee, and tea canisters that line the opposite counter, running from large to small, in perfect order, like the kids in the picture frame at Jackie's house.

"She's not getting any better. I can't get through to her. I'm trying, I really am. But I can barely get her to look me in the eye, and if I do manage that by some miracle, I just end up blowing it anyway—say the wrong thing, do the wrong thing."

He looks at me, at a total loss, not seeing that there's something he could do to solve all our problems. "She'll get there," he says uncertainly.

I've been crafting a new plan for us over the past couple of weeks, and I tell myself now's the time to deploy it. "She talks, just not to us."

"She's talked to me," he admits. "A little, anyway."

I take a breath, try to fortify myself. "I think we need to come home, Aaron."

"But . . . how?"

"You. Don't you see it? You're nineteen, you're an adult. You could technically be our guardian."

He stares at me, squinting. "Brooke, I don't think . . ." He pauses, and because I can't handle hearing him finish that sentence, I keep talking, try my luck with the honesty card once more—time is running out, after all, the summer nearly over.

"Aaron, I don't want to live at Jackie's, okay? Maybe that's selfish. But I don't. Not for another day, not for however long this whole thing is going to take. She's fine. Ray's nice. The house is perfect, I should be grateful. I get that, all right? But when I'm with them, all I can think about is how we don't fit in there, how we don't belong, how we're these giant charity cases."

"You know that Jackie and Ray don't feel that way—they love you guys."

"We don't know that," I argue. "Jackie and I don't even get along. Besides, that's not the point. I'm saying *I* feel like shit around them. I know I should feel so safe and secure, but it's the complete opposite. And I know Callie feels the same way," I lie, remembering that convincing Aaron hinges on her welfare. "And I really think she'd be doing better if we were *all* together."

He sighs loudly, shakes his head. "You honestly think it would be better for Callie to be here—after everything that's happened?"

"I don't know. It's still our home, isn't it? I'm just saying we have to try something. She's not getting any better at Jackie's. It seems like she's only getting worse. She acts like she hates me." I pause, afraid I might be losing him. "And what happens when Mom comes home? Are we just going to sit back and lose the apartment?"

"We don't know when she's coming home," he says, looking at me like I'm stupid. "*If* she's even coming home."

"She's coming home, Aaron—of course she is."

"There's a real possibility that things won't go the way we think they should."

"Look, I called Mom's lawyer, and he said that we could—well, *you* could—apply for Dad's social security benefits. That would help with expenses. And you have your jobs. And I'm working now too. And he said that the temporary-guardianship thing can be changed so that you're our legal guardian."

"Jesus, Brooke—what are you doing calling Mom's lawyer about this stuff?"

"I'm trying to figure out a way to keep us together. Because I'm telling you, it's not working—none of it is working. Not at all."

He's nodding, though he's stopped looking at me and now has his eyes fixed on the floor.

"Please think about it before you say no," I plead. "You know, I never thought I'd say this, but I want to be *here*—in my own room, with my own things, in my own home. It's like too much is changing, I—I can't even keep up." I have to stop because I can feel the tears starting to simmer behind my eyes, obstructing my throat, making it harder for the words to find their way out of my mouth. "It wouldn't have to be like you're *really* taking care of us. I mean, we'd be doing it together—you and me." My voice catches, in spite of my best efforts to hold it together. "Remember, you and me? Remember when there was a time we used to get along, when you still liked me? It wasn't that long ago."

"Hey," he finally says, snapping out of his trance. "Look, I know we haven't been tight in a while," he says, pulling me into an awkward hug. "It didn't have anything to do with you. I wanted to get out of here, that's all. I wanted to get away from *him*. Never you." I can't help but wonder if he's talking about moving out or if he's talking about that day on the roof. "I'm sorry," he adds as we pull apart. "Maybe I never actually told you that, but I didn't think I had to."

I'm relieved to hear him say it finally—to acknowledge the fact of it, that all of that really happened, that he really did turn away from me and it wasn't my imagination. "No, you forgot to tell me that part!" I say, uncertain if I'm angry or sad, or both. Then an old reflex takes hold. My arm extends involuntarily and I punch him in the shoulder too hard, catching him off guard and sending him reeling backward.

He winces and yelps, "*Owwshit!*" catching the handle of the refrigerator door, which swings open fast, making him stumble like he's on roller skates, falling down directly on his butt.

I smack my hand over my mouth and mumble, "Oops," unable to stop the laughter erupting from somewhere deep in my center. I reach out my hand to help him up, but he pulls me down along with him. I trip over his legs. And suddenly we're both keeled over on the floor, cracking up, wheezing, contagious, like it always used to be when we were kids, our laughter filling in all the rooms and the empty spaces that were afraid they'd been forgotten.

Every time our laughter slows and I think we're going to stop, all we have to do is look at each other and we start up again for no reason. My abdomen expands and contracts too violently, sending waves of nausea through my body, which hasn't laughed like this in years. "Okay, stop—ow, stop, my stomach hurts!" I gasp.

By then we're both sitting cross-legged on the kitchen floor. It feels like something has shifted, like some jagged edge of bedrock in our foundation has just now settled into place, and perhaps, at last, we've reached a cease-fire in our ongoing cold war.

He sighs as he extends his arm toward me, holding his hand with his pinkie sticking out. It takes me a moment to understand the meaning of this gesture, uncertain what exactly we're pinkie-swearing over. This is another thing we haven't done in years—I guess somewhere along the way we must have learned that pinkie promises were not, in fact, the most binding of agreements.

"What?" I ask, squinting at him.

"Come on." He tips his head toward the space between us, extending his arm a little farther. As I reach my hand out and lock my pinkie finger with his, he looks me in the eye, no trace of playfulness in his voice when he says, "I'm in."

FALL

ARTIFACTS

JACKIE CAME THIS MORNING armed with muffins and pastries, coffee, juice, and old cardboard boxes from the shop that previously contained bulk shipments of things like napkins and paper cups, plastic eating utensils, and coffee beans. It's the very last weekend before school starts up, and Carmen and Jackie have been here all day helping us get the apartment in order, getting our things moved back in and making room for Aaron in our parents' room.

I pull on the string that hangs from the ceiling of their closet and step inside as the light flickers on. Mom's dresses and blouses and skirts take up at least two thirds of the space. Her shoes are laid out on the floor, left and right, in two neat rows. On the other side are Dad's clothes, his uniforms lined up one after the other. I reach out and run my fingers along the sleeve of one of the black police shirts he wore every day. I carefully press my face against the starchy fabric, realizing that this is the closest I've come to hugging my father since I was in elementary school, and it's the closest I'll ever come again. Then, like a reflex, I stretch my arms wide and gather all my mom's clothes up at once and fall into them, breathing her in, missing her so much it feels like she's the one who died.

"Oh!" Jackie says, suddenly standing behind me.

I turn around, letting go of the clothes so abruptly one of Mom's dresses slides off the hanger, the entire wardrobe left swinging back and forth on the rod.

"I'm sorry, didn't mean to scare you," she says, holding out a stack of garment bags folded over her arm. "I was just bringing you these."

"Thanks." I take them from her and lay them down on the bed. Then I scan the room, trying to devise a plan for how to go about clearing the jewelry and spare change from the tops of their nightstands, how to empty the dresser drawers, and then there's the perfume and cologne and makeup and toothbrushes in the bathroom. It has to be done, but as I run my fingers over these mundane items, they feel more like artifacts, remains of another life and another time, that should not be disturbed.

Jackie was against the whole thing, naturally. But Aaron and I went to see Mom and we explained everything. She heard us out, and while she didn't seem particularly thrilled with the idea either, I don't think she had the energy to debate the issue. She looked back and forth between us, lost in her thoughts. Then she shook her head and said, "I don't know. You kids do what you think is best for everybody. I don't know," she repeated. "Not anymore."

"How about I help you in here?" Jackie says, looking around the room at everything that still needs to be done.

Also lacking the energy to debate the issue, I tell her, "Sure."

We're all at it for hours; small fragments of conversation punctuate the time, bringing us out of our minds and back into the present for a reprieve. We manage to box things up we won't be needing. I make so many trips up and down the stairs to our tiny storage unit in the basement that my legs begin to feel like putty.

The last remnants of daylight are streaming in through the open windows, painting a band of gold light across the living room wall. Jackie has postponed leaving for as long as humanly possible. She stands in the living room clutching her purse, reminding us for the thousandth time: "Your mother agreed to this on a trial basis. I'm only twenty minutes away, if you need anything—really, anything. And I'm going to be checking in. I'll be a pain in your ass," she tells us, wagging her finger.

"We know. Thank you for everything, Jackie," Aaron tells her.

"Bye, Callie," Jackie calls across the room.

Callie raises her hand and waves. Another small victory for us all.

"And, Brooke," she says, directing her attention at me. "See you tomorrow for your shift?"

I nod.

At last she leaves. I think we all take her exit as the cue we've been waiting for, the one that allows us to cave into our exhaustion. We each find a place to sit, simultaneously. Me on the floor, Carmen on one end of the couch and Callie on the other, and Aaron in the armchair that used to be Dad's spot. It feels wrong to see Aaron sitting there—and maybe he feels it too, because he sits there for only a second before he sinks down to the floor with me.

Carmen's been making polite small talk with me all day, but

she's been acting like Aaron is invisible. Which means they're in some stage of fighting; I can't tell if it's the beginning or the end.

"So, Brooke," Carmen says, breaking up the groggy silence that's washed over us. "Getting excited about school?"

"I guess!" I say it with the same level of enthusiasm as if I'd said, *Yes, absolutely! I can't wait.* But the thing is, I'm not excited. I'm glad, sure. This was never about excitement. It was about strategy, about creating a way for me to exit, to leave, to get out. I can tell from her puzzled expression that my answer wasn't good enough. So I try again. "I mean, yeah. Yes," I repeat. "I'm excited."

That earns me a smile.

"And, Callie, how 'bout you, babe?" Carmen says, louder. "How's your summer been?"

She's been talking more and more every day since we decided on coming home, but Aaron and I sit up straighter, silent as we wait to see what will happen. Callie stares at the coffee table, her face unchanging, as if she hasn't heard, her arm dangling off the edge of the armrest, too still. And just when it seems like one too many seconds have passed and she isn't going to answer, we hear the two most marvelous words pass across her lips: "Fucking hot."

Aaron and I share a triumphant smirk—of course no one is going to reprimand her use of the f-word.

"That's for fucking sure, right?" Carmen says, giving me a wink. She shifts her gaze to Aaron, who's smiling at her with soft eyes. She purses her lips, then stands abruptly. "I guess I should get outta here too."

Aaron stands up slowly and sighs. "I'll walk you out." Their footsteps on the stairs fade until Callie and I are alone again.

I open my mouth to speak, but all the things she's still not telling us sit like a giant wall around her. She raises her eyebrows at me, making her eyes wide, as she crosses her arms, silently asking, *What?* I walk over to the couch and sit down. "It's good to be back home, isn't it?" A stupid, generic question, but it's the only thing I can think of to say.

She stands and looks out the window, focusing in on something. I turn around so I can see too. Down below, on the sidewalk in front of our building, Aaron and Carmen look like they're arguing, their voices too faint to hear what they're saying. Carmen keeps her hands on her hips, and shakes her head as she looks off into the distance. Aaron throws his arms out to his sides, then turns away from her, taking a few steps in the opposite direction. She stares at his back for a moment, then spins around and walks away. When Aaron realizes she's leaving, he starts walking after her fast, but then stops short and stands there, frozen.

I feel like I'm watching a play, something choreographed, steps on a stage.

"That doesn't look . . ." But when I turn back around, Callie's gone. "Good," I finish, talking only to myself. The stench of cigarette smoke wafts up through the window. Looking back down, I see that Aaron now sits on the front step, hunched over with his elbows planted on his knees. The sun drops below the buildings, casting a deep shadow over the street. He brings the cigarette to his mouth, the burning tip glowing brightly as he inhales.

I wait for a while. I plan on asking if everything's okay, but he doesn't come back up right away. In my bedroom I pull out the stack of eight different summer reading books I was supposed to have been plugging away at over the past two months. Then I pull out the gigantic AP Psychology book I ordered online the day I found out I'd be going to Jefferson, before all of this happened. I even had it delivered priority. I planned on reading it cover to cover over the summer. I planned on memorizing everything. I wanted to be prepared. I wanted to show my new teachers how worthy I was of being there. But I haven't so much as peeled the plastic wrap off.

I feel a tiny point of pressure pinch somewhere inside my rib cage—the familiar knot of panic, the shortness of breath. I rifle through my desk drawer until my hand finds the smooth plastic bottle. I quickly twist the cap off and pop four almost-expired aspirins into my mouth. Then I place my hand over my heart. I breathe air into that small bundle of tangled nerves, and something inside of me seems to loosen its grip, the pressure in my head and chest and lungs beginning to retreat.

I grab the book and my favorite orange highlighter and bring them out to the kitchen table, where I'll wait to talk to Aaron. I sit down and rip off the vacuum-sealed plastic wrap, flip open the cover, and start reading the introduction. I uncap my highlighter and mark a passage. I'm halfway through the second unit—"Memory"—when suddenly I look up. Outside it's darker. Time has passed. Aaron still hasn't come back.

My eyes ache from reading for so long. I blink hard a few times. I'm tempted to call it a day and go to bed. But no, I have a little more in me, I decide. Just need to rest my eyes for a minute. I fold my arms over the hefty psychology book and lay my head down. Only resting my eyes, I tell myself.

FAULT LINES

I AWAKE WITH MY face in the folds of my textbook and glance at the clock. It's 5:30 a.m. Aaron is asleep on the couch in the living room. I gather my things from the table and on my way to my room peek inside Callie's. She's sleeping with her covers thrown off despite the cool night air. I glance at her desk—my old desk—and see my old globe. A memory arrives in my mind like it has been on pause, waiting for me to hit play.

I see myself as a thirteen-year-old in the room, back when Callie and I still shared it, back when Aaron lived with us the first time. Before the day on the roof, before he moved out, before I took over his room and claimed it as my own.

I remember how I'd run my fingertips up and down the lines of longitude, across the lines of latitude. But one moment rushes forward.

It was October; I was in eighth grade. I had just spun the globe and set my finger down slowly, letting it skim against the molded surface. A sandpaper sound emitted from the sphere until finally it slowed to a stop, spinning to a time in the future. I took a breath and moved in closer to get a better look.

"So?" Callie asked me. "Where are you going to live now?"

"In the middle of the Indian Ocean." I sighed, genuinely disappointed. Sometimes the middle of nowhere happened. Then again, sometimes it was Bali or Fiji. Sometimes Quebec or Malawi. Hawaii was my favorite. I looked at the big island dreamily and sighed again—I was big on sighing back then—"Someday." I added *Indian Ocean (?)* to the list that I kept in the back of an old notebook. It was pages and pages long by the time I stopped, by the time I realized I was going to have to stay put, at least for a while.

I walked over to our bookcase, cradling that precious globe in my arms like a baby—my only connection to the great, big world out there, a world full of better places, places I'd rather be, places that I was convinced were waiting for me—and set it back down in its spot on the top shelf.

I turned to Callie, my face suddenly serious and pinched in now that my daily allotted daydreaming time was over. "You have your geography test tomorrow, don't you? What is it, capitals?"

She moaned and rolled her eyes—she'd been getting really good at that—and simply continued playing with her dolls on her bed. With a Barbie in each hand, she thrust the one on the right forward at arm's length so that it was facing me. "You think that because you're in eighth grade and I'm only in fourth, you can tell me what to do!" her Barbie accused me in a voice slightly higher than Callie's, her whole plastic body being shaken for added emphasis. "Just because *you're* the smartest person in your class doesn't mean that I should be smart too!" Then the Barbies went back to talking among themselves, an indecipherable murmur passing between them.

"Shut up," I mumbled, so casually that neither Callie nor the Barbies seemed to hear me.

Then there was a big crash out in the living room, shaking the walls and the floor like an earthquake, like a fractured fault line on my globe had just cracked the whole world wide open. I jumped, but Callie barely seemed to notice.

Mom shouted, "Stop it!" She was already crying. "I told you I don't have it! Listen to me. I swear. Please, calm down."

"Don't!" he screamed—*screamed*. "Lie. To. Me." Every word matched with a *bang-slam-bash-boom*.

Callie started humming.

Money.

He always thought she was hiding money from him. She might have been too. But it was *her* money, after all.

"Mrs. Allister's gonna call the cops again," Callie said in her singsong voice, more to her Barbie than to me.

"Did you study?" I asked her, trying so hard to ignore what was happening on the other side of our bedroom door. I walked over to our laptop to turn the volume up on the music. Underneath the arguing and the music and Callie's humming, and me pretending like nothing was happening, I could hear the steady rhythm through the wall our room shared with Aaron's. It was the bump-bump-bumping of Aaron lying on his bed tossing a tennis ball against the wall and catching it, over and over again.

"Sorta," she finally answered.

"*Sorta* . . . is not good enough," I scolded, as I thought was my duty. "Nebraska?" I asked her, even though I was almost unable to hear myself think through all the layers of noise reverberating through the house.

Callie rolled her eyes and fell over sideways onto the bed.

Here we go.

"I don't wanna do this," she moaned again, opening her hands dramatically to let the Barbies fall lifeless to the floor with a dull clatter.

"*Nebraska*," I demanded.

"Omaha," she growled into her pillow.

"Wrong. Lincoln." I lay down on my bed, across from hers, on my stomach, getting fully into quizzing mode. "Rhode Island?" I asked, some part of me taking pleasure in the structure of it all—the rightness of having clear, definitive answers. I could feel myself kicking my feet, swinging them up and down, alternating, left-right, left-right, left-right.

"No, Brooke. *Pleee-ease.*"

I threw my ancient Care Bear at her head. "Come on!"

"*Ow*," she whined. "Providence, jerk!" She threw it back at me, but I blocked, and it ricocheted off my arm into the wall, then fell softly onto my bed, before tumbling soundlessly onto the floor with Callie's Barbies. She stuck her tongue out.

"Vermont?"

She shrugged—she could never remember Vermont, for some reason.

"Montpelier. You can remember because the end of 'Ver*mont*' is the beginning of '*Mont*pelier.' Got it?" She continued to stare at me, expressionless. "Okay, Kansas?"

"Toe-picker!" she shouted—she really did enjoy annoying me.

"It's Toe-*peek*-a. Topeka, okay? Be serious, Callie. New York—you *better* know this one."

I watched this little smirk twisting up the corner of her mouth, a dimple indenting her cheek, and I could read it on her face—she was probably daring herself to say "New York City," like the last time, but decided against it. She took a cue from me and sighed through the word "Albany," managing to stretch it out over one long syllable.

"Yes. Tennessee?"

"*Nasssshhhh*-ville" she said, sitting upright again, suddenly alert, bouncing up and down, having found a way to amuse herself.

"Right. North Dakota?"

"Bisquick!" she shouted, totally losing it, dissolving into that stupid full-body laugh of hers that was nearly impossible to withstand without joining in. I bit down on the insides of my cheeks to keep from smiling.

"Fine. Enough, okay? Are you done?" I waited until she stopped. "All right, Arizona?"

She gazed up at the ceiling thoughtfully, trying to come up with something clever. But then the door slammed, giving the whole apartment one last rumbling aftershock. I could hear his footsteps on the stairs. And Mom gasping through her sobs in the living room.

My eyes closed. There was a tiny ice pick somewhere deep in my brain, jabbing away at my frontal lobe. I buried my face in my folded arms. My legs went limp as they flopped down against the bed. It was over. It hadn't been that bad. It wasn't always super awful; sometimes it was just loud more than anything. But no matter how bad or not bad, it always affected me the same, stirring up all kinds of chaos inside of me, the way a storm churns up all the mud and scum at the bottom of the river.

"Phoenix," Callie answered.

On the other side of the wall the bouncing of the ball had ceased, and I could hear Aaron wrestling his window open—a clang followed by a screech, always. Then his careful footsteps pinged the metal stairs of the fire escape. He was on his way up to the roof to smoke.

I lay there, trying to still the rolling waves of anarchy surging through my body.

"*Phoenix*," she repeated, louder. "Brooke, Phoenix!"

Something took hold of me then, as it sometimes did. I lifted my head to look at her, and when I opened my mouth, it was someone else's voice. "Shut up, Callie—just *shut up*!" The words raked through my throat like fingernails on a chalkboard, sending chills up and down my spine. "*Shut! Up!*" I screamed into my pillow, the words strangling me.

She did. She shut up.

Without another word she got up and switched the light off, turned the computer speakers down.

By morning Mom had cleaned everything up, like nothing had ever happened, and Dad was sitting at the table with a bowl of cereal, already showered and dressed in his uniform, looking clean and composed, polished and calm. I used to love the way he looked in the mornings, almost like it was truly a new day, like maybe things could be different, like maybe we could all start over and be better.

He looked up from the paper as we walked in.

"Hey, kiddo," he called out to Callie.

To me, he gave a single sharp nod.

"Hi," Callie mumbled, rubbing the sleep from her eyes.

I rushed out past her, trying to ignore the cool suspicion on my father's face as he looked at me. My wet hair was pulled back in a tight ponytail that swung from side to side, smacking me in the face as I lugged both of our backpacks out and set them down by the front door. "Callie, go get dressed first, then eat your cereal. You have twenty minutes, so hurry—I'm not going to be late again!"

"Calm down," Dad said through a mouthful of cereal. "You have plenty of time."

"Not really." I sighed as I bent over to tie my shoes tight. I looked up just in time to see Dad shoot me a warning look, a courtesy he never afforded Mom.

"Both of you come sit. Eat your breakfast," he ordered. "Aaron!" he shouted.

"Dad, I still have to make our lunches," I protested. "And Callie takes for-*ever* to eat."

"I said"—his face flamed pink for a moment—"come sit. *Now.* Aaron!" he yelled again.

We sat. And finally Aaron emerged from his bedroom. Thankfully, because I was about to run in there and drag him out if he made Dad call his name one more time. He didn't say anything as he slumped into his seat at the table. Dad's face cooled off then.

"Shouldn't we wake up Mom?" I asked.

This time Callie shot me a warning look.

"Let her sleep," he said, folding the paper in half and setting it on the table next to his bowl.

"But . . . ," I began, my eyes fixed frantically on the time on the stove. "But isn't she going to be late if—"

"What did I *just* say?" He brought his fist down against the table so hard that my spoon jumped out of my bowl. Aaron sat up straighter. I could see him clench his fist in his lap, preparing to step in if this suddenly blew up.

"Sorry," I mumbled.

"Don't be sorry, stop with the worrying. Let the parents do the worrying. You be the kid, all right?"

I could feel my jaw muscles clench as I nodded carefully, clamping down on the words already in my mouth, begging to come out.

"Good morning," Mom yawned, coming out of their bedroom wearing her fuzzy purple bathrobe and matching slippers—the ones we picked out from some catalog for Mother's Day two years earlier. I turned around in my seat to look at her. Her eyes were still puffy from last night's crying, but that was all. No marks on her face, which was always good.

Dad looked up but didn't speak to her. "Say good morning to your mother," he ordered us instead.

"Good morning, Mommy," Callie and I said in unison.

"Morning," Aaron added, a second too late and a tad too unenthusiastically. Which, we knew, was all it really took to set Dad off when it came to Aaron.

Dad grabbed Aaron's wrist abruptly, making him drop his spoon, splattering milk across the table. "What's this?" he asked, inspecting Aaron's hand in his own.

"What? Nothing," Aaron mumbled, quickly using his free hand to sop up the stray drops of milk with his napkin.

"You need to cut your fingernails." It wasn't a simple observation, though; it was an accusation. "What have I told you about that? And what did you do, sleep in those clothes? You look like you just rolled out of bed. You don't take any pride in your appearance."

Aaron snatched his hand back and ran it over the front of his shirt. "No," he said quietly. "It's just wrinkled." Then he smoothed his hair back and tucked the unruly strands behind his ears, all of us anticipating what would come next. I tightened my ponytail, in case Dad happened to examine my appearance.

"Ally, the boy needs a haircut. Unless you *want* to look like a girl?" Even Aaron knew not to answer that. "Listen," he said sharply, jabbing his finger into Aaron's shoulder. "You clean up before you step foot out of this house. Can't have you walking around town looking like a bum. Understood?"

Aaron nodded.

Mom sat in her spot next to Dad at the table and poured herself a glass of orange juice. Both Callie and I saw the gray-blue bruise circling her wrist as she reached across the table. "No problem, we can go after school." She smiled like things were just perfect. "Right, Aaron?"

He nodded again.

Everyone was finally quiet. And I remember thinking that if we could stay *just like this*, then everything would be fine. I ate my cereal one Lucky Charm at a time, trying to make it last a little longer, not even caring about the time on the stove or our unmade lunches or being late to school.

RAVENS

LATER THAT DAY AT WORK I'm exhausted. Thankfully, it's been a slow morning. Jackie's had me detailing the espresso machine and the coffee grinders. She told me that today would be the day I'd learn more on the register; up until now she's had me on menial, pointless tasks.

The bell dings. I hear Jackie call out across the shop, "Hey, Owen!"

They make small talk as he comes behind the counter and pulls an apron over his head, tying the straps behind his back, working his O charm on her, too. I do my best to make it seem as though I haven't taken notice of any of this. And then I feel their eyes on me. I look up again only because I hear my name.

"What?" I ask.

"I was just telling Owen how you're going to be picking up a few hours here and there."

"Oh. Yeah," I tell him. *Stellar, Brooke.*

"Sweet," he says in this way that makes me feel like he thinks the idea of working with me is the exact opposite of sweet.

"Nice to meet you," I offer.

He looks at me, a slow grin turning the corners of his mouth upward. "We've gone to the same school since kindergarten," he tells me as he pulls on his JACKIE'S hat over his now-shoulder-length dreads. As he stands there in front of me, with his brown skin and deep eyes, I can see why all those other girls, even guys, are in love with him. I can't help but think about how much simpler life would be if I could just have a crush on him too, like everyone else.

"Yeah, but . . ." All right, so I look stupid. That's okay, I tell myself. It doesn't matter. I pretty much always look stupid when it comes to my fellow Riverside students. "Well, anyway. Not anymore. I'm going to Jefferson this year." I don't know why I'm saying this; I realize how snotty it sounds the instant it's out of my mouth. I am seriously socially impaired.

The phone rings behind the counter and Jackie goes to answer it. Then Owen and I are left standing there together.

"Why would you wanna do that?" he finally asks, as if going to Jefferson is the worst idea he's ever heard.

I don't know how to explain the million reasons why. "Well, they offer a lot more AP classes there," I tell him.

"Maybe, but they got nothing on the Ravens, let me tell you," he answers. "I guess you probably don't care about football, though."

"Not so much," I admit. "Sorry."

"It's cool." He shrugs. "To each their own, right?"

And this has officially become the longest conversation I've ever had with a fellow Riverside student since my lunch table of friends-by-proxy all graduated at the end of my freshman year, except for Aaron, who had dropped out by then. I open my mouth to answer, but the bell dings again, and as I turn to look, my stomach flips when I realize who it is.

Jackie whispers, holding her hand over the phone, "Owen, help Brooke with this one, will you?"

I walk up to the register, Owen so close behind me I can feel him breathing. I want to hide behind him. Because Monica B. is standing there, tapping on her phone, sunglasses still on, looking nothing like that awkward little girl who was my friend for a few hours in sixth grade.

"Hey, O!" she says, finally looking up from her phone, pushing her sunglasses up on top of her head. "Wait, I'm mad at you. You didn't come to my party last weekend," she accuses.

"I know, I know, my bad. Between practice, work. Couldn't make it. Sorry. Next time, I promise."

"Fine, I guess I'll forgive you," she teases.

"All right, thank you," he says, playing along. "You know Brooke?" he asks her.

She looks at me for the first time. I know she remembers. But she looks through me, squinting, turning her head as if she's having trouble placing me. I hate her so much.

"Anyway," Owen continues. "What can we get for you?"

That was supposed to be my line, I gather.

"Can I get a medium coffee with a shot of hazelnut? And . . ." She scans the rows of doughnuts and pastries in the display cases but then says, "That's it," probably just because she doesn't want Owen to know that she actually eats food sometimes.

I stare at the register. I found the coffee button. But dammit, I don't know what to press for the extra flavor—there's no flavor button.

"Right here." Owen reaches across me and presses one of the buttons on the screen.

"Thanks," I tell him, hating every moment of this. "Uh, okay, so that will be—"

"No, you hit total first," he interrupts.

I find the total button. "Okay, so that's—"

"Here. Keep the change," she says, sliding a five-dollar bill across the counter, as if that's easier than watching me fumble through a simple order.

"I'll finish—it's okay," Owen tells me. "You can start the drink."

He flashes me a quick sympathy smile; his eyes seem to be telling me I can relax. And for a second I wonder if it's because I'm acting like this is the first time I've ever been in public, interacting with other people, if it's because of those old rumors, or if it's because he knows about my parents. It's been on the news, of course, and in the paper. I've forbidden myself from looking it up online, so I don't know how much is out there, how much people know.

I try to focus on pouring the coffee into the cup—a simple task, something I can control. But suddenly my hand twitches involuntarily, making me spill the coffee, which burns my hand in one hot, sharp slice—making me drop the cup on the floor, the coffee splattering everywhere.

"Oh, damn!" Owen murmurs, slamming the cash drawer closed as he rushes over to me.

"Careful!" Monica B. adds, though I'm sure her concern is for her coffee and not me.

I will time to speed up, just this once, but it refuses. Then I will everyone to stop staring at me, but they won't. I study the place on my hand where the skin feels like it was suddenly lit on fire. Jackie hangs up the phone and is standing next to me in the puddle of coffee.

Owen takes over, pours the coffee, adds her stupid flavor shot, and snaps the lid on, so effortlessly.

"Here," Jackie says, pulling me over to the sink and holding my hand under a stream of cold water. I watch as the water circles the drain, spiraling down into that black hole. Part of me wishes I could dive in too, and then part of me thinks maybe that's what's already happened. I glance over to see Monica B. and Owen exchanging their good-byes. "See you in school tomorrow," he tells her. She blows a kiss to him as she walks out the door.

I feel the beginning of a headache coming on, its familiar tightness crawling along my hairline. I try to breathe, in and out, slowly. I try to shove down all these murky old feelings that are churning up inside of me, a volcano preparing to erupt. That's the last thing I need while I'm trying to be normal. I silently tell myself to hold on, a few more hours, then I can go home and be myself.

Owen has now appeared with a mop and slides it back and forth, sopping up the spilled coffee. "Don't worry, that happens to me all the time," he tells me.

"Really?"

"Well, no," he admits.

Jackie laughs. Then Owen starts laughing too. Slowly I realize I'm smiling, and that lava in the pit of my stomach is beginning to cool.

JEFFERSON HELL

JEFFERSON STARTS AT 7:15. It's only fifteen to twenty minutes in the car, but I have to take the bus, forty-five minimum. That doesn't include the time it will take to actually get into the school and make my way to homeroom. That has to add at least four or five extra minutes, I imagine. I calculated it all out, so that if I catch the 6:15 bus, then that should leave me with about ten minutes to spare.

I check my phone again. The bus is thirteen minutes late now. My palms are sweating, the exact change clenched in my fist. The whole rest of my life starts today, and I'm late for it.

By fourteen minutes.

Now fifteen.

"Perfect!" I growl only to myself, since there's no one else around at this ungodly hour. My whole day is already completely screwed, and I haven't even spoken to another human being yet. I check my phone again. Sixteen minutes. There's absolutely no way on earth I can be on time at this point. No way at all.

"Shit!" I hiss.

I start dialing the 1-800 number listed on the timetable posted at the bus stop, prepared to give someone at the Department of Transportation an earful, but just then I see the crosstown bus round the corner and rumble toward me at a snail's pace.

In my dream I would have been arriving at my shiny new school and checking in at the office, not bouncing up and down over potholes in the road on a smelly bus with sticky seats and no shocks whatsoever. In my dream I would not have been crouched down in my seat at the back of the bus, discreetly peeling the wrapper off a half-smashed granola bar, taking small bites so the driver wouldn't catch me eating on the bus.

In my dream I would've been the first person to arrive—my spot claimed, front and center—fresh notebook ready, the top of the first page already labeled with the date and *AP Psychology*. I would have introduced myself to my new teacher—Dr. Robinson—properly before class began. *I'm going to be your new star student.* I would have wanted her to know that up front. First impressions. They're everything. And you get only one shot at them.

But in real life that's not what's happening. What happens is I get off the bus at my stop twenty-two minutes late. What happens is I have to run—literally *run*—from one end of campus to the other while trying to read the map I printed out on Jackie's printer last week. I get lost trying to find the main office, even though I had the whole thing planned, even though I had everything figured out. When I finally find the office, get myself signed in, and secure a late pass, I am informed I've missed homeroom altogether, so I race down the unfamiliar halls, peering in through each door's small, rectangular window as I pass classroom after classroom, none of which seems to be mine.

"Two fourteen, two fourteen," I hear myself breathe, my eyes frantically scanning the room numbers. I feel my chest wanting to collapse, my lungs not used to me running like this, my mind not used to having the things I've planned fall apart. That's the whole point of planning.

I reach the end of the hall and I still can't find it. I've passed 212, 213, 215, 216, but not 214. I go up and down the hall two more times, so sure it should be here—so sure my mind is playing tricks on me. I stand still for a moment in the center of the hall, close my eyes, and take two deep breaths. When I open my eyes, the classroom is right there; it's been right in front of me the whole time: 214, reads the placard next to the door. So relieved to have finally found it, I jump into action and bust through the door, but in my single-minded hurry I've forgotten about the rules—the ones about first impressions. The ones about acting normal.

I can almost hear the echo of the teacher's last words still hanging in the air before the door slams against the wall with this horrible screeching, clanging, metal-on-metal wail. Everyone falls utterly silent as I face an entire room full of strangers.

The door finishes slamming closed with a final hollow *clang*.

Dr. Robinson, according to the name listed on my schedule, spins around with this look on her face—I can't tell whether she's pissed or amused. Or worse, both. A sudden deep splinter chisels its way across my skull, throwing the whole room off-balance.

"Glad you could join us"—she raises her arm in the air, bending it at the elbow and squinting at the watch on her wrist—"twenty minutes late. We were just going over a bit of housekeeping. Please." She takes the late pass I'm stupidly holding out to her and waves her arm in the direction of one of the few empty seats left in the entire room. "Brooke Winters," she reads from the pass as I step forward.

If this were a dream, it would be the one where you show up naked to the really important thing and you realize you've shown up naked only when everyone starts pointing and laughing. Except this isn't a dream. It's a nightmare, only worse. Because it's real.

So I do end up with that front-and-center seat anyway. And I'm definitely making a first impression as I squeeze my way through the narrow aisle with my enormous backpack and my heavy breathing and my hair a wreck and my not-new clothes sticking to my skin because I'm sweating my ass off from running all the way across campus. I slide into the vacant spot. The girl next to me has all her supplies neatly organized in front of her. Textbook, binder, notebook—I glance at the top of her page, and sure enough, it is clearly labeled with the date and *AP Psychology*—she is me, just twenty minutes earlier. She is me, coming to this class from another life, a better life.

"*Oh-em-gee*," I hear someone whisper behind me as I take my seat, followed by snickering.

The girl next to me throws a "*Shh*" over her shoulder.

"As a general rule," the teacher begins, loud enough to block out all the whispers and the pounding of hammers in my head, "I do not repeat myself. But I will say, *once* more"—good God, her eyes burn me—"I do not tolerate lateness of any kind for any reason. If I can manage to make it here on time, I expect the same of each of you. And if for whatever reason you can't make it here on time, you will not be allowed to stay—after today, that is—and you will be counted as absent, and you will have detention." She finally breaks her gaze away from me to look at her watch again. "I have seven fifty-two. I suggest synchronization."

Then she lets out this maniacal chuckle.

"But seriously," she continues. "Unless you enjoy public humiliation"—her eyes fix on me once again—"you need to be in your seat, ready to go, by the time that bell rings. Another serious note: There will be no phone rings, beeps, or buzzes of any sort. And finally, I highly encourage you to find a study partner. This is a college-level course, remember. We will be covering everything from how your brain stores memories to how you fall in love. I will not slow down. This class is a well-oiled machine. I've been teaching it longer than some of you have been *alive*."

There's something in the way she utters that last word, "*alive*," that makes it sound like some kind of threat. She holds a packet of stapled-together papers high up over her head and takes a step forward. "This syllabus is your bible. Know it. Follow it. Do not lose it."

I look around—everyone has one except for me. The girl next to me slides hers toward me in the space between us. I look up at her for the first time and suddenly realize how long it's been since I've looked someone in the eye. I try to muster a smile back at her, taking note of her straight posture and perfectly smooth bronze skin, a streak of purple running through her shiny black hair. The sides of her head seem to have been recently shaved and are just growing back in, leaving a thick mane of wild hair on top, which she runs her hands through, flopping all that hair over to one side.

But just as I'm trying to drag my eyes away from her, I feel this gust of wind blast by my face, like a sword cutting through the air—Dr. Robinson slaps the syllabus she was holding flat on my desk, making me jump back in my seat. And she stares me down with this expression on her face like she's caught me cheating, and is really thrilled about it too.

I want to stand up and call a time-out and explain everything—how I, too, care deeply about punctuality, and how I did the math and all the calculations added up; I built in loads of extra time to account for all the mishaps, but somehow it still wasn't enough. I want to tell her how hard I try. All the time, at *everything*, and still it's never good enough. A one-minute time-out is all I need, but she keeps going.

"Papers are worth fifty percent of your final grade. Midterm, fifteen percent. Final exam is twenty-five percent," Dr. Robinson continues, my mind barely even able to catch up. "And for those of you doing the math, the final ten percent of your grade comprises all the miscellaneous punishments I will dispense at will—that means attendance, quizzes, participation, and punctuality, which I believe we've already discussed, though I'd be happy to reiterate that one more time if anyone is still fuzzy on my policy?"

No one makes a sound.

Promptly after class I find the nearest restroom. I lock myself in the closest stall, drop my backpack to the floor, lean up against the back of the door, and squeeze my eyes shut tight, focusing on breathing and not panicking and not regretting my decision to transfer here.

I hear the bathroom door screech open. Then somebody knocks fast three times on the back of my door, sending vibrations up my spine. I take a deep breath, clear my throat. "Just a minute."

"No, I know," a girl's voice says. "Are you okay?"

"Yes," I answer simply, unemotionally. I turn around, unlock the door, prepared to open it casually yet triumphantly, but all that ends the second I see who's standing there. The girl from class, the girl with the hair, the up-close-and-personal firsthand witness to my public shaming.

I give her a polite nod and walk past her to the sink. I look up into the mirror—God, my hair is all frayed and coming loose from my ponytail—I can't believe I showed my face in class looking like this. I pull the triple-wrapped elastic band out in one swift motion. I hear strands of hair snapping as it falls past my ears and onto my shoulders, down my back. My scalp sighs. I massage my head for a moment, trying to soothe the spots that have pounded all morning. I wish I'd had the time or the energy to get a haircut before school started.

"It really wasn't that bad," the girl says, appearing next to me.

I meet her eyes in the mirror and really look at her. I was able to give her only a sideways glance when I sat down, only long enough to notice her haircut, the shock of purple. Her flawless skin shimmering. But here, our reflections side by side, I can't *not* notice the rest of her. Her eyes, for one thing. They're this insane color—a sea of blues, greens, and browns—a pattern of sunbursts and halos that sparkle so brightly, especially against her rich terra-cotta-toned skin. I'm positive she has to be one of the most beautiful people I've ever seen in real life. She has this glow that emanates from her like a visible aura. Or maybe she's just exaggerated in comparison to me. I turn my attention back to myself: my bloodless pale skin, my eyes dull and flat. I look completely worn out, used up, tired—the faint, shaded half-moons under my eyes have deepened since this morning.

"Well, it wasn't that good, either," I finally answer. I try to brush it off with a little dose of sarcasm, but damn, I don't sound convincing at all. I start to pull my hair back into its familiar ponytail, wrapping the band once and pulling my hair through, twice, pulling my hair through again, then I stretch it, preparing for the third round—but it snaps like a flimsy rubber band, stinging my fingers and making my hair fall down. I toss the broken strand of fabric-covered elastic into the garbage, brace myself against the cold porcelain sink, and look down into the black hole of the drain.

"The woman's a legendary hard-ass," she continues. "She was just using you as an example. That was all for show. It didn't mean anything, really. By next week she'll have someone else she's picking on."

I look up at her again, wanting so badly to be able to believe her, to be able to respond, but how can I even put into words how much is riding on my success here? Thankfully, she fills in the space instead.

"And forget about those girls, okay? Really. Please don't let them get in your head—I hope they're not in your head." She grins as she looks at me. "I like your hair down better, by the way. All crazy like that—not everyone can pull that off." She runs her hand through her own hair again, this time flopping it to the opposite side.

Sidestepping her compliment, I clear my throat and try to smooth my hair back with my hand. "They're not in my head," I tell her. "I don't even care about that. That stuff is, like, the very least of my worries, so . . ." I stop myself from saying anything more, like *I didn't come here to make friends*, then add, too late, "Thanks, I mean."

"I'm Dani, by the way." She extends her hand. "A junior. And you're . . . new?"

I take her hand. "Brooke. I'm a junior too. I just transferred here from Riverside."

"Really, why?" she asks. "I mean, *welcome*, of course. But it must be weird to transfer halfway through like that."

"Well, Jefferson offers the best AP classes." She's nodding in this way that tells me she's expecting more of an explanation. "It's not like I'm some genius or anything, I'm just trying to get a jump start on college. And they didn't offer a lot of the classes at Riverside. Like AP Psych, for example." Oh my God, I can't stop my mouth. "That's what I want to go to college for, at least I think I do. Or it's on my list, anyway"—earlier versions of my list included paleontology and marine biology, and there was a time when I thought I'd be a veterinarian, a sculptor, a pilot—"so it just made sense to take AP Psych now. You know, here. Now. So . . ." I pause.

"Wow," Dani says, shaking my hand fiercely. "So what's wrong with you?"

I think my face must be hovering between expressions. "Oh. Right, I know. Sorry, I just—I tend to ramble when I'm nervous, I guess."

She laughs, showing all her teeth, so loud that it echoes through the whole bathroom, bouncing off the tiles and sinks and mirrors. "No, I mean, anyone who wants to be a psych major really just wants to figure out exactly how crazy they are, right? That's my theory, anyway. That's what my older sister's going to school for, and she's basically nuts. So"—she raises one eyebrow, finally letting go of my hand—"what's wrong with you?"

As I look at her, I feel all my dread and doubts retreating back, way back, a smile hijacking the muscles of my face. "What's wrong with me?" I repeat, trying to come up with something witty. "Do you want that alphabetically or chronologically?" I hear myself say, an unprecedented lightness in my voice. I don't know what's happening to me. I don't know who I am right now, and somehow that feels . . . terrific.

"Ha!" She raises her eyebrows. "Well, I'd actually *really* love to hear it chronologically, but since the bell is going to ring in, like, thirty seconds, we might need to start with the *A*s. You may have noticed that I tend to ramble as well?"

"Then, I'm in good company."

"I'd like to think so," she says. "So . . . study buddies?"

I feel my head nodding up and down before I've even had the chance to weigh out the pros and cons. "Deal," I tell her.

The bell rings.

"'Kay. Later, then."

As she turns to leave, I want to follow behind her and ask her why she's being so nice to me. I want to tell her I like her purple hair and ask about her eyes—did she get them from her mother, from her father? I want to stop time and savor this feeling. But she pushes through the door without another word. I check my reflection in the mirror once more—I swear I have a subtle glow to my cheeks, a gentle sheen bouncing off my loose hair. Like maybe something from Dani has rubbed off on me.

*

At lunch I consider going to the nurse's office. For a moment I miss my old school—I miss the predictability of it, miss knowing my place, knowing that I can sit in the empty seat at the table in the far corner and no one will bother or question me. I can read and be left alone. I don't have that here. But as I'm lurking outside the door of the nurse's office, scoping out the two beds with thin foam pads covered with starchy white sheets and protective paper, and deciding on an ailment that will get me out of lunch but not send me home, I hear my name being called. When I turn around, Dani's standing there.

"Dibs," she says, or at least that's what I think she says.

"What?" I ask, looking back and forth between her and the boy who's standing next to her—he's wearing skinny jeans, and his hair has been carefully sculpted so that it hangs down across his forehead at an angle. He's taller than both Dani and me, and he looks like he just stepped out of a magazine shoot for something really trendy and expensive.

"We're calling dibs on you," she explains. "Before anyone else snatches you up."

"Um. Dibs. Okay. Is that a good thing?" I ask.

"Hell yeah," she says. "This is my bestie, Tyler. Tyler, say hi to Brooke," Dani instructs, looping her arm with his.

As I open my mouth to say hello, a trio of guys runs up, tearing through the hall like a hurricane, and shoves in between us, yelling at everyone, "Are you ready? Are. You. Ready. Are you ready?" I plaster myself against the wall to avoid being trampled; meanwhile, Dani scrunches her nose up as she watches them proceed down the hall, and says simply, "Jocks."

I guess some things stay the same at every school.

"Welcome to Jefferson Hell," Tyler says with a polite nod of his head, barely even batting an eye at the commotion. "I think we're in chem lab together, right?" he asks.

"Oh." I try to recall, but my mind is still in a whirlwind. "Yeah, I think so."

"Are you brainy? Because I suck at chem—I could use a partner who won't let me blow myself up," he says, completely serious, as if blowing himself up is something that happens all the time.

"Um . . . yeah, I—I guess."

"You're sitting at our lunch table," Dani says. They start walking, but I can't seem to make my feet move. I look back and forth between the two of them and the nurse's office. "Come on," she calls over her shoulder.

"It's taco day," Tyler adds with a shrug. "They're pretty good."

I feel something like gravity pulling me toward them.

REBELS

WHEN I GET HOME, the apartment is quiet. Callie's not home from school yet. I drop my backpack off inside my bedroom door and go into the kitchen for something to drink. I'm surprised to see that the wooden fruit bowl that sits on the table is overflowing—an uncharacteristic cornucopia of bananas, apples, oranges, even pears. I open the fridge. It's full of food. Mom always did the grocery shopping in small, frequent trips. Maybe spending small amounts of money at a time was easier to get past Dad, but then again, maybe she just wanted more reasons to get out of the house. I know that's why I always wanted to go with her, despite the fact that I kind of hated going to the store—too many people to bump up against, too many unknown variables, too many things that could go wrong.

Thinking about this major grocery trip that Aaron embarked on all by himself makes me smile. Because Aaron going grocery shopping means he's on board—*really* on board. It means I'm not in this alone.

I reach for the full carton of orange juice and pour myself a glass. I start walking toward the living room but stop short, remembering the rules. Dad never allowed drinks anywhere in the house except the kitchen. We used to be allowed when we were kids, until the day Aaron spilled purple grape juice on the carpet and Dad went ballistic, and Mom cried over it as she scrubbed but could never completely remove the stain. There was an immediate ban put in effect. No drinks other than water were to be allowed in any of the carpeted rooms. That was one of the rules Mom enforced—I guess maybe she did it to avoid any further occasions for Dad to lose it over grape juice stains. Or was it Callie's grape juice? The whole memory seems to stretch out like Silly Putty, morphing in my mind, and for some reason I can't put all the parts back together, can't remember clearly the order of things, and that makes me feel slightly insane.

Maybe it's that mild dose of insanity that takes hold of my limbs as I stand at the threshold between the linoleum and the carpet. Something mildly rebellious moves me forward. The juice sloshes dangerously from side to side against the edges of the glass as I tiptoe over to the couch and carefully set it down on the coffee table. I sit back and watch as the movement on the surface of it stills. I might have to work up the courage to pick it back up again to actually drink it. But, somehow, drinking it seems beside the point now. It takes my eyes a second to find that faded grape juice stain, but there it is, a small patch on the carpet, only slightly discolored, slightly darker, almost invisible. You might not even be able to see it if you didn't know to look for it.

But that's when my gaze catches something else—Aaron's

sneakers by the door. I'm standing before I know why. I call his name. No answer. Something about his sneakers just sitting there side by side doesn't seem right—doesn't *feel* right. If he'd left, he'd be wearing them. And if he were home, he'd have put them away, because, again, we're not allowed to leave things lying around the house, especially potentially dirty things like shoes.

I call his name again, bounding from room to room. I enter our parents' bedroom. The bathroom. I throw open the shower curtain. Nothing. He's not here. But then why this sinking feeling? Why this pounding in my chest, why this nervous electricity surging through my veins, keeping me searching? I'm standing in the hallway, trying to find any logical answers to these questions, trying to catch my breath, when out of the corner of my eye I see something flutter in *my* bedroom.

I step inside, unable to place the movement at first. Until it happens again; the curtain blows out gently, the flap of a bird wing. The window's open. I know I didn't leave it open. It's not safe because this is the fire escape window—you never leave that window open when you're not here. Aaron's the one who told me that when I moved into his old room, after he moved out. He told me always to keep it locked, especially at night—yet here it is, not locked, not even shut, wide open.

I'm outside. Before I've had time to scare myself out of it, I'm scaling the rickety black and rusted metal stairs in my socks, my heart slamming against my ribs.

No.

I realize I'm whispering it, breathing it over and over. *"No, no, no, no, no."* I realize then what I'm afraid of. My legs move too slow, but finally I'm scrambling over the brick ledge of the roof, my body tired and out of practice, half expecting to see Aaron passed out, barely breathing, nearly dead and shoeless.

I scan the rooftop, but he's not there. My eyes rise to see him standing near the ledge on the far side of the building, opposite me, the expanse of stained concrete between us seeming to stretch out forever. "Aaron!" I scream, unable to control the volume of my voice, the pitch, the panic. And just as I'm about to run and scream again, *Stop! Don't jump!* he turns around, a cigarette in his mouth. He seems to move in slow motion, pulling one hand from his pocket, bringing it to his lips, scissoring the cigarette between two fingers, the other hand falling from the brick ledge to his side.

"What?" he calls back, suddenly seeming not so far away after all. "What's wrong?"

"N-nothing," I stutter as I look around, seeing that, in fact, nothing *is* wrong. "My window was open" is all I can think to say.

"Oh," he mumbles. "Sorry, I tried not to mess with any of your things. I just wanted to come up. It's been a while."

I nod, though he's turned his back to me, so he can't see that I'm nodding. I stand next to him now, my hands gripping on to the edge of the brick wall—the only thing keeping us from falling to our death. I don't like the way he leans over it, resting his elbows there so casually; I don't like that far-off look in his eyes. I follow his gaze, trying to see the world below the way he might see it.

There's the wide swath of green—the park one block over, where we used to play for hours while our parents were fighting. I can't see the swing set or the playground from here; the cover of trees is too thick. But I trust they're still there, sunk in that urban beach of sand where we used to play pretend, making believe we were explorers or pirates, stumbling onto forgotten shores after an ill-fated night at sea had left us shipwrecked. In the distance I can see the line of skyscrapers downtown, like a fence for the city, and wonder if anyone is looking out those windows right now, in our direction, wondering about us.

"You ever come up here?" he asks as he exhales a cloud of smoke.

I wonder if he knows that I was the one who found him. I wonder if he realizes that *that* was the last time I was ever up here. But I only shrug and say, "Not much."

The moment of silence between us fills up like a balloon about to burst. Some kind of urgency takes hold of me, squeezing my heart like a fist. I need for him to tell me that he'll never try anything like that again. I need a guarantee. I need him to tell me that he's okay now, that I don't need to worry about him so much, and that shoes left by the door don't automatically mean something terrible is happening.

"Are you okay?" I manage to ask.

He turns to look at me, as if he's surprised by my question. "Yeah, I'm okay. Why?"

"I don't know," I lie. Then, thinking quickly, I add, "It seemed like you and Carmen might be fighting, is all."

He smiles a little and crushes his cigarette against the strip of hardened mortar between two bricks. "She's not exactly thrilled with our arrangement here."

"Why?" I ask, the word coming out more defensive than I meant it to. "Doesn't she understand that we need to stick together right now? She could even move in, too, for all I care."

"Thanks, kiddo." I wonder if he realizes that's what Dad always used to call us, but I don't point that out. "We'll be fine. This is just our thing. I fuck up, then she gets mad, and then she forgives me. Then I fuck up again, she gets mad, forgives me—it's the way it is."

"So she thinks you moving back in here to help take care of us is you fucking up?"

"Maybe." He shrugs, shaking his head. "I don't know. I guess she thinks it's all too much to handle—correction, too much for *me* to handle."

"Is that what you think?" I ask, though I'm not sure I want to know if it is.

He opens his mouth but doesn't answer right away, like he's debating several different responses. "We'll be fine," he repeats, and it's not clear whether he means "we" as in him and Carmen or "we" as in us.

Then he takes the pack of cigarettes from his shirt pocket and gently taps it against the palm of his hand twice; three are loosened, extending from the pack like tiny skyscrapers of varying heights. He brings the pack to his mouth and pulls one out with his lips. His hands tremble slightly as he lights it.

"I thought you quit," I say.

"I did," he says with a laugh, looking off into the distance again. He clears his throat—always his tell that something else is up. "Got a call from Mom's lawyer today. No real news yet. They're waiting for a date to be set. But he needs me to come and fill out some kinda paperwork for the guardianship thing. Not a big deal. Standard stuff, I guess. Make it official and all. I just wanted to keep you in the loop, right?"

"Yeah." I pause, not sure what to say. "Good, I mean. Thank you."

He nods silently and flicks his cigarette. The ashes seem to float, suspended on the air for a moment before they descend toward the ground. "Hey, new subject, okay?" he says, an uptick in his voice. "How's the fancy-pants school?"

"It's good, I think," I tell him, happy for the topic change. "Or it will be, anyway. I get the impression the teachers do not mess around—I think it's gonna be tough, but that's the whole point. That's what I wanted."

"Well, you're a masochist, so—sorry, go on."

"It's cleaner. Bigger. Everything's new and shiny and high tech. Lots of screens everywhere. Smaller classes. More teachers, fewer students. They seem like mostly assholes—"

"They are everywhere, aren't they?" he interrupts.

"Except . . . there were maybe a couple of nonassholes—one for sure."

"A nonasshole?" he repeats, a smirk pulling up the corners of his mouth as he considers this for a moment. "That's pretty high praise coming from you."

"Too soon to tell, but there's potential."

"Potential, even," he marvels. "Might this potential nonasshole be . . . a guy?" he asks, elbowing me in the side, with this stupid grin on his face.

I try to cover my mouth with my hand, but I can't quite stop myself from smiling. "Shut up, it's not even like that."

"Oh wow—it is, isn't it?" he teases, pulling my hand away from my face.

"No, for your information, it's not. I'm talking nonasshole

friend potential—acquaintance potential, nonasshole study partner potential."

He turns his head to the side and squints at me like he doesn't quite believe me. I don't quite believe myself, either.

"Not everything is about a guy, you know," I tell him.

He nods, sticking his cigarette into a dirty pot full of old soil and ashes, whatever once lived there now long gone.

We don't say anything else as I follow him down the fire escape and through the open window, across my bedroom and into the living room. He immediately catches sight of my orange juice glass sitting there on the coffee table. I wonder if he thinks much about that grape-juice-spill day, if he could still find that old stain. He doesn't say anything about the orange juice I left out, though, as I bring my glass to the kitchen table.

"You know," he says, not looking at me as he pours himself a glass of juice from the refrigerator. "It would be okay. I mean, if it's *not* about a guy."

"Yeah, I'll keep that in mind," I try to joke, but I'm aware that neither of us laughs.

"Good," he says, taking a reckless sip of his own orange juice as he passes me on his way over to the couch. He sets the glass down on the end table, without a coaster, even. I join him, taking my glass back into the room with me. He turns on the TV, the volume higher than was ever allowed, and we don't mention the fact that we've both suddenly become freaking rebels here.

AQUARIUM

MY FIRST WEEK AT Jefferson *Hell*, as the locals refer to it. The first week back home. I'm doing okay, I reassure myself. I've been finding my way around, keeping up with homework, and the buses have been relatively on time. I've even had a lunch table to sit at all week—that's more than I can say for my old school.

We're *all* doing okay. No fights. No arguments. Balanced meals and everything. I'm starting to feel things falling into place. The first step to getting our lives back on track. We just need to keep everything running smoothly a little while longer, I tell myself, until Mom can get back home.

That's what keeps me safe in my little bubble, an invisible barrier between me and everyone else, between me and all the shouting and the excitement of weekend plans, and these hundreds of people who have known one another forever. People who don't know anything about me. It's better this way, I assure myself. Less complicated. But as I tack that last thought onto the never-ending monologue that continually runs through my mind, something bursts through, a needle popping the delicate bubble that surrounds me.

"Hey, Winters!" Dani throws her arm over my shoulder, nearly making me drop the stack of books I had perfectly balanced in the crook of my arm. I stoop to catch them before they topple. "I was calling you back there."

"Oh, sorry. I—I didn't hear you," I stammer like an idiot. This has happened every time she's spoken to me all week—as it turns out, we have AP American History, AP English, and AP Calc together too.

"That's all right. As long as you weren't ignoring me," she adds with a lightness in her voice. She glances sideways at me as I struggle to reposition the stack in my arms. "Can I . . . carry your books for you?"

"No, that's okay. I got it."

She rakes her fingers through her hair, messing it up in a way that somehow makes it look even more incredible, shrugging as she mumbles, more to herself than to me, "Well, I tried."

Seeing her so often is making it so much harder to ignore those old feelings creeping up inside of me. In the past, anytime I ever really, truly let myself *think* about it, there always seemed to be all these walls standing in the way. I always thought, what did it matter anyway—there was no use in trying to sort it out if there wasn't anyone *real* my feelings were attached to. It was nothing more than a concept, a theory, impossible to prove. But I'm beginning to see that this thing with Dani is no theory, not something that's going to fade away, not something I can simply distract myself from. Because it's not just a safe, depthless crush; I actually like her.

But the truly terrifying part is that I'm pretty sure she likes me, too. And lately those walls don't seem so tall anymore.

"So, did you need something . . . or something?" I ask her, hating myself for how nervous she makes me. I try to keep us moving down the hall, toward the doors.

"You in a hurry or what?"

"Actually, I kind of am. Sorry, I have a bus to catch. I need to get home." Which is true. Really, I should be *racing* to catch the bus, because I need to get Callie to her appointment with Dr. Greenberg. I regret volunteering to take her now, especially when Jackie offered to do it. But it's not like I can explain any of that to Dani.

"Oh, you take the bus? Well, you know, I'm one of those really obnoxious spoiled brats who got a car for her sixteenth birthday—used, but still." She pauses before she continues. "And by that I mean I could give you a ride home."

"*No*," I tell her, too quickly. "I mean . . . no, thank you. That's okay. I'm fine with the bus, I just—I need to get moving, that's all." I take a few steps forward.

"Oh. Okay, sure," she says, walking alongside me now. "I was just going to give you my number. You know, in case you . . . well, just in case."

Another "just in case."

"Just in case of what?" I ask her, realizing how suspicious I sound only after it's already out of my mouth.

She squints at me before a smile breaks out across her face. "I don't know! What, you want, like, actual concrete scenarios? Just in case of . . . *whatever*. Maybe you wanna talk or hang or have a homework question?"

"Right, of course. Thanks. Can I get it from you Monday, because I really—"

"Need to go," she finishes, cutting me off. "I know, I know. Here, why don't you let me get your number instead?" Pulling her phone out of the back pocket of her jeans, she stops walking and looks up at me, her mouth twitching like she's about to laugh. "Jeez, is that *okay*?" she asks when I don't say anything.

"I guess," I tell her.

"You're sure?"

"Sure," I lie, even though everything inside of me is arguing back and forth as I recite my number to her.

"Okay, I'm texting you. That way you'll have my mine, too." She starts tapping out a message on her phone, grinning at the screen before looking up at me. "I won't keep you any longer," she says, hitching her chin in the direction of the front doors.

"Thanks. Sorry," I say, feeling my phone vibrate in my pocket as I begin jogging away.

"Have a nice weekend!" she calls after me.

When I turn to look at her, she's standing there in the middle of the hallway, rocking back on her heels, her thumbs threaded through the belt loops at the waist of her jeans, so casually. She raises one arm to wave. Suddenly disoriented as I turn back around, I nearly slam right into someone.

I have to run to make up for the time I lost talking to her. I reach the bus just as the doors are folding shut. I find a spot with two empty seats and slump down, out of breath, finally able to let go of my books. My arms ache, fossilized into ninety-degree angles. I have to bend them out gently, curling them up and down, as the blood rushes back toward my fingers with a tingle.

The window has been left cracked open, and as the bus gains speed, a cool, welcome breeze fans my face. I feel my phone again, vibrating in my pocket, but I close my eyes, basking in this rare moment of stillness, which, for once, doesn't feel quite so scary.

Callie's lying on the couch when I get home, flipping through the channels. Another thing we've never really been allowed to do, unless we're sick, like really sick—like doctor's-note, stay-home-from-school sick.

"Hey," I call to her.

She doesn't even look away from the TV.

"Where's Aaron?" I ask.

She gives me a shrug.

"Work, probably," I answer myself. "Look, we have to leave in, like, three minutes, so . . ."

She stabs the on/off button on the remote with her thumb and hoists herself upright, as if getting off the couch is the most taxing activity she's ever had to complete. Tossing the remote onto the coffee table, she stands and walks into the kitchen, without a word.

I barely have enough time to drop off my books and backpack, go to the bathroom, wash my face, grab a speckled banana, and pop a couple of ibuprofens before we have to rush downstairs to catch the next bus across town to Dr. Greenberg's.

"So, first week. How's school been going for you, Cal?" I ask her, needing to raise my voice over the rumbling bus engine, the road noise, the blur of idle chatter. "Are some of your friends in class with you?" I try.

A single nod, barely discernible.

"Has anyone, you know, asked you . . . about what's going on with Mom and everything?"

She turns to look at me, her hazel eyes seeming to turn black as they bore into me. "You mean like *you*?" she asks, more words strung together in a row than she's spoken to me in months, which is a relief, despite the iciness of her tone. "No," she answers, slowly turning her head away from me to stare out the window again.

The bus lurches, jerking us forward in our seats, as it comes to a grinding halt to let one last person aboard.

I open my mouth, but I can't think of anything to say that won't offend her. I wish she would fill me in on the hidden criteria she's worked out in her head—which topics are off-limits and which are still fair game. I think back to that rainbow day, when I was so close. I've been losing ground with her ever since. We sit next to each other in silence as the bus dips and rocks down one street, then the next.

I reach over Callie to pull on the cord as we near the corner building where Dr. Greenberg's office is located. We descend the giant steps of the bus, still wordless. I follow Callie into the building, then into the elevator—she presses a button and the number seven illuminates—and the doors slide open with a ding. I follow her through another door and into a waiting room, all the while silent. The tension between us pulled taut like a rope being tugged back and forth. Words only pit us against each other, both of us yanking in opposite directions with equal force.

"Callie! Right on time," the woman behind the reception desk says, the volume of her voice filling the room, each syllable placing strain on the fragile places in my head, threatening to overpower the soft washout effect of the pills. "Dr. Greenberg will be right with you. Please have a seat."

There's a giant fish tank in the corner of the room. How did I not notice that before? It's taller than me. Not only a fish tank—it's much fancier than that—an aquarium. A habitat. Bright and luminous, fitted perfectly in the corner like it was built specifically for this room. Real plants swaying in the currents created by the humming, motor-powered water pump, and neon-colored fish swimming in circles, charting a path that leads to nowhere. I know from my brief foray into planning out a future career in marine biology that these are tropical fish. I wonder if fish can miss the sea, even if they've never lived there. If something instinctual tells them, *This isn't real, this isn't what life is supposed to be like.* Probably not, I decide as I take my seat near an end table stacked with magazines.

Callie sits down directly next to the aquarium and traces her finger along the glass, tracking the path of a flat, disk-shaped blue-and-yellow fish with long, flowing fins.

"Hey," I whisper to Callie. "Is that new?"

She looks at me, wide eyed, and shakes her head like I'm the stupidest person in the world. I want to ask her if she likes them. The fish. Ask if maybe she'd like to get a small fish tank at home. But I feel that rope once again between us, pulled, stressed, and inflexible.

A phone rings behind the reception desk. "Callie?" the woman calls out. "Dr. Greenberg is ready for you."

Callie stands and walks toward the door, says "Thank you" to the receptionist, but doesn't even bother to cast so much as a glance in my direction. I catch a quick glimpse inside the office as she slips through the door. I see a desk—one of those big, old wooden desks—bookcases lining the walls from floor to ceiling, a leather couch overflowing with big pillows, and a table by the window filled with houseplants, green and sprawling. And then the door closes.

I hear muffled greetings exchanged. I strain my ears. I try to switch casually to a seat next to the door. The woman comes out from behind the reception desk, giving me a suspicious sideways glance as she switches on the sound machine that sits on the table next to the door—the white-noise setting. She could've at least given me rain forest or thunderstorm.

She goes back to her desk without so much as a word. I'm half afraid she's going to kick me out. I reach into my bag for my AP English textbook and thumb through the unit on the Romantics so I have something to distract me from her sporadic glares in my direction.

Behind the door, underneath the foamy static of the machine, I hear a small chirp of a laugh followed by the raucous roar of unselfconscious male laughter, accompanied by Callie's signature hiccup-cough-chuckle sequence, the kind she reserves only for truly funny circumstances.

Un-freaking-believable.

I slam the book closed on Lord Byron and march up to the reception desk. The nameplate reads simply, INGRID. "Ingrid?" I begin. "After Callie's appointment I need to speak with Dr. Greenberg about something." She stares up at me with blank, unblinking eyes. I am so goddamn sick of people not responding to me. "It's about Callie," I add impatiently, an audible edge to my voice. "Five minutes?"

She sighs.

"Three minutes?" I feel my fists clench at my sides. "It's important."

Reluctantly she shifts her bored gaze from my face to her ancient computer screen, double-clicking her mouse. "There's a chance he'll have a few minutes before his next appointment. But in the future you really need to schedule appointments ahead of time."

I clamp my mouth shut on the words in my mouth. *It's not an appointment.* Instead I force a smile and tell her, grudgingly, "Thank you very much."

Back in my seat by the door and the noise machine, I feel my phone suddenly vibrate in my pocket. I reach for it. I have eight missed messages from Dani.

The first is from 2:20, while I was still standing in front of her:

This is me, busy girl.

Watching you run away from me right now . . . Wow. You almost just plowed a kid down in the hall! You really are in a hurry. Ha.

Then 2:25: GURRRRL, you are SUPER serious!

Hmm, what are we going to do about that??? lemme think . . .

At 3:33: Hey! It's dani. Remember me? Your brilliant study buddy? Umm . . . are you getting these?

OMG, you gave me a fake number, didn't you? Ouch.

And 4:51: OK, now you're giving me a complex :(

JK . . . well, sort of ;)

I stare at the words for a long time. They make me smile, against my will. But how do I respond to this girl, this girl who's normal enough to think *I'm* somehow normal enough to know how to do this—whatever *this* is? How do I respond to frowny face and winky face?

Hi, I begin.

I delete. I try again.

Hey

Delete.

Oh, hi

Wrong—delete.

Sorry, just saw this

Delete, delete, delete, delete.

I start typing at least a dozen messages, but no words are adequate, no words make me seem cool enough, sane enough. No words leave me feeling safe. Because no matter what I write, I'm opening myself up to something I'm not sure I can actually handle. Not right now. And maybe not ever.

Just then the door opens. Callie walks through, followed by a short-statured man. His jacket has elbow patches, and his thinning hair is speckled white. "Well, you must be the famous *Brooke*," he says, stepping toward me.

"Famous?" I repeat, pocketing my phone as I stand.

He shrugs noncommittally. "What can I say, I lead a sheltered life. Please, come on in," he says, his smile never fading as he holds his door open.

Callie eyes me suspiciously.

"I'll only be a minute," I tell her.

No response.

I cross over to the other side of the door. It feels warmer in here, softer, dimmer. Maybe it has something to do with the fact that this room is lit by lamps, rather than the overhead fluorescent lights of the waiting room that make everything look vaguely neon, not quite real, like we're in a fish tank ourselves.

He closes the door behind us and walks past me to take a seat on the couch. He crosses one leg and holds his hand out, gesturing to me. "Please, make yourself comfortable."

I take a seat opposite him.

"So, what's on your mind?"

"Um," I begin. "Well, thanks for agreeing to see me on such short notice. I just wanted to check in, I guess."

He nods slowly, uncertainly. Waiting, as if I haven't finished my sentence.

"About Callie," I clarify.

"Oh. Sure." But then he still doesn't respond.

"I mean, I guess I wanted to see how she's doing."

"Well, how do *you* think she's doing?" he asks me.

"I don't know. Seems like school is maybe going okay. At least, we haven't heard any differently. But at home, I don't know, she just seems so . . . angry."

"Hmm." He nods again. "And what about you, are you angry?"

"Me? *No.* I'm saying *Callie* seems angry."

"Okay. Well . . . what makes you think that?" he asks.

"*Well,*" I say pointedly, "it's pretty clear. I mean, every time I try to talk to her, she shuts it down. Like, with me in particular. But she's obviously talking, right? I mean, she talks to *you*. She must be talking enough at school to be getting by. I've seen her mumble stuff to our brother. But she won't talk to me. It's like she's mad at me for something, and all I'm trying to do—all anyone is trying to do—is help."

He reaches for the notepad and pen that have been sitting next to him. He scribbles something, then looks back up at me. "Go ahead." He gives me another encouraging, bobbleheaded nod.

"That's it." I can feel my pulse speeding up, feel that vein near my temple beginning to throb. "I'm—I'm asking *you* a question."

"About Callie?"

"Yes, about Callie." I can feel my tone sharpening, my patience dwindling. "Is she doing any better? Because it doesn't seem like it."

"I really can't talk too much about it, but I think she's making progress, yes," he finally answers.

"Okay, great. Then, what can I be doing differently?" I ask him, hearing the edge in my voice making me enunciate each syllable. "I'm constantly walking on eggshells around her and still nothing I do is right. Everything I say is wrong."

Nods. Again. "You know, why don't you come back next week? Just you. And we can talk more about all of this."

"Next week? But what am I supposed to do in the meantime? I mean, I don't need a whole appointment, just—do you have any tips?"

He stands and removes his glasses, then wipes them on his shirt. I stand as well, since it appears I'm being kicked out. He looks me in the eye. Without his glasses as a barrier, this silent exchange feels too intimate somehow. "Sometimes if people seem like they need some space, that might be exactly what they need."

"So you're telling me to give her space?"

"Not necessarily. Maybe it's you who needs space." He frowns, turns his head slightly, then shrugs once, as if to say, *Hmm, beats me.*

I take a deep breath and hold the air in my lungs until my chest aches, trying to think of any response that won't come out sounding mean and snarky. I exhale, unable to think of a single one. I'm seriously beginning to wonder about the psychiatric profession as a whole.

"We'll talk more next week," he assures me, placing his glasses back on his face as he ushers me out into the waiting room, where Callie sits in her spot next to the aquarium, jiggling her foot back and forth like she wants to jiggle right out of her body. The fish swim frantically behind the glass, flapping around, seeming to mirror her movements.

Dr. Greenberg whispers something to Ingrid. I keep one eye on the agitated fish while Ingrid and I toss days and times at each other. Finally she hands me a card to remind me of my appointment next week: Wednesday at 3:00. On the ride home I don't even try to talk to Callie.

But I do decide right then and there that I'm going to let Jackie bring Callie to her appointments from now on. I will call the office on Tuesday afternoon and tell Ingrid something's come up. School, work, transportation, et cetera. Dr. Greenberg is going to be useless anyway. He doesn't get me, I can tell already, doesn't get our family, but then again, no one does.

CONSTELLATIONS

THE SHOP WAS SLAMMED only an hour ago, the Sunday after-church rush. But as the crowd begins to thin, all that's left is Callie, Aaron, and Ray. They seem to be here all the time recently, which, I suppose, is okay. I suspect, like me, Callie and Aaron sometimes feel weird about being at home, like when they remember about grape juice stains on the carpet or a particular crack in the wall . . . things we'd rather forget.

I had to work, but Callie and Aaron wanted food, so we walked here together—the first time we'd been out walking like that since we were little. We cut through the park, but there wasn't much to say to one another.

She called this morning. Aaron talked to her first. Then he put Callie on the phone. I don't know what Mom said to her, but I heard Callie say "Yeah," "Fine," and "Okay." That's it. Then she passed the phone to me.

Mom sounded distracted. Exhausted. Defeated. I tried to cheer her up. I told her that things were going great and tried to be upbeat. "Callie's doing great—she's back at school. And I love my new school too. I'm making friends. Things will be great once you're back home, Mom," I told her. Great. Great. Great.

"Brooke?" she said weakly. "I just want this to be over."

"We do too."

She was quiet—I wondered if she was crying. I heard a click on the line. And she said she had to go.

"I love you, Mom—everything's going to work out. You'll see, okay?"

"I love you, too."

Dial tone.

I feel like I've been dragging a hundred-pound shadow behind me all day.

Aaron and Ray sit next to each other at the counter, talking, their voices low. I'm purposely wiping down only the tables within earshot of where they're sitting so I can eavesdrop on their conversation. I glance over at Callie, who sits alone at a table for two in the corner with her legs pulled up to her chest. She's pretending to do homework, with her books open in front of her, but all she's really doing is staring out the window at the park across the street.

I remember what Dr. Greenberg said about people needing space. Maybe he wasn't so wrong about that one.

From what I've gathered, Ray wants to help Aaron get a job at his company. Sounds like it would be a sweet gig for Aaron. Full-time with benefits, holidays, sick time. A *real* job—a grown-up job. This would be perfect. But perfect means pressure, means getting our hopes up; it means there's a good chance this won't work, because if there's one thing Aaron's not good at dealing with, it's pressure.

"You know, the boss is doing a big hiring in the next couple months," Ray tells Aaron, then takes a sip of his coffee. "Getting ready for the holidays. Supposed to be one of the busiest years. Or so they say," he tells him with a shrug. Ray is such a *dad*. I find myself smiling at him in spite of myself. He's the kind of dad I always dreamed about, the kind of dad I used to imagine was trapped somewhere deep inside of ours. Jackie appears then, walking over to them with a freshly brewed pot of coffee. She fills Ray's cup up to the top without even asking if he wants more. I guess that's the kind of thing you just know about someone when you've been married for so long.

"Yeah, but a place like that . . . I would need to get my GED to even get an interview, wouldn't I?" Aaron asks, prepared to pull out every excuse not to take advantage of this help we're being offered. Dad's social security benefits help a lot, but it still isn't nearly enough. We're struggling. And every day that passes, the bills keep piling higher and higher. I'm making only enough at Jackie's to cover some of the utilities. I want to yell at Aaron, shake some sense into him—*Do whatever you have to do, just try*—but I bite my tongue, focusing hard on the coffee-stain rings that seem to be permanently fused to the surface of the table I'm working on.

"I know you'll think I'm meddling, Aaron," Jackie begins, the coffeepot hovering over his cup. It seems like he's practically living off coffee and cigarettes these days.

"That's because you *are*, dear," Ray interjects, patting Aaron on the shoulder as he stands. He wanders toward the door like he's not in much of a hurry to get wherever he's going.

"Well, too bad, so sad!" Jackie pretends to yell at Ray's back as he leaves.

He raises an arm in the air, but it's unclear whether he's shooing her or waving good-bye—either way, it somehow manages to be a loving gesture. The bell on the door dings as he opens it. "Bye, girls," he calls out. "See ya, Owen," he says just before the door swings closed.

"All right," Jackie admits, "I am meddling—I'm a meddler. Here's the thing," I hear her tell Aaron. "I signed you up to take the GED at the Adult Ed Center." She pulls a folded piece of paper from her apron pocket and slides it across the counter. "That has the dates and times of the tests. You be there. I mean it." She points a stern finger at him, like a warning.

"Yeah, but—" he starts to protest.

"Dude, I'd listen to the lady," Owen mumbles, pushing a mop across the tile floor as he moves in between us. He looks up at me with a grin and then raises his eyebrow in this mischievous way, like we're suddenly the best of friends. "She'll hunt you down if you disobey—she's the Godmother," he says, pretending to whisper in Aaron's ear, but talking more than loud enough for Jackie to hear.

"Yeah, yeah," Jackie mumbles, her voice flat and monotone. "Get outta here," she teases as she swats at him with her hand. "Hey, where's your hat?"

"See what I mean?" he says, looking back and forth between me and Aaron, pointing a thumb at her as he pulls his folded-in-half JACKIE'S hat out of his back pocket. "Vicious."

"Little punk," Jackie mutters. Then she refocuses her attention on Aaron and sighs. "Good kid. Like you."

"Jackie, look," Aaron begins. "I appreciate what you and Ray are trying to do, but—"

"But what?" she interrupts. "You'd rather do things the hardest way possible? Rather do it all alone? Struggle? You're stubborn." She points her finger again. "Just like your . . ." But she stops herself from finishing.

I feel my blood getting hot on Aaron's behalf, almost like I can feel his blood inside of me, simmering. "I'm not like him," he finally tells her, a tiny tremble in his voice that I'm pretty sure no one else can hear but me.

"No—no, Aaron." She places her hand on his arm and squeezes gently. "It wasn't an insult. Your father was . . . a complicated man. Not all bad. Not all good. You know? Just like the rest of us."

He shakes his head, looks down into the bottom of his coffee cup.

"So, what is it, then?" she asks him. "You think you can't pass the exam, is that right?"

He turns around, as if he can feel me listening. I look away.

"Huh?" she prompts, shaking his arm like a little earthquake.

"Yeah, maybe," he admits, so quietly I almost can't hear him. "So?"

"So . . . you're wrong. You'll study. You're a smart boy."

Then she smiles that award-winning toothpaste smile at him and adds, "I really wish you could've known him when he was your age. He was a different person then." I wait for Aaron to detonate. But, thankfully, the bell on the door dings, interrupting her.

I consider telling Aaron that I'll help him study, but something keeps me standing here, silent. Maybe it's because I'm starting to get really sick of taking care of everyone else. Sick of feeling responsible for everything that goes right, everything that goes wrong. So I stand here, feeling so weighed down I can't even move, with both of their backs facing me.

Jackie picks up the pot of coffee, tousling Aaron's hair with her free hand before walking away to greet the new customer.

Then it's the three of us: me, Aaron, and Callie, forming a triangle in the empty space. A constellation. Something invisible holds us in formation, keeping us from moving toward one another, but keeping us from moving away, too.

"Brooke?" Jackie calls across the room, snapping me out of my trance. "Can you give me a hand?"

Somehow I didn't notice that there's now a line forming at the front counter. When I look back, both Aaron and Callie are watching me. While I'm rushing to fill coffee and tea orders, I see Aaron, out of the corner of my eye, walk over and sit down at the little table with Callie. His back is to me, so I can't tell what he says to make her laugh. But she does.

I have the overwhelming urge to scream at the top of my lungs, to shout both of their names, get them to turn around, to look at me and see that I'm my own person and I have my own life and I'm so sick of worrying about them all the time. But I don't. I reach into my pocket for my phone instead.

Hi, Dani! Sorry, I forgot to respond the other day. How's your weekend going?

She writes back nearly instantly, and I start to feel a little lighter: going great now, girl! you?

OK . . .

what r u doing right now? wanna hang?

I can't. Sorry. At work.

bummer :*(

I take a deep breath, fill my lungs with air, releasing it slowly as I type what feels like the riskiest words I've ever dared even to think: I was going to stay after school tomorrow to study in the library. Wanted to let you know. Just in case . . .

I lower my phone as the screen fades to black, trying, unsuccessfully, not to get my hopes up as I wait for a response. Just when I begin to think this reckless experiment has become an utter failure, as I'm shoving my phone back into my pocket where it belongs, I hear the most wonderful one-note chime. I fumble to get my phone out of my pocket, nearly dropping it.

i'll be there! :)

I smile to myself, the screen glowing at me like a signal from a different star across the galaxy.

FREAKS

I LOOK OUT THE WINDOW. Fall has swooped in silently, like a fever breaking. And overnight the trees have taken on the appearance of bursting into flames—oranges, reds, yellows—the whole world suddenly combustible.

I reserved a table for Dani and myself in the library. It's become our ritual over the past couple of weeks. I have exactly fifty-two minutes before the next bus leaves. We're going to cram in one last study session for our first psych exam of the semester, which, Dr. Robinson warned the class, is going to be a "make or break" kind of exam.

I check my phone for the time and see that Dr. Greenberg has left another voice mail. That's the third one in two weeks. Each time he calls, I let it go to voice mail. He's concerned. He wants me to reschedule. I don't call back, over and over again. You'd think he'd get that I'm not going to return the call. I delete the message.

Dani's three minutes late.

Waiting is the absolute worst. When I'm waiting, I'm stuck

in the present. I can't lie to myself when I'm in the present. When I think about *now*, I can't help but accept how complicated everything has become. I don't have enough space in my mind to keep track of everything. School, for one thing. I had no idea how much more work these extra AP classes were going to be. Then there's Aaron, Callie, Mom—always Mom, there in the back of my mind—taking up all my thoughts. Being in the present is like coming up for air, and coming up for air only makes me realize I've been suffocating. Easier not to breathe at all, like maybe with enough practice I can learn to live underwater like those aquarium fish, lie myself into believing things are okay, that this is what life is supposed to be like.

"Hey, sorry." Dani comes in like a whirlwind of energy, talking fast. "Tyler's having an existential crisis over some boy he met online." She starts explaining more about whatever it is that's going on with Tyler and how he thinks he's being catfished, but I'm having trouble paying attention—the air in the room feels too thin. "What's wrong?" she asks.

"What?" I clear my throat. "Nothing," I lie.

"Are you sure?" she asks, squinting like she's trying to see me better. She pulls out the chair opposite me.

"I just have a lot on my mind, I guess. Sorry." I quickly try to wall up those soft places inside of me, the ones that want to show themselves too often these days, especially when I'm with Dani. She sits down and lets her arms fall against the table, and the series of silver bangles lining her wrists clang, making so much noise people turn to look.

Whenever she's around, I feel like people are looking. But

then again, whenever she's around, I'm always looking too. I could try to build up an immunity to Dani, and then I wouldn't have to feel my insides turn to gelatinous mush every time I saw her, except for the fact that I don't really want to be immune anymore.

I shrug and tell her, "Family drama," as if it could ever be that simple. I try to laugh, but it falls apart in my throat, and somehow I think I might actually start crying in front of her. I feel my chin tremble in that way it does. "God—sorry!"

"No, don't be sorry," she tells me, her voice gentler and quieter than I've ever heard it before. "Seriously, what's going on?" She reaches across the table to touch my arm.

I dab my eyes with my sleeve before any of those traitorous tears can fall. I try to rearrange my face so that it's smiling, but my voice sounds all weird and mangled when I speak again. "I'm fine. I'm seriously, totally, completely fine."

"No you're not."

"I think it's just this damn exam," I tell her, slamming my book closed too loudly. Her face turns so open and soft as she gazes at me, no hint of a smile on her lips, no joke on deck in her mind. "Stop looking at me like that, I am fine. Robinson has me freaked out! That's all, okay?" I realize I'm raising my voice only when this boy at the next table swings around in his seat, a crazed look of study stress in his eyes.

"Hey, do you mind having your breakdown a little quieter, please?"

Dani spins around in her chair so she's face-to-face with this kid. She stands then, shouldering her bag, and starts collecting up my things in her arms before I even know what's happening. "Come on," she tells me. As we pass the boy at the next table, she extends her arm all the way and holds up her middle finger inches from his nose.

My pulse quickens, a dull throb echoing its beat in my temples. I'm a little scared this is about to blow up into something dangerous—because that's what usually happens—but the boy only shakes his head and looks back down into his open textbook. Dani pushes forward, full speed ahead, walking tall, taking long, confident strides out through the doors of the library.

"Dani," I call after her, trying my best to follow behind her as she leads the way down the hall. "Thanks, but you didn't have to do that, you know."

She stops and turns around so abruptly I almost run right into her. "Sure I did. He was being an asshole."

That's when I realize something else about Dani. She isn't just beautiful and cool and smart and funny—she's tough. Like, the real kind of tough. Not the insecure, defensive, covering-up-fear-and-weakness kind of tough, which is what I've always thought of Aaron, and Dad, even. Or maybe that's what I've always secretly thought of myself, too.

She's the real thing, more real than I could ever hope to be.

"Come on, let's get some air." She grabs my hand like she's been reaching for my hand for years, like it's the most natural thing in the world. I let her lead me through the corridor and down the stairs—I think I might let her lead me anywhere.

It's only once we're sitting outside on the bench under this enormous tree that she does let go, gently placing my hand in my own lap, leaving my fingertips electrified. "Okay, you have my undivided attention. Go. Tell me."

"What, are you being my therapist now?"

Her face remains still, like a frozen pond. "No, I'm being your friend. I know I'm always joking around and everything, and you really don't know me very well, but I'm serious when it comes to serious stuff. So, what's going on?"

"Nothing, really. I'm just upset because I think I'm going to have to drop a couple classes." Not a complete lie, anyway.

She purses her lips as she considers this. "Would it really be so bad to have a little extra time? Especially when you can spend it hanging out with your awesome new friends, like me?"

"Not when you put it like that," I say, trying not to smile too much.

She somehow manages to wait the perfect amount of time before speaking again. "Is that really all that's wrong?"

"Not exactly," I admit.

"Well, I'm here. Happy to listen."

I open my mouth, no idea what I'm going to say. "My dad," I hear my voice tell her, seemingly without the permission of my mind. "He died a few months ago. Unexpectedly. And . . ." I swallow hard, somehow convincing myself I'm telling enough of the truth. "It's been really tough. My little sister isn't doing well with it, and my older brother moved back home to help out. We're all still adjusting. And changing schools right now—even though this is what I wanted—it's just been hard." *Having you sitting next to me like this, looking at me like that, is also hard*, I don't say.

After a moment of silence her voice cuts through; solidly, smoothly, she asks, "What happened to your dad?"

I guess I've never thought of what happened as something

that happened to *him*. I've been thinking of it as something that happened to our mom, and to me, and to Callie and Aaron. "He was stabbed." True enough. "He was a cop." Also true, although I'm fully aware that grouping those two facts together creates an entirely inaccurate picture of what happened. It's an omission, just on the safe side of a harmless white lie.

She nods, and chews on her lower lip as she watches me. "I'm sorry," she whispers. "One of my uncles was in the military. He died overseas—was killed, I mean. It's been so hard on my aunt and my little cousins, the whole family. I know it's not exactly the same. How's your mom holding up?"

I shrug. "I'm not sure," I tell her.

Then she wraps her arm around my shoulders and inches me closer.

I think I might go into cardiac arrest.

There are these little whispers in my head telling me I should leave, telling me I'm letting her get too close, telling me how dangerous this is. Those are the voices that guide me in everything I do; they've always been dependable and sturdy. But right now I want them to shut the hell up. I lean my head against her shoulder. I let myself stay that way—*she* lets me stay that way. And we sit here. For once I really don't give a damn about those voices, and I don't care what anyone who might be passing by thinks of me.

The afternoon breeze flows around us and up through the leaves, rustling gently, drowning out the noise of people coming and going on the pathway that lines the lawn behind us. I relax. So calm I could almost fall asleep, except for the other part, which is that I also feel wide awake. It's in this moment that I actually *want* to tell Dani everything. With that thought there's a strange sensation in my stomach. Something like a knot being untied in the center of my body that starts radiating outward, untying smaller knots everywhere. In my throat. In my brain. In my hands and fingers, in my arms and legs, and heart.

"You think I'm a total freak?" I finally ask, lifting my head off her shoulder.

"Yeah," she says softly, not even pretending to think about it. A smile is forming at the corners of her mouth. "But I already thought that."

I sit up straight and do my best to play along, pretend to be offended. "Oh really?"

"Of course. Considering the first time I saw you, you were storming into Robinson's class like some kind of rabid animal on a rampage. You had this wild look in your eyes. So. Yeah. My first thought: *Freak. Total freak.*"

"Wow, thanks. I feel so loved."

"You should, because my second thought was, *Oh fun, I hope she sits next to me*. Because, well, I guess I happen to like freaks."

"Good for me, I guess."

"And me too."

As we sit here laughing, the whole rest of the world falls away. But I hear something, a muffled noise that doesn't even register right away—a ring tone. It's the alarm on my phone. Which means the crosstown bus is leaving right now, and I had to be on it if I was going to get to work on time.

"Oh shit!" I jump up and grab my bag. "I have to go, sorry. Sorry, sorry, I have to go!" I start running. I turn around once and wave. She's standing there next to the bench. "Sorry!" I yell one more time.

I cannot miss that bus.

I run as fast as I can across the wide expanse of cool grass and shade trees that make up the campus, past the rows of buildings, finally reaching the corner stop just as my bus is pulling away. I manage to conjure up one last burst of energy and really make a break for it, screaming and waving my arms over my head. "Wait, wait! Wait, don't leave!" I run up alongside the bus as it's gaining speed, pounding my fists against its metal body. I look up, on my very last ounce of adrenaline, and right as I'm about to lose hope, I see a woman look down at me through the window. Then I watch as she shouts something to the driver.

The brakes squeal, bringing the bus to a stop. I let myself slow down to a jog, before I mount the three giant steps, gasping as I tell the driver, "Thank you, thank you so much." I collapse into the closest empty seat and try to catch my breath. And twenty minutes into the ride, even though I'm breathing normally again, my heart is still pounding at this wild pace. All light and fast and skipping beats.

It stays in a frenzy as I walk the two blocks to Jackie's from the bus stop. It stays like that through each cup of coffee I pour. And it stays like that as I climb the stairs to our apartment hours later. Even as I put my key in the lock and turn. As I lie down in bed that night, I place my hand on my chest and try to will it into calmness. Then I reread the messages on my phone.

Dani: what up, cinderella?

Me: What?

Dani: you just up and ran away. what, fairy godmother waiting?

Me: Oh. No, had to catch my bus.

Dani: ah, i see. it was the pumpkin. hate that. ;)

Me: Had to go to work. Didn't want to be late.

Dani: ok. just making sure I didn't scare you off. def wouldn't want that.

THE TEST

"MORNING, CINDERELLA," DANI GREETS ME, already sitting in her spot when I walk into the classroom the next morning. We're the first ones to arrive, even before Dr. Robinson. She smiles as I set my things down next to her. And there goes my heart again, speeding up like I've just had a shot of espresso injected directly into my bloodstream.

"Hey." I decided I would try to act like nothing had happened between us yesterday afternoon. "Good morning," I add. Because, after all, nothing really did happen. As I sit down, she looks at me like I should be saying something. "How are you?" I try.

She wrinkles her forehead and smirks at me as if that's a ridiculous question. Then she sits up straight, interlaces her fingers so her hands are folded together neatly on top of her desk, and says, "I'm fine, Brooke," her tone stiff and edgy. "How are you this morning?" she adds, an automated quality to her voice.

"Um . . . okay," I tell her, uncertain about this tension I feel coming off her. "What?"

Her posture slumps back down and she unlocks her hands, running one through her hair. "Nothing, you just . . ." She stops herself, like she decided against whatever was to come next. "Never mind."

I begin pulling my things out of my backpack, but I can feel her eyes piercing me the whole time.

"So, you ready?" she finally asks, almost her normal tone again.

"Ready?" I repeat.

"For the test."

"Oh. Right." I try to laugh, but it sounds like this demented gurgling in my throat. "Let's hope I am."

"Hey, you never told me, where is this mysterious workplace, anyway?" she asks, a strange change of topic.

"You wouldn't know it."

"Or you don't *want* me to know it," she counters, that edge back in her voice. "Is it classified information, or what? Top secret?"

"No, it's not that. You can know. I only meant that it's in my neighborhood, and I wouldn't imagine you'd even know where it is."

"Yet you're still not telling me!" she says, her eyes wide, looking like they're changing from blue to green to brown every time she raises her voice. "I thought we were finally getting to be friends?"

"We *are*."

"Well, this is the kind of basic information friends tend to know about each other. Where they live, where they work, hobbies, interests, et cetera," she says.

"Why do you sound like you're mad at me?"

"Because every time I see you, it's like we're starting from scratch. We have this big moment yesterday, and then you come in here acting like it's the first time we've ever seen each other—it's impossible to get to know you!" She crosses her arms and leans back in her chair, looking straight ahead.

It takes several seconds for her words to sink in, for me to understand what they mean. I've never had anyone want to know me so much that they would get mad about it.

"Okay, fine. I work at Jackie's Coffee and Bakeshop. It's over by Riverside Park. And I live in an apartment two blocks from there."

"Fine. Thank you." She unfolds her arms and pivots toward me once again. "And you're right, I'm not sure where that is!" she shouts, though a smile brightens her eyes. "I live ten minutes north of here in one of those obnoxious subdivisions with big houses that all look alike! And I don't have a job because I'm spoiled and my parents give me an allowance!" She pauses and takes a breath. "There, now wasn't that fun?" she yells, throwing her arms up in the air.

I can't stop myself from grinning. "You're a little crazy, you know that?"

"Well, that's the perfect amount, isn't it?" she says.

"You're the only person I know who can yell and laugh at the same time!"

"It's only because you happen to be adorable and incredibly frustrating all at once!"

I open my mouth, not sure how to answer, but just at that moment Dr. Robinson appears in front of us. "Good morning, ladies." She holds up a thick manila folder, bursting with photocopies, which I imagine can only be the test. Giving the folder a little shake, this delightful twinkle in her eye, she asks us, "So. Are we terrified yet?"

Hell, yes.

⁂

After the bell rings, and everyone is scrambling to leave, Dani waits for me by the door, and asks, "How did we do?"

"I don't know," I tell her as we exit the room and spill out into the noisy hallway. "At first I thought I did okay, but then after I handed my test in, I started thinking some of those were trick questions."

"Yes, exactly!" she says, her voice carrying over the hallway chatter and the echo of lockers clanging. She walks next to me, her pace too leisurely for my comfort. "Like some of it was too logical? But then I started thinking maybe *that* was the trick. To make us think that what we thought was right was too simple so we would change our answer to something more complicated, when really we had it right the first time. If that even makes sense."

"Frighteningly, I completely followed that."

"See? That's why this works," she tells me, waving her hand back and forth between the two of us. And she looks at me in this way, like she's saying something more than what her words are telling me.

I can do nothing more than look down at my hands, studying my fingers like they're foreign objects, the way they're interlaced, squeezing together, twisting around one another, bone against bone.

"So, are you going to homecoming on Friday?" she asks.

I snort, thinking she has to be joking. "No, definitely not."

"Perfect. Then, it's settled. You're coming out with us. Me and Tyler. Every year we go to this big party at the Spot. And usually my sister goes with us. But this is the first year she's not here—she's away at college—and we really need a third person. You in?"

"What's the Spot?" I ask her.

Dani grabs my arm, making us both grind to a halt. "You've never been to the Spot? Okay, now you *have* to come," she says, nudging me in the arm. "Every year they do this crazy alternative homecoming—I'm telling you, you haven't lived until you've attended the Spot's annual unhomecoming."

I open my mouth to answer—*no* is my default setting—but I don't know how I'm supposed to say no to her, especially when there's a small part of me that can actually imagine myself being there with her—that is, if I were someone else entirely. "Thanks, but I really probably can't make it, Dani."

"Why not?" She lets go of my arm, but she's not about to let me off the hook that easily.

"It's just hard for me to get out. I have to take the bus, and it's a long trip, and if I don't time it exactly right, then I'm basically stranded, so . . ." I trail off, because when I look up and meet her eyes, I'm unable make the words come out. Not when she's standing this close, with her eyes not letting me look away, her right arm brushing up against my left, activating this total-body power surge sequence that immobilizes my brain. She squints at me like I'm still speaking, like she's still listening.

"Okay," she begins. "Well, I have a car and I'd be more than happy to drive us. So, that problem's solved. What's the next one?"

"What do you mean?"

"I mean, I get the feeling you have at least four or five more complications lined up." She lowers her chin and raises her eyebrows at me. "And unless one of those complications is that you can't stand me and you don't want anything to do with me, then let's save ourselves some breath, not to mention mental energy." She stares at me, waiting for a response. "That's not the real problem, is it?" she finally asks.

"No," I tell her. "Of course not. That's not it at all."

"Okay, then. It's settled! I'll pick you up at eight." She starts walking away before I can say anything else.

"I'll try, all right?" My voice gets lost in the noise of the hall, so I'm not sure if she hears me, until she turns around.

From the other side of the hall she yells, "Something tells me if you really try, you'll make it happen."

"Do I have to dress up?" I call out.

"Nope," she answers. She's grinning now—she knows she has me. "Adorably frustrating!" she calls out as she rounds the corner.

"So, are you actually going to this homecoming thing?" Tyler whispers next to me in chem lab as the teacher writes out formulas for our experiment on the board at the front of the room.

"I don't know, probably not." I glance over at him for a second while I try to decipher the numbers and letters and symbols on the board.

"That's not what Dani says." He twists in his chair so that he's facing me, not even pretending to pay attention.

"She doesn't seem to want to take no for an answer."

I can feel him staring at the side of my face. When I turn to look at him again, he's narrowing his eyes at me.

"What?"

"Can I just ask you something, once and for all?" he whispers, leaning in.

I shrug. "I guess."

He hesitates but then says, "Are you?"

"Am I . . . what?" I whisper back, keeping my eyes on the board.

He scowls, letting out this loud sigh that turns heads in our direction. "Are. You?"

"Am I what?" I repeat, getting annoyed that he's distracting me from my notes.

"Shhh!" someone hisses from the front of the room.

"Oh man," he breathes, pinching the bridge of his nose like his eyes hurt from staring at me so intently. "Okay. I *am*," he says pointedly, which finally makes me look up at him.

"You are . . . ?"

"Oh my God," he gasps. "*Gay*, Brooke. You knew that, right? Please tell me you're not *that* clueless."

"Oh." I look down at my notes, then back to the board, anywhere but *at* him. "Right. Yeah. I mean, I guess. I mean, I guess I didn't really think about it," I lie.

"So?" He nods slowly. "I'm asking, are *you*?"

"You're asking if I'm—if I'm g-g-g—" The word gets stuck in my throat, and then I can't finish because he bursts out laughing. Loudly.

"I'm sorry if my lesson is getting in the way of comedy hour back there!" our teacher yells, hand on hip. "Don't make me separate you—this isn't preschool!"

"We're sorry," Tyler apologizes, still giggling. "Won't happen again." When she turns back around, he stutters, "G-g-g-g-g—" accompanied by a full-body shudder, like he's being electrocuted.

"*Shut up*," I whisper, people turning to stare at us again.

"So, are you?" he whispers so quietly I can barely hear him, even though I'm right next to him.

I open my mouth, but I have no idea what to say. "I don't know," I finally tell him.

He raises his eyebrows and turns his head slightly, looking at me like that's not a real answer. Except that's the *only* answer I can give him. To say no would be a lie, but yes would be to cross that line between fantasy and reality, and I'm pretty sure that there would be no turning back. I don't think I'm ready to be that real yet.

"I don't know, okay?" Now someone shushes *me*. "Is that not allowed?" I ask, feeling defensive, hearing it in my voice.

"It's allowed. Just a friendly inquiry," he says, pivoting in his seat to face the front of the room again. He hitches his chin in the direction of the board. "Hey, quit messing around and pay attention, will you? My life is in your hands, remember?" he jokes, laughing quietly to himself.

FAMILY DINNER

AS I WALK HOME from the bus stop after school, a dense patch of gray and black clouds rolls in overhead. The wind howls past me, blowing the leaves from the trees like they're nothing more than dandelion fluff. My hair whips around my face. I can smell it in the air, taste it—that wild, earthy flavor—a storm, a big one.

I make it to the steps of our building just as a team of crisp brown leaves lifts off the ground and charges toward me, until it crashes full speed into the bottom step and falls lifeless to the ground. Then the first fat, freezing drops of rain fall down against the sidewalk. *Splat, splat, splat.* Then. Monsoon.

Upstairs the apartment smells amazing. I can hear the sizzle of something simmering in a pan in the kitchen. The windows in the living room have been darkened by the clouds overhead, and the rhythm of the rain outside is muffled into a soft hum. The feeling is unfamiliar. Comforting, warm, cozy. Like maybe this is what people mean when they talk about *home*.

I close the door behind me, and Callie turns around in her

seat at the kitchen table, throwing a casual "Hi" in my general direction.

I reciprocate with a "Hey," careful not to sound too excited about her greeting. Leaving my shoes and jacket and backpack by the door, I make my way to the kitchen to find Aaron standing there in front of the stove. "Smells good," I tell him.

"Thanks." He glances up at me and smiles. "It's just spaghetti, though. The sauce is from a jar."

"Well, it smells great. I'm starving," I add, trying to stretch out this good feeling as long as possible. Twenty minutes later, the three of us are at the kitchen table, and Aaron keeps clearing his throat like he's working up the nerve to break some kind of bad news. Bad news about Mom, I'm sure, about the trial.

"There's this thing on Friday," I begin, thinking that maybe if I can talk long enough, then Aaron won't ever get the chance to tell us whatever it is he doesn't want to tell us, and then we'll never have to know, and we can hold on to this moment.

"Oh yeah?" he asks, too interestedly, as he twirls a bunch of jumbled stands of spaghetti around his fork over and over, around and around.

"A dance thing. Whatever. I might go, I don't know."

"You *should* go," he agrees.

"Maybe," I say, and I wonder how much longer we can feign interest in this pointless conversation. "It's not like I have my heart set on it or anything."

At this point Callie rolls her eyes and tears off a bite of bread between her teeth, looking back and forth between Aaron and me like we're some kind of preverbal cavemen, not speaking a real language, but just grunting and snorting and pointing.

"No, go. I mean, why not, right?" he says, finally putting that twirled and retwirled forkful of spaghetti into his mouth.

"Yeah?" I ask. "Well, maybe."

Callie sighs loudly.

After a few seconds of silence, chewing, and swallowing, Aaron clears his throat once again. "So, listen. I saw Mom today."

Callie sets her fork down with a clang against her plate and crosses her arms over her stomach, sitting back in her seat.

"Aaron, you knew I wanted to go see her too," I tell him, careful not to yell.

"It wasn't a visit like that. Her lawyer wanted me to go talk to her. She's getting cold feet, I guess. She wants to take the plea bargain instead of having the trial."

"Why would she want to do that?" I ask.

"I don't know," he mumbles. "I think she just wants this to be over with. We're trying to convince her that they need us to testify—all of us. You know, to prove that it was self-defense. Jackie's going to. So am I. Tony, too. Except Mom doesn't want you guys anywhere near this, even if it's going to hurt her case."

"That's ridiculous!" I shout.

He scratches his head and sets his fork down on his plate. "She wants to protect you, I get that, but—"

Callie lets out this small noise, a cross between snort and laugh. Her eyes tick back and forth between me and Aaron.

Ignoring Callie, I answer for us all: "We'll do whatever we have to do."

"Speak for yourself," Callie hisses, her voice low.

"What?" I ask, not used to her voluntarily offering up so many words at once.

"I'm not lying for her," she says, wrapping her arms around her body so tightly her muscles tremble, something menacing going on behind her eyes.

Aaron looks at me, confused. "Who said anything about lying?" he asks, that familiar edge of irritation rising in between the words.

She looks back at us, her eyes dark, her jaw set, and repeats herself through gritted teeth. "I'm. Not. Helping. Her."

I feel my breathing slow to a stop, my brain unable to process what she's saying to us.

"Are you serious right now?" Aaron asks, barely able to stay in his seat. "Callie, she's our mother—we *have* to help her."

I'm sitting there, getting caught in a familiar cross fire, my head foggy, because this is not happening. Our little sister can't turn on us, not now, not when we need her.

"And who was he?" Callie says, her voice not having reached this volume in months and months. "Some random stranger?"

My head feels like a drum being pounded, word by word.

"Just because *you* guys hated him," Callie continues, gaining steam, "doesn't mean he deserved to die!"

"No one said that," I tell her, but I can't make my voice loud enough to be heard.

"So it would better if Mom were dead right now?" Aaron asks, his voice getting louder. "That's what you're saying?" He pushes his chair out and stands, like he's going to walk away, but then he doesn't.

"Stop, you guys," I try, but no one seems to hear me.

Callie stands now too and swipes at the angry tears on her cheeks. "Why does anyone have to be dead?" she challenges, getting louder.

"You guys, stop!" I try again, my head surely about to implode.

"I don't know, all right?" Aaron shouts over me.

"Shut up," I tell them. "Stop it, both of you!" I yell, now standing in between them. "Shut up! Just. Shut. Up."

Callie and Aaron stand on either side of me, all of us breathless. Then they both take a step away from me, like *I'm* the bad guy, when they're the ones who are fighting. Callie spins around and stomps off to her room. When she reaches her door, she turns around and braces herself with one hand on either side of the doorframe, her voice straining when she says, "I hate you!"

Then *crash*. Her door slams shut.

"Why does this happen every time we try to act like a family?" Aaron asks, though I don't think he expects an answer, because he turns away from me before I can offer one. He stacks our three plates, one on top of the other, all the delicious food being smashed and splattered, and walks into the kitchen. I open my mouth to say something—what, I'm not sure—but the sound of the plates crashing into the sink makes me jump.

After a few seconds I hear the water running. I walk to the doorway and have to raise my voice over the clanging dishes: "Let them know that I'll do whatever she needs, tell them whatever they want to know. She doesn't have to keep me out of it—please tell her that. Okay?"

"Yeah," Aaron mumbles, not looking up.

✳

I go into the bathroom, open the medicine cabinet, and swallow three aspirins. Then I close my bedroom door and lie facedown in bed, listening to the pattering of rain on the window as I wait for the pills to kick in. She said she didn't remember what happened. I didn't believe her at first. But then I did. And now . . . now I don't know.

I must have dozed off, because I awake to muffled voices. I lie here for a while, listening. I drag myself up from my bed, my head noticeably better, though not all the way. I sit at my desk and pull out my homework; putting my brain to work drowns out their voices, drowns out the dull leftover ache of words pounding through my head. Everything's quiet now, even the rain has stopped.

It's almost midnight when I come out of my room again. Aaron's sitting at the table hunched over this giant GED study guide that I've seen him open only in five-minute increments over the past few weeks.

I go sit down next to him. He doesn't look up.

"Sorry," I offer, even though I'm not really.

"I'm trying. I really am," he says, picking up the study guide, as if offering up proof.

He is trying, I can see that. "I can help you, Aaron. Studying—it's sort of one of the only things I'm good at."

"Nah," he says, pushing the book away. "Thanks, though. I gotta get up early tomorrow." He stands abruptly, already walking away before I can answer.

UNHOMECOMING

DANI AND TYLER ARE talking the entire car ride, but I have no idea what they're saying because their voices are competing with a billion formless thoughts that flow through my body to my brain all at once, jumbling together, so that I can't parse out anything coherent, anything that remotely makes sense.

Less than ten minutes after she picks me up, Dani is pulling into a big, crowded parking lot. There's a neon sign at the entrance of a giant warehouse-looking building that flashes THE SPOT, THE SPOT, THE SPOT, over and over again. We've only just stepped out of the car, and already my eardrums vibrate with the sound of the music pounding.

"Okay, listen up. Both of you," she announces as Tyler trudges up behind us. "I plan on having a good time tonight. So no excuses from either of you—we're dancing, *all* of us, and we're going to have fun. Got it?"

"Yes, drill sergeant," Tyler murmurs unenthusiastically, raising his eyebrow at me—the corner of his mouth hooking up into a smirk, which makes me laugh.

"Come on." She reaches for my hand, pulling me along, and I suddenly feel like such a normal girl doing normal things. Then she drapes her arm across my back and around my shoulder, something between us buzzing with new energy.

I stop laughing then. I stop breathing, because Tyler's stupid voice has lodged itself in my head, whispering, *Are you? Are you?* over and over again. I focus on the fresh air. I swallow gulps of it, trying to fuel my mind back up with oxygen. And when we get to the door, I have no choice but to let her do the talking, because I've been rendered speechless by the weight of her arm across my shoulder. She tells the bouncer at the door that we're here for the Unhomecoming Dance and then pays my cover charge for me. I notice that Tyler pays his own.

"Thanks for getting that," I yell over the music as the bouncer draws a thick black *X* on each of our hands as we enter. But under my words there's a thought brewing—one that makes my heart skid through a few beats—*Is this a date?*

Being inside this club is like being inside of a giant speaker. I swear I can almost see the sound waves hammering themselves out through the air, ricocheting against the walls. But that's probably just the flashing lights. I move in close to Dani and have to shout in her ear, "I'll pay you back!" Except I can barely even hear my own words once they're out of my mouth. I have to repeat it two more times before she hears me, and then she shakes her head, gives me the thumbs-down, and grabs on to my hand again, leading me through the sweaty bodies jumping around, covered in glitter, spilling their drinks.

The three of us huddle in a circle and Dani holds her hand

out to Tyler, as if she's waiting for him to give her something. He reaches into his pocket and pulls out a little bottle of hand sanitizer, squeezes a glob into his own hand, then Dani's. Then Dani grabs my hand and turns it over so Tyler can give me some as well.

"You guys . . . ," I caution, feeling my eyes widen as I look around. "What if we get caught?"

They look at each other and start laughing hysterically, rubbing their hands together until the black *X* disappears.

"Drinks!" Tyler shouts. Then he walks off into the crowd. We follow in the direction he went until we get to the bar. Dani gets me a drink—it's pink. She orders one for herself and Tyler, too. I have no idea what it is, but when I bring it to my nose, it smells fruity and toxic, all at the same time. We stand there next to the bar and she holds up her glass, and then she reaches over to position my arm so that I'm holding my glass up as well, and yells: "To unhomecoming! And to us surviving our first Robinson exam!"

"Cheers, y'all," Tyler sings.

Dani clinks her glass against mine, then Tyler's, then takes a sip.

I do the same. I'm too embarrassed to admit this is my first adult beverage.

It's like I can feel it traveling through my veins immediately, both warm and cool. It sizzles when it reaches my chest, and gives me the chills when it reaches my brain, then it's inside of me, moving everywhere, working its way through my extremities, untying all those knots. I take another sip.

The three of us move through the bodies again, out onto

the dance floor, except this time it's like I'm swimming with the current instead of against it. Dani leads us to the very center of the place, the source of the pulse that pounds through the walls and floors and me. The DJ—a girl, superthin, with wild, curly hair that sticks out in every direction—is up on this elevated platform like a deity, surrounded by turntables and equipment and adoring dancers. She has her eyes closed. With one of her hands she holds a heavy-duty set of headphones to one ear only, and she raises the other arm in the air, moving it back and forth to the beat that she's creating, like she's conducting some invisible orchestra. Then she opens her eyes slowly, like she's waking from a dream, finding Dani immediately. Then Tyler, then me. She smiles, mouthing the word "Hey," and she holds her arm still as she points at us, a strangely warm, welcoming gesture. She gently absorbs the momentary stillness into the rhythm and goes back to blissing out, everything in her body thumping along smoothly, in total harmony with the music.

"That's Kate!" Tyler shouts. "Dani's ex!"

My heart plummets. My whole body goes still. That girl is older than us, cool, confident, clearly so *out*—the exact opposite of me. There's no way I can ever compete.

"They're totally over, though!" he assures me.

I take another sip of my drink—no rules, I remind myself—and soon enough it begins to feel like I'm drinking the music, too. It works its way into my blood and my bones; another burst of fire and ice flows through me like electricity. I think about the now again, because this is a place composed solely of nows. In this moment—in this now—I have no past, I have no future. And I don't know why, but somehow this is one of the most comforting thoughts I've ever had. I take another sip, and another.

The next thing I know, somehow this place has taken me over, and my body moves on its own. I am dancing. The bass goes crazy—faster, somehow louder, more intense—like a veil has been torn off the whole world, making everything that much clearer, that much sharper. I jump up and down with them like I was made to do this. I'm laughing so hard, except I can't even hear myself. We hold on to one another's hands, flying them up above our heads like flags through the air and the sound waves. And it's like we become one person, and we become one with the people all around us, one with Kate, up there on her pedestal, one with the building, and one with the music and the air and lights. We all breathe the same breath; our hearts beat the same beat. There's no such thing as time. Just now. Right now. Dani leans in and kisses me on the cheek. And I never want this song to end.

The rest of the night is a blur, but in a good way—a fantastic dream half remembered. As I lie down in bed and close my eyes, I replay the movie of this night on the walls of my eyelids, feeling connected, as if there's an invisible thread still tethering me to that place, to Dani.

Then comes my favorite part. The part where Tyler and I are standing outside waiting for Dani to pull the car around, the perfectly chilled autumn air flowing through me, our backs against the brick wall, and Tyler looks at me, his eyes slightly glazed, and says something I didn't know I needed to hear so badly. "You know Dani likes you, right?"

I open my eyes. I am here in my bed. I place my hand over my heart, but it's almost like it's beating outside of me now. In the floor and ceiling and walls. *Boom-boom, boom-boom, boom-boom*, contracting and expanding in pairs. I hear its pulse in my ears, whispering this one word over and over, like a bass line: *NowNowNowNowNow.*

AVALANCHE

I FORCE MYSELF TO go into work. The bell dings overhead as I walk through the door, assaulting my eardrums like a giant gong. The smell of dough and sugar makes my mouth salivate but my stomach nauseous. There are only a couple of people in here, a man sitting at the counter, a regular, and a woman doctoring up her to-go coffee. I let myself exhale; maybe this will be an easy day. But then Owen approaches from the other side of the counter, tossing a rag somewhere underneath.

"Hey, you!"

I wave but don't say anything as I make my way behind the counter. When we're face-to-face, he starts laughing like he knows some big secret about me.

"What?" I ask.

"You're totally hungover, aren't you?" he says, leaning up against the doorframe, watching me too closely as I clock in on Jackie's computer.

"Is it that obvious?"

He laughs again. "I thought you were supposed to be a Girl Scout or something."

But before I can answer, Jackie suddenly appears behind him, carrying a tray full of pastries drizzled with chocolate and vanilla icing. "Brooke!" she shouts, making my head throb once more. Her smile fades, though, as she looks at me. "Oh, sweetie, do you feel okay?"

"Yeah, I'm fine," I lie.

Owen walks away, snickering.

"Hey, so I'm dying to know," Jackie begins, lowering her voice. "Did Aaron say how it went? We've been playing phone tag all day."

"How what went?"

"The exams."

"I don't—I don't know what you're talking about."

"He had the GED tests this week." Her brow creases as she looks at my face. "He didn't tell you?"

I shake my head no, but I can't shake this nameless dread that's suddenly creeping up through my veins, poisoning my blood.

"Well, that's strange," she breathes, her eyes crinkling up around the corners. "He better not have forgotten about it with everything else that's going on."

"I'm sure he didn't," I tell her, and I mean that. Because he wouldn't just forget—he's been studying, even. The only reason he wouldn't have mentioned it is if something happened, something worse than forgetting. I can feel it like something collapsing under my feet, the beginning of an avalanche.

✳

When I get home that night, I find Callie sitting cross-legged on the living room floor, grinning as she messes around on her phone. I ask her where Aaron is and she doesn't even look up; she raises her arm and points to the hallway, where my bedroom door is open, light on.

"Thanks," I tell her.

The window's open. I stick my head out and hear voices from up above. Carefully, I maneuver myself through the window and onto the platform of the fire escape. The higher I climb, the louder they get. They're laughing. When I crawl over the brick ledge, I see Aaron and Mark, in two lawn chairs set up near the edge of the roof, their feet kicked up on the wall.

I planned on asking Aaron about the exam, but as I get closer, I know I'm not going to be able to talk to him about that tonight. They have a collection of empty beer bottles sitting in a cluster on the ground next to each of them, an overflowing ashtray on the plastic table that sits between them. Mark mutters something I can't quite understand, but whatever it was, it makes Aaron fall forward, wheeze-laughing, just like he did that day in the kitchen with me. A twinge of jealousy pokes me in the side.

I must make a noise, because they both turn around at the same time.

"Hey, Brooke," Mark calls out to me. "Did you bring us some scones?" he asks, referencing my work uniform, and they both start cracking up again.

I try to smile. "Nope, sorry."

"Hey, sorry—just realized," Aaron says. "Your window, right?"

"It's okay," I tell him, stepping closer, trying to act casual. "What's . . . uh . . . going on?"

No one says anything.

Mark shrugs. Aaron takes a sip of beer. When he looks up at me, I see a flash of something. I recognize it immediately. It's one of Dad's favorite looks, a gaze designed to make its object feel infinitesimally small and scared and useless.

"Nothin', little sis," he answers. "What's goin' on with you?" There's some kind of weird, under-the-surface antagonism exchanged between us. I think Mark must pick up on it too, because he stubs out his cigarette and stands, stretching his arms over his head like he's been sitting for too long.

"I'm takin' off, man," Mark says to Aaron, and then reaches out to do that dude-handshake thing.

"You don't have to leave," Aaron says, standing up now too.

"Yeah, it's getting late. But listen—think about it, right? What we talked about. It's no problem, dude. No problem at all."

"Thanks, I will."

"See ya, Brooke," Mark calls out as he climbs back over the wall and down the metal steps that creak, one by one, under his weight.

"Sorry to break up the party," I tell Aaron, but he doesn't answer. "What was Mark talking about just now—what are you thinking about?"

"Nothing. He might have a job for me, that's all."

"Well, what about the job with Ray?" I ask. "What about getting your GED and everything?" I add, though something tells me I shouldn't go there right now.

"That's . . . uh . . . not happening," he mumbles, scoffing.

"Why not?"

He doesn't say anything to me as he gathers up the empties

and tosses them into the plastic garbage can in the corner, the glass bottles making a racket as they fall against each other one by one.

"I'm just saying—" I start, but he interrupts me.

"Yeah, what *are* you saying?" he snaps.

"I thought that was the plan, right?" I ask, feeling my patience slipping away with each crack of glass against glass. "What, are you mad at me now? For coming up here, ruining your good time?"

"No," he answers. "I'm not mad you came up here. It's just so obvious you're standing there judging me. Which, by the way, you have no right to do, especially after the way you came home last night. So if you have something to say, say it."

"I'm not judging. I was worried that something happened!" I yell over the glass clinking. "I always worry when you're up here," I add, except I don't think he hears me.

"Well, don't!" he says, turning around to face me. "Don't worry about me so much. I feel like you're always watching me, waiting for me to fuck things up. Guess what? I fuck up sometimes, okay? I already feel bad enough about it, and it makes me feel ten times worse when you look at me"—he points at my face—"like that."

I wish I could see how I'm looking at him, because then I could try not to do it anymore. "What are we even talking about? I'm not judging anything!" Although that's not completely true. "The only thing I'm ever trying to do is keep everything from falling apart."

"How, though?" he snarls. "It's already apart, Brooke! Why can't you see that? It's broken, okay? There's no saving this." He throws his arms open and turns in all directions, as if he's trying to gather up everything around us—the air, the roof, the building, the street below—all of *this*. Part of me wonders if he's talking about our family or Mom or maybe just himself.

"If you really believe that, then what are you even doing here—why did you agree to come back?"

Something settles inside of him as he looks at me, his anger suddenly transformed into sadness, weighing him down. He shakes his head, as if he's trying to find the answer. "Because you asked me to," he says.

We stand here, silent, on opposite sides of an invisible line. There are so many things I want to say, but so little I think he'll hear.

"What's going on with us?" I finally ask. "Why are we all fighting so much?"

He shrugs and shakes his head and smiles sadly as he looks up at the sky. "Maybe it's just in our blood."

He starts walking toward the fire escape, and I know I have to say something—I know we can't leave things like this. "Aaron. Wait, okay?" He stops and turns to look at me. "I disagree. It's not broken. I think it can be saved. I really do." I'm not sure if I'm talking about our family as whole, or our mom, or him, or all of it.

"I know you do." Something in his voice, in the way he says those words, makes me suddenly doubt myself. He swings his leg over the wall, then disappears, his footsteps fading as he descends the stairs.

OLD MONSTERS

I WENT DOWN INTO the storage unit in the basement and rifled through the stacks of plastic bins full of various holiday decorations and pulled out the one with all the Halloween stuff. I brought it upstairs and started taking the contents out, one by one. Old monster costumes and face paints, plastic pumpkin baskets for trick-or-treating, bundles of fake white spiderwebs and little black spiders.

Callie walks into the room, regarding the pile of stuff with contempt.

"Hey," I say to her, doing my best to sound optimistic, doing my best to mend whatever it is between the two of us that keeps on breaking over and over. "I thought maybe it would be fun to go out this year. What do you think?"

"I'm twelve." She pauses. "Not two."

"What are you talking about? Halloween's your favorite."

"Oh, okay. If you say so." Then she walks into the kitchen and says, almost as if she doesn't care whether I hear her or not, "I must be wrong, then."

“Okay,” I mutter to myself as I start piling all the stuff back into the box—the witch costume from second grade, the devil one from fourth, Callie’s Barbie princess one from kindergarten, a rubbery decayed-flesh mask from a zombie ensemble, the eye patch from when Aaron was a pirate. Then I see something I almost forgot about. There, at the very bottom, bundled in a heap. My homemade Peter Pan costume from sixth grade.

Everyone was into fairies that year—it was all about Tinker Bell. But I wanted to be Peter Pan. So I asked Mom if we could make my costume that year. It was one of the few crafty things Mom and I ever did together. She wasn’t that good at sewing and neither was I, but together we were really proud of this “project,” as she called it.

Green leggings and a green leotard—those were easy enough to come by. But Mom made the skirt, layers of different shades of green fabric, sewn together so they looked like strips of leaves and whatever other greenery we imagined might be appropriate for a girl version of Peter Pan. And then, of course, the signature hat with a feather—Mom made that, too. And my favorite part: the shadow.

Mom bought a cheap black sheet and laid it out on the living room floor. She had me lie down on top of it with my arms and legs spread out, and she drew the outline of my body in chalk. Then she cut it out and sewed a strand of ribbon into the neck so I could wear it on my back like a cape, my shadow trailing behind me. I remember telling her about how Aaron and I would run as fast as we could at the park, checking behind us to see if our shadows could keep up.

She threw her head back and laughed as we sat on the floor, cutting out my shape on the sheet. She rarely ever laughed like that, so that’s probably why I remember it so well. That was the year Dad decided I was too old to dress up for Halloween. I'm not sure why he decided, right then, when I was already in the stupid costume and ready to leave with Callie, that this was suddenly a new rule. I remember him making me go back into our bedroom and change into regular clothes.

As I looked at myself in the mirror one last time, I decided it was probably my turn anyway. Maybe, I thought, there was a finite amount of meanness in him, and if he took some of it out on me every once in a while, then maybe there would be less for Mom, less for Aaron. So I went out with Callie that Halloween, dressed as myself, and I didn't complain.

Almost as if Mom can sense how much I'm missing her right now, the phone rings—the landline. And no one ever calls the landline—the only reason we have it is for her phone calls. I trip over the Halloween stuff to reach it in time. I answer, and it's the recording that always comes on. I press one to accept the charges.

"Mom?"

"Brooke, I'm here," she says, her voice so much stronger than the last time we spoke.

"You sound good," I say.

"Well, I've been feeling better lately."

"Good," I tell her. "I can tell."

"How are *you* doing?" she asks.

"I'm good. Pretty good, I guess. I mean, we miss you. I was just thinking about you." She's so quiet I start to think I've lost her. "Mom? Hello?"

"I'm still here." She pauses. "Brooke, I have something I want to tell you."

"Okay?"

"I've had a lot of time to think in here over these past few months," she begins. "And I don't think I've been fair to you kids—to *you* especially." Her voice shakes as she tries to talk louder. "It all finally made sense to me."

"What . . . what did?"

"I look at you, and I see you trying to take care of things and be responsible"—her voice catches—"trying to take care of me. I've put too much on you. I always have, and that's not right."

"Mom, you know I don't feel that way," I tell her, but that's not the truth.

"That's exactly what my mother did to me. My whole life was taking care of her. And I hated her for that, Brooke. I don't want you to hate me. And I certainly don't want you to *be* me. And that's what I see when I look at you. I see you turning into me, and it scares the hell out of me."

I keep opening my mouth to interrupt her, to argue with her, but I don't know what to say. I want to tell her all the ways she's wrong. I want to tell her to take it all back right now.

"Brooke, I want you to stay away from here from now on."

"What? No, Mom—"

"I mean it. I don't want you to visit me. You see me here, like this, and you think you have to fix this for me, but you can't. I don't want you to take care of me anymore. I'm going to take care of myself now. All right?"

"No," I repeat. "I need to see you, Mom," I tell her.

"Just until everything is settled. I need you to stay away. For you, and for me, too. I love you. That's why I'm saying this."

"That doesn't make any sense. *No*," I repeat, trying to get her to hear me. But she doesn't. "Mom?" I try again. "Mom!"

"I have to go now. I love you."

"Mom, don't hang—"

But it's too late. She did. She hung up.

HARVEST

"YOU KNOW HOW I'M LEFT-HANDED?" I ask Dani as we sit next to each other in her car outside my building. We made a deal—I would stay and work with her until the library closed, and she would give me a ride home every day.

Weeks have passed since unhomecoming, and each day we hug good-bye, letting it linger a few extra seconds, and then I stand on the top step and wave as I watch her leave, feeling like some vital part of me is slipping away. And then my whole life is stuck on pause, unable to move forward until I see her again.

Maybe it's the deeper chill of the air today, something about all the fallen leaves staining the sidewalk with their last shreds of pigment, the bare branches trembling in the wind, that makes everything feel so urgent. These are our last moments together before Thanksgiving break, and if I have to wait five more days to tell her, I'm fairly certain I'll lose my nerve, fairly certain something inside of me will die.

Or maybe it's just because I need something to make sense,

need something to feel good. Fall is supposed to be the harvest. A time to reap the fruits of the seeds we've sown. Which means I need to say something. I need to say it now, before my heart ruptures, before one more minute passes and the ripeness that is now turns to decay.

"Mm-hmm," she hums, lowering the volume on the radio.

"Well, when I was little, I tried to teach myself to write with my right hand instead, because I wanted to do it the *right* way, you know. I didn't want to be different. But it was so hard. Too hard. Impossible, actually. So then finally I broke down and accepted it: *I'm left-handed*."

"Yeah," she says, grinning. "I can totally picture it."

"Well. Being with you is like that."

She looks at me uncertainly and then asks, her voice soft, "Like what?"

"Like I've been living my whole life in this right-handed world, where everything felt slightly off, everything a little too difficult, out of sync in this way I could never really explain or understand."

"Okay," she says.

"And now—when I'm with you, I mean—everything feels right, easier. Like I've always been looking to the next thing, waiting to finally get to that place where I'm supposed to be, but when I'm with you, I feel like I'm already there. I've never had that before." I dare myself to look up at her. "Do you—do you know what I'm talking about?"

I wanted her to know: I'm in. But now that it's all out of my mouth, this interminable silence stretching out between us, all I want is to rewind and tell her "Happy Thanksgiving" and "See you

Monday" and do our cute but counterfeit hug number, then get out of the car and wave to her from the top step like every other day. I grab on to the door handle, and as I'm about to make my escape—

"I think I do . . . ," she begins, the corners of her mouth almost curving upward, but not quite. "But I just made my peace with the fact that we were only going to be friends."

My mouth suddenly goes dry as a desert. I lick my lips. "Oh," I manage. "Okay." I'm about to sprint from the car when I feel her taking my left hand in her right, our fingers weaving together, and God, it's like my hands never knew what they were made of, what they were made *for*, until now.

"It's just that sometimes I get this strong *Back off* vibe from you, so I've been trying—not very successfully—to forget about it."

"I don't want you to forget about it," I admit to her, and to myself, out loud, at last.

She doesn't say anything. Instead she leans in slowly, closes her eyes, and presses her lips against mine. Her fingertips against my face, my cheek, send a trail of sparks along my skin. Our mouths fit together effortlessly, like our hands, missing puzzle pieces.

When we finally pull apart—forced only by the need to breathe—I look at her and it's like I've known her my whole life, but then again, in this other way it's like I'm looking at her for the first time. Maybe it's because of the way she's looking at me. Like I'm someone different than I was only minutes earlier.

I realize I'm right in the middle of one of those earth-shattering, life-altering, mind-melding, world-rocking moments you hear about that you think can't possibly be real. I try to memorize it all—her face, the way her lips are parted, the sound of the wind, a siren faintly wailing somewhere blocks away, footsteps crunching through the leaves on the sidewalk—these things are the beginning of my life. My real life. Finally, starting now.

I don't know how I make myself get out of the car, how I force myself to say good-bye. She waits until I'm inside before she pulls away. When I close the front door behind me, I stand there staring at the rows of mailboxes that line the entryway. I touch my lips. They're pulsing. They're alive. And so am I, for maybe the first time in my life.

WINTER

DOLLHOUSE

"YOU SEEM NERVOUS." Dani looks at me in the passenger seat as we drive away from school. She's taking me to her house for the first time. Her parents wanted to meet the "friend" she's been spending so much time with, and honestly, I'm happy to be away from home for an evening. The trial is about to start and none of us—not me, Aaron, Callie, or even Mom—are on the same page anymore.

"That's because you're *making* me nervous," I tell her. "What are your parents like?"

"My parents are accountants."

"That's what they do. What are they like?" I ask again.

"They're *like* accountants. They're nice. They're not cool. Our house is boring and looks the same as every other house on our street. And I have two guinea pigs," she adds, as if owning guinea pigs signifies something unredeemable about someone's personality.

"So?"

"So I'm just giving you fair warning. You might have been

under the false impression that I'm more interesting than I probably really am, okay?"

"Stop," I tell her as I stroke her hand. "I've never seen you like this. What are you so freaked out about?"

"I should live somewhere more like your neighborhood. It has so much character. It's eclectic and funky. The buildings are old—"

"Yeah, old and dirty?" I interrupt. "It's *so* great. You have to make sure you lock up all your doors and windows. You get to take the bus everywhere . . . it's really funky. Walking up a thousand stairs to get to your house every day—now, that's character."

"Why do you sound like that?" she asks. "All sarcastic or something?"

"Because. Come on, my neighborhood is not cool, I promise. You know, it's not a *bad* thing to live in a nice neighborhood," I tell her, but I hear it too—a tinge of something in my voice—not sarcasm exactly. Something more sour than sarcasm. I swallow it down. "Hey, stop worrying, this will be fine." I rub her shoulder and smile sweetly, burying that bitterness somewhere deep in my gut.

"Okay . . . this is me," she says, pulling her car into the driveway of a house that looks like something out of a magazine. Tall, made of brick and siding, with a big, beautiful wraparound porch, complete with a swing and wind chimes and bird feeders, shutters flanking every window, a big tree in the front yard that's lost all its leaves. And, sure enough, it really does look pretty much identical to the houses on either side. It reminds me of Jackie's neighborhood, except everything is a lot newer, a lot bigger, fancier.

When we walk through the door, everything is neat and clean and orderly, just as it was on the outside. And bright. Lots of windows with matching curtains. Smells like flowers—lavender, maybe—though I don't see any. We take our shoes off in the entryway, and Dani hangs our heavy jackets on the coatrack next to the door.

"Okay," she whispers. "Brace yourself."

"Danielle?" I hear a woman's voice call. "Danielle, is that you?"

"Yes, it's me," she yells as I follow her through her living room, decorated almost entirely in blue—all different shades of it. Blue couch with blue pillows, a blue abstract painting on the pale blue wall. "And Brooke is here too."

"Hold on!" I hear, the voice sounding like it's getting closer. I hear a small crash in the next room and then a muffled "Ow, damn!" before a woman emerges from the doorway. She's a full head shorter than both me and Dani. As she comes closer, I can see bits and pieces of her in Dani—the same smile, the same voice. She has amazing deep-brown eyes and shiny black hair pulled back into a french braid, her skin the same bronze tone as Dani's, except deeper. She's wearing a skirt suit with panty hose and no shoes, her jacket unbuttoned to reveal a white satin shirt underneath that it looks like she was in the process of untucking when she ran in here.

"Brooke, finally!" she shouts, walking right up to me and throwing her birdlike arms around my neck, as if we've just been reunited after years of being apart. I feel a jolt, a spark in my chest, a small electric shock—trying to remember the last time someone hugged me like this. Even though this woman is essentially a stranger, I don't want her to let go. I try to gather this up for my memory, save it, and store it somewhere cool and dry. There for me to pull out another day when I need it.

When she releases me, she still holds on to my arms, as if

she senses, somehow, how much I've been longing for a mother. "We are so happy to have you," she tells me, her voice soft, like she's talking to a little kid. "Danielle's father isn't home yet, but he's looking forward to meeting you too. Danielle never brings friends home anymore. We keep asking her, 'Where's Brooke? Why don't you invite your friend Brooke over?'"

"Okay, Mom—let her breathe, please." Dani steps in between us and gives her mom a hug. She's so casual about it, but I guess she must get hugs every day. She mumbles "Sorry" to me under her breath. A petty monster of jealousy begins to creep up my spine, one vertebra at a time.

"Oh, stop!" her mother tells her, swatting at her arm lightly. "I'm a mother—it's my job to embarrass you. Right, Brooke?"

"Right," I agree. "It's nice to meet you, too."

"There. See?" she says to Dani, waving her arm in my direction. "She said it's nice to meet me."

"Yes, yes, yes," Dani moans. "I heard. Mom, look, we're going to go upstairs and study until dinner, okay?"

"Fine, hide her from us—that's fine. I just got home myself. I need to get out of these clothes!" she calls after us, already halfway out of the room.

Dani narrates for me as we move from space to space: "Dining room, where we never eat unless we have company." Then she leads me from the formal dining room through a kitchen with shiny new appliances and a sliding glass door that leads outside to an enormous backyard. "Kitchen, obviously. Kitchen table, where we *always* eat. Outside, grass, garden, pool, blah, blah, blah." She talks fast and walks even faster, as if this is all too humiliating for her to bear. Then down a hall she points to doors: "Basement, where there's a game room nobody uses. Bathroom. My parents' room. Their office—where they keep the good liquor," she whispers behind a cupped hand. "Now. Upstairs. Almost there," she says, lowering her voice, taking the stairs two at a time.

"Okay, we're in the sanctuary now," she announces, slightly out of breath as she reaches the top step.

"One minute forty-five seconds," I say, looking at the place on my wrist where a watch would be. "You could probably shave off at least five seconds if you skip the kitchen portion of the tour next time."

She takes my face in her hands and looks at me straight in the eyes for a moment. Then she reaches for my hand and leads me into this loft area that the stairs spill out into, a closed door on either side. There's a window seat straight ahead, and bookshelves and a big red couch with lots of pillows, a TV with some kind of complicated gaming system hooked up to it. There's a huge dollhouse that sits on a table in the corner, looking suspiciously like a miniature version of this house. And next to the dollhouse, the guinea pig habitat.

"So this is my pad. My sister and I have the whole upstairs. Of course"—she gestures to the closed door on the right, big foam letters spelling out V TORI 'S ROO—"she's away at college now, so it's just me. And Bonnie and Clyde," she adds, pointing at the two balls of white-and-gray fur nested into a kingdom of cedarwood chips.

"I like Bonnie and Clyde. Victoria, is it?" I ask her, trying to read through the missing letters.

"Tori."

"Okay, *Danielle*," I tease.

"Dani," she corrects. "No Danielle—not ever."

"Okay, *Dani*," I relent, sensing she's not joking about this one. "You miss her a lot, don't you?" I ask, though I don't tell her that I can relate to missing a sister.

She nods, then turns toward the door on the left: DANI S R OM. "She's my best friend. I know that's totally dorky, but it's true. It's actually kind of ridiculous how much I miss her," she tells me, trying to cover up her sadness with a laugh. "You may have noticed I don't exactly have all that many friends."

The terrible thing is, I didn't really notice. But now that she's mentioned it, it's not like I ever see her hanging out with anyone other than Tyler. "Why is that?" I ask as I follow her into her bedroom. "You're a nice girl."

"Ha, ha," she deadpans, pulling me in and closing the door behind us. I barely have time to look around before she's kissing me, her hands finding my waist. I kiss her back, running my fingers through her hair, my favorite part the soft, downy fuzz that's growing in from when she shaved it before school started.

"Hey," I say softly, pulling away. "Aren't I supposed to be the one with all the evasive maneuvers? Not that I don't like your maneuvering, but . . ." I step away from her to take a look around her room—posters line every inch of every wall, floor to ceiling, so that I can't even tell the color of the wall underneath. Bands I've never heard of, movie posters for movies I've never seen, quotes, art, pages torn from books. "Now, your room definitely feels a lot more like Dani than the rest of your house."

"I'll take that as a compliment," she says, coming up behind me and threading her arms around my waist, pressing her mouth against my neck.

"You should." I walk up to her vanity—formerly white wicker but now covered with bumper stickers that overlap one another so they can barely be read. A mirror is framed by snapshots. "Is that her? Tori?" I ask, looking at one that features a younger-looking Dani with black, shoulder-length hair standing next to another girl who looks almost identical to her, except maybe a little older and with their mom's dark eyes. "And you . . . look at your hair—oh my God!"

"Yeah, that's us."

There are other pictures too. I recognize a few people from school. But not anyone I ever see talking to Dani. Yet here they all are, smiling, laughing, shouting together in these pictures. I decide not to ask what the deal is. If she wants me to know, she'll tell me.

"Your mom is adorable. You know that, right?"

"I do," she says with a sigh. "I know. She's very sweet."

"You must get your eyes from your dad, though."

"My eyes?" she repeats, batting her lashes dramatically.

"Yes, your beautiful eyes," I tell her. "I've been a huge admirer of them since the first day of school, you know."

"Oh really?" she says with a wide grin, pulling me over to her bed. We lie down side by side. I feel her let out a long breath of air. She has glow-in-the-dark stars plastered all over the ceiling, arranged in haphazard clusters. "Yes, I have my dad's eyes. He's white, by the way—not sure if I ever mentioned that. Don't want you to be surprised when you meet him. I mean, a lot of people don't realize. My mom's side of the family is from India. But she grew up here."

"You never really told me that," I say. "But I guess I kind of figured."

"He's nice too," she adds. "You'll see."

I prop myself up on my elbow so I can see her face. "All right, I have to ask. Why do you seem so damn sad about your parents being nice and sweet?"

"They're nice, they're sweet, they love me, they take care of me, feed me, clothe me, all of that, and I'm grateful, I really, really am. But . . ." She stops, inhales through her nose. "I'll always be Danielle to them."

"So they don't know that you're . . . that we're . . . you know . . . *together*?"

"Oh, they know!" She laughs, bitterly, in this way I've never heard from her before—it sounds so wrong coming from her.

"What do you mean?"

"I mean, everything is all on the surface with them."

I nod, encouraging her to tell me more.

"I came out to them in eighth grade. I sat them down at the dining room table, Tori next to me for moral support, and I flat-out told them, no two ways about it, I'm a lesbian. They sat there, listened, then asked if I wanted ice cream. Never talked about it again. They've never acknowledged it, never asked any questions. It's like they pretend it never happened. That's just the way it is."

She hoists herself up from the bed and walks over to the mirror to look at the pictures again. "You know, I used to have tons of friends," she tells me, her smile wavering, making it clear she's trying not to cry. "When I was this person"—she holds up the photo of herself with shoulder-length hair—"but that person's gone, and so are all of those so-called friends."

"They stopped being friends with you when you came out?"

"Not exactly," she says with a shrug. "They just sort of faded slowly, one by one. But I still had Tori, and later, Tyler, and somehow that was enough."

"Until this year," I add. "Right?"

She nods and bites her lip, trying not to cry. I stand and walk over to her. I put my arms around her, the way that I've needed these past several months. "I don't know what I would've done if I hadn't met you, seriously," she whispers into my hair.

"Yeah," I tell her, "I know."

"I guess," she says, sniffling as she lets go of me, "the thing that bothers me most about my parents is they should be able to understand. You know, their families were not okay with the two of them getting married. My mom's parents wanted her to marry an Indian guy. My dad's parents thought they we were too different from each other—they didn't get it, they worried about things like, what religion would their grandchildren be raised in, stuff like that, you know?"

I nod.

"But they loved each other and they did what was right for them. I've always really respected that—respected *them* for that. Except now they can't see that I need to be different in the same way that they needed to be different from their parents. They can't see me." She lets herself sink down onto the small stool at her vanity mirror. "It's so frustrating!" She pulls a tissue from the box that sits on the desk and wipes her eyes. "They're such hypocrites, sometimes I can't stand it."

I kneel down on the floor so we're at eye level. "I see you," I tell her.

"I see you, too."

No she doesn't, my brain argues. I do my best to ignore it.

We eat in the dining room, the room Dani said they use only when guests are here. The food is great. Her parents are perfectly lovely and sweet and polite, and she does have her dad's eyes. But she's right; they don't see her at all. They don't want to see her. This is no dollhouse after all. I look at Dani across the table, feeling like maybe we're more alike than I thought, like maybe someday I could let her see me, too, all of me.

SEEKING WATER

SINCE FOURTH GRADE I'VE missed two days of school, and that was only because I was contagious with strep throat. I've never even considered skipping school before. Until today.

Dani has been texting all morning with updates about all the stupid stuff I've been missing—Robinson yelled at a student, student cried; someone dropped a lunch tray in the cafeteria; a kid was sent to the principal's office for making sex noises in AP American History; Tyler's wearing mascara and got really mad at Dani for pointing it out; and so on.

I told her it's a flu-like thing. Which is believable, probably brought on by the sudden cold snap. The second week of December and we're in the single digits, which seems wrong when there isn't even any snow on the ground yet.

I had to wait until the seats filled in, so I could sneak in the back of the courtroom without being seen—Mom was very clear, she didn't want me here. She told Aaron, Jackie, and her lawyer to keep me away. But I couldn't force myself to go to school and sit there through all my classes and pretend like this was an ordinary day.

Aaron sits at the very front, Jackie and Ray next to him. There's a table with Mr. Clarence, Mom's lawyer. He turns around and says something to Aaron. I see Aaron shake his head, and then he nods—what they're saying, I can't tell. I notice that Carmen isn't here.

People start talking all around me, chattering, and that's when I realize it: They're bringing my mom out. She's thinner, lighter, like she might just float away, if not for the two officers flanking her. They each hold on to an arm, as if she's dangerous, in need of being kept under control. She's wearing a blue dress, one with a tiny flower print, the one she used to wear to work all the time. I watch them escort her to the table, where Mr. Clarence pulls her chair out for her. She sits and then turns around to look at Aaron, but she doesn't say anything. Then, as if she can sense I'm here, her eyes flick up in my direction, almost *at* me. I duck my head quickly, watching her scan the faces around me once more before turning back around.

Behind me I hear a raspy whisper: "I'm hiding too."

As I turn around, the voice and its words sink in slowly. Caroline. My grandmother. I open my mouth, but no sound comes out. I turn back around, trying to remind myself how to breathe. I have trouble paying attention knowing she's right behind me, the keeper of family secrets, the cause of so much pain, according to Jackie and my mom.

A whole group of cops in uniform are in the seats on the opposite side of the room. A few rows ahead of me I see Tony, sitting in between two people. He is the only police officer on my mom's side. I know those can't be good odds. I see Mrs. Allister from downstairs, her signature permed puff of old-lady hair on the top of her head. Both Mr. Clarence and the other lawyer make their statements. Various people are called up to the stand—it seems like everyone is an expert on something.

It all feels very tame, anticlimactic, until Mr. Clarence calls a woman up, Dr. Montgomery. He approaches the witness stand, addresses the doctor with a casual tone. "You know, one of the first things many of us think whenever we hear about a woman being abused by her husband is, why did she stay? Why didn't she tell someone? Why couldn't she simply ask for help? Can you explain it—for those of us who have a hard time understanding—what is the thought process here?"

"You're absolutely right, it can be extremely hard to understand, especially for anyone who's never experienced it firsthand. It's not just about the physical abuse," she tells Mr. Clarence. "Before Mr. Winters ever struck Mrs. Winters for the first time, he had already beaten her down emotionally, mentally—destroyed her confidence, made her feel worthless, like everything that was happening was her fault. . . ."

I try so hard to listen, but her voice goes in and out. Something's happening to me—each word is like a punch in the stomach, a slap in the face, a kick in the teeth. They echo over and over, pounding like a stake being driven into the side of my head. I'm suddenly plagued by an overwhelming rush of nausea through my whole body—not only my stomach, but in my throat and arms and legs—every part of me feels sick somehow. I notice my body tilting; I lean forward in my seat, my head feeling so heavy I think I might fall all the way over. But there's a hand, strong on my shoulder, squeezing lightly, pulling me back from the edge of wherever I went just now. When I'm sitting upright, Caroline lets go and rests her hand on my back for a moment.

When the other lawyer gets up to ask Dr. Montgomery questions, there's this tone in his voice; it's hard to say what it is, but it sounds so familiar. It feels like he's bullying her—the same way Dad would bully Mom, making every word out of her mouth sound stupid, sound like a lie, twisting and bending every point she tries to make. Why didn't Mr. Clarence get a male doctor to testify? That was stupid of him. They're not taking her seriously. She's too young, too pretty, too honest. She steps down from the witness stand looking defeated.

Before I know what's happening, I feel motion behind me, chairs shifting; they're calling Caroline. She makes her way up the aisle and my mom turns to watch her. I wonder how long it's been since they were in the same room. It takes her a while to get up there—the same shuffling gait she had at the funeral, like maybe one of her legs doesn't quite cooperate.

Once she gets situated and swears on the Bible, Mr. Clarence asks about the first time she ever noticed that something was wrong between my parents. I expect her to tell a story like the one Jackie told me. But right away it's clear that's not going to be her story.

"Allison was a senior in high school—they'd been going together for a while at that point. One night she called me from this diner where the kids used to hang out. It was late for a school night. Eleven o'clock maybe. She wanted me to come and pick her up—which was strange because she never asked me for rides, she was always very . . ." She pauses, trying to find a word. "*Independent*, never wanted help with anything. She told me they'd gotten into a big argument. She said Paul suddenly started yelling at her, calling her names. And then he left her all alone and told her she couldn't leave until he came back. She said she'd been waiting for three hours and the restaurant was closing. And I asked her . . ." She stops abruptly.

"Please, take your time," Mr. Clarence tells her, something in his demeanor softening.

"I said, 'Sweetie, why are you staying there?' I didn't understand why she wouldn't just *walk*. It wasn't very far, a block away; she used to walk there all the time. And I remember she whispered this part so quietly I could barely understand her, like it was too humiliating to say it any louder . . . she *couldn't* walk home because he took her shoes and her coat. It was January."

I watch the faces of the twelve jury members. No one looks impressed. Like maybe they don't get how messed up that was. They look hungry and bored. Maybe Mom wasn't so wrong about wanting to keep me away from this.

When the judge calls a recess, I rush out of the courtroom to avoid being seen. Outside I stand on the steps of the building and fill my lungs with freezing air. As I exhale, I watch my breath turn to fog. I can't help but imagine what I might feel like if I were standing here without my boots and my coat right now. I try to take as many deep gulps of air as I can—that familiar old suffocating, straitjacket feeling wrapping itself up inside of me.

"Too cold to snow."

I turn to my left. Caroline is standing there. She's bundled in a puffy mauve parka and a knit hat and scarf, and the kind of gloves you buy at any drugstore for ninety-nine cents. Between her fingers she holds a long, slender cigarette.

"What?" I ask.

"The weather. It's too cold to snow."

"Oh."

"Do you mind?" she asks, nodding at the space between us—at least the length of one tall person.

I'm not sure if she's asking whether I mind her smoking or if I mind her standing next to me. I shake my head, because honestly, I have no good reason to deny her either. She takes a deep, long drag from the cigarette, her cheeks sucking inward and her eyes squinting against the wind.

"I was a weather girl," she says. "For two years, when your mother was a baby. Channel four."

"You were a meteorologist?" I ask.

"No. Just a weather girl—a weather*caster*," she corrects, bending her gloved fingers twice, air-quoting with a cigarette. "Never finished my degree, but I was close."

"W-why not?" I ask, not sure if my stutter is from the chatter of my teeth or how surreal it feels to be standing next to this woman with whom I share DNA and not much else.

"I got pregnant in my last year of college," she says matter-of-factly, puffing away. "So I dropped out and got married. Got myself hired for the news anyway. I was young then—pretty. I don't think anyone cared that I actually knew what I was talking about." There's a wistful half smile on her lips that makes her look so much like Mom. "But then I started getting hit in the face too much to be on television anymore." She shrugs, then side-eyes me, checking for my reaction.

I nod and mumble something that might sound like "Oh."

"Well, it's actually not that it's too *cold*," she continues. "You hear that, but it's really all about the moisture in the air. The colder the air, the less moisture there is for the water vapor to form snow crystals, so that's why it usually won't snow if it's this cold. But it has to do with moisture, not temperature."

"Huh," I mumble, finding it increasingly difficult to be verbal. I wonder if cold has an effect on speech, too.

"It all starts way up in the atmosphere," she says, looking up into the thick gray sky. "A tiny particle in the air—dust, something like that, pollen, whatever—all it takes is for one droplet of water to stick to it. It freezes. Then it travels down, collecting the water vapor in the air, forming more ice crystals, more and more and more, and water does what it does . . . ," she explains, as if there's one obvious, known fact about what water does.

I nod.

"That's why no two are alike—that's true, you know, not just an overprecious metaphor—each individual snowflake has its own journey down to the ground. A million tiny factors make each one different." She takes one long last inhale of her cigarette. "You're planning on college, right?" she asks me, breathing out a thin stream of smoke after the words.

I nod again.

"Good." She tosses her cigarette to the ground, stomping on it like she's crushing a bug. "Well. Not sure if you like science, but . . ." She pauses, looking up at the thick layer of clouds sitting above us, as still as a picture. "If you ever get the chance to look at a snowflake under a microscope, you have to see it. It's magical." She bends over with some difficulty, wobbling slightly as she picks the cigarette butt up off the ground.

I look at the clouds too. I have a million things I want to know, but I can't think of a single question. So I ask the only coherent one that comes to me: "Do you think it'll snow soon?"

She raises her head to the sky, shielding her eyes with one hand, studying something there that I can't see, and says thoughtfully, "Pretty soon."

It's silent in the space between us as we both look out at the traffic on the street. Out of the corner of my eye I see her breaths on the air, coming in quick succession, and it makes me wonder if she's breathing heavy because of the smoking or because of me—if I'm making her as nervous as she's making me.

"I do like science, by the way," I blurt out, an afterthought.

She turns to me, stares for a moment. "Are you okay?" she asks. "Earlier. Inside." She gestures toward the building looming at our backs and pantomimes her head dropping forward, like mine did in the courtroom.

"Oh. Yeah, I just—I get these headaches sometimes."

She nods knowingly, sympathetically. "Migraines. I get them too. It's the stress."

"What did you mean, what water does? What does water . . . do?"

"Water," she begins, shaking her head slightly, a deeper crease forming in her brow as she tries to put it into words, "water's always seeking water. It's like gravity, magnetism—water attracts water."

She searches my face to see if I've understood, but I'm not sure I have.

"Well, think about rivers. Every river leads to the ocean—that's their whole purpose, trying to find a way back to the ocean. They cut through rock, move mountains to do it, but they always carve out a path"—she moves her hand through the air, a zigzag line like a fish—"to reach that other body of water out there."

"Right," I hear myself mutter, agreeing, realizing how much sense that makes, vaguely remembering having learned that at some point.

"Funny thing is," she continues, "people do that too, don't they? But then again, look at what we're made of." She starts laughing but chokes out a deep, lung-rattling cough instead.

I feel myself nodding. It's strange, I feel like we're having multiple disjointed conversations at once, yet they all make sense and I don't mind. She doesn't seem like the pill-popping, criminally negligent drunk that Jackie described. Maybe a little odd, but then again, so am I.

"Are you going back in?" I ask her.

"In a minute I will." She reaches into her purse and pulls out a leather pouch that clasps like a change purse; from it she produces another long, skinny cigarette. "I never did mind the cold," she adds. "Are you going back in?"

I look back at the building. "I don't think so."

“Maybe I’ll see you here tomorrow, then?” She smiles, a hopeful lift to her voice.

“Yeah, maybe.” I begin to descend the stairs of the courthouse, unable to remember if the bus stop is to the left or to the right, like if I were a river, I wouldn’t know for sure which way to flow to reach the ocean.

STAINED

I CONSIDER GOING TO school late. But as I sit down on the couch, the warmth slowly returning to my body, I realize I'd rather just sit here and do nothing. I slink out of my boots and gloves and scarf and coat. They sit there, forming a puddle on the floor. Like I've melted away and all that remains is this small pile of personal effects.

I sink into the couch cushions, their soft, massive arms folding around me. My eyelids feel so heavy, like I've been drugged by the day. I try to keep them open, but they drift and set, as they often do, on that pesky faded grape juice stain, before closing.

When I open my eyes again, I'm ten years old. It's Sunday morning. Cartoons on TV. I've just stashed Callie in our bedroom. I closed the door behind me quickly and stood there in the hallway trying to become invisible, trying to blend in like a chameleon, fading into my surroundings, becoming undetectable.

"What, you think you're a tough guy, huh?" He pushed Aaron. Hard. "Big man, are you?"

Aaron had thrown his cereal bowl at Dad only seconds earlier.

If I was ten, Aaron was thirteen. Still small—too small, too scrawny—and Dad was like a giant advancing on him. I think Aaron must've been aiming for his head, but he never was particularly good at throwing things, so the bowl hit Dad in the back instead. It made a dull, soft thud and then clattered to the floor, sending the spoon flying across the kitchen.

Dad turned around. He let go of Mom, whom he'd already backed up against the wall. I watched soundlessly from the hallway as the scene unfolded in slow motion.

"Leave her alone!" Aaron yelled, trying to hide the trembling of his voice under sheer volume. I thought I might pee my pants, I was so scared for Aaron. But a small spark of hope flickered alive inside of me for just a moment—the hope that maybe this would work. After all, it wasn't like anyone had ever actually tried to stop him before. Maybe it could be that simple. Maybe Aaron was onto something.

Dad shoved him again, though. Aaron stumbled backward, and as the two of them spilled into the living room, that little light inside of me was snuffed out, almost as soon as it had ignited. Because of course Aaron couldn't stop him; Dad wasn't going to suddenly flip a switch in his head and wake up and see all the damage he was doing.

Aaron tried to stand his ground. A stupid idea. He should've been running.

Mom was calling both of their names, yelling for them to stop, but it was suddenly like there was no one in the world but Dad and Aaron. Everyone seemed to fade into the background: Mom and her pleading; Callie humming quietly behind the closed door; and me, frozen there in the hall—even I had finally faded away. And there was no place else in the world except our living room, the space between the two of them, no sounds but Dad's voice, shouting:

"Come on! You wanna hit me? Do it like a man. You get one free shot—do it now," he demanded, this deranged smile distorting his face. He bobbed his head up and down, holding his arms open, beckoning Aaron forward, repeating over and over, "Come on. Hit me. Hit me. Come on. Now—*now*!"

Something in Aaron's eyes went all steely and hard, and I wanted to scream, *Don't! It's a trick!* but I wasn't even there anymore, so I couldn't say anything. And it was too late anyway. Because everything sped forward, happening too fast to stop. The flat, sloppy sound of flesh against flesh: Aaron's fist crashing into Dad's face. But Dad had some kind of force field around him. He didn't even flinch, didn't miss a beat before he hit Aaron. It was so quick I barely saw how it happened; one second Aaron was standing and the next he had collapsed like that tiny, weightless bird from the hospital, smashing into an invisible glass wall—crumpled on the ground, wings broken.

By then I'd rematerialized in the hallway, still guarding our bedroom door. I flattened myself against the wall and tried not to make eye contact as Dad walked toward me. Didn't matter, though; it never did. Because he just looked through me as if I weren't there anyway, and I knew that was the best I could ask for.

And then the worst part.

He threw a glance over his shoulder as he walked away, and

mumbled "Loser" under his breath, like Aaron wasn't even worth enough for him to bother saying it to his face.

My legs trembled as I walked over to where Mom knelt on the carpet next to Aaron. The coffee table had been knocked over, and with it, Callie's entire glass of grape juice, which was now sinking into the carpet fibers. Mom touched Aaron's hair, saying, "Why did you do that? Why?" She looked back and forth, frantically, between Aaron and the growing purple stain, like she couldn't choose which one to save. She said something to me, but all I could hear was that word echoing in my head: *Loser, loser, loser*. All I could see was Aaron lying there on the living room floor.

"Brooke!" she yelled at me. "Get something!"

"What?" I stood there, not knowing what she wanted me to do. "Get what?"

"A towel, something. Anything! Go, now."

I ran into the kitchen, slipping in the spilled milk from Aaron's cereal bowl, and grabbed the dish towel that was hanging from the handle of the refrigerator door. When I returned, Mom had Aaron sitting up, her hand on his back. I knelt down next to them and brought the towel to Aaron's face, trying to decide how best to approach the blood coming from his nose, his mouth. But Mom snatched the towel from my hand before it touched his skin.

"Help him up!" she snapped at me. Then she grabbed my wrist, replacing her hand on his back with mine. She turned away from us, on her hands and knees, and folded the towel in half, pressing it down against the carpet, sopping up the grape juice. "Get him to his room"—she was crying hard now—"before he comes back."

Aaron was out of it. I was glad. Because maybe that meant

he hadn't heard what Dad called him, maybe he hadn't noticed that Mom seemed more concerned about the stain setting than his bloody nose and split lip.

"Come on," I told him, struggling to pull him up. He wobbled as he got to his feet. We took a million shuffled steps to get to his bedroom. When we finally did, he fell onto his bed and bounced with the mattress, gasping like he hurt everywhere. His left cheekbone was already bruising up, his eyelid swelling fast.

Ice.

I ran back out to the kitchen, this time sidestepping the puddle of milk. I grabbed a bag of frozen peas from the freezer and wet a bunch of paper towels in the sink. I wanted to say something to Mom, but she didn't look up; she just cried, and scrubbed and sprayed the spot with carpet cleaner. I closed Aaron's door behind me and sat next to him on his bed. I tried to wipe the blood off his face with the paper towels, but he kept pulling away.

"Are you okay?" I asked, but that was a stupid question.

"My fucking hand," he moaned as he sat up slowly, raising it, wincing as he tried to move his fingers. It was so swollen and bruised all over I was sure he'd shattered every bone.

"Does it hurt?" Another stupid question.

But as he inspected the damage, I watched his mouth twisting upward slowly. He was smiling as he said, "It feels like someone strapped a firecracker onto my fist and it exploded."

"Here," I whispered, handing him the bag of peas. "Your face—it looks really bad."

"Good," he said, his voice tight.

"What?"

He laughed, struggling to focus his one nonswollen eye on me. "He did exactly what I wanted."

"But, Aaron—" I began, but he cut me off.

"I can take it, all right? What I can't take is just standing by, doing nothing, trying to stay out of his way. There's no staying out of his way—he won't let that happen." He paused, gingerly cradling his hand in the nest of frozen peas. "I can't pretend anymore."

I understood. Sort of. He'd never thought he could win. That wasn't the point. I tried to think of anything I could say to try to plead some sense into him. "He'll kill you."

"He'll kill *her* if I don't—it's only a matter of time. You know that."

I shook my head, my eyes getting hot, stinging with tears. No, no, no—we weren't allowed to think those kinds of things. Aaron was breaking all the rules.

"You don't have to be scared," he told me. "I don't want *anybody* to be scared anymore. I got this. I promise," he added, holding out the pinkie of his good hand.

I couldn't decide if I thought he was really brave or really, really stupid. Reluctantly I reached out and wrapped my own pinkie finger around his.

Something pulls me back through time, abruptly, tearing me away from Aaron and his bedroom and his promise. It takes me back to the day in the hospital—that bird smashing into that glass window. I hear the sound of it—that horrible thud over and over again. The crack and crash of it. My mind reverses, then fast-forwards. Now it's Dad's footsteps on the stairs as he leaves. Mom crying somewhere, muffled. Then a key in the door.

My eyes fly open. And it's now. I'm still slouched on the

couch. My things still sit in a pile next to the door. My neck aches, my head kills. I sit up straight. I reach for the remote and quickly turn the TV on.

When Aaron opens the door, I'm almost expecting to see a small thirteen-year-old version of him. He looks down at my stuff sitting in the doorway but doesn't say anything. He closes the door behind him, pulls his arms out of his coat, and drops it on the floor next to mine, another silent nod to our solidarity, I guess.

"Hey," he says, his tone not so much casual as it is exhausted. I feel the cold coming off him in waves as he plops himself down on the couch next to me. He yawns through the word "Jesus," sighing as he rubs his eyes. Then he turns to look at me, surprised, as if he didn't fully realize I was here.

"What?" I ask, wondering if there's any way he can tell where my mind has just been, where my body was earlier. "How did it go today?"

"Wait, should you be here right now?"

"Oh. Um, I came home—I have a headache." Not a total lie. "So how did it go?"

"Fucking sucked."

"Why, what happened?" I ask, pretending I wasn't there for at least part of that torture.

He shakes his head, opens his mouth, but nothing comes out at first. "It's not going well, Brooke. It was like every person who got up there to testify—the other lawyer twisted everything they were saying, made Mom look . . ." But he stops himself from finishing.

"Look . . . what?" I ask. "Guilty? Crazy? Stupid?"

"Yeah," he says quietly. "All of the above."

We both look away. I turn the TV back off and set the remote down on the table.

"Sorry, I'm just trying to tell you the truth," he adds. "I don't want you to be scared."

And in the forbidden part of my brain I hear the sentence that followed: *I don't want* anybody *to be scared anymore.* I wish I couldn't remember so clearly now—I wish I'd kept that memory locked up tight and safe. "Are you?" I ask, some new surge of bravery stirring in my gut, daring me to trespass once more. "Are you scared?"

His gaze travels across the room, and I think maybe his eyes set on that goddamn stain for a second before he lets his head fall back against the couch and closes his eyes. He doesn't have to say yes.

I watch him in profile, and suddenly the entire puzzle of him clicks into place. He couldn't keep pretending anymore—he told me as much, but I don't think I really knew what he meant until now. Because I think for the first time in my whole life I'm beginning to see things clearly, feel the way things really are, the way things have always been.

I've been pretending along with Mom for years, scrubbing out all the stains alongside her, trying to erase all the ugly things as if they never existed.

TRESPASSING

WHEN I ARRIVE AT the courthouse the next morning, Caroline is waiting for me outside. "Still no snow," she says. In her gloved hands she holds out a book. "Here, I brought this for you."

I look at the cover as I take it from her; it has shades of sky blue with a series of white snowflakes printed in rows: *Snow Crystals*. "You brought this for me? To keep?"

She nods. "To keep, yes."

"Why?"

"Well, your birthday's coming up, isn't it?"

I nod, wondering how much she really knows about us all—clearly more than we know about her.

"There you go. My father gave it to me for my tenth birthday. That edition's from the sixties, but it was first published in 1931. Bentley," she says, pointing to the name on the cover. "Snowflake Bentley, you ever heard of him?"

I shake my head and open the book—in the upper right-hand

corner of the first page, in the kind of precise, neat, loopy cursive they used back then, blurred blue ink spells out: *This book belongs to Caroline.*

"He was a strange person—dedicated his whole life to photographing snowflakes. They're in there, thousands of them. When I was ten, I wanted to grow up to be just like him. Life doesn't always go as planned, though, does it?" she asks, but before I've had a chance to respond, she adds, "Well, shall we?"

We take our seats in the back row; this time we sit next to each other. We wait, our own silence drowning in the chatter that surrounds us. The air feels thicker today, denser, less open space for hope to breathe.

"Thank you," I finally say, holding the book on my lap.

"You're welcome." It scares me that I'm starting to get used to the sound of her voice, her different facial expressions, that I could close my eyes right now and clearly picture what her face looks like when it's smiling. Or maybe the scariest part is that I already can't do that with Dad. It gets harder to remember his face every day.

Like yesterday, the guards bring Mom into the courtroom. She gives Aaron a small, sad smile. Mr. Clarence pulls out her chair again. But as she moves around to the other side of the table, she raises her head. She looks directly at me, then to my right, at Caroline. She freezes. Her face blanches. Her jaw drops open for a moment, then clenches tight. She feels her way into the chair, not taking her eyes off me until she's seated.

She leans in toward Mr. Clarence. I see her mouth move—what

the words are, I can't tell—but she's talking fast and gesturing with her hands. He turns and looks in my direction. Followed by Aaron and Jackie and Ray and Tony. They all stare at me—I'm not supposed to be here. I'm trespassing again. I'm tempted to stand up and shout out, *I'm sorry*. Only I'm not sorry. Not this time.

Mr. Clarence turns back toward her and talks with his mouth close to her ear. She's shaking her head no, no, no. He whispers something to his assistant. Now Mom spins around and reaches out across the bar that separates the courtroom—the lawyers and my mom and the judge—from the regular people. She grabs Aaron's hand, holding on so tight; she doesn't say anything to him—she only nods. Then she looks at me once more, and even though her chin trembles and her mouth collapses, there's something in her eyes—some new strength. Resolve, maybe. The guard is walking over to stop her from touching Aaron. But just then the judge comes in and everyone has to stand, then sit back down.

I hear Mr. Clarence's voice: "Your Honor," he says, "permission to approach the bench?"

Both Mr. Clarence and the prosecutor walk across the room to where the judge sits. The three of them talk in hushed tones. Then the judge steps down from behind the platform and enters a door in the back wall, Mr. Clarence and the other lawyer buttoning their jackets and following behind.

"What's happening?" I say to no one in particular.

"I don't know," Caroline whispers back.

Aaron looks over his shoulder at me, an expression on his

face I cannot name. I hold my hands up, palms facing the ceiling. *What?* I silently ask. He shakes his head: *Don't know.* Next to me, Caroline fidgets, tapping the tip of her thumb against the tip of her ring finger, over and over.

"What's happening?" I ask again. Except she doesn't answer this time.

The buzz of whispers—of everyone asking everyone else what's going on, why they went into the judge's chambers—is deafening. I keep thinking the door is opening, but it isn't. It's my mind playing tricks. I close my eyes, trying to keep the hammers in my head from taking over completely. In my mind I try to recite things. True things. Facts that can't be distorted the way my mind likes to distort things sometimes, especially things that shouldn't change, like memories, like the truth, like time.

The state capitals—I go in geographic order, starting in the northeast and fanning out from there, but I get lost somewhere in the Midwest. Next I try the elements of the periodic table; I remember a song we learned in middle school: *There's hydrogen and helium . . . then lithium, beryllium . . . boron, carbon everywhere, nitrogen all through the air*. But all that comes to a screeching halt because my eyes open. Caroline has her hand on my shoulder. Everyone is standing all around me.

"What—what's happening? Is it over?" I ask.

"They're clearing the courtroom. They're asking everyone to leave. We have to go," she tells me, standing and folding her big coat over her arm.

"But—" I begin.

"I know, but we have to do what they say right now."

We file out of the room. I look back and I see Aaron and Jackie and Ray standing up as well. I try to see my mom, but everyone's in the way. I struggle to find her face. I can only catch glimpses. It feels like she's slipping away, being carried out by a high tide, only I'm the one who's moving.

The hallway is packed with people, both sides of the room suddenly all mixed together, but then they disperse, thinning out gradually, breaking off into smaller groups. It reminds me of fire drills at school—there's this panic and excitement and confusion in the air. I stand here with Caroline and wait for Aaron to find me. Finally I see him, walking toward me, finding breaks in the wall of bodies standing around, wagering guesses.

"Aaron, what's happening?"

He shakes his head. "I'm not sure. I couldn't hear everything she said." He pauses and nods, an acknowledgment of Caroline's presence.

Jackie and Ray find their way to us now. And suddenly it feels like it's me and Caroline against the three of them. I feel like I've been caught consorting with the enemy. I take a small step away from her and she notices.

"I think . . ." Aaron stops himself, as if saying it will make it true. "I think she wants to change her plea."

"Oh Lord." Caroline breathes through the words, and I start to worry she might pass out, because she wobbles and puts her hand to her forehead. Jackie helps her over to one of the marble benches that line the hallway. As they sit there next to each other, Jackie puts her arm around Caroline, and though I can't hear what she says, it seems like she's trying to comfort her, like she's forgiven whatever transgressions Caroline might have committed in the past.

We stand there in the middle of the hallway, me and Aaron, staring at our shoes. I would say something, but there are no words left, no more questions to ask, nothing else to know.

GLACIERS

THE DEEP, METALLIC CHILL of winter seeps into my skin, settles into my bones—the cold cuts like a knife, but I don't care. I've been walking around the park for hours.

Along the bank of the river, the water looks clearer than usual, flowing violently, as if it's fighting so hard to keep moving, to avoid freezing. The sky is getting darker—the days are shorter all the time. In the distance the clouds churn slowly, deliberately, gradually turning from white to gray to black.

She did it. She changed her plea to guilty. Guilty of voluntary manslaughter. Ten years. State prison. She'll be eligible for parole after five years—that was supposed to be a consolation. "It could've been worse," Mr. Clarence told us. "Much worse."

But how?

How could she do this?

Doesn't she care about what happens to us?

Does she even care what happens to herself?

These answerless questions run on a loop in my head as I

complete lap after lap around the park, my feet pounding against the frozen ground, getting nowhere, hating her. Hating her so much I don't think I'll ever be able to feel or think anything else for the rest of my life. I don't remember leaving the courthouse. I don't remember how we got home. I don't remember if I said good-bye to Caroline. I remember I was still clutching that snowflake book when we sat Callie down in the living room. And when we told her, she didn't say anything at first. I thought maybe all the progress we'd been making would be reversed and she'd stop talking altogether again.

But that's not what happened.

She sniffed and tucked her hair behind her ears and said simply, "Okay," as if we'd just told her we'd be ordering out for pizza, or something. Then she stood and walked into the kitchen. We heard some dishes clanging and the refrigerator door opening and closing. Water running. I looked at Aaron, as if to say, *What the hell is she doing?* And he shrugged and shook his head in that way he always does when he doesn't give a shit. I set the snowflake book down on the coffee table, stood, and walked into the kitchen to find her ripping open a packet of hot chocolate and pouring it into a big mug—one with penguins, her favorite—the half-full bag of mini marshmallows open on the counter next to her. She turned to look at me. "Want some?"

I didn't answer. I couldn't. I backed out of the kitchen and into the living room. I put on my coat and scarf and gloves and walked out the door. Aaron didn't ask where I was going and I didn't tell him either. I came to the park. Dani texted me about a million times. But I turned my phone off.

I keep circling this giant boulder in the very center of the park. I examine it from all angles and it brings back all these memories of Aaron and me when we were kids—the boulder seemed even bigger then. We'd convince each other that we'd found fossils of baby dinosaurs embedded within the surface, or we'd jump off it, pretending we could fly. There's a little ledge carved out of the side that used to be a good foothold for climbing, but now it's the perfect height to take a seat.

I walk over and sit on that timeworn shelf. I pull my knees into my chest and let my back rest against the solid wall of ancient rock—no doubt deposited here by some glacier during the Ice Age, though I'm sure it doesn't contain any baby dinosaur fossils. As the cold mass cradles me, shielding me from the wind, it makes me wonder if there was a moment when all of this could've gone another way. Maybe that moment was two million years ago—that glacier could've veered slightly and set a whole different path for the river our ridiculous town was built up around. It could've curved in the direction of the coast and turned this whole city into a wide, deep cut in the earth, with this boulder sitting at the very bottom of a lake, miles below, no one ever knowing it even existed. And then my parents wouldn't have lived here, their parents wouldn't have lived here, and all the ancestors before them, all the people who found this place, would never have lived here, and Allison and Paul would never have met, maybe never even existed. I wouldn't exist either. And maybe that's a reasonable price to pay not to be here in this mess, feeling the way I feel, right now.

Then again, maybe that moment was the day he left her stranded without her shoes at that restaurant when they were our age. Maybe if Mom hadn't given him another chance. Maybe that was the day it all could've changed. Or maybe it was the fight between Dad and Aaron, the one that caused the grape juice stain. What if Dad had seen me standing there, scared, in the hall and realized how wrong he'd been? Maybe it was the day I found Aaron on the roof. Or maybe if Mom had left. Moved in with Jackie when Aaron was a baby.

It seems like there should be a specific moment in time. A clear event. A point in our history when they could've chosen another path. Something we could look back on now and know for sure, *Yes, this is where it all went wrong.* Or maybe it was all like a slow-moving glacier, the escalation, the damage it was causing underneath indiscernible to the naked eye. Maybe Caroline was right about people being like water—it does what it does and there's no stopping it.

HAPPY BIRTHDAY, LIAR

I STAY HOME FROM SCHOOL the rest of the week. I lie. I tell Dani I'm still sick. She asks if I need anything. She offers to make me soup. She wants to bring me my missed assignments, share her notes. But I tell her no. No thank you. That's okay.

On Friday she texts again: r u sure? I don't mind . . .

I'm fine, really. Thank u tho <3

sighs well . . . i'm sitting outside of your building right now

"Shit," I whisper. I look around. It's not too crowded at Jackie's today. "Hey, Owen?" I call into the kitchen.

"Wassup?" he answers, not looking up from the counter where he's dividing a pie into eight perfect slices.

"Could you cover for me? Five minutes. I need to make a quick phone call."

"Uh-huh," he mumbles, still not looking up from his work.

I grab my coat and go outside into the cold to call Dani.

She picks up on the first ring. "Hey."

"Hi, so listen . . . I'm not actually at home. I'm at work."

"I know, your brother told me."

"My brother?"

"Yeah. I just met him. We ran into each other. He was coming in. I was looking at the names on the mailboxes, trying to figure out which apartment was yours."

I feel my heart pounding, the sensation in my fingers retreating, a tiny panic attack coming on. I can't speak. I can't hide. I'm caught. She's going to know everything about everything. *What did Aaron say to her?*

"I thought you were sick?" she asks.

"I—I am. I mean, I'm not. I was. But I'm not now. It's just—it's been a weird week."

"Why are you lying to me?" she asks, except she doesn't sound mad. She sounds like she's asking a rational question, but it's not one that I'm prepared to answer. Thankfully, she keeps talking. "You don't have to do that. I would *always* rather know the truth. If you're having a weird week and you need some space, just say that. Don't lie to me. Don't push me away like that. Not when we're finally getting somewhere."

"Okay," I whisper, unable to understand how she always makes honesty look so easy. "I am having a weird week," I tell her. "But I don't need space. Not from you, anyway. I couldn't really bring myself to go to school. It's complicated family stuff. I'm sorry."

"Don't be. Hey, go back to work. We'll see each other later, all right?"

"Okay."

"I love you."

I almost hang up. I'll pretend I didn't hear, that I hung up before she said it. Silence.

"Fuck," she finally says. "Okay . . . that was totally idiotic."

"No, it's—it's okay."

"I shouldn't have blurted it out over the phone like that."

"No, it's okay," I repeat.

"I mean, I *do*. It's just—I wanted to say it differently."

It's like I'm incapable of saying anything else: "It's okay."

"Um. All right. Look, do you mind if I hang around here until you get out of work?"

"No. It's—"

"*Okay?*" she finishes for me.

I laugh, or try to, anyway. "Yes."

As I walk home from work, there's this stillness in the air, like a breath being held. Snow is coming. I can taste it, can smell it, can feel it all around me. I see Dani's car outside but no Dani. I call her from the street, but she doesn't answer. I walk down around the corner. Not there, either. My thoughts jumble up and my heart leaps into my throat as a fresh wave of panic settles in my bones. There's no sign of her. I start imagining something bad happening. She's way too friendly, too open, too honest—someone could easily lure her into something shady. And then I start to think maybe this means I must love her, too. I call her one last time, then I go inside. I run up the stairs, preparing to enlist Aaron in a manhunt. I hear whispers coming from underneath the door. It's dark inside as I push it open. My hand glides along the wall, feeling for the light switch, when all the lights are suddenly flipped on at once, accompanied by a chorus of "Surprise!"

I jump back and drop my bag on the floor. Standing at the kitchen table are Aaron, Callie, Jackie, Ray . . . and Dani. I'm so relieved I want to run to her and throw my arms around her. But then I start to panic all over again, because here she is in my apartment, the place I keep all my secrets, too close to everything I want to keep away from her.

They're all staring at me, smiling hugely, and wearing these pointed paper-cone hats, and there's a banner made of shiny metallic letters strung across the ceiling that reads: HAPPY BIRTHDAY BROOKE.

"Oh my God, what is this?" I finally say as the shock dissipates.

"Surprise!" Jackie repeats, throwing her arms wide open as she steps aside and reveals this gigantic square cake sitting on the table behind them, lit with what appears to be a hundred candles that flash and pop like Fourth of July sparklers. "I know, I know, we're a few days early—but hey, that's the surprise, right?"

Dani croons, "Surprise," her voice smooth and gorgeous. She pulls me in for a hug and whispers in my ear: "Happy birthday, liar." When she lets go of me, she's smirking.

"I can't believe you guys did this." I figured we'd all made a silent agreement that we were going to skip my birthday this year, considering the circumstances. I barely remembered it myself.

"We all need something to celebrate right now, and what's better to celebrate than you, my dear?" Jackie pulls me by the hands closer to where the cake waits, awash in the glow of frantic sparkling light. "Now, hurry—hurry before the wax drips!"

As if that's their cue, they all begin singing at the same time.

I really have no choice but to step forward and blow out the candles. Make a wish. It comes to me, not even a thought, a flash of a thought, a feeling. I wish for more of this—*this*—what's happening right now, whatever this is. I blow as hard as I can to make sure I extinguish all seventeen candles in one shot. Otherwise my wish won't come true—at least, that's what Aaron told me when we were little. That last candle flickers, fighting it off, but then finally it forfeits. And they all begin clapping. I look up at their faces, each of them watching me, smiling like they're truly happy, like they're all having fun somehow.

Jackie makes Ray take about twenty million pictures of the cake, and of me and Aaron and Callie standing there with our arms draped over one another's shoulders. Then one of me and Dani—our first picture together.

Jackie made the cake. I've only ever had birthday cakes that came out of a box, where all you need to do is add a few ingredients and top it with a can of frosting. This one is special—it is flawlessly decorated with ribbon-like ornamentation along the edges, billowing flower shapes, and red cursive that spells out HAPPY BIRTHDAY BROOKE! surrounded by little birthday balloons and frosting roses.

"Happy birthday," Aaron says, smiling at me as if we've never had a fight in our lives.

"Surprise," Callie whispers in my ear as she hugs me.

"I hope everyone likes cream cheese frosting," Jackie says as she plunges a knife into the cake, dividing it into perfectly symmetrical squares. "And there's a layer of ganache in the center. I hope you like it."

I'm not sure I even know what ganache is, completely, but I

tell her, "It's my favorite," and I mean it. I can smell the sugar, taste it in my mouth before I even take the first bite.

Never having had anyone around—no aunts or uncles, no cousins, no grandparents—I always felt like the Winters began and ended with us. Something about that made the world feel small. Too small sometimes. For a moment I wish Caroline were here too. I wonder if this is what it feels like when people talk about family. Is it like this? How it almost feels like things will work out, like things will somehow be all right after all, in spite of everything?

As we eat our cake, I look out the living room windows. We all see it at the same time. The snow. I kneel on the sofa to get a better look, and Dani scoots right next to me, her fingers grazing mine, a volt of electricity flowing between us, our breath fogging up the window as if it were one breath we were sharing. Everyone watches for a moment as the snowflakes fall slowly, weightlessly, like tiny white feathers from the sky.

"Sure is pretty," Jackie says with a sigh.

"Beautiful," Dani whispers.

"Yeah," I agree, but then I catch Dani looking at me, not the snow. As I look at her, something inside my chest does this crazy little flip. I look around to see if anyone else noticed. Aaron watches me, this amused smirk contorting his face.

There are even a few presents. I keep telling everyone, "You didn't have to do this." Jackie and Ray give me this really pretty, long, expensive, designer-looking sweater—a plum color, soft, with a hood and a belt—the kind of thing I imagine, once you put it on, you never want to take off because it's so warm and cozy and perfect. I don't think I've ever owned anything this nice before—most of my clothes come off the clearance racks at discount stores. "I love it, thank you," I tell Jackie. "It's too much, but I really do love it."

Next it's Aaron's. He slides a big gift bag across the table. "You didn't have to get me anything," I tell him. I look at the folded paper tag, hoping it's going to say something like *From Aaron & Carmen*, but it doesn't. It makes me nervous that she's not here, just like she wasn't at the courthouse.

"Just open it," he groans, pretending to be impatient.

I dig into the tissue paper until my hands pull out a messenger bag. It's soft and smooth to the touch and smells like real leather, not that plastic, rubbery scent of faux leather that I'm used to. There's no way he could afford this—I'm about to tell him so, but when I look up at him, he looks so proud of it, so happy. I shake my head at him, pretending to disapprove, but I think it's obvious how much I love it.

"All those damn books you're always carrying around, I figured you could use a new bag, right?"

I reach over to give him a hug, and all I can say is "Thank you."

Callie hands me a big, rectangular object wrapped in Christmas paper with a big blue bow on top. It has all the telltale signs of a book. "*Callie . . .* ," I begin, but stop because I can tell she's also proud of her gift.

I peel the bow off the top and stick it on my shirt, like a pin. I carefully tear the paper off to reveal a shiny hardcover world atlas, an image of the earth suspended in black space on the cover. It's thick and heavy. The scent of ink and paper—that new-book smell. There's no way she could've bought this for me either. Jackie must've given her the money. It's one of those gifts you never realized you wanted until you have it. I want to believe this means there's still something to salvage with Callie, because if she remembers the days when I would dream of other places, then maybe she also remembers the days when things were better between us.

"It's perfect," I tell her. "Thank you." I wrap my arms around her, and she lets one hand rest on my back for a second.

"Well, since I'm a surprise guest to the surprise party, I don't have anything for you today . . . except for homework," Dani announces. "But that's not really a gift. So you'll just have to wait for mine."

"I'm glad I happened to run into you, Dani," Aaron says. "I've been hearing a lot about you."

"Let me guess, all bad?" she jokes.

"All good, I promise." Except he's looking at me while answering her. He can be perceptive when he wants to be.

After presents I take Dani to my room. As soon as I adjust the door behind us, leaving it open a crack so we're not being too suspicious, she starts talking right away. "Don't be mad, okay?" she whispers. "I swear, your brother twisted my arm. He came downstairs and practically pulled me out of my car. I really had no choice but to stay."

"It's weird to have you here. But I'm glad you are. I really am, but there's something I should explain—" I begin, but she cuts me off.

"You don't have to explain anything. Your family is so awesome. Aaron, Callie, your uncle Ray. I love it here, I love *them*. And . . . hello? You guys call your mom by her first name? I mean, come on—that's so badass. This explains so much about you."

"No, it's not that . . ." I stop midsentence. Because if she thinks Jackie's my mom and Ray's an uncle and we have some kind of hippie, twenty-first-century family dynamic where we all treat one another like we're individuals worthy of some kind of sophisticated system of respect, then maybe I should let her go ahead and think that. It's not like I've told her some big lie; I'm simply letting her believe something that isn't quite true.

"What?" she asks when I don't finish.

I want to keep Dani out of it. Not for her sake, but for mine. She's my one last uncontaminated thing, this single remaining fragment of my life that can belong to me alone, that doesn't have to be tainted by my family. I'm willing to lie a little to keep it that way.

"Nothing," I finally answer. "I just wanted to tell you that they don't, like, know about us—about me."

"Oh totally, I got that. Don't worry."

We gaze into each other's eyes for a moment. "All right," I say with a sigh, forcing my eyes to look anywhere else. "So this is me. . . ."

She takes a turn around the room, her fingertips grazing the cover of the snowflake book that sits on the corner of my desk. "Not at all what I expected. But then again," she says, turning to face me, "you're not at all what I expected either."

"Is that a *good* thing?"

She smiles and nods enthusiastically. She takes a step toward me, and because it feels like she's going to either kiss me or tell me "I love you" again, I back away, a reflex, and swing my door open wide. "Let's get back out there, okay?"

"Oh. Sure," she says, looking down at her feet instead of at me. I should apologize, I should explain, I know I should tell her the truth.

Dani's a big hit with everyone. No one mentions Mom or Dad, and I'm thankful for that. After everyone leaves, Aaron comes to my room and knocks twice on my open bedroom door.

"Come in," I tell him.

He does. Then he sits down on my bed next to me, my presents between us. He looks at me as if he's waiting for an answer to a question he hasn't asked.

"What?" I ask.

"So that was her, huh? Your girlfriend, right?" When I don't answer, he laughs, giving me a light punch in the shoulder. "Hey," he says. "You seem happy."

I can't help but smile. But it's immediately coupled with guilt. "Is that bad?" I ask him. "It feels like I don't have a right to be happy, with everything that's happening."

He shakes his head. "No, it's not bad. Not at all."

PUSH

I DIDN'T SET MY ALARM before going to bed last night. I wasn't in a hurry to start this particular day, because it's my real birthday. One more thing that my parents are missing, one more piece of evidence that time is going to keep on moving ahead, that we'll have to keep pushing forward without them.

I hear the phone ringing, muffled on the other side of my closed door.

Aaron's talking. I pull my pillow over my head and consider sleeping through this whole day. But someone's knocking on my door.

"You awake?" Aaron calls to me.

I roll over, force myself to get up.

When I open my door, he's standing there with the phone. "It's Mom," he says, holding it out to me. "For you." I stare at the phone—wish that I didn't still want to hear her voice so badly, wish I could cut her off, cut her out for good. "Take it—she might not have long," Aaron whispers, covering the mouthpiece.

"Hello?" I grumble.

"Brooke, happy birthday, sweetie."

"Oh, is it suddenly okay to talk again?" I ask her, my words turning sharp.

"Don't do that," she says.

"Why? You can do whatever you want, but I'm not allowed to?"

She scoffs. "Please, I can't do whatever I want—I can't do *anything* I want." I hear her breathe into the phone. "Talking to you is one of the few things I can still do, so please just let me."

"Well, I don't want to talk to you." I have to stop to catch my breath before I continue. "How could you? How could you just throw it all away and give up like that?"

"Brooke, I was only trying to make things right for everyone."

"That wasn't what was right! That was selfish—we need you here. You're the mother, we're the kids. Don't you understand that?"

"Yes, of course I do. But I need you to understand that I had to," she tries to explain, but I won't let her—not this time.

"*No.* No, it's too late. I hate you for this, I really do."

"Don't say that, please. Look, they're moving me next week. To the state prison. And I really would love it if you would come visit me before they do."

"Are you serious?"

"Brooke, I—"

But I hang up. I push her away this time.

I try to go back to sleep, but my mind won't stop replaying every word. I have to take some pills for my head to quiet all the noise. And eventually I'm able to fall back to sleep. I don't get up again until dinnertime.

NEW YEAR

"IS THIS CRAZY?" I whisper, my cheek against Dani's shoulder as we stare at the ceiling of her bedroom, lined with soft, white twinkle lights. The falling snowflakes make *tink-tink-tink* tapping sounds against the windowpane, accentuating the deep, middle-of-the night silence that has washed over the world. I imagine the snowflakes crystallizing way above the surface of the earth, beginning as specks of dust and water droplets, like Caroline said.

"You don't have to whisper," Dani tells me, her voice sounding extra loud. "It's just us up here." That's true. Her parents are tucked away downstairs, fast asleep, no idea that after dinner we snuck a bottle of champagne up to Dani's room and toasted everything we could think of—us, Tyler, Bonnie and Clyde the guinea pigs, New Year's Eve itself. We even drank to a promise that since we were starting the new year together, we would end it together as well, and the year after that, and the year after that. We were laughing so loud for a while, her parents were probably downstairs wishing, hoping, pretending, we were giggling over boys and not each other.

But now we're calm. Lying here, breathing together—her exhale is my inhale, my inhale her exhale—is so perfect I can almost pretend that I live here with Dani, that we have our own little loft apartment, that it's two years from now and we're both in college, living out life exactly as I've planned in my dreams. I can almost convince myself that I really belong here. That life is okay. Dani lifts her head from the pillow and looks at me. She traces the tip of her finger along the necklace she gave me for my birthday—a thin silver chain with a sparkly snowflake charm dangling from it—her touch sending shivers throughout my whole body.

"Why would this be crazy?" she asks, her voice strained from all the talking and laughing and champagne and kissing.

I shrug. "I don't know," I whisper again. "Just never thought . . ." I realize I've started this sentence without actually knowing the ending. I stop talking.

"Never thought what?"

I shake my head. "I'm not sure. I guess I never thought I . . . ," I try again, but still the ending isn't there.

"Never thought you . . . were . . . *gay*?" her voice lifting on that last word. "Because you really, *really* are, Winters," she says, losing the voice to a new bout of giggles.

I feel myself smile. "'Really, *really*'?" I repeat, raising my head to look at her. "Really?"

"Oh, big-time, yeah," she tells me, still laughing as she pulls the covers up around us.

I kiss her cheek and lay my head back in its spot—that soft curve between her shoulder and her collarbone. Then I kiss her neck. And she kisses my forehead. "That wasn't what I was going to say, though." I take her hand in mine, and our fingers wrap around one another. "I was going to say I never thought I'd be this happy."

This time she whispers, "Me neither."

We listen to the microscopic symphony of snowflakes and silence. Neither of us speaking, neither of us sleeping. As if time is standing still once again. Only this time I never want it to pick back up. I want to stay just like this forever. I want to tell her I love her. *Love.* It's so huge, so monstrous, so dangerous and unknowable. No. *Not now*, I tell myself, *don't ruin this moment*. Her breath spaces out to an even, steady rhythm.

"You know," she says, her voice sleepy and scratchy, "you still never said why this would be crazy."

I close my eyes tighter and I wonder how much longer she'll let me get away with not answering her questions.

"What's it like?" she whispers, even though she just said we didn't have to be so quiet.

"What's what like?"

"What's *life* like? What's life like for you, I mean? You realize you're still frustratingly private, right?"

"I am not," I lie.

"*What?* Please, you don't talk about your family or what's going on at home—you always say 'family drama' or 'it's complicated.' I mean, I wanna know this stuff. I want to know what it's like with your father being gone. That. What's that like?" she asks. "I can't imagine how I'd feel if my dad died. I'm not trying to pry; I just want you to know that I'm here."

Being so close to her seems to loosen my grip on all those things that should never be said out loud. Or maybe it has something to do with the half bottle of champagne getting warm in my stomach. "You know those tightrope walkers you see, like at the circus or something?" I ask.

"I'm serious," she says, exasperated, her whole body tensing.

"No, I am too."

"Okay. Sorry, go ahead."

"It's like you've been walking along on this tightrope your whole life. And you always thought you were doing it all on your own. Keeping your balance, putting one foot in front of the other. You look down sometimes and see the ground, but you never really worried about it. One minute you're walking along, same as always, and then the next it's like suddenly you can't find your footing and you realize that you weren't doing it all alone like you thought. Something was there keeping you up—*someone*." I stop and wonder if I'm telling the truth; sometimes it's hard to tell.

"Keep going," she whispers.

"But pretty soon you swing your weight an inch in the wrong direction, only to realize there's nothing there anymore. You see yourself teetering from side to side, but there's nothing you can do. And then, finally, you just fall. And it's like you keep falling and falling through the air and there's nothing to hold on to, and all you want is to hit the ground so you know where you are again, but you don't—you can't." There's this pang in my chest, interrupting the dull, steady ache that always seems to be there, making the words get caught in my throat. I swallow hard. "It's sort of like that, I guess."

"Brooke?" Dani pulls me closer and whispers into my hair. "You can hold on to me."

So I do. I hold on, tighter and tighter.

"I used to think that if my dad died, I wouldn't really care, I wouldn't feel anything. It wouldn't really be any big loss." I volunteer this information, not so much because I want her to know, but because I need to say it. Out loud. Just once. Need to own it.

"Why?" she asks softly. I listen for it, but I don't hear any hint of judgment behind her words.

"He wasn't . . ." I stop because I'm treading dangerously close to the truth, to letting her see all my hiding places. "He wasn't the greatest person most of the time. I was pretty much scared of him my whole life—everyone was. Sometimes I thought it would better if he just died. But it's not."

"I don't know how to ask this, but was your father abusive or something?"

I've never really assigned a word to what he was. There were never any words that quite fit. No words that could ever explain *enough*. "I—I guess," I whisper. "I mean, it's not that simple."

"I know," she says, but she doesn't.

"You think I'm a horrible person?"

"Never."

It feels like I've only blinked when Dani's shaking my shoulders, whispering my name. "Brooke, wake up. Wake up, your phone."

I open my eyes. Dani's shoving my phone into my hand. I look at her alarm clock. It's 3:17 in the morning. I look at the screen on my phone: Jackie. My brain puts the pieces together too slowly. But once it does, I bolt upright. "Hello? Jackie? What's wrong?"

"Brooke, hi. I'm here with Callie."

“Why? Is she okay?” I ask, struggling to get out from under the sheets.

“Yes, yes. Everyone’s okay. We’re at the apartment. Callie said she’s been trying to reach you—she’s fine, just a little upset, is all.” She pauses. “Brooke, Aaron’s not here. Have you spoken to him? Is it unusual that he wouldn’t come home?”

Her words echo in my head and something twists inside of me like a snake coiling up through my abdomen, constricting around my lungs, making it hard to breathe, then around my throat, strangling my voice.

“What is it?” Dani whispers.

“No, I—I told him—I mean, I texted him—that I was staying over at Dani’s house. No, he—he should be there,” I stutter through the words; I feel the world tilting. “Something’s wrong. He should be there. I’m coming home.”

“No, Brooke, calm down. That’s not necessary, I promise. Have your sleepover. Everything’s . . . under control,” she says, but she’s distracted by something that’s happening over there, across town, where I’m not—where I *should* be. “I’m sorry I called. I didn’t need to bother you with this. I thought maybe you knew something. Look, I’ll leave a note for Aaron. And Callie’s going to stay at my place tonight. Okay?”

“Okay,” I repeat. “Thanks, Jackie, I’m sorry.”

Dani turns her bedroom light on and stands in front of me, wearing only her underwear and a thin spaghetti-strap cami. She wraps her arms around herself like she’s scared and cold—like she needs a hug.

“It’s not your fault,” Jackie tells me. “It’s no one’s fault.”

Yes it is, I say to myself.

"We'll talk in the morning. Go back to sleep. Don't worry, please. Bye, Brooke."

My hands are shaking. I open my mouth, but she hangs up before I can tell her that she needs to check up on the rooftop.

"What's going on?" Dani asks as I hang up and scroll through my missed messages.

Callie, 11:55: Did you tell Aaron you weren't coming home? Just woke up and he's not here.

Callie, 12:34: I'm fine by myself, but thought you should know

Callie, 1:45: Hello?? Now I'm worried abt both of you . . .

Callie, 2:12: You guys suck. I'm calling Jackie.

Nothing from Aaron.

Dani's following me as I pace her room. She's saying my name, but I can't even answer because I'm trying to get dressed while calling Aaron at the same time. I'm muttering to myself—I might even be muttering to myself that I'm muttering to myself. I'm pressing all the wrong buttons. I feel like I'm losing it. I manage to pull on my pants one-handed. I need to find him. His phone goes straight to voice mail.

"God damn it, Aaron! Where the hell are you? Call me back the second you get this—the *second* you get this! I need to know you're okay. All right? Call me back, just call me back." I hang up. I throw the phone into my open bag on the floor—it bounces out and makes a noise too loud for three o'clock in the morning at a nice family's house. "God, fuck!" I whisper-shout as I bend down to pick the phone back up, checking to make sure it's still on. I stuff it into my pants pocket instead.

Dani reaches out to grab my hands, but I twist away from her, pulling my shirt over my head, not caring that it's on inside out. "Sorry, I—I just need to get home."

She stands in front of me and turns her head, this concerned look on her face, and she walks toward me even though I'm backing up. "Come here, sweetie. Come here—okay, just slow down." She pulls me in with both of her arms, crushing me against her breasts and ribs and stomach. I bury my face in her neck, craving the softness of her, and without warning, without permission, I feel my lungs contracting, my throat constricting, my eyes welling up. My body wants to cry. But my mind cannot let that happen. She holds me tighter and tighter, until it stops feeling good and starts to feel like she's suffocating me, drowning me, pulling me under.

"Stop, okay?" I whisper, my mouth next to her ear, my words crashing, hard, against her neck. I close my eyes. "Please, I can't breathe!" I yell. And as I pull away, too roughly, I catch the look on her face. Her eyes are wide, stunned that I yelled, because I've never let her see that side of me before, the side with all the secrets.

"Okay, you're scaring me now," she says, crossing her arms.

"This isn't about you!" I snap. "I mean—God, can you just give me some space for a minute?"

She doesn't say anything. I'm hurting her and I know this and still all I want to do is yell at her for not understanding. Even though I know it's not her fault for not understanding, because I never told her the things that she would need to know to understand in the first place. I want to climb back into bed and feel her breathing and listen to the silence and her heartbeat and the whispers of falling snow. But I'm not allowed to have any of those things. And I hate the world, and my life, and me, and even her a little bit, for that.

"Look, I'm sorry. I'm sorry, Dani. Okay? I really, really need to go home. Now. It's an emergency. For real. Please, can you just take me?"

"Yeah," she breathes, looking at me like she's not sure she knows who I am. "Okay," she whispers, reaching for the clothes she wore yesterday, scattered across her bedroom floor. "Okay," she repeats to herself as she gets dressed.

GHOSTS

"CAN YOU DRIVE ANY FASTER?" My tone is clipped, my words too sharp for the cold, icy, empty streets and the middle of the night.

"No. The roads are slick. I'd rather get you there alive." I feel her looking at me. "You have to tell me what is going on. I want to help—I'm trying to help you—why are you so upset?"

"It's my brother. He didn't come home."

"Why is that such an emergency?"

"You wouldn't understand, okay? And I can't explain it right now."

"Well, try."

I breathe in deeply, through my nose, and exhale slowly from my mouth. "Our sister was alone. She's only twelve. I can't understand why he would do that unless something bad happened, okay? I need to find him before—"

"Before what?"

"Can we please just stop talking?" I am exhausted, yet wired, and too tired to be so wired. I feel all wrong in every way.

"But I don't understand. What about your mom—I mean, where's she? What am I missing?"

"Can we *please* stop talking, Dani?" My patience grows more slippery with every word.

"Fine. Okay, stop yelling, though—you're making me nervous, and I can't drive when I'm nervous!"

"I'm not yell—" But of course I am. I keep my mouth shut until we get there.

She slows to a stop in front of my building. The fresh snow makes everything look like a dream. Makes me want to slow down and turn to her and cry and kiss and beg her to forgive me. It makes me want to tell her to keep driving and take us somewhere, anywhere, far away. It makes me want to leave it all behind, forever.

"Let me at least come in with you," she says, unbuckling her seat belt.

"No. Please, I need to handle this by myself, okay? Thank you, but—oh my God, there he is!" I open the car door and try to run to where Aaron's just rounded the corner. My feet slide on the ice, and I struggle to keep my balance. "Aaron!" I call out, my voice getting lost in the air as it swirls around us.

"What?" he whispers into the silence, not bothering to quicken his pace to reach me sooner.

I hear Dani calling my name behind me.

"Where were you, dammit?"

"I'm right here, you don't have to yell," he says, several feet away from me now. "What's wrong?"

"You didn't answer your phone!" I shout. "I was scared—Callie was scared, I mean."

"It died." He pulls his phone out of his pocket and waves it around. "What? Is she okay?"

I walk closer to him, trying to see his face more clearly, but he's all in shadow. "Callie didn't know where you were. She called Jackie to pick her up."

"What for?" He shrugs through the words. "You're here."

"I wasn't here—I texted you that I was staying at Dani's."

"Okay, well, I didn't know!" he says, getting defensive.

"Where were you?" I repeat.

"I went out. Is that a crime now?" he asks, as if that's a question I can answer. "It's not that huge. Callie's okay, right? You're okay. I'm okay. So calm down, all right?"

"Brooke?" Dani says again.

"What?" I shout, turning around to see her looking at me in that way—maybe the way I was looking at Aaron that night on the roof—that makes you feel like a total worthless piece of garbage for disappointing the one person you want to love so badly.

"Brooke, Jesus," Aaron says under his breath.

"I'm sorry, but please go, Dani. Okay?" I say.

"I'm just trying to help," she says, her voice so small. She walks toward me cautiously, and I want to believe that she's being careful because she's afraid of the ice, not me. She holds my leather messenger bag out at arm's length.

"I know. I'm sorry, I'm sorry," I keep repeating. I walk over and try to pull her in for a hug. "I'm sorry," I whisper against her cheek as she pushes away from me, like I'm suffocating her this time. "I'll explain everything. Later. Okay? *Okay?*"

"Okay," she finally answers. She gets into her car, closes the door, and pulls away slowly. I wave to her, but she looks straight ahead. Everything's left quiet in the wake of our voices.

Aaron walks up the steps, then brushes the snow off the top step before he turns and sits down. He looks out over the rooftops at the half-moon, barely visible through the thick clouds.

I follow his lead and brush the spot next to him and sit as well. The snowflakes float down around us, the muteness of winter finally setting in. In the streetlight it looks like dust, a fine white powder, a million tiny stars twinkling as they fall.

"Listen, you can't be like that," he finally says.

"Like what?"

He shakes his head slowly as he looks at me, disapprovingly. "She genuinely cares about you. Don't start treating her like shit."

"I—I'm not—I didn't mean—"

"Yeah, I know!" he snaps at me. "Believe me, I understand. You didn't mean to, right? You're sorry—who does that sound like?" He reaches into his coat pocket and takes out his cigarettes. "It's not okay to take your shit out on other people. For fuck's sake, haven't we learned that by now?"

"Why are you saying this? You act like I've done something terrible. You're always fighting with Carmen."

He turns his head and looks at me like he wants to yell but just doesn't care enough to actually do it. "Yeah, that's why you should listen—I know what I'm talking about. You and me, Brooke, we need to be careful with people. Callie, too."

"What do you mean?"

"I mean you have to watch how you treat people. You have to watch how you let people treat you. They're in us, both of them." He pauses while his words sink their way into my brain slowly. Then he adds, "We split up weeks ago, by the way. Not exactly breaking news."

"I'm sorry."

He shrugs in response.

"How come?" I ask, trying to make my voice softer, gentler.

"I don't know. No reason. A million reasons," he mumbles through his cigarette. "Better question, why are you all freaked out and yelling at your girlfriend? And me, too, by the way? This is not exactly a catastrophe here," he says, looking around at the sheer calmness surrounding us.

"No, but it could have been—"

"But it wasn't," he says, cutting me off.

"But it could've been! You don't even know what I'm talking about, do you?" I feel myself start to laugh—needing some kind of release for my frustration.

"What?" he asks me, trying to be comforting but getting frustrated himself. "What are you talking about, then?"

"You, Aaron! It was the worst moment of my whole life. Finding you on the roof. Did you know it was me?" I finally ask the question that has been on the tip of my tongue for two years.

His brow furrows in confusion, as if maybe this is one of his memories that he keeps locked away.

"You do know what I'm talking about, right?" I ask when he doesn't answer.

He hesitates. "No. I mean, yes, I know what you're talking about. I didn't know it was you, though." He brings his cigarette to his mouth again, looking out across the street, and says absently, "I don't really remember much about what happened."

"Well, I can't forget it," I tell him. "I think about it all the time. And I think about what would've happened if I hadn't come up and found you. And I get scared it could happen again—I'm scared about that all the time."

He nods, but he doesn't say anything. It's so quiet I can hear the paper and tobacco sizzle as he inhales deeply. "Can I ask you something stupid?" he finally says, his voice amplified by the cold and the snow and that silence they create together. I nod. "Do you . . ." He stops to laugh at himself. "Do you believe in ghosts?"

"I don't know," I tell him. "Why, do you?"

"Sometimes I think I'm being haunted. Possessed or something."

"By who?" I ask, even though I already know the answer.

"I can hear his voice in my head. Always there, pushing me around. 'Loser,'" he mimics, almost perfectly, Dad's deep baritone voice. "'You little girl, you stupid idiot, be a man.'" I watch his nostrils expand as he inhales, his mouth opening slightly on the exhale. "Sometimes I look in the mirror—I see his face. Then again, I guess he was haunting me long before he was dead. It got better after I moved out. But now, being in this goddamn place again . . . he's everywhere I turn. Starting to feel him get inside my head again."

"Aaron, I—"

"And I don't want you to be haunted like that, not by him, not by me, not by some screwed-up thing I did on the roof."

"I'm not," I lie, feeling the ground slipping out from under my feet.

"I think we need to call it, Brooke," he blurts out. "This is over. You can't say we didn't go down without a fight."

"It's not over. I mean, can't she appeal?"

"No, she can't appeal. She pleaded guilty. You can't appeal that. It's done, Brooke. It really is. And we can't stay here—*I* can't."

"Aaron, please. You can't leave. Please." I grab on to his arm. "Please? I need you. I'm sorry that we fight. I'll be better, I'll be more understanding. I'm trying too, you know?" I feel this overpowering desperation taking hold of me. I'm begging. I can hear it in my voice and hate it.

"No, stop." He pulls his arm away and stands, seeming so tall, so far away from me already. "Listen to yourself, Brooke. You know, lately, if you're not sounding like Dad, you're sounding just like Mom."

"I do not!" But he's not listening; he's backing away from me, toward the door.

"Look, I'm wrecked, okay? I'm sorry," he says one last time, leaving me alone outside in the cold at four o'clock in the morning.

I watch as the wind drags the snow across the street in slow motion, S-like patterns, quivering snakes, making the invisible air visible. It's strange how absence can take up so much space sometimes. I guess that's what ghosts are. I stay outside until I get so cold I can't stand it anymore.

CRASHING

IN THE MORNING I put on a pot of coffee for Aaron. I eat a whole bowl of cereal and sit there at the kitchen table, feeling okay about the silence. I'm planning out my talking points for the conversation we're going to have. We'll both be more rational in the daylight. We'll figure it out. We'll make a new plan.

But then all of a sudden my eyes fix on something. A sheet of lined paper folded in half like a tent. It's been sitting there right in front of me this whole time; my name is scrawled out across the front.

I unfold it, but the words don't make sense at first.

Brooke,

I'm sorry. I swear I tried my best. I'm sorry I couldn't say all of this to your face. If I had, I wouldn't be able to leave. I'm taking that job with Mark. It's out of town. I wasn't going to go with him, but I realized tonight that I have to. I can't be here anymore. Neither can you. We all need to leave this place. You and Callie need to go to Jackie's. Jackie and Ray are good people and they want to help. Let them.

This is not forever, I promise. I just need some space to get my head together. Forgive me someday?

-Aaron

The paper slips between my fingers. It hits the table with a hollow tap and then flutters to the floor, shifting something in the air around me. I march into the hallway and throw open the door of my parents' room. The bed is made perfectly. The closet empty. The bathroom clean.

I walk back out and look around. Everything is different. New. Raw.

All my worry, my fear, it all turns, like some kind of previously contained fire inside of me, suddenly raging out of control in all directions. I sweep both of my arms across the kitchen table, throwing everything to the floor: dishes, apples and oranges, the full cup of now-cold coffee I poured for Aaron. I knock the chair over too. It feels good. I don't care if it breaks. I don't care if *I* break. I don't care about anything, anyone.

In my ears I hear something—something loud and terrible. I cover them with my hands. And then I realize that loud, terrible noise is me. I'm yelling, screaming, crying. I'm throwing things. I'm pacing. I want to punch a wall—so bad. The inside of my chest feels like it's freezing and burning at the same time.

"Why?" I'm yelling. "Why?" I'm shouting. "Why?" I'm sobbing

until I can't tell anymore if I'm even saying it out loud. I've slowed down, like someone struggling against quicksand. I'm suddenly taken down; I'm lying on the floor, part of the debris.

Someone's knocking on the door. I cover my ears again, but I can still hear it.

Knock-knock-knock. Louder, louder, louder.

"Hello? Helloo-ooo?" It's Mrs. Allister. "It's Mrs. Allister. From downstairs. I heard some commotion." *Knock-knock-knock.* "Just making sure everyone's okay."

"Go away," I whisper.

"Hell-ooo?" *Knock-knock-knock.*

"Go *away*," my voice squeaks.

I've hit the ground—literally, metaphorically, and everything in between. I've finally stopped falling. I take a good look around me. At the mess I've made. It looks so much like the aftermath of my dad on some psychotic rampage. I feel my heart start pounding inside my chest, banging, thumping wildly. Then, abruptly, it slows, slows too quickly, so quickly I'm afraid it's going to stop. I close my eyes. And then I'm gone.

"Hoooh-leeee *shit*." I open my eyes. Callie's standing over me, wearing her coat and gloves and scarf, her overnight bag slung over one shoulder. I'm flat on my back on the living room floor.

"What the ef happened in here?" she asks, almost laughing, but not quite.

"Callie?" I say, uncertain of my voice, my body, my anything. Because it feels like I'm waking up, not from sleep, but from my whole life.

"What happened?"

"I—I fell," I whisper, pushing myself up to sitting.

"Fell?" she repeats, raising her eyebrows. "Are you hurt?"

My head feels like it has cracked open once and for all. I hold it between my hands, trying to put the pieces back together. "No." I clear my throat. "When did you get here?"

"Just now. Jackie dropped me off. Where was everyone last night? Why didn't anyone call me? I was worried. Where's Aaron?" she asks, looking around suspiciously.

I stand, shaky on my new feet, on my new ground, testing it like ice with each step, not sure if it's solid or if I'll fall through again.

She stands in front of me, crossing her arms, and we're nearly at the same eye level. When did she get so tall? "Are you having a breakdown?" she finally asks, surveying the damage.

"No, of course not." But she looks at me like she's not convinced.

"Dr. Greenberg says people don't break *down*, they're really breaking open. So. It's not that bad, if you are." She reaches for the chair to turn it upright.

"No offense, but I don't think I should be taking mental health advice from a twelve-year-old."

"It's not *my* advice. And I'll be thirteen next month, anyway."

"Fine," I relent, beginning to gather the miscellaneous pieces of broken things at my feet. "But I'm not breaking down, or breaking open, just so you know."

She scowls and shrugs. "Fine."

"Look, Callie. I need to tell you, Aaron left town this morning, but—"

"What?" she interrupts, her face draining of all color.

"Remember his friend Mark?" She nods, then sits down in the chair she just turned over. "Well, they're doing a job together and he'll only be gone a few days—it was a last-minute thing," I lie.

"When will he be back?"

"I don't know. Soon. A few days. A week, tops." Or at least, that's how long I figure he might need to cool off and realize he can't just leave us like this.

"Are you sure?"

"Sure about what?"

"Are you sure that he's really coming back?"

"Yeah, of course."

She opens her mouth but then shuts it. Then she stands without a word, walks to her room, and closes the door behind her.

CONTRAPASSO

OUR ENGLISH TEACHER FURIOUSLY scrawls a word out on the whiteboard at the front of the room, her letters in all caps: *CONTRAPASSO*.

"Who knows what this means?" she asks, turning around, searching for recognition. "Come on, who's taking Latin?" Radio silence. "Has anyone bothered to read *Inferno* over break? Anyone at all?"

I look at Dani. We bothered to read it. We read it out loud together as we sat on her bedroom floor with our legs crossed over each other's; we took turns as we lay in her bed with our feet touching.

She could answer this question. So could I. But we don't.

"It means 'punishment,'" some guy shouts out, not bothering to raise his hand.

"Yes, but more specifically than that?" she asks, a glimmer of life lighting up her face momentarily.

He shrugs in response.

The teacher looks annoyed. It's Monday—the first Monday after winter break—everyone looks annoyed. It's cold, gloomy, and gray, and no one gives a damn about Dante. "All right, are your brains still on vacation? Someone look this up," she demands.

I see a few students flip idly through the pages of our textbook. Our teacher lets out a long sigh and starts writing more words on the board.

"It comes from the words *contra* and *patior*. Anyone? It translates to 'suffer the opposite.' And it's one of the major rules in Dante's Hell. What does it mean, though?" she asks.

I roll it around in my head a few times. It means me looking across the room at Dani. It means having her ignore me. It means me telling her to leave me alone when I meant to say *I love you*, when what I really meant was *Don't leave me alone like everyone else—I have this hole inside of me that's getting so big I think it might swallow me up*. But I didn't tell her that, either. I yelled, I scared her away, and then I ignored her phone calls. So now I'm suffering the opposite.

I wonder if that's what Dante had in mind.

Probably not.

When the bell rings, Dani bolts out of her seat, like she did in AP Psych, and like she did in AP American History, where it felt as though we were having our own private civil war from opposite sides of the room.

"Dani! Will you please talk to me?" I ask, catching up with her in the hall.

"I wanted to talk to you," she finally says, turning to give me the coldest glare I've ever seen. "That's kind of why I was calling you all weekend. Because I wanted to talk. I don't anymore, in case you couldn't tell."

Tyler joins up with us as our hallway spills into the main thoroughfare that leads to the cafeteria.

"Hey, Brooke," he says, wincing—clearly, he's heard all about our fight. Dani walks ahead of us, faster, until she disappears into the crowd.

I turn to Tyler, at a loss. "I don't know what to do."

"You better figure it out, this shit's bad for my complexion."

"You've known her longer than me. Tell me what to do, please?"

"Did you lie to her?" he asks. "She thinks you lied to her."

"I didn't lie," I lie. "I mean, I didn't mean to. It's more like I haven't told her the whole truth about some things."

"Well, then it's easy. Just tell her the whole truth."

"That's the opposite of easy," I tell him, suddenly losing my voice.

"Look, why don't you keep your distance till the end of the day, at least? I'll work on her for you. Call her tonight, okay?"

I took Tyler's advice. I didn't go to lunch. I went to the nurse's office instead. I told her I had a migraine, which, as it turned out, got me a lot more sympathy than a simple headache—it got me out of school early. I've been missing so much school lately that somehow it has stopped seeming so important.

But when I get home, I'm greeted by a notice stuck on my door with a crooked piece of clear tape: 7-DAY NOTICE TO PAY. From the landlord. I rip it down, but I'm afraid it's already been seen by our neighbors—one more thing to be ashamed of.

Damn you, Aaron. He could've mentioned in his little goodbye note that he didn't pay the rent. There was some cash Aaron left in an envelope that I found mixed in with the debris I threw off the table, but I thought it was extra money, since it clearly wasn't enough for rent. Aaron didn't care what would happen, apparently. Just like Mom.

Or maybe this is Dante's *contrapasso* at work again: I freaked out, lost my temper, wrecked the place, scared the neighbors. But it was all because I wanted to stay. I wanted us all to stay. Therefore they're trying to kick me out. A just punishment, according to Dante.

Well, screw Dante. Screw Aaron, too. Screw Mom and Dad.

I start making calls before I've even closed the door. I leave a message for the landlord. "There's been a mix-up, I'll have the rent to you this time next week, I promise." I bring Mrs. Allister's paper to her, sure to give her extra smiles and pet her cats. "Oh, the noise—that was nothing. I fell trying to move the furniture by myself—that was stupid, huh?"

By the time I get back upstairs, Callie's home from school. She's eating cereal from the box, the volume on the TV too loud.

"Can you please turn that down?" I shout.

She turns it off instead. Then leans back into the couch and stares at me.

"What?"

"Are we getting kicked out?" she asks, tilting her head in the direction of the letter that I stupidly left out on the coffee table.

"No, of course not. We just had a mix-up with the rent this month, that's all."

"Where's Aaron?" she asks, her voice flat and hollow.

"I told you already, Callie. He's out of town for a few days."

"It's been a few days."

"Well, I don't know exactly when he'll be back. Remember, he said it could be a week."

"No, you said that. He didn't say that. He didn't say anything. He's not answering his phone."

"He's probably busy, Callie—he is there to work, after all."

"But where's *there*?" An uptick in her voice. Is it anger, worry, frustration? I'm not sure, but it sparks all those things in me.

"What do you want me to say? I'm not sure, okay? He didn't tell me."

"This is . . ." But she stops short before finishing, shakes her head instead.

"This is what?"

She stands abruptly, brushing past me on her way to her room.

I make endless calculations. I call Jackie and beg for more shifts. I scrounge up every last bit of money hiding in piggy banks and coat pockets and dresser drawers and even in the basement laundry room. Miraculously, I come up with $35.32 in under an hour. I add in my paycheck from last week and the social security check. If I don't pay the electric or buy any more groceries, I'm short only $75.00.

"Okay," I whisper to myself, hunched over my calculator and pad of paper, chewing on the end of my pen. It's possible to keep this going for at least the next month.

I have to squint to see what I'm doing, and then I realize that's because it's getting dark outside already. I've been at this for hours. And even though *this* is shit, somehow I feel invigorated. Because here's a problem that has an *actual* solution. Whether I'll be able to solve it is another question entirely, but at least I know, as of right now, what has to be done.

Unlike those other problems. People problems. Mom. Aaron. Callie. Dani. Those are trickier to fix, maybe impossible. School problems are another thing, but in a different class of trouble. I make myself a grilled cheese for dinner and eat it on the couch, watching the snow fall down outside the window.

FREEZING

I PLANNED ON TALKING to Dani first thing, but she wasn't in class this morning. So I'm sure to make it to chem lab early. Tyler walks through the door right before the bell and slides into the seat next to me. Without looking at me, he says, "Oh good, you are here. I thought you might have suffered a stroke last night, or something."

"What?"

He pinches the bridge of his nose and squeezes his eyes shut for a moment, a gesture of exasperation I've noticed he sometimes does. "Okay, you know I love you girls, but this kind of drama is exactly why I don't *love* you girls."

"Um. Okay," I say, trying to act casual as I set up our beakers and test tubes, adjusting the ring stand for our experiment, double-checking to make sure the Bunsen burner is turned off.

"I'll have you know I did some of my best work on her. She was this close"—he brings his thumb and index finger together so they're barely touching—"to forgiving you. Why the hell didn't you call her? Now she's mad all over again, and I don't know if I can go through this another time. I don't do stress, as a policy. But dammit, this is giving me heart palpitations."

Looking at the strained expression on his face, which is usually so placid and smooth, I cave in. "I'm sorry, really. I was planning on it, but—"

"Listen. Don't make excuses. She hates them. And I'm not so fond of them either."

I'm sure I flinch at his tone, the way he interrupted me—he's serious. Which means Dani is too, which means I've really messed this whole thing up.

"I'm giving you tough love, all right?" he explains. "Don't screw her over. And don't make me choose sides, because I'll choose hers, and that'll blow because I happen to like you. That's all I have to say." He sets the Erlenmeyer flask in between us, as if that officially marks the end of this conversation. "Except do your hair like that more often." He flips my loose hair over my shoulder.

When I get home from school, I go straight to my room and call Dani. Except, listening to the ringing on the other end, I feel like a different person than I was only a few nights ago, when I was safe in Dani's bedroom, her arms around me, her wanting to know me—and me wanting her to. With each unanswered ring I feel myself being swept farther and farther away from her. So much has changed I don't know how I'll ever get us back to where we were. I know I probably don't have a right to be mad, but I am. I don't have the time or the energy to be dealing with this. Everyone's shutting me out—Mom, Aaron, Callie, now Dani—and I'm starting to think maybe it's better that way.

I hang up without leaving a message.

✳

I'm a mess at work. Dropping things and screwing up orders. It's just me and Owen. Jackie's not here—she's been here less and less lately, which, I guess, is one of the perks of being your own boss. I haven't seen her since before Aaron left, haven't talked to her since that night on the phone. She called me this afternoon, but I didn't answer and she didn't leave a message.

I keep thinking any minute she's going to drag us out of our apartment, but as each day passes, I have a feeling Aaron didn't tell her that he left. I've called him about a thousand times, but no answer.

I'm only half here tonight, I can't concentrate, I'm not paying attention. The line is suddenly out the door. People are impatient. I feel like I'm moving in slow motion. I'm supposed to be taking orders, manning the register, and Owen is supposed to be in the back, doing prep and dishes and whatever else needs to be done in the back. Weak spots in my head start to crackle, those old fault lines buckling under the weight of my thoughts.

Owen must hear people complaining and making a fuss. That must be why he comes out of the kitchen, why he's standing next to me now. "Chill," I hear him tell me quietly, his voice smooth and cool. He reaches out and places his hand over mine. We both look down. My hands are trembling. "It's okay. Just chill," he repeats.

He starts joking with the customers, turning on the *O—O—Ohhh* charm, getting drinks and to-go orders lined up, diffusing all the tension, somehow, in a matter of seconds. We don't have to discuss it, it works—he takes care of the angry people, and all I have to do is focus on taking their money, no small talk, no chitchat, just business.

Some of them got so pissed at how slow I was going that they left. And then a bunch of them leave their cash on the counter the second Owen gets their stuff, not willing to wait around any longer for me to ring them up. I have four different pockets in the front of my apron, and so I stuff four different piles of abandoned money into the separate pockets and try as best as I can to make a mental note of their corresponding orders.

It seems like we get that whole line of people taken care of in no time at all. And when it's just us again, he looks at me for too long, like he's waiting for an explanation. When I don't offer one, he says simply, "You good?"

I say "Yes" even though I feel my head moving back and forth, not up and down.

"So, what—is this about that punk-rock chick who came in here last night?"

"Punk-rock chick," I repeat, my stomach sinking slowly. "What punk-rock chick?"

"Some girl. She asked for you. I told her you weren't here. Then she asked if your *mom* was here."

"Oh my God," I whisper. "What did you tell her?"

"Nothing." He shrugs. "Didn't get a chance. Jackie came up and started talking to her—seemed like they knew each other. They sat over there"—he points with his chin toward the table in the corner by the windows—"and talked for a long time."

"Oh my God," I repeat, my hand flying to my mouth. That's why Jackie called—not to bust me, but to ask me why Dani thinks, *or thought*, she was my mom. Maybe that's why she didn't come to school today. Why she didn't pick up when I called her.

After work I take my time getting home. I cut through the park, which I know is probably not a great idea after dark, but I don't even care. Under the trees it's so still and quiet, everything sparkling under a fresh layer of snow. As I walk along the river-bank, I realize it's actually too quiet. When I look down, it's more like a picture of the river than the real thing—an image on pause. It's finally frozen over. The whole world is in suspended animation. Maybe now I'll have a chance to catch up.

When I get home, I see Dani's car parked outside. As I cross the street, she unrolls her window and sticks her head out. "Get in, okay?"

I do. It's warm in here, the heat on full blast, the radio playing softly. "Hey."

"Hey," she repeats. "Sorry I didn't answer when you called."

"That's okay."

"I was so mad at you I didn't know what to say." She reaches over and takes my hand. She pulls my glove off and wraps her warm fingers around mine. "But I'm not now. I want to understand."

"I know you talked to Jackie. I assume she told you everything." I pause, giving her a chance to respond, but she only nods. "I planned on telling you what was going on, but there was never a good time."

"Yeah, but how could you not tell me something so huge? You let me believe Jackie was your mother. You let me believe your father was killed while he was working, like it was some kind of accident."

"It was an accident." I let go of her hand now. "What, like I know every last thing about you?"

"No, but that's only because you haven't found certain things out yet, not because I'm keeping important things from you."

I look away, shaking my head. Dani will never understand.

"Look, I am sorry I was so upset the other night. I snapped at you and I shouldn't have. I know you were trying to help. But there's all this stuff between me and Aaron that I couldn't explain right then."

"Well, if you had told me before, you wouldn't have had to explain it right then when you were upset. I would've already understood what was going on and I could've helped, instead of you flipping out on me."

"Yeah," I tell her, "I know."

"Can you explain it to me now?"

I shake my head. "This isn't fair," I mumble. "None of this is fair."

"No, it's not fair—here I am thinking we're getting close. Thinking I know you and you know me, and what we have is real," she says, her words speeding as she continues. "I told you I love you."

"I have very little control over anything in my life right now, and you don't get to dictate what I tell you about myself and when I tell you."

"You think withholding real stuff about yourself gives you some kind of power? That's extremely messed up."

"No. You're twisting what I'm saying, Dani! It's not about us or you—it's about *me*, my life. God, can't anything just be about me?" I yell.

"Sorry, but no, our relationship—if that's what we're even calling this—can't just be about you." She crosses her arms and stares out the window. "You deserve better. That's all I came here to say, Brooke. I don't want to fight. I just wanted to tell you that you deserve better than all this stuff you've had to deal with."

"Do I?" She reaches for me, but I pull my arm out of her grasp. "Thanks a lot."

"Why is that a bad thing to say?"

"Because, don't you see? I'm one of them!" I tell her, raising my voice. "So what you're really saying is that *you* deserve better."

"I am not," she argues.

"We're not even having the same conversation right now, do you know that?"

"Well, what is the conversation you're having?"

"What I'm trying to say is that it's like you have all this information now. But you don't even know what any of it means—you say you understand, but you don't. Because you went behind my back and talked to Jackie instead of me—"

"I tried to talk to you!" she interrupts, but I keep going.

"And you say you want to be close, and you want to *know* me, but . . ." I stop to catch my breath. "Honestly, I feel like you've never known me less than you do right now. So, congratulations."

"You're right," she says, smiling sadly. "I don't know this person. Not at all."

"Then we're in agreement." I crack the door open. The cold rushes in, not just into the car but into me; it gets into my blood and organs, freezing over my insides just like the river. "Good-bye, I guess."

I shut the car door. Then up the stairs, one by one. I unlock the door. Callie's asleep on the couch, TV blaring. I don't bother turning it down or shutting it off. I go straight to my room and close the door behind me.

As I start undressing, every layer feels like a piece of armor that has been weighing me down. I get lighter and lighter. I reach into my apron pockets, and when I pull my hands out, I'm holding a wrinkled ten-dollar bill in one and a five in the other. In the other two pockets, three singles and a twenty.

Shit.

But as I lay it down on my desk next to the envelope with the rent money, it adds itself up in my mind, an involuntary reflex. I look for a moment. I can give it back—I *will* give it back. Just not yet. I flatten out the extra thirty-eight dollars and stick it in the envelope with the rest.

CRYSTALLOGRAPHY

IF YOU'RE ABSENT FROM school for more than three days in a row, you need a doctor's note when you go back. I read that in the student handbook before I started at Jefferson. That's why I knew I'd be okay if I stayed home the rest of the week. I told myself I was giving Dani space to be mad at me. Giving myself space to work things out in my head.

The thing I didn't count on while pretending to be sick was *actually* getting sick.

Maybe it's karma, or *contrapasso*, or whatever, coming back to bite me in the ass. For stealing, for skipping school, for lying, for being mean and crazy, or for any number of things. Maybe that's why Callie leaves. I can't put up a fight, or at least not much of one, not when I'm laid up on the couch, half-empty bottle of NyQuil nestled in the crook of my arm, a steady pounding in my head, alternating between chills and fever that turn my blood to ice, then fire, alternately.

"Where are you going?" I croak, my throat raw from all the

coughing I've been doing. I lift my head from the pillow to see her walk across the living room with her coat and scarf and backpack. At first I think maybe I've slept through the entire night out here, but no—I look around, the streetlights are shining in through the windows—it's still nighttime.

She turns toward me and states matter-of-factly, "It's been a week. He's not back. I'm not staying here anymore. I'm going to Jackie's."

"What?" I struggle to sit upright. "Callie, he'll be back. He said he'll be back. We can manage until then."

She shakes her head. "I'd rather stay at Jackie's."

"He's coming back, though. He'll be back and then things will be . . ." I stop short because I hear my voice, though it's so sore it barely works; it's close to pleading again, sounding just like Mom, the way she'd beg Dad not to leave.

She squares herself, plants her feet into the floor, and stands in front of me. "I'm. Not. Staying." Her words are so firm, her voice so commanding, as if it's taking a lot of resolve, almost like she's standing up to me. Then I realize that's exactly what she's doing.

So I watch her leave. And though it takes all my strength, I manage to twist my body around on the couch, my muscles aching and strained from whatever illness has seized my body. I watch as she gets into Jackie's car. I watch as the red taillights fade fast into the falling snow, like static. I turn the TV off and sit in the dark for a while—I don't know how long—and I watch as the snow comes down faster and faster, the light from the street reflecting against the blanket of microscopic crystals, casting a cool blue glow inside the apartment, so that I don't even need any lights to see.

I get up to go to the bathroom and make myself some more honey lemon tea, in hopes of repairing the damage to my throat, in hopes that with enough of it I might get my voice back in time for work tomorrow afternoon—even with the extra cash I accidentally brought home, I can't afford to miss a day of pay. I put my mug into the microwave and press start. And then I stand there in the kitchen and try not to think of all the terrible things that have happened in here.

I find my feet moving away, taking me to my room. I turn on the light and look around. "What did I come in here for?" I whisper, my voice seeming to echo and bounce back at me. That's when I spot the snowflake book—the gift from Caroline. It's been sitting in the same place on my desk since I brought it home from the courthouse. I pick it up and it feels heavier than it should, but I know that's just because I'm sick and weak and all drugged up. I hear the *beep-beep-beep* of the microwave—two minutes and thirty seconds have passed, yet all I did was walk to my bedroom and stare at the book.

I shuffle back out in my slippers and pajamas and the blanket I have draped around my shoulders. By the time I reach the couch, carrying my tea in one hand and the book in the other, it feels like I've run a marathon.

I open the book and see that faded blue ink in the top corner again: *This book belongs to Caroline.* I flip to a section: "Crystallography of the Snow Crystal." All about the observation and classification and properties, the crystalline structure of snow, and temperature and humidity—who knew there was even such a thing as crystallography? My eyes strain to read in the dim glow of snow light. So I flip through page after page of black-and-white images of individual snowflakes. They look ghostly, otherworldly, beautiful. Some are like stars and flowers, others like shattered glass or spiderwebs, fossilized remains of something forgotten and extinct, some kind of organism in between plants and animals. Thousands of them, like Caroline said—they're obsessive, mesmerizing, unsettling, all in this weirdly tame way.

Maybe this Bentley guy had the right idea. I study the picture of him on the inside cover. Snow dusts his coat and hat and gloves—he's cold but smiling, hunched over the camera. Yes, I think he was onto something. Living alone. Just him and his snowflakes and his obsession. Not hurting anyone. Simple. Maybe the Winters family was meant to be alone like that—isn't that when we all seem to run into trouble, when there are other people involved?

I close the book and turn my attention to the real snowflakes that get stuck to the outside window screen, like insects in a web. One by one they get caught. They stay there, frozen in place for a little while, before they begin melting and freezing all over again, the heat emanating through the window from inside the apartment, warping them. Watching it happen, over and over, lulls me into a state of peace, a rare calmness settling over me.

Maybe I'll be a crystallographer, I think as my eyes close. I'll learn all about snow and microscopes and cameras—I'll learn how to be cold, how to be alone. Someday.

LANDLINE

EVERY DAY IS CLOCKWORK: school, Jackie's, pocket a little extra cash, have a coughing fit, get a massive headache, swallow some pills, study in the empty apartment. Pretend I'm doing okay. I've managed to keep it going for almost a whole month, all on my own.

While Aaron has yet to return any of my calls, he did send some money for rent, so I guess that's something. I don't know how he knows I'm still here—he must have someone, somewhere, checking on me. Which means he must still care in some small way. Maybe it's Carmen or Mrs. Allister from downstairs.

But something feels different on the walk home from school today. In fact, the whole day has felt off.

The landline is ringing.

I can hear it as I walk up the endless stairs to our apartment, my lungs ragged and still not functioning at capacity due to this cold that doesn't want to go away. I drop the keys on the floor, pick them back up, try the lock again. Finally I make it inside. I race to the phone.

"Hello?" I say into the receiver.

The connection is bad. Static. But on the other end I hear pieces of the words: ". . . a collect call from . . . inmate . . . correctional facility. . . . To refuse this call, hang up. To accept this call, press one now."

I press the one button. Then I press the receiver to my ear even closer. Don't want to miss a word. The automated voice says, "Thank. You." There's a click on the line.

Then, "Hello, hello? Brooke, are you there?"

I feel tears stinging my eyes. *I miss you. I love you. I need you. I hate you. I'm sorry.* I keep opening my mouth to speak, but it's like a hand is reaching up the back of my throat, strangling the words out of me.

"I don't have long," she says, and pauses, the line crackling. "Say something. Please. I miss you." And then I hear it: She's crying. She sniffles loudly and coughs like she's trying to catch her breath. "Brooke," she whispers. "I love you."

I slam the receiver down. Hard. But then I pick it back up immediately and bring it to my ear. "Mom?"

But it's just the moaning, empty dial tone.

My voice echoes back at me, spiraling through the kitchen. I hang up again, softly this time. I run my fingers over the gentle crater in the wall next to the phone—the spot where Dad's fist once landed. I sink down the wall onto the linoleum floor. I think about the way Dad's hand looked the day he died, his body sprawled out only a few feet from where I'm now sitting.

The phone rings again. I look up at it, but it's too late. I can't reach it. Aaron was right. There's no saving this. It's too late for us. The phone rings and rings and rings. Ten times, twenty times, a thousand times. I cover my ears. I close my eyes. I can't feel my insides. I'm cold now. Frozen solid.

GLASS SHATTERS

"WHERE'S YOUR BROTHER?" Jackie asks as I arrive at their house for Callie's thirteenth birthday party. "How did you get here—I thought you said Carmen was going to drive you."

I forgot about that lie.

"Plans changed. Aaron had to work," I lie again. "I took a cab."

"He had to work on your sister's birthday?" she asks in disbelief.

Callie walks up and, miraculously, covers for me. "Yeah, he called this morning to say happy birthday—he told me he was sorry he was going to have to work tonight."

I don't know why she did that, but I'm thankful. I give her a small smile and she nods. Maybe Aaron's talking to her. Maybe she's the one keeping him in the loop.

Being here is like walking directly into a tornado, twisting me back in time. I keep pulling my birthday sweater around me, tighter and tighter, trying to shield myself against the tornado's pull. I want to ask Callie why she lied for me. But I can't get a second alone with her.

After cake and presents Jackie corners me in the kitchen. "You know, I have had the damnedest time getting ahold of Aaron these last few weeks. Will you tell him he needs to stop by and see me?"

"Why?" I ask.

She widens her eyes and looks around, like the answer should be obvious. "We need to talk about Callie."

"What do you mean?" I ask, playing dumb, as if nothing's wrong at all—a technique I've learned to master over the years from watching Mom do it.

"What do you mean, what do *I* mean?" she says, her voice sharp, yet still trying to be quiet so Callie doesn't hear us. "I mean . . . what's going on over there that Callie doesn't want to live there anymore?"

"We're okay," I lie. "I think Callie got mad at us over the whole New Year's Eve thing."

"Are you sure?" she asks. "It seems like more than that."

"I'm sure," I lie.

"If it's not working out, that's okay, but then we need to make proper arrangements for everyone."

"Everything's working out, Jackie."

"Okay, but let your brother know I need to speak to him." She pauses, looking at me like the liar I am, but thankfully, she drops it. "You know, they moved your mother. I talked to her on the phone today. She said it's actually better there than in the jail. She has more privileges, a little more freedom now."

"I don't really care," I try to tell her as gently as possible.

"Well, she's asking for you, and we're planning on heading up there next weekend. So let me know if—"

"I don't want to see her."

"*Brooke* . . . ," she says.

"Am I not allowed to be mad about what she did?"

"Of course," she finally relents. "Just think about it. Let me know if you change your mind."

"I'm positive I won't."

She nods and squeezes my shoulder, then walks back out into their dining room.

Ray drives me home, and I'm thankful that he doesn't try to make a bunch of small talk with me. He looks straight ahead, and I look out the window.

We've reached that part of winter when we haven't had much new snowfall, so all the old snow has started to pile up on the sides of the roads like miniature gray mountains, turning to slush in the streets, no longer white and shimmering, magical crystals, but cold mud, contaminated with all the grime and debris of the frozen months. The trees look like skeletons of their former selves. It seems like the longest time of the year, these weeks of ugliness.

We cross the bridge, and as we drive past the shop, I can see Owen through the window, laughing with the lady who works weeknights when I'm not there. Ray and I exchange our good-byes, and he reminds me again to call if I need anything.

I trudge up the stairs slower than usual. I leave my coat on the floor. I stand in the living room for a minute. I dare myself to go into Callie's room, my old room, our old room, for the first time since she left.

The door creaks as I push it open. I flip the light switch on and enter.

It's pretty bare. Nothing on her desk or walls. Her bed is made, but even her dolls and stuffed animals are nowhere to be found. I open one of her dresser drawers. Empty. I open another. Empty. I open every last one—they're all empty. Everything's gone. Even the books in the bookcase. Half of them are there, but I realize as my fingers travel over the spines, all the ones that remain are mine. I pull my globe down from the top shelf, and a layer of dust brushes off against my sweater as I cradle it in my arms.

When did she take everything? She must've come back with Jackie. She couldn't have gotten everything out on her own, even if she was doing it in bits and pieces.

It hits me hard.

She's not coming back. None of them are coming back.

I try to rewind the evening, but I can't remember if I even said good-bye to her when I left Jackie's house. Did I say happy birthday? I must have. I sink down into her bed, fall onto my side, and bring my knees to my chest, my body curved around the globe. I hold on so tightly—that hollow sphere that used to hold so much potential, so much wonder, now just feels fake.

I bury my face in her pillow, missing her so much, even though I was with her less than an hour ago. I feel something hard—I reach my hand underneath her pillow and pull out that silver picture frame from Jackie's house. The picture of all of us together, smiling and happy. I study it for a moment. Then I chuck it across the room. The glass shatters as it hits the wall.

I wake up at nine in the morning, still in the fetal position in Callie's bed. I missed my alarm. I missed the bus. I missed all of first period.

The sun is streaming in through the window, its light unfiltered in a way I haven't seen in months, suggesting the constant cloud cover of winter has finally lifted. The sky hasn't been this clear in so long I almost forgot how blue it can be.

I should be rushing to get to school, but I'm not. I'm changing out of yesterday's clothes and getting into my pajamas instead. What's the point? I'll stay home and study, I tell myself.

I don't study. I clean up the broken glass. I set the picture frame on the coffee table in the living room. I sit with my books open and think about Aaron and Callie, and Mom and Dad. I think about how only half a year ago, my greatest hope, my biggest goal, was just to get the hell out of here. And now I can barely make it out the door. What is it? Is it like the water thing Caroline talked about? Water seeking water. Is that what keeps me here when it seems everyone else is floating away, fleeing, finding other water to attach to?

It's nearly four o'clock when I have an idea. It comes to me so suddenly I jump up off the couch, my books falling from my lap. I go into the bathroom and pick my shirt up off the floor. I strip down to my bra and underwear, pull the shirt on over my head, then shake out the jeans I wore yesterday and step into them.

I gargle with some mouthwash quickly and catch a glimpse of my face in the mirror—pasty and tired, my hair scraggly and tangled. I pull it into a sloppy ponytail, splash my face with cold water. I grab my sweater off the couch and push my arms through. Fold my coat over my arm and race down the stairs. If I hurry, I can catch her in time to have a few minutes alone with her.

When I reach the bus stop, I put my coat on, my breath coming fast and heavy, white puffs of air escaping my mouth. I keep an eye on the time. As we cross back over the bridge, the whirring and squealing and screeching of the bus stopping and going, letting people on and off, makes me feel alive, like my body is once again a living, breathing organism, like I can try to be part of something again.

At last I make it to the corner—I'm the first one off the bus. I race across the street and through the doors of the building, then into the elevator, pounding on the close-door button over and over. It dings at the seventh floor and I get off, my feet flying.

Just as my hand reaches for the doorknob, it turns from the other side, yanking my arm as it pulls open. I stumble right into Dr. Greenberg and Ingrid, all bundled up in their coats and scarves and gloves, ready to leave for the day.

"Oh!" I shout, jumping back, scared and out of breath. "Sorry, sorry, I—I was looking for Callie. I was going to pick her up from her appointment," I tell them, hoping they believe me.

"Brooke, Callie comes in on Fridays," Dr. Greenberg answers.

"Right," I mumble, stopping myself from asking the question on the tip of my tongue, which is, *Isn't it Friday?* "Okay, sorry—I must've gotten it mixed up." I feel my throat closing up around the words. I take a breath, but it gets stuck. I start hacking and coughing so hard I have to brace myself against the wall. "Sorry," I manage to say as I'm gasping for air, fishing in my coat pockets for a lozenge. I hold it up so they can see—*I'm okay, I have a remedy, don't worry.*

"Here, why don't you come in for a moment," Dr. Greenberg says, stepping aside so I can make it through the doorway. "Ingrid, you can go—I can close up. We'll just be a minute."

"All right. I'll see you in the morning, then," she tells him, then to me, a weary, "Take care."

I sit down in one of the waiting room chairs and unwrap the cough drop, while Dr. Greenberg gets me a Dixie cup full of water. I drink it slowly, the coughing fit finally subsiding.

"Sorry," I croak. "I've been trying to get over this cold thing for weeks." I clear my throat. "Thanks."

He sits down across from me, the aquarium illuminating his face in waves. It's weird to be in a waiting room after hours, no fluorescent lights, no phone ringing. "You know, I've tried calling you several times. Have you gotten my messages?" he asks.

"I don't think so. Well, maybe," I lie. "Sorry, I've been really busy. School and work and everything."

"No, I understand. It sounds like you've had a lot on your plate."

"Yeah, sorry."

"You're saying 'sorry' a lot," he says as he leans back into the chair, crossing his leg.

I'm about to say "sorry" again, but I stop myself.

"Which makes me wonder if there's something you're feeling bad about, perhaps? Is that what brought you here today?"

"No," I lie. "I—I told you. I came to pick up Callie."

"Well, I'm glad you did. I'm in no hurry, if there's something on your mind."

"I can't pay you," I blurt out.

"Well, good thing this isn't an official appointment, then." He laughs, which makes me relax a little bit. "Seriously, we don't need to be talking about money."

"Okay."

"So, what is it that brought you here?" he asks.

"I told you—Callie."

"Yes, but why did you want to pick her up? It seems like you've been going out of your way to keep your distance from my office."

"I don't know, I guess I was feeling . . ." I trail off, suddenly not quite sure how I'm feeling, exactly.

"Yes?" he asks when I don't finish.

"Alone."

"Mm," he hums, nodding slowly. "Good answer."

"Which is weird," I continue, "because sometimes all I want in the world is to be left alone. Other people make things so complicated. But then I'm finally alone and all I want is other people around."

"Well . . . ," he begins, then looks off in the direction of the aquarium. "'You are born alone. You die alone. The value of the space in between is trust and love.'" He meets my eyes and shrugs.

"Cheerful."

"Yes, it kind of is, actually."

"Is that Freud, or something?" I ask, somehow managing to joke, even though I'm pretty sure I've never felt quite so low in my whole life.

He lets out a small chirp—that same laugh I heard with Callie that day behind the closed door. "No, an artist said that. Louise Bourgeois." Then he slinks out of his coat and pulls a notepad from his briefcase. "Go on."

I do. I don't know why, but I do.

SPRING

REASONS

I RIFLE THROUGH MY desk drawers like a madwoman. I hid it months ago, after we moved back in. But I know I kept it—that small scrap of paper. My hands run over all kinds of objects, erasers and pens that no longer work, Post-it notes, and old flash cards.

But . . . there. Now I remember, as my fingers grasp for the small box of paper clips. I folded it up into a tiny square and stuck it inside. I dump the entire box out on my bedroom floor; my fingers sift through the pile quickly. I unfold it and read the words again:

Caroline. Just in case.

She answers on the first ring, like she has been waiting for my call all this time.

We arranged to meet halfway between where she lives and where I live. She offered to pick me up, but I told her no. I wish I'd let her, though, because it's pouring down cold rain now.

I go into the diner, at the corner where she said it would be. I shake my umbrella off at the door and lower the hood from my face. She's already here, waiting with a cup of coffee in a booth in the corner, wearing a fuzzy sweater and corduroys.

"You made it," she says as I approach. "Thought the rain might keep you."

"It was okay," I tell her, sliding into the seat opposite her. "Hi."

"Hi," she echoes. "I ordered you a water—I didn't know what you'd want."

"Thank you." I unwrap the plastic straw from its paper wrapper so that I have something to do with my hands.

"I'm glad you called. I wasn't sure you would," she admits.

"Me neither," I tell her.

She starts laughing, followed once again by a bout of hard coughing.

"Are you okay?" I push my glass of water across the table toward her.

Still smiling, she shakes her head and holds her hand up, sliding the glass back to me. "I'm fine," she's finally able to say after the coughing subsides.

"You're probably wondering why I called," I begin, though the whole way here I wasn't able to answer that question myself.

"There doesn't have to be a reason—just coffee is reason enough." She waves her hand in the air, getting the attention of the waitress, who comes directly over to the table.

"What are you drinking, hon?" the waitress asks me.

"Just coffee," I answer.

We wait until she brings it back before either of us says anything else. It's a comfortable kind of silence, like I remember from our conversations at the courthouse.

Caroline watches as I doctor it up with lots of cream and sugar, anything to dilute the actual coffee taste. She grins at the number of sugar packets I pour in. "I'm actually not much of a coffee drinker," I explain.

"I didn't used to be when I was your age either."

More silence.

"I really liked that book you gave me," I say. "Thanks again."

"It's special, so I'm glad you liked it."

Another silence.

"Can I be honest with you?" I ask.

"Definitely." She takes a sip of her coffee and looks me straight in the eye, unflinching. "Life's too short for anything else."

"You don't seem at all like the person I've heard stories about."

She nods as if she understands everything I've heard about her. "I don't claim to have been the best person in my day. I really wasn't a very good mother, I'll tell you that much. Allison saw a lot that I'm not proud of—I can't defend myself for any of that." She takes another short sip. "Except to say that people change."

I want to believe her, but I'm skeptical.

"Or rather, people *can* change. I know I have. But people have to change themselves—you can't make them change. That's where I went wrong. I kept thinking I could change her father. That's why I stayed so long. But I couldn't, and eventually I became the one who was changing—changing into someone I didn't much like, in fact. She hated me for staying, your mother. But then she went ahead and did the same exact thing, waiting around for Paul to magically become a different person. Followed right in my footsteps," she says, shaking her head sadly.

"She thinks I'm following in hers," I admit. "Or at least she did, anyway. Do you think that?"

"Well, I don't know you well enough to say." She pauses. "But I'd think if you're even asking the question, then you're most likely on the right track."

I shrug. I hear myself say, "I told her that I hated her the last time I talked to her."

"I can imagine you had your reasons. I can think of a couple myself," she answers, not at all surprised. I'm beginning to think maybe she's one of these people who have seen so much they've become unshockable. "Did you mean it?" she asks.

"I think I meant it when I said it. I don't think I do anymore, though."

She nods again, as if everything I've said is totally understandable, like maybe I'm not such a terrible person after all. "Like I said, people can change."

We sit and drink our coffees together, allowing for the random exchanges and breaks of silence. It feels easy, simple. When we finish, Caroline pays the bill, and she offers to give me a ride home. But I tell her no; it's stopped raining by then.

"Call again," she tells me, giving me a one-armed hug as we part at the door. "It can be just coffee. Or any other reason."

THE THAW

MARCH IS ALWAYS A BATTLEGROUND. Trying to fight off spring, get a stronghold overnight as the puddles turn back from water to ice. Winter is sneaky that way.

As I'm waiting at the bus stop, with the sun peeking over the tops of the buildings, new light filtering through the bare branches of the trees in the park, I hear this *pop*. This crack like an earthquake—something snapping, breaking. I jump and duck my head, covering it with my arms. Then silence. I look around, but there's no sign of any disturbances. But it happens again, louder this time, echoing, sounding close yet faraway, like it's everywhere and nowhere.

Another crack, another snap, another break. I smell it in the air—something like rain and dirt. The river ice is breaking. It happens every year, but I guess I'm never outside when it does. Behind closed doors it never sounded so violent.

I have at least five minutes before the bus. If I hurry, I can make it over to the park. I'm crossing the street, rounding the corner, before I've even made up my mind.

I keep slipping on the black ice that lines the pathway down to the riverbank, but manage to keep myself from falling. It's louder and louder the closer I get, drawing me into its urgency.

When I reach the edge, the ice is giving way, huge pieces of mosaic churning and tumbling over themselves to get downstream. The water level along the bank rises right before my eyes, so quickly that I have to take a step back. I'm consumed by a vision of the river overflowing, swallowing me up, carrying me off, drowning me along the way. I step back again. And again, and again. Until I'm not taking steps anymore; I'm running. I exit the park and cross back over to my side of the street, looking behind me the whole way, just to be sure.

I look up in time to watch as the bus pulls away from the curb. Shit. I'm going to be late. Again.

"Ms. Winters . . ." My head snaps up from the sign-in log. It's Mrs. Murray, my guidance counselor. I've been dodging her for weeks. She wanted to sit down with me after I dropped those extra classes at the beginning of the semester. She told me to make an appointment with her whenever it was convenient for me. But there never seemed to be a good time.

"Hi, Mrs. Murray."

"Do you have a moment?" she asks.

"Well, I'm—I'm late, so . . ."

"Yes, I see that. Please," she says, leading the way to her office. She lets me in first, then follows me inside and shuts the door. "Have a seat," she tells me, sitting down across from me, in her vomit-colored three-piece suit, her hair unraveling from the bun knotted at the back of her head, somehow already looking sick of me. She thumbs a file folder full of papers and sighs, shaking her head.

"Is that mine—my file, I mean?" I ask.

She nods. "I've been trying to reach your guardian. Aaron Winters—is this an uncle?"

"No, he's my brother."

"I see. Well, he hasn't returned any of my phone calls," she says.

"Oh, really?" I say, pretending to be confused about the situation. "Well, he's been pretty busy."

"I'm your guidance counselor and I'm pretty busy too. And part of my job is to make sure you're doing okay." She pauses, expecting a response. "You've been missing a lot of school recently. Have you been ill, or is it something else?" she asks.

I recognize these questions. They pulled this on me at my old school. Fishing. Trying to see if something's "going on" at home. When I don't answer, she raises her eyebrows and says, "Or maybe you've just been truant?"

I despise her with every fiber of my being, for ambushing me, for her headshaking and phony concern, but especially for using the word "truant."

"Either way," she continues, "this number of absences is unacceptable."

"I'm not quite sure what that means. I've had the flu a couple of times. But I've been keeping up with schoolwork and everything. I can't really help it if I've been sick, can I?"

"Look," she begins, sitting up straighter, "you have to meet me halfway here—a quarter, an eighth of the way, even. Give me something, *anything*, to work with," she says, clasping her hands together.

"Your teachers are concerned about you. You started off very strong, and now . . . well, your work has tapered off." She stares at me while I consider this for a moment.

"Like I said, I've been sick. But I'm better now, and I just need a little time to catch up."

"Did you know if you have more than ten unexcused absences, you could be in danger of not having enough credits to pass the year?" she asks.

I shake my head no.

"This is serious. I need to speak with your brother. We need to get some documentation for your absences—that is, if they're legitimate."

"I thought you only needed a note after three days in a row."

She grins. "I see you've brushed up on the rules."

"Not really," I lie. "I just like to be informed."

"Good. This is me informing you that you've already accumulated thirteen unexcused absences since December. And that doesn't include the days you've been late or gone home early, which are adding up as well."

"What?" My voice is raised, I know, but I can't help it. "How? It couldn't have been that many already."

She nods emphatically. "No, I assure you, it is. I'm looking at it right here." She flips the printout over and slides it in front of me.

I can't believe what I'm seeing; it's true. I scramble to find some kind of response. "Well, once I explain to my brother, he can write a note and sign them and—"

"Yes, do that. I'll still need to speak with him, of course." She reaches across the desk and draws an arrow in red pen. Once. Then twice. "But see these—these two weeks you missed three days in a row. For those you need doctor's notes. The rule is three or more, not more than three, by the way."

Those are the week of the trial and then the week of my breakup with Dani. When I look up, Mrs. Murray is eyeing me like she's some kind of bird of prey. She knows I'm trapped. In another life I would've commended her for being such a stickler about the rules. But this isn't another life.

"No problem," I tell her, careful not to let on how screwed I really am. "Can I get to class now?"

"Of course." She stands with a smile, and so do I. "Remember, I need to see your brother. In person. Have him call me, please. Will you?"

I find Tyler at his locker before chem. "Dude," he says as I approach. "You look like crap."

"I feel like crap, thanks for noticing." I drop my bag on the floor and kneel down next to it, rifling through the mishmash of papers crumpled at the bottom. "I need help," I tell him.

"Yeah, I'm not even going to touch that one."

"With midterms. Mrs. Murray ambushed me today. I've gotta find a way to step it up." Finally my hand finds my stash of aspirin. I twist off the childproof cap and shake three white pills out into the palm of my hand. "Because apparently it's common knowledge among the entire staff that I'm fucking up in all areas right now."

"What do you mean?" He closes his locker and stands there, looking down at me, waiting for me to answer.

"I don't know." I throw the pills into the back of my throat and down them with a swig from my water bottle. "Does it ever just feel too hard some days?"

"What, school? Shit. Yeah."

"Not school. Just life, in general."

He crouches down next to me, and looking at me more seriously than he ever has before, he says, "Honestly, now. Should I be worried about you?"

"What, I'm just venting."

"Yeah, I know. But should I be worried?"

"I'm not trying to off myself, or something—not with three stupid pills." I laugh, but he doesn't. "Relax. I have a headache, that's all."

"Well, you're not in school half the time anymore. You look like you haven't slept in a year, you're currently sitting on the dirty-ass floor popping pills in your mouth, and you're asking *me* for help studying. There are so many things wrong with this picture."

"It's aspirin. And I'm kneeling, not sitting," I tell him as I pull myself up to my feet.

He stands as well and examines me for a moment, narrowing his eyes.

"Think of it as us studying together, not you helping me. Does that make it easier?"

"It makes it less weird," he counters as we begin to walk down the hall toward chem.

"Weird because of Dani?"

"No, weird because you're acting weird right now," he says matter-of-factly as we enter the classroom. Our teacher is already talking, even though the bell rings directly after we walk through the door.

"So, do you want to or not?" I whisper as we take our seats, not sure if he realizes he still hasn't given me an answer.

"Oh. Yeah," he finally says. "I mean, of course I will. This weekend good?"

I nod, and mouth the words, "Thank you."

BLAME

DR. GREENBERG TAKES IN a deep breath through his nose. "Last time we were talking about your mother." He reaches for the notebook sitting on the table next to him and flips a page. "You were telling me about how your father would beat her. Talk to her like she was stupid. Take her money. Take her shoes so she couldn't leave—"

I have to stop him there. "I never said 'beat.' And I didn't *see* that shoe thing," I correct. "I told you that was something my *grandmother* said in court."

He moves his glasses up to the top of his head and looks at me. "Okay. Well, but what's the difference?"

"Nothing. I'm just saying that's not what I said. It sounds worse when you say it like that."

"Worse than what?"

I shrug. "Worse than it was, I guess."

"Well . . . ," he starts, then stops, then starts again. "Okay, but it really was pretty bad, wasn't it? I mean, your mother *is* in prison and your father *is* dead."

"When you say it like *that*, yes." I can feel myself losing my patience.

"Well, how would you say it?"

I study him closely. "I would say it was an accident."

"You don't know that, though, do you? Isn't that what you said caused all the tension between you and your sister? You wanted to know, and she couldn't tell you."

I cross my arms over my stomach. I don't know how we got into all of this again. I only came here to see if he could write me doctor's notes. I swear, the last time I was here, I must've been delirious from that lingering fever. Otherwise, why would I have told him so much?

"'He blamed her for everything,'" he reads from the page. "That's what you said. And then I asked if you blame her." He looks up at me. "You never answered."

I blame her. And him. I blame them—their weakness, together. I blame the sun and the moon. I blame the year, the season, the month. I blame the hour of the day.

"I blame her . . . ," I begin, not knowing what I'm about to say, "for not being here now."

It's so silent I can hear Dr. Greenberg breathing. I can hear my pulse pounding in my ears. I can hear Ingrid's voice carry through the thin walls.

"Maybe I thought that if we could all agree that it wasn't her fault, then I wouldn't have to blame her?" I say it like a question.

"There's no right answer, Brooke." But before I can respond, he continues, asking, "What about Callie and Aaron? Do you blame them for not being here now?"

"They're coming back," I tell him, my voice clearer, louder, trying to cover the fact that this is one more thing I don't know for sure.

"Okay," he concedes. "But let's just say they don't. What would that mean?"

I shrug. I reposition myself in the chair so I can see the clock on the wall. It's 4:40. I follow the slim red second hand all the way around the circumference of the clock to 4:41.

"Brooke?"

I look up again. The clock suddenly says 4:45.

"Why do you think they left?" he asks.

"I told you, they're coming back!" I nearly shout, though not quite. "Aaron's only out of town, doing this job thing. And Callie is only at Jackie's until Aaron gets back." Except I think Dr. Greenberg doesn't even believe me. I check my volume, force myself to turn it down a notch before answering his question. "I think they just wanted to give up."

"Give up on . . . ?" he prompts.

"Give up on us—our family, our mom." *On me.*

"But you don't want to give up?"

"I'm trying not to. I mean, isn't this what family's supposed to do? You're supposed to be there for each other through anything." I stop because I can feel my head starting to pound.

"Well, I think there's a difference between giving up and letting go."

No there's not.

"What would happen if you let go?"

A tiny bell chimes from somewhere behind Dr. Greenberg's desk. Time's up.

I pick up my bag and prepare to stand up, leave, and possibly never come back again.

"Wait—wait right there. We have time. What were you about to say? What are you feeling right now?"

A few moments of silence pass between us as I try to find a way to express all that I'm feeling right now. But no words can make sense of how much I want things to go back to the way they were, even when things were bad. Or how much I want to leave—how sometimes I wish I could burn the whole place down, take a wrecking ball to it. No words to explain how I feel all those things at the same time, all the time.

"If I really let go"—my voice catches, even though I'm trying so hard to be brave—"I'll never have a *home* again, that place you hear people talk about—that safe place to land. That's over for me."

"I'm curious, is that really what it felt like before?" he asks.

I think about it for several moments, but I refuse to give him the answer I know he wants, the answer that I know deep down is true.

"I have to go to work," I tell him, rushing out, not even bothering to ask about those damn doctor's notes.

TINY STORM

THE SMALL COWBELL STRUNG to the door with Christmas ribbon dings softly as two cops walk through. I see their uniforms before I see their faces. The air is suddenly sucked from my lungs. Because for a moment, a millisecond, a nanosecond only, my mind forgets and I think that one of them is my dad. But then my brain kicks in and I realize for the millionth time, in the millionth way, it can't be.

I return my attention to the woman in front of me. She gives me that passive-aggressive *I'm in a hurry* scowl I've come to recognize so well. "I'm sorry, what was that again?" I ask her.

"Large coffee and one of those cinnamon rolls. To go. Please," she adds, looking down at her wallet.

I pull a sheet of wax paper from the cardboard box underneath the counter and grab the cinnamon roll farthest back, squeezing my fingernails gently into the dough as I shove it into a paper bag. The coffeepot crackles and hisses like a tiny storm as I place it back on the burner, and it's more like that is what's happening inside of me.

I snap the lid on snugly and tell her "Three seventy-five" as I slide the cup and bag across the tile countertop.

She lays down a five, mumbles, "Keep the change."

I turn away, pretend to count the number of blueberry muffins that must be rationed throughout the night, while I slip the five into my apron pocket.

Turning around, I grab a rag from the bucket under the sink and start wiping down the counter in slow, circular movements. Then all the surfaces on my side—the sugar canister, the cream dispenser, the coffeepots, the register—for the hundredth time tonight.

I'm despicable, I know.

The first time was an accident, a mistake, but it's become easier and easier. The trick is not ringing up the order at all. No one will notice money missing that was never supposed to be there in the first place. The trick is to spread it out across a bunch of small orders. It's not like I don't feel bad about it—I feel *horrible*. But rent is due again, and I'm already late, and I honestly don't know how I'm going to pull it all together before getting another one of those scarlet-letter notices taped to my door.

"Behind you," Owen says as he brushes past me with a fresh tray of chocolate-glazed something. The thick, sugary scent wafts up through my nostrils and sticks in the back of my throat.

"Slow tonight," I muse halfheartedly, my usual Owen small talk.

He casts a sideways glance at me over his shoulder and grins. He shakes his head slowly, then he turns his back to me. "You're slick. You know that? Very slick."

I swallow hard, watching him fill in the pastries, the word sinking into my brain, slow like honey. "What?" I utter, pretending

I didn't hear him, pretending I'm not completely taken off guard, pretending those aren't dangerous words he's speaking. But Owen is quiet as he finishes arranging the new pastries. And then he leans up against the wall and stares at me as if *he* asked *me* the question instead of the other way around. "*What?*" I repeat, louder.

He gives me another one of his noncommittal headshake gestures and walks back into the kitchen, wordless. I brace myself with both hands on the counter. Inhale one-two-three-four, and exhale one-two-three-four. Inhale. And exhale. I try to count slowly, by Mississippis, like Dr. Greenberg taught me, but I can't even get past two Mississippi. I try to rehearse in my head what I can say, how I can explain, or even better, lie. But I can't do that, either. So my feet begin to move in spite of my brain, taking one step, too fast, into the kitchen; they slide across the wet floor.

"Careful!" he shouts, looking up at me for only a moment, his eyes wide. "Floor's wet."

I grab hold of the counter and regain my balance. He dunks the mop into the dirty gray water, the muscles in his forearms contracting as he squeezes the excess water out. Then he slaps the mop down against the floor, pushes it back and forth, slopping left to right and left to right.

"Owen, what did you say?" I ask as calmly as I can.

"I *said*"—he enunciates precisely—"be *care*ful. Floor's wet."

"No, I mean before."

"Oh." He stops, and stands the mop up straight, crosses his arms over the top of the handle, and squints hard at the air above my head with this puzzled expression on his face. "You have to be more specific. I've said lots of things before."

I'm not amused. I cross my arms.

"Look, I know what you've been doing," he finally says, returning to his mopping.

"I don't know what you're talking about, Owen," I lie.

"Well, how 'bout that? I'm guessing *I* don't know what I'm talking about either, huh?" he says, staking the mop into the floor with a splat.

"Owen, I need this job, so whatever you *think* you saw—never mind, fine!" I scoff, reaching down into my apron pocket. "Here, take it! Happy?" I yell, throwing the five-dollar bill onto the floor in the space between us.

He looks down at it and shakes his head, then looks up me accusingly. "You have Jackie wrapped around your little finger. She thinks you're a friggin' angel."

"It was a couple dollars, okay?" I lie. "It's not like I'm some mastermind. And I'm going to pay it back."

The bell dings out in the shop. A woman's voice shouts, "Hell-ooo?" But I can't move, can't end this conversation. Not without some kind of resolution.

"You have a customer," he says.

I finish up her order without any pleasantries; no fake-outs with the register, no extra "Have a nice night." When I go back into the kitchen, he's not there. But the five-dollar bill is sitting on the counter next to the giant tubs of frosting and doughnut fillings, pressed straight, wrinkles flattened, waiting for me either to take it or to return it to the register, where it belongs.

Movement in the periphery catches my eye. Owen stands at the back door of the kitchen kicking at the triangular wooden doorstop. He wedges it under the bottom to prop it open, even though he knows that's not allowed—Jackie says it's a violation of the health code or something. But a cool breeze rushes in, and I suddenly feel like I could lie right down on this dirty floor and fall asleep for a million years. He stands there with his back to me, looking out, a silhouette against the early-evening sky, craning his neck left and right, stretching his arms one at a time across his chest.

I walk toward him, my insides tightening with every breath. I take a gulp of air, but my lungs turn to steel. I open my mouth to speak, but my tongue is just a soggy clump of paper. My eyes begin to fill with water as I watch him. Feeling my entire universe unraveling before me, I pull my sleeves down over my hands and dab at the tears before they can spill over.

He takes exactly two steps toward the dumpster out back, drawn to a defunct, formerly yellow mop bucket that's sitting next to the dumpster, destined for a landfill somewhere. He maneuvers the dirty old thing with his feet like a ball, gliding it gently back to the door, and me. He stops the bucket and steadies it with his foot, just on the edge. In one sharp movement he presses his foot down quickly, flipping it over—gracefully somehow. Then he sits down on the top of the dingy bucket and stretches his legs out in front of him. But he still doesn't say anything—if he's trying to make me squirm, it's working.

"So?" I ask.

He inhales the fresh air, closes his eyes, then exhales.

"*So?*" I repeat, louder.

"Yeah. So. What's your deal, anyway?" he asks, looking at the dim sky, at the tiny pinpricks of light, muted as they peek through the veil of thin clouds. It's been staying light later, another sign that spring is winning the battle.

"My *deal*?"

"Yeah, your deal." He finally cuts his eyes at me. "Klepto?"

"Klepto?" A klepto would steal *things*, not money, but I guess pointing that out wouldn't exactly help my case.

"What then, just stickin' it to the man?" he jeers.

"Sticking it to the *man*?"

"That's really annoying."

"What?"

"*What?*" he mimics. "You keep repeating everything I say."

"Actually, you just repeated what *I* said."

That gets me a smile. "I know about your mom, and all. Brutal," he says under his breath, mumbling the word into one syllable.

I'm not sure which thing it is he's referring to as brutal: the fact that my mom's in prison—not jail, but prison, and will not be getting out anytime soon—or the fact that she killed my father with the kitchen knife, or that my family is split into pieces, scattered like broken glass.

"Owen, *listen*—I'm not going to do it again, okay?" I look at his face, not certain if I mean it or not, or if I only mean it right now. "I'm really not," I say anyway, maybe more to myself than him. "So do you think you can keep it between us? Please? Can you just forget what you saw?"

He breathes in deeply then, reluctantly looking at me. "If you do it again, I can't cover for you. I need this job too. And who do you think Jackie will blame when she figures it out, me or you?

Think about that next time." Then he stands up and brushes past me without another word. The yellow bucket glides across the grease-stained pavement, moved by some invisible force. I sit there and watch. Try to breathe.

At closing time Owen locks the front door behind us. He mumbles, "G'night," and we part ways as usual. Except tonight, as I look at his back walking away from me, I think about how I've been seeing too many backs walking away from me lately.

"Hey, Owen?" I call after him.

He stops and turns around but doesn't come any closer to me. So I have to shout across the parking lot.

"How come you never talked to me? I mean, when we went to school together?"

"How come you never talked to *me*?" he asks, not missing a beat.

I think about it. "I don't know," I finally answer. "I guess I thought people had made up their minds about me a long time ago."

He nods as he considers this. "You always acted like you wanted to be left alone. That's why people never talked to you."

"I guess I did," I shout across the space between us—it feels weird to be shouting one of the most intimate and honest conversations I've ever had with anyone. "Want to be left alone, I mean."

He nods again but doesn't say anything.

"So, are we friends?" I ask, realizing how stupid and childish it sounds only after it's out of my mouth.

He takes one step closer. "If we weren't, I'm telling you we would not even be having this conversation." It's only right now, in this moment, that I realize something about him. He has tons of friends not just because he happens to be talented at sports or great-looking; they like him because he's nice and honest and a genuinely good person.

On my walk home the chill in the air feels purifying, cleansing, like drinking a cold glass of water when you're really thirsty. I have the strongest urge to call Dani, but I don't. I sleep better that night than I have in months.

STARTING OVER

THE PARK IS BEGINNING to come back to life. Small green buds dot the trees. Ducks and geese and birds and squirrels are suddenly everywhere, kids playing again, climbing on the big boulder, parents yelling, joggers shuffling, the river running strong, things beginning again, starting over.

I came here to study—I have my whole messenger bag full of books and notes. I'm sitting under a tree along the river. The ground is damp and I feel it seeping through my jeans, but I don't mind; it's good to be outside, breathing fresh air.

I try to work on my calculus, but I can't concentrate.

Dr. Greenberg has planted this weed of a thought in my mind that I cannot kill. What would it mean to let go? Maybe letting go is like the ice finally breaking. Maybe I'm thawing slowly, like the rest of the world; maybe I'll just crack open and release it all, start over again too.

I lean my head against the tree trunk and close my eyes.

Somewhere a little girl is crying. It takes me back to this day when Aaron and I were little. It was one of the many times we came here, holding hands as we crossed the street, while Mom and Dad were busy fighting.

I remember we found these fallen branches and made them into swords for one of our pirate duels. We were pretending to have a sword fight, and he was letting me win, as usual, when these big kids came up to us. They called us babies and snatched our swords out of our hands and broke them in half, stomped on them so they snapped like they were nothing more than twigs.

Aaron always seemed so much older than me, but he really wasn't—that's something it's taken me a long time to realize. We were both little, I was almost six and he was maybe eight or nine. Being little didn't stop him from being pissed, though. He marched right up to the ringleader of the bullies—who couldn't have been much older than us, maybe nine or ten—and demanded that he go find us new swords. But of course they weren't about to do that. They all got a good laugh, though. Then the four boys circled Aaron and started pushing him back and forth, taunting and shouting as he bounced against them like a pinball, unable to break free or even gain his footing.

I've always remembered the part about the bullies breaking our sticks and Aaron being pushed around, but I forgot there was another part to it. I never remembered exactly how we got out of there.

I had just started crying right before Dad showed up.

He entered the scene like some kind of superhero, I remember now, still in his uniform. He swooped in and pulled Aaron right out of there, so stealthily no one had even seen him coming, not even me. We stood behind him and watched as he closed in on the kids.

"What's going on over here?" he said, not yelling but speaking loudly, firmly. He had his hands on his hips and towered over them, casting a long shadow. "Huh? You think it's fun to beat up on little kids half your size? Four against one? Let me tell you something, that doesn't make you tough, that makes you a coward—you know what that means?" he demanded, moving even closer to them.

They were terrified. They nodded frantically. "Yes. Yes, sir. Yes, Officer," they replied, their voices cracking and shaking.

He lowered his voice then and bent over so that he was face-to-face with them and said, "I'm always watching—you won't know I'm here, but I'll be watching you." He glanced over his shoulder at the two of us and winked. I don't think I've ever felt safer, more proud, more vindicated, than I did right in that moment. When I looked up at Aaron, he was just watching in awe, his mouth hanging open in a smile.

"If I ever, and I mean *ever*, see you beating up on these kids, or any other kids, ever again . . ." He paused at exactly the right time to let the fear sink in. "I will take you to jail. That's right. What do you think your parents would think of that? Huh, you hear me?"

Emphatic nodding and another round of "Yes, sirs."

He stood upright again, so tall and straight. "All right. You remember that. Now get out of here before I change my mind and arrest you all right now. Got it? Yeah? Go, then."

They ran.

When he turned around to face us, I ran up to him and hugged his legs. He was laughing as he picked me up—I could feel it vibrating in his chest; I can almost feel it now. "You okay?" he asked me, touching my cheek where my tears had been.

"Yep," I told him, and I leaned my head against his shoulder.

"What about you? You okay, bud?" he asked Aaron, taking his chin in his hand to get a better look at his face.

Aaron nodded. "Yeah, I'm okay."

"All right, then. Come on. It's time for dinner."

He patted Aaron's head and carried me the whole way home.

I open my eyes.

Back in the present. The river seems to be rushing even louder now. Faster. I look around. Everyone seems so far away, and the sky is now populated with a team of deep-gray clouds. I start packing up my things, uncertain anymore if I made up the ending or if it was real. If I ever talk to Aaron again, I'll have to ask him about it.

OUT OF HIBERNATION

"SO THIS IS WHERE you live?" Tyler says as he steps into my living room. I spent the morning cleaning and straightening and organizing. I couldn't believe how disgusting I'd let it become. "Dani said it was normal. I didn't believe her, though."

"What do you mean, why wouldn't it be normal?"

"You're such a control freak, I figured you probably lived in a sterilized bubble, or something. Guess you're really human after all," he says, this sly grin on his face.

"Thanks, I guess. Come on in."

We get set up around the coffee table. We tag-team it. Tyler's the point person for calculus. I'm in charge of English and chem. Both of us suck in history, so we decide to tackle it together. We're at it for hours. It feels good to work hard again, to be good at something again.

As it begins to get dark outside, I'm aware of a gnawing feeling in the pit of my stomach, but for once the cause is not worry, it is simply to tell me how hungry I am. "Wanna take a snack break?" I ask Tyler.

"Good God," he says, closing his laptop. "I thought you'd never ask."

I raid the kitchen, which is admittedly devoid of much within a valid expiration date these days. "Tater Tots and Pizza Rolls?" I call out to Tyler, finding the only halfway respectable items left in the freezer.

"Perfection!" he yells back.

Twenty minutes later I'm dumping the sizzling Tater Tots and Pizza Rolls onto two plates, which I bring to the table. "Brain food is served," I announce.

He takes a seat next to me, and I suddenly realize how nice it is to have someone else around. "Where is everybody?" he asks. "I thought you had, like, ten siblings or something?"

"Two." I laugh, blowing on a Pizza Roll before putting it in my mouth. "But it's just me now."

"What do you mean? It can't just be you," he says, selectively searching for the perfect Tater Tot.

"It is," I admit.

"How?" he says, clearly still not taking me seriously.

I shrug. "I honestly don't know."

He stares at the table for a few seconds before he looks back at me. "But how?" he repeats, popping the Tater Tot in his mouth at last.

"I don't know. I mean, I've been lying to everyone about it, so I'm not sure anyone really knows. I'm probably getting kicked out soon, though, so I won't be able to hide it much longer."

"Holy shit," he breathes. "I don't know the details, obviously, but you can stay at my house if you need a place. My mom would be cool with it, I know she would."

"You would really do that? Even though you're Dani's friend?"

He stares at me, unblinking, as he pinches the bridge of his nose. "For such a smart person, you can be so completely dense sometimes."

"Why? Or is that a totally dense question?"

"Yes, it is. Because I can't believe you still can't seem to comprehend the fact I'm *your* friend too, Brooke."

"Oh" is all I can say.

"Oh? That's it? You're not gonna tell me I'm your friend too?"

"No, you are. You definitely are, you're one of my only friends."

"Dork," he says, tossing a Tater Tot at me.

I catch it and throw it back at him.

"Okay, change of subject. What are these?" he asks, tapping his finger against a stack of photos from my birthday party that have been sitting there for months. Jackie had them printed and gave me copies. I haven't even looked at them yet.

"Nothing, just stupid pictures from my birthday," I tell him, trying not to remember how great that day was.

"Thanks for inviting me, by the way," he jokes as he shuffles through them, smiling at some, and then he stops and flips one over so I can see. It's the photo of me and Dani. Our first picture together. She has her arm around me and we're both smiling so hugely. I take it from him, but I can only stand to look at it for a second before I have to give it back. He studies the picture closer and says, "You two are so cute."

"'Were,' you mean," I correct.

"You miss her?" he asks.

I let my head fall into my hands for a moment. "Yeah," I groan. When I look up, he's grinning at me. "What?"

He sighs and pops a Tater Tot in his mouth. Then he slides the plate closer so I can snag one for myself, never answering.

"How do you manage to stay so damn calm all the time?" I ask him, wondering if I could ever learn to be like that.

He shrugs. "I'm simply on a mission to not have a bunch of wrinkles by the time I'm twenty-five. I plan on looking this good for a long time. I told you before, I don't do stress. Unlike you"—he touches the spot in the center of my forehead, between my eyebrows, with his index finger and pushes ever so slightly—"a girl who's on her way to getting a big, fat worry line right there."

I laugh, shake my head. "I guess I pretty much blew it with her," I admit to him, and to myself.

"Listen, she's just hurt. And if she didn't still care, she wouldn't still be complaining about you to me. Every. Single. Damn. Day."

"If you say so."

"I do. I also say, you need to come out of hibernation and start fixing things."

"I wouldn't know where to begin," I tell him.

"Just apologize. And be honest with her—that's all she wanted in the first place. You realize that, right?"

"I guess so," I admit.

"So, suck it up. Do that, and I bet she'd be willing to give it another go—but don't tell her I told you to," he warns me, flinging another Tater Tot in my direction.

CAROLINE

HER APARTMENT IS NOTHING like I imagined it would be, yet it suits her perfectly. Everything here looks like it would've looked better in a different time. Not unlike Caroline herself.

"Well, it's not much, I know. But it's home," she says, slapping a throw pillow into shape on her couch.

"Is this where my mom grew up?"

"No. This is where I grew up. My parents lived here. I bought the place from my father when my mother died."

"Is he still alive? Your father. My great-grandfather," I add, hearing how strange these words sound coming out of my mouth.

She shakes her head but doesn't offer up any further information. I follow her into the kitchen, where she pours two glasses of iced tea from a pitcher—a warm golden brown, with ice and wedges of lemon floating at the top. "Want to sit outside?" she asks as she hands one of the glasses to me.

She leads the way back through the living room to a sliding glass door that opens to a small balcony with a concrete floor and wrought-iron bars that form a fence around it. We look out over a courtyard that has a big, L-shaped inground pool in the center, surrounded by tables and umbrellas and those outdoor lounge chairs that have the adjustable backs. There's a man skimming it. And when he looks up, he waves at us. Caroline waves back and then turns to me as we sit in two metal chairs that are slightly rusted at the edges, their cushions flattened and well worn. "Pool opens next week. You and the others are welcome anytime. Aaron and Callie," she adds, like it's strange for her to say their names as well.

"Thanks, I think Callie would like that."

She nods but doesn't say anything else.

"Do you work?" I ask, trying to think of anything normal to talk about.

"I work at the college."

"You're a professor?" I ask, impressed.

She laughs hard, then starts coughing like before, hacking like she can't catch her breath. "No," she finally manages. "Although, once upon a time I thought I would be. No, it's administrative. Nothing too exciting. But it pays the bills."

"Do you live here by yourself?"

"You ask a lot of questions—but that's a good thing. No, as a matter of fact, I have a boyfriend who lives here too. He's not here right now, but you'll meet him another time—we'll have you over for dinner. Do you have a boyfriend?"

"No . . . but I have a girlfriend. Or I did, anyway. I don't know. It's complicated." I wait for her reaction; I know a lot of older people don't get it. A lot of younger people don't get it either.

"Good. It's good to have someone," she says, not batting an

eye. "I'd like to meet her sometime. When things are less complicated, that is."

"That'd be nice." I pause and consider how to frame this delicately. "Are you sick? I can't help but notice the coughing. Are you *okay*, is what I'm trying to ask."

"I'm old."

"Yeah, but are you—"

"Dying?" she finishes. "We're *all* dying. Most of us just don't know what we're dying from." She pauses, then smiles. "I have emphysema. Some days are worse than others. I have oxygen in there"—she hitches her head in the direction of the sliding door—"if I really need it. Sometimes I do."

"Do you ever think you should quit smoking?" I ask, gesturing to the cigarette case and the lighter in her hand.

Smirking, she shakes her head, pulls one of those long, slender cigarettes out, and lights it. The tendrils of smoke snake around her head like fingers. "It's my one remaining vice. My father always said"—she lowers her voice to a deeper pitch—"'You're allowed one vice in life, Caroline, so choose wisely.'" She wags her finger, grinning as she mimics her father, this man I'll never know.

She looks off for moment before turning back to me. "He told me that when I married your grandfather. At the time I didn't know people could be vices. But they can. I told your mother the same thing right before she married your father. That was the last time she ever spoke to me. Well, until now." She sighs sadly. "Of course, I wasn't the most credible person back then. So I can see why she didn't listen."

"But you changed," I remind her.

"That's right," she begins. "I've been clean and sober for over twenty years. I quit all that stuff when your mother got pregnant with your brother. Not that she was speaking to me then. But children change things. I knew that firsthand. And I wanted to be able to be there if she needed help. So I kicked her father to the curb for the last time, and then I kicked all the other stuff that was bad for me. Except these." She shakes the cigarette in her hand above her head.

"That must've been hard," I tell her.

She nods. "It was, but not as hard as it would have been to just keep going. You know, in that way I can understand how your mother could've done what she did—but mind you, that doesn't mean I think it was right. It was obviously wrong, there's no question about that. It can be hard to figure out the right way to get free sometimes."

I let a wave of silence wash over us, her words sinking in, and I start to think maybe I understand a little bit too, because after all, haven't I been doing the same thing—trying to figure out the right way to get free?

"Do you talk to Mom now?" I finally ask.

"Yes, I've gone to visit her a few times. I was surprised I was on her visitor list. But I was."

"Do you think I am? After everything?"

"I know that you are." She pauses to take a long, deep drag of her cigarette. "Would you like to go with me next time?"

"I think I would, actually."

"Okay," she says, swatting a fruit fly away from our glasses.

"I came here to—well, I came here for a lot of reasons, but mainly I came to ask a favor." I take a sip of my iced tea, trying to clear my throat so that the words come out easier. It's sweet and sour, sugary and lemony, all at the same time. "It's hard for me to ask for help, I guess."

"You get that from me," she says with a patient smile. "You can ask. Whatever it is, you can ask me."

"Well, things have gotten kind of . . . *bad*. At school, they need to meet with my guardian because I have all these absences. But Aaron left. And honestly, I don't even blame him anymore. And I think I'm probably about to get evicted from the apartment. Callie went to go stay with Jackie. And I know she'd let me stay too. But I don't belong there. And I'm so sick of being where I don't belong." I pause, inhaling deeply for the important part. "And I thought maybe, I don't know, maybe I might belong here. With you."

She's nodding before I've even finished my sentence, and I think I see her eyes watering up, just barely. "Brooke, I think you might belong here too. So if you're asking if you can live here with me, I'm saying yes."

"Really?"

"Yes, really."

"Your boyfriend won't mind?"

"Hell no, this is *my* house," she shouts, with a laugh. "And you know what else?"

"What?"

She crushes her cigarette in the tin ashtray on the table. "I think I might actually try to kick these damn things after all."

COMING CLEAN

"YOU'RE AVOIDING ME." I swing around, startled by the voice as I exit our building. Jackie. She stands there waiting for me like she's been camped out on the steps all morning.

"I'm not avoiding you," I lie.

She raises her eyebrows and continues standing in my way, holding two to-go cups from the shop. She hands me one. It burns my fingers even through the corrugated sleeve. She sits down on the top step. I know I don't have a choice but to sit next to her. "So, where are you off to?" she asks, carefully removing the plastic lid from her coffee.

"Nowhere," I lie again. Across the street the park is in bloom, the brightest greens coming to life everywhere. There's a light scent of cherry blossoms in the air, so faint you could almost miss it. I'd be enjoying it all right now if I weren't aware of Jackie sitting next to me, seeing right through me.

"Listen, I have to ask you something, and I need you to tell me the truth."

Instantly I feel my stomach leaping up through my throat.

"Jackie, I'm sorry. I'm really sorry. I'm going to pay you back every cent, I promise."

"Pay me back?" she asks.

"I don't even know how it started. It was a mistake at first, and then I just . . . ," I gasp, the guilt strangling me. "I feel terrible about it. I never should've started. But I stopped, I really did. And it will take me a while, but I will pay you back—I kept track of how much it was because I was always going to pay you back."

"Brooke, what are you talking about?"

"Well . . ." My voice catches in my throat before I can say anything else. "Wait, what are you talking about?"

"I'm talking about what Callie told me this morning. She said Aaron moved out."

Overhead a flock of geese fly in formation, squawking one after the other, putting our conversation on pause.

"So, is that true?" she says loudly as the geese gradually fade away beyond the park and the trees.

I nod, biting my lip, afraid to speak.

"I don't understand why I'm only hearing about this now. You cannot be living here alone. Do you have any idea how irresponsible and dangerous—"

"No, I know," I interrupt. "But it's—it's going to be okay."

"You're damn right, it will. Because you're coming home with me right now."

"No, just hear me out. I have a plan. I've been talking with Caroline. And I'm going to move in with her."

"Brooke, Ray and I would be more than happy to have you come live with us. You know this, don't you?" she asks, cupping my chin in her hand. "Things are going really well with Callie. And there's no reason—"

"I know, and I appreciate the offer, and all. And I'm so grateful that you're helping Callie like this, because she really needs you, she needs parents. But this is something I want to try—this is something I need to do."

"For tonight you're coming home with me. You have to talk to your mother about this. She is still your mother and she has a right to know what's happening."

"Okay, I will. I promise."

She nods, taking a sip of her coffee. "So, what were *you* talking about?"

I take a deep breath—I have to tell her the truth now. My voice is shaking as soon as I open my mouth. "I've been stealing from you, taking money at work," I admit, burying my face in my hands because I can't look her in the eye. "I'm so sorry," I blubber. "I just wanted to keep the apartment. It seems stupid now. It was so wrong. But I know exactly how much it was—I'll pay you back with interest, I swear."

She pulls my hands away from my face and looks at me, hard. I can tell she doesn't want to believe I would do that—take advantage, break her trust, waste her generosity like that.

"I'm sorry," I repeat. "I will never do it again. I feel so terrible and I really am so, so sorry."

"I know," she finally says, relenting, and puts her arm around me. "I appreciate you telling me. I'm sure that was hard to admit."

We sit there like that for a while, and for the first time I think I'm seeing Jackie clearly. Seeing how much she really does love my mom, how much she only wants to help, how much she truly cares.

THE BUILDING IS A massive structure, imposing, like a factory. Caroline drove us in her ancient car, which smelled of motor oil and leather and old smoke. We hummed along to an oldies station on the radio and kept the windows rolled down. Even though we didn't talk much, there was something so comforting about the whole thing.

We had to pass through a series of checkpoints, metal detectors, and wands, forced to empty our pockets, and take off our shoes and belts, and lock up all our belongings in tiny lockers, like the kind they have at bowling alleys or skating rinks. It's all done in a very orderly and civilized fashion, which I greatly appreciate, the line moving along smoothly and steadily. The officer behind the reception desk checks our IDs and the paperwork Caroline hands her.

"All right. Fill this out. Read over these policies and make sure you understand them. Initial and date the bottom of the page when you're done. Your visitation supervisor will collect the forms when they call you back. Wait over there. Listen for this number," she instructs, circling a number on one of the pieces of paper in red pen and pointing to a pair of solid-looking double doors. There's an old tin sign that reads VISITORS in bold, sharp letters.

Caroline and I sit in a cluster of hard plastic chairs, becoming part of an assortment of people—all ages, shapes, sizes, and colors—each of us here to visit a loved one. Some of them look very average, some scared, and others *scary*, seeming as if they should be the ones being visited rather than the other way around. What's most shocking to see, though, are how many kids are here, some who are even younger than Callie, dressed up like it's picture day at school.

I suddenly remember this thing my social studies teacher said last year. She was talking about how famous works of art or historic landmarks act as these "great equalizers." How everyone is the same staring up at the ceiling of the Sistine Chapel, or standing in front of the Pyramids at Giza, or approaching the Grand Canyon. No one is better or less important than any other person, regardless of where you come from, how young or old you are, how rich or poor. At the time I hoped I might experience something like that one day. As I scan all the faces here, I realize that this is another one of those great equalizers—all of us waiting here together for the same reason, no room in the spaces between us for our differences.

The seconds drain out of the minutes so slowly they seem to morph into hours, slipping into years, decades, centuries, before they call us back. The guard stands in another doorway opposite the one we came through, this one looking more heavy duty, more like the type of door you'd imagine prisons to be made up of, doors that are barriers, not passageways.

We follow him through the massive entrance; a steady pulse

of buzzes and clicks punctuate the static over the two-way radio clipped to his belt. As the guard leads us down a long, cavernous hallway, he calls over his shoulder, "Bright, sunny day out. Taking you to the outdoor visitation area today. Which is much nicer," he explains as we cross another checkpoint and are admitted through yet another door that leads to an identical hall.

Then we turn a corner abruptly, and there's a door right there in front of us. "You'll have one hour," he tells us. There's a beep and the light on the sensor next to the door turns from red to green.

This is it. The moment I've been waiting for. And dreading. Part of me wants to keep pretending this isn't real, this isn't happening. The door swings open, and at first I'm blinded by the sunlight. I shield my eyes as we follow the guard through one last chain-link gate, which spills out into a wide, open area with tables and groups of people sitting and standing and smoking. A tall fence encloses the whole space, a layer of barbed wire lining the top. The sun leaves no dark corners forming shadows, nowhere to hide—every inch of this place is visible from every other inch.

"Where is she?" I ask Caroline.

"She's over there," she tells me, and I try to follow the direction she points in, but my mind can't make the connection because the only person *there* is not my mother. My feet move toward her slowly, my legs struggling against a strong current. But as the distance between us closes, I start to recognize her again, underneath the washed-out blue jeans and buttoned-up work shirt and her hair pulled back into a braid. I step forward cautiously, my shoes scraping against the concrete as I drag my feet.

She pulls me in with both of her arms, no longer handcuffed, like the last time I visited her in jail, before the trial. She's crushing me against her. I bury my face in her neck, and without warning, without permission, I'm sobbing. Not just crying, not just tears, but full-body shuddering. She holds me tighter and tighter as I finally let myself feel the weight of how much I've missed her, how much we've lost.

Caroline's hand is on my back, rubbing a gentle circle, sturdy and sure.

When we pull apart, Mom is smiling. And she looks more beautiful than ever.

"Mom," I finally say, still holding her hands, which feel more solid than before, no longer thin and soft and delicate. She looks tough, strong somehow—unvarnished in this way that I've never seen before.

"Come. Please, come sit down." She leads us over to a circular picnic table where we sit and stare at one another, no one knowing where to begin. "Look at you, honey. You look so much older. How is that possible?" she says with a laugh. She reaches out and tucks a stray strand of hair behind my ear.

I try to frame out the question in my head, not sure how to ask, as I look around at the other inmates. "Mom, how is it here? I mean, are you okay?" I ask, barely able to get the words out.

She looks around too, then nods. "It's okay," she finally answers. "I'm okay. I really am." She looks up at the sky, shielding her eyes with one hand, and breathes in deeply. I track where her eyes lead, but there's nothing there. Not a cloud passing overhead, no distant planes drawing white lines through the sky.

She looks down at her lap and I watch her swallow hard,

like she's downing a mass of words—all the secrets about herself that she's never told me, secrets about what happened, secrets that maybe she's even kept from herself. Tears start to pool at the corners of her eyes, and I can see something beginning to separate in her, from the inside out, like stitching coming lose, revealing a glimpse of something vibrating low and deep inside of her.

"Why don't I give you girls a minute," Caroline offers, patting my mother's hand before she stands and walks over to an empty table several feet away.

Mom clears her throat and wipes her eyes. "You know, I never thought things would end up like this. This isn't what I dreamed my life would be when I was your age. I had goals, plans, dreams. None of them involved this."

"You shouldn't be here."

She shakes her head and looks down again, says, "Maybe, maybe not, but I am."

"Tell me it was an accident, Mom," I whisper.

"It was, of course it was. I didn't wake up that day thinking that was how it was going to end. It's so hard to explain. He pushed me too far and I reacted. I wasn't thinking about what would happen next, I just . . . ," she gasps, running out of breath. "I was *always* thinking. I never stopped thinking, not even for one second, not even in my sleep. I was always worrying, constantly, trying to plan out ways to keep the peace, to make things better. That was my whole life."

She stops, and just when I think she's about to spill open, she pulls the edges of herself back together and looks me in the eye. I want to tell her that I know what that feels like—it feels like a strait-jacket, like you're suffocating, like you can't breathe, ever.

"But not then," she continues. "Not in that moment. I needed to *do*, not think, just do . . . something. It *was* an accident, honey—I swear it was. And it was wrong. So I'm okay with being here." She takes my hands in hers and holds on tight, forcing me to look at her. "He wasn't an evil person, I hope you know that."

"I do," I say, barely.

"I didn't want him to die," Mom continues. "I just needed to live. I don't expect anyone to understand that."

I swallow hard. I feel my head nodding, but I can't find any words to say—there are no words that are enough. Nothing I could say would explain all the ways that I understand, or all the ways I never will. There's nothing I can say to explain how losing Dad—something that made no sense—has ended up making everything else make sense. How it's shifted everything in all our lives, everything inside of me, forever.

"You don't have to say anything," she answers for me.

I feel closer to her than I've ever felt before, yet there's this vast distance between us, all at the same time, with love and hate and everything in between. I want to leave her here the way she's left us, but I also want to hold on and never let go. She's like a stranger in this one way, but in another way she's more real than she's ever been, more alive than I've ever seen her. Not only my mother, but someone else, someone more than my mother could ever have been, someone bigger, more honest, stripped down in this way that's raw and powerful and terrifying and fragile. She's free now, in her way, somehow.

AMENDS

I TELL MYSELF TO be brave, be bold, be honest, one more time, as I press my finger against the glowing doorbell next to her front door. And after a pause I hear this muffled chiming from inside—*ding-ding-dong*.

Caroline's car pulls out of the driveway slowly.

I wait. But no one's coming. I ring the bell again. I hear footsteps. A girl answers the door. Not Dani. But I recognize her from the pictures in Dani's room. Her sister. She looks different in person—shorter than Dani, more like their mother's height. And her hair is long and flowing.

She greets me with a "Hey, you're not our Chinese food."

"Oh, no," I say with a laugh. "I guess I'm not. Is—is Dani here? I'm Brooke."

She opens the screen door to let me in. "Yeah. I know who you are. I'm Tori."

"It's nice to meet you," I offer.

"Same here, come in. Dani, you have a visitor," she calls out over her shoulder as I step inside.

“So, I guess your semester’s over?” I ask as we stand there.

“Yeah, I got in yesterday, actually. We’re catching up on sister time. Movies. Takeout. You know.”

I smile, hoping that one day it can be like that between me and Callie again.

“*Hey* . . . ,” Dani says slowly, stopping abruptly as she enters the room, “what are you doing here?”

“I don’t want to interrupt you guys, I—I wanted to see if we could talk for a minute?”

Dani looks at Tori, who looks at me. “I don’t mind,” Tori tells us.

“Okay, come on.” Dani leads the way through the house and up the stairs like she had that first time, except she doesn’t speak a word until we reach her bedroom. “Fine. I’m listening,” she finally says, turning around and crossing her arms.

“I’m sorry,” I begin. “I’m so sorry about the way I acted, the way I treated you.”

She stares at me—clearly, that’s not going to be good enough.

“You were the first person to make me feel like I could be myself, that I could have a life that didn’t revolve around what everyone else needed me to be. And I don’t think I knew how to handle that.”

I stop, waiting to see if she has anything to say. But she doesn’t.

“I guess I wanted to keep you separate, outside of all the chaos. I didn’t want all the other stuff going on in my life to touch what we had. ’Cause it was so good. It was so good and I can’t believe I screwed it up, because all I wanted was to protect what we had.”

She sits down on the edge of her bed and stares somewhere around my knees. I don’t know if she’s hearing me. If I’m being clear.

"I was afraid," I admit to her.

"Afraid of what?" she asks, finally meeting my eyes, and I see all the hurt that's still there, the pain I caused.

I shake my head. "Of being honest, being happy. Afraid of letting you in. Afraid you wouldn't love the real me, with all the drama and baggage."

"Well, so what's changed now?"

"Everything." I hear a laugh behind my words. "Everything's changed and . . . I would really love to have you back in my life, but *really* in my life this time."

There's this unbearable silence.

"Listen," she begins, "we were about to do this whole sister movie-marathon, junk-food thing, so—"

"Oh. Okay, I'll—I'll go."

"No, I was asking if you want to stay?"

"I wouldn't be messing up your sister time?"

She shrugs. "I have her for the whole summer," she tells me, a very small smile beginning to emerge. "But this doesn't mean we can just pick up where we left off, you know."

"I know," I tell her. I don't think we could even if we tried.

I get home from Dani's that night feeling so full of something—gratitude, maybe? Hope? Or maybe a little bit of both. I open my bedroom window and climb out, making my way up to the roof. I take my phone out of my back pocket.

Looking out over our neighborhood, I realize that this is the last time I'll ever be up here, the last time I'll ever see things from this vantage point again. I try to memorize it all. The moon is full and low in the sky and looks so much bigger, so much closer than usual, more gold than silver tonight. And I think about how the moon's gravity affects the tides of the oceans, pushing and pulling at the water, and I wonder if it has a similar effect on people, too.

I dial his number. It rings and rings—I expected nothing different.

An automated message answers, telling me, in yet one more way, that my brother "is not available. Please leave a message after the tone."

"Aaron, it's me. I promise I'm not calling to yell at you. I wanted to say that I'm thinking of you. And also . . ." I pause—I want to ask him if he's looking up at the sky like I am right now, but I don't. "You were right. I have to leave. And I am. I'm moving in with Caroline. Just wanted you to know. I hope you're okay. I hope you're doing better now." I can feel my voice trembling, so I let the rest of the words tumble out quick and messy: "Okay, Aaron. Call me when you can. Love you, bye."

LETTING GO

I SIT DOWN next to Callie at one of the old plastic tables outside Jackie's. She's reading a book, drinking a smoothie, letting the sun spill over her.

"You're not working?" she asks, taking note of my regular clothes.

"Not today. Is that the mango one?" I ask her, gesturing to her drink. "It my favorite too."

She slides it toward me and I take a sip.

"What are you reading?" I ask.

She flips the book over to show me the cover: *Little Women*. "Getting started on summer reading early—I blame you for that," she adds, trying not to smile.

"I'll take that as a compliment," I joke. "Hey, can we talk for a sec?"

"Okay," she answers uncertainly, setting the book facedown on the table.

"You know, Callie . . ." I take a breath before continuing. "I guess

I've been realizing that maybe I haven't really been there for you. I mean, wanting us all to be together isn't the same thing as us being there for each other. Does that make sense?" I ask. "I think I got confused about what was important."

She nods. "Yeah, I know."

"I wanted to tell you, I went to go visit our grandmother—Mom's mom."

"What?" Her eyes go wide. "I thought she was *dead*."

"Why did you think that?" I ask, laughing.

"Don't know. Just assumed, I guess." She pauses, pondering this new information, then asks, "What's she like?"

"Um . . ." I try to figure a way to describe her. "She's kind of odd, actually. But nice. A good person. We've been talking, and I wanted you to know I'm going to move in with her."

She holds up her hands, as if pushing something invisible away from her.

"No, no, I'm not asking you to go with me. But she wants to meet you."

She nods, listening more closely.

"You know, she has a pool. Not *hers*, really, but at her building. It's very blue. Shaped like an L. It has a diving board. And Caroline—that's her name—she wants to invite you over to go swimming sometime."

Now she's nodding and smiling.

"Sound like fun?"

"Yeah," she says, and pauses before she continues. "You could finally teach me how to dive."

"I could," I agree. "I will." I wait a few minutes, let the silence settle things between us. "Well, I'm gonna go—I have to take care of some last things at the apartment. Pack up what's left. Is there anything you want me to keep?"

She shakes her head.

"Okay." I give her hand a squeeze and she lets me. "Later." And as I look at her, I finally see how much she's changed too, just like the rest of us.

On the walk home—my last walk home—I think about how the spring suits Callie. It makes her brighter, like something inside of her is in bloom, something coming back to life. And maybe we're all like a season in that way. If we are, then Aaron would be the fall—all fiery and fickle, complicated and beautiful in his own way, in this way that lets me forgive him for doing whatever he needs to do to keep going. And me, maybe I'm most like the winter. Maybe I need that stillness, as much as I've tried to fight it. I need it like oxygen, that quieting of the world around me, so I can finally listen to myself.

Mom and Dad. I think they're both like the summer. And maybe that was the problem. They were too similar; they needed the same things from each other. I have to think that their love was like the sun, warm at first, comforting, peaceful. Perhaps they thought they could bask in each other forever, but they burned too hot, too fast, too bright, until all they had was a fire that raged out of control, uncontained and wild—dangerous. And maybe I have a little of that heat inside of me, too. But I have enough of their good parts in me, I think, to balance out.

Dani and Caroline are waiting downstairs, both of their cars full. I stand in the doorway, one foot in the past, one in the future, my last cardboard box perched on my hip. Inside, it contains my globe, the atlas and the leather bag from my birthday, the snowflake book, and the picture of all of us together in that fancy silver, now glassless, frame. And for once time isn't jumping backward or forward.

I think about how I've finally learned something here after all. About what love is and what love isn't. It's not so monstrous, not so dangerous and unknowable—not something to fear. And it's not as simple as just finding someone else to hold on to; it's not letting that other person crawl into those hollow spaces inside of you. I think love also means you have to stand on your own for a while, stand with yourself and *for* yourself, before you can ask someone to stand there next to you. I think maybe that's the trickiest part, and that's where our parents got it wrong.

There's a line. Between right and wrong, truth and lies. But that line moves every second; every moment of our lives it seems like we're just drawing more and more lines that we swear we'll never cross. Until we do. And I guess we all have to live in the gray area, the space between the lines, between darkness and light, good and bad, love and hate.

For so long all I wanted was to be free. But it never occurred to me that I was the one who was holding on, that I'd be the last to let go. I take one more look, in the here and now. And I say my silent good-bye to every crack in every wall. Good-bye to every stain, every mark, every scar. As for the memories, I've boxed them up too, and I'll take them with me.

I close the door gently—letting go, at last.

AUTHOR'S NOTE

This book was inspired, not by one real-life story, but *many*. Every minute, twenty-four people become the victim of domestic or intimate partner violence—affecting twelve million people in the United States every year. It is estimated that a child will witness nearly one in four of these acts of violence. Studies show that children who are exposed to violence in the home are more likely to be abused later in life.

Domestic violence is often referred to as one of the most "predictable and preventable" crimes, yet there is still so much silence, stigma, shame, and misunderstanding surrounding this kind of abuse. Although this book is fictional, what I hope it illuminates is that behind every statistic are real people with real lives and real struggles. The cycle of abuse can be extremely difficult to break free from; leaving is never simple or easy.

If you or someone you know needs help, you are not alone.

For free, safe, confidential 24/7 support, call the National Domestic Violence Hotline at 1-800-799-SAFE (7233) or visit thehotline.org. Help is also available at loveisrespect.org, which operates the Teen Dating Abuse Hotline (call: 1-866-331-9474 / text: loveis to 22522).

ACKNOWLEDGMENTS

It feels like this book has been in my heart and on my mind forever, but I didn't actually start writing it until 2013. I had to put it away many times, often for long periods, when it became too difficult to keep telling this story. And without the following people, I honestly don't know how I ever would have finished.

First and foremost, I thank my readers—some of you I've had the privilege of meeting face-to-face, and others via e-mail, tweets, messages, and posts. Please know that your kind, thoughtful, supportive words, and the personal stories you have shared with me, mean more than I could ever say—thank you for always reminding me why I write.

To my agent, Jess Regel, you continue to be the best champion a writer could possibly hope for, and I feel so fortunate to have you and Foundry Literary + Media in my corner—thank you for, well . . . basically, *everything*.

Deepest thanks go to my brilliant editor, Rūta Rimas. For your belief in this story, for your guidance and insights, and for always seeming to know exactly in which dark corners to shine a light, I cannot thank you enough.

Thanks are also due to Justin Chanda and the excellent team at Margaret K. McElderry Books, as well as the entire Simon & Schuster Children's division—from the talented designers, copy editors, and proofreaders, to all the dedicated people on the library and education, sales, marketing, and publicity teams—it takes a village to raise a book, and I'm so grateful to be a member of yours.

Many thanks to Holly Summers-Gil, Judy Goldman, Shannon M. Parker, and Bryson McCrone for reading early drafts or portions of this book—your encouragement, feedback, enthusiasm, and friendship have made all the difference. To Heather Summers, not only are you one of my best friends, you are also one of the most devoted Domestic Violence Advocates there ever was—thank you for your important, yet often thankless work, for our *long* talks over the years, and for reading and providing feedback on this book when it was still kind of a mess. And Margo Smith, thank you for sharing your knowledge of criminal justice, and for talking me through the legal stuff I was sure I'd never get right.

I'm also grateful to the following people for making what is often referred to as a "lonely" profession a lot less so, and for welcoming me into an amazing community of generous, talented authors: Amy Reed, Robin Constantine, Jaye Robin Brown, Megan Miranda, Megan Shepherd, Rebecca Petruck, Brendan Kiely, the Nebo Retreaters, the Sweet16ers, and all the incredible YA authors with whom I've had the honor of serving on panels—I have learned so much from each of you.

And last but not least, thanks always to my family, to my dear friends, and to the many people, come and gone, who have taught me lessons in letting go.